BURNING CRYSTAL

BOOK FIVE OF ECLIPSE COURT

SHIRLEY MEIER

To Mr. Hall who first told me I had all the tools I needed to write... and to Ms Walsh who encouraged my love of literature.

CONTENTS

ACKNOWLEDGMENTS

To Karen Wehrstein for their gracious assistance and to all the beta readers and role-players who gleefully threw themselves into the fray!

ABOUT THE BOOK

Minis, his little brother, and his brother in spirit, Gannara are still on the run. Driven away from the Healer's Island by a Mahid sighting, they head to the last place anyone would think they would go.

To Yeola-e, the conquering country of Arko.

It is still too dangerous and they finally try hiding in the other last place; Arko the City itself.

Minis is both the rising young writer for the Pages, Minakas Akam and in public a wild, street courier boy on cheap looking skates with blue hair and a nose ring. Surely no one will recognize him, or find them now.

But the problem with healing and growing up is realizing you still have responsibilities and Minis is about to skate face-first into the last thing on the Earthsphere he wants to do.

1

GODS AND TAPESTRY AND WORDS

THE ODD, ONION-SHAPED DOMES OF BRAHVNIKI ARE REALLY PRETTY in the morning mist. We're tied up on the opposite shore and the swarms of little boats that sell or buy anything that might fit in such a little floating barge, that beleaguer the incoming ships, are all out-harbour, beyond the tax-line.

I'd never seen Brahvniki before. At least as far as I remembered. My healer on Haiu Menshir, Initaeran told me I was doing really well. She said that I was going to heal fast probably because it was strangers who took me away and tortured me, rather than my own family. "It is less of a betrayal," she'd said in her gentle, brutally direct Haian way. "Less of a betrayal than the ones who should love you and raise you. Granted you will have to re-learn trust on a number of levels."

Minis, Spark of the Sun's Ray in Exile, after the Sack of Arko, doesn't realize yet that he's one of the best people I know to re-teach me trust. Even in the golden and gem-decked cess pit of the Marble Palace, he did the best he could not to hurt me. He even helped me after his father had… done too many brutal things to me, to remember.

I remember lying on the foot of Mini's enormous bed in the Heir's Rooms. I had been glad he'd put the barricade of pillows between us and he was all the way on the other side of the mattress. I didn't have to touch anybody. His nurse would see that I was fed and clean and comfortable.

Minis'd cry in his sleep sometimes. I always woke up when there was noise. I was supposed to and if I hadn't someone might have hurt me worse.

Who was I trying to fool? Someone? *Kurkas* would have hurt me. Not Minis.

Initaeran said. The Mahid would just want me focused on Kurkas. Just Kurkas. No one else. And no one else was supposed to exist. The walls in my head tried to go up again.

Nowadays the walls were more like lacey holes of pain and the awfulness dripped. The think is... yes, think, not thing.

The think is I can see and feel through the Mahid awfulness. There's people on the other side. Minis, kind of wrapped in this garbage but holding his hands to pull me through. And you know... he doesn't realize that he's hanging on to the pain that holds him in the wall.

He has to let go, to pull me through. Not really. I could walk through myself but I LIKE Minis. I won't leave him in the *shen*, however much he thinks he should be there. Deserves to be there.

Somebody – my *semanakraseye,* the leader of our country, Chevenga, gave him a bridge out of the *shen* and *kyash* and Mahid pain. Pain like lava and a black wall that you can't see past. Anything on the other side just does not exist. But Mahid don't understand that tears can reach past pain. Tears can reach through sorrow. Love is a force like water wearing away stone. When the water and salt have passed the stone is gone with them.

Tears do not destroy stone, but transform it, make it part of themselves. It's one reason that torturers fear them and try to dry them up. Tears are more powerful than pain and they know it. Sometimes it takes an ocean of tears to wear away pain and torture but that is what happens. Ultimately torture drowns in tears.

I turned from the rail and flung one arm around Minis and another around Ili, his little brother. "I'll bet there's a good library or two here. There's dozens of stories for Minakas Akam to uncover and write out of here, preserved here and unknown in Arko, because Arkan Imperators have strangled the histories in their infancy!"

～

I tighten my arm around Gannara. He is the strong one of us... him and me, I mean. Ili just coming up on his first threshold and is all right. I'd throw myself in front of Ili to save him and won't hesitate. He's innocent in a way I can plaster over. *Dear Gods. Dear Selinae. You already know. I will sacrifice myself for Ili. You know that.* He is my little brother. The best thing I can do, even as we run away again, is take him into the heart of Yeola-e where these free thinking people live.

Slaves must agree to be slaves. People must submit themselves to be slaves, or they will not be slaves long. They die.

Without fear of death and *Hayel* and eternal smothering, no one would allow the torture of the flesh. Perhaps no one would allow the control of the soul. Gods. Gods and Ancestors and Eternal Selestialis... I cannot. Gods. I cannot submit myself to You because I am myself. Perhaps I know too much.

You cannot be the tiny Beings that human minds can understand. You cannot be the miniscule minds that encompass humanity. You MUST be bigger. You must be more than can fit inside the narrow, ugly, controlling words that rest inside the stone walls and the iron minds of man.

~

The letter paper lay creamy smooth against the desk and the words, the ink, flowed from Kyriala's pen in a way she was still thrilled with. Thrilled that she could. Thrilled that women in Arko could read and write for themselves. If anyone asked she could say she was just practicing. Wherever in the world that Minis was, she couldn't mail it, couldn't know. The Marble Palace hadn't asked, with threat of truth-drug, if she knew where Minis was, for a long time. But they might. One never knew. So she would write the letters into the void, though she'd store them away in her practice books, not able to bear burning them.

Burning them seemed too final, too much of an abandonment.

Dear M,

My words are flung into the void. But I cannot cease thinking them. I try and reduce the majesty of the Gods to single strokes of thread but the only way I can see Them is in the gathering of all threads.

M, where are you? I am lost. Mama said a day would come when I wanted someone to cling to who wasn't her. I need more than just my mama. I want someone who I've been to *Hayel* and back with. I need a physical human man to throw my arms around, to keep the dark at bay.

What am I saying? Another caring soul who would hold me to my life and my dreams instead of letting me fall into my nightmares. I don't understand what I'm longing for. What is it about human dreams that make the nightmares so much stronger, so much clearer? Why can we see the depths of darkness so much more clearly?"

Why may we not see *Selestialis*? Are we blinded? We peer into the light and are afraid and our fear makes the light blinding.

M, I am angry. I will stare into the light and dare it to blind me! I refuse to let the darkness silence me any more than the darkness and his blindness silences the canary you sent me. He sings in defiance of all. Light, dark, cool, warm. He sings. It is his choice. Faced with darkness, he sings.

Since you and Gannara and Ailadas delivered me safe home, my world has been too narrow. When we escaped from the Mahid and were on the road I could see so much more. Minis. Wherever you are... be safe. Wherever you are... be happy. My mother thinks in terms of the next stitch. I dream of tapestries and vast landscapes of thread, the hanks and tangles and smooth, vast sweeps of story... I'm sorry. I will never send this. I don't understand.

I look at my sewing basket and I see a mass of threads and colours and I wonder if the God see us as single threads in the tapestry They are weaving. Other writers, I now know, have said this... but words are more powerful than stitches... M... I can do nothing here, but create. I weave and stitch a vision of what I wish. Not what is, but what I wish. Is that not what authors do? Weave a world out of words of all colours that they wish rather than worlds out of single types of thread?

I wish and want my world to be my word. Is this wrong? Is
this odd?

There must be more than I have been taught by the approved
priests and *dekinas,* the *Fenjitzas* and the new *Fenjitza.* I quote:
"The manifest works of thy fingers..." Goddess I am confused.

2

LIBRARIES IN BRAHVNIKI AND VOMIT IN MY HAIR

WE FOUND A LOVELY ROOM IN A TOWER HOTEL HALF-WAY UP THE city's bluff, looking across the wide river with the ferries going back and forth to the Benai Saekrberk. In Brahvniki, so heavily influenced by the old Zak Empire, all the tower rooms were seen as less expensive and cheaper, rented mostly by foreigners.

The walls along the harbour were high grey stone, the remnants of the old Empire and had served them well enough they'd successfully defended the city a few years ago against the abortive Thanish war. The Benai Saekrberk also had its walls going down into the water, the soaring white towers drawing the eye away from the old fortress monastery.

The great library in the Benai is built below ground and instead of big windows to let people read they have these *kraumaks* everywhere... the old style ones were made of a certain type of stone but the modern ones were originally clear Arkan glass and glowed white instead of green or yellow or red.

So the reading cubicles are these tiny, private brick or stone vaulted rooms, dark except for the clear, bright reading lanterns. The other lamps below were just as odd.

The librarians, all Brahvnikian monks -- or *Vra* -- swear the lamps need daily prayers to give off their light. They say the light comes from two things, neither of which burn and thus do not damage walls and paper with smoke or fumes. Every day the lamps need to see the sun. The tops are full of a green liquid like algae in a scummy pond, and the *Vra* set them in rows outside, on the south wall racks built especially for them.

The Brahvnikian sign for a library is one of these conical lamps. There is one outside... a big one... before the library doors and it glows white/yellow for half the night. So the front door of any of their libraries is always built facing south.

But like every other Great Archive it had the same hushed atmosphere and the familiar whiff of books, plus the delicate perfumes in the mortar that the *Vra* architects included in every sacred building. It was nice to know they thought the same way I did about books.

It was amazing how much one could learn from tax and court records. It was interesting that the Imperator of Arko... long before there was a huge Empire... actually came on a State visit to the Great Dragon of the Zak in Brahvniki. That was Eighth Kurkas, meeting with Great Dragon Valentin. I didn't recognize the name until I wrote it down as it would be spelled in the Imperial Archive—Falantinas.

It looked like the two leaders arranged trade, around an Enchian Empire land-route that had held a monopoly and tolls.... hmmm. I would love to ask Ailadas but I couldn't write him, since he would be duty bound to let them know he'd received correspondence from me.

But I would only indulge myself in researching the ancient *volksmoots* that eventually replaced the Great Dragons for a little while. The most consistent and long-term voting country, who still practiced it into modern days, was that of Yeola-e. I would follow the track of the effect of the vote on the surrounding countries. Most of the old empires and countries were 'great' only in name, claiming territory where there were no people to populate it.

~

Selina we had already seen but this time we took a river boat heading east. It was the river Ereala and the flat-boat had the promising name of 'Chagae's Dreams'. I hadn't realized that the boat was empty of passengers for a reason, since the whole middle of the barge had been empty and waiting for the bags of grain or stooks of 'maranth I'd imagined.

Chagae, the merchant owner, had gotten an exclusive contract to ship a brand new herd of *Kaeryal* to the north mountains. They were long-necked and fuzzy, with camel faces. Yeolis had used them in the south mountains but not in the north at all and in the catastrophe of the war, the Yeolis had decided they were too useful to not use them in the whole country, setting out to breed them up in numbers.

I was surprised that the owner was willing to sell me passage, since she was a war veteran with a missing forearm, but she hadn't offered the story and I had not asked. But she had asked if I had heard what she was shipping and I had said no. She'd smiled and taken our passage money.

Now I realized why. *Kaeryal* not regularly groomed do not smell bad. They even have tidy toilet habits, choosing one spot to defecate. But. They spat up the contents of their stomachs if they didn't like you. They were amazingly accurate. It couldn't have been the colour of my hair that set them off because they didn't spit at Ili. Chagae and her crew were mostly on the shore, leading the draft-horses towing the barge. At least a bucket of water dipped out of the river to wash my head with – again -- wasn't salt.

And I was lucky that all of the intact males had had their fighting teeth removed so they didn't try to sneak up on any of us and either rip our ears or privates off. A charming trait no doubt encouraged and bred for by Hyerne women. Of course I wouldn't miss my most hated organs.

"So, Minakas, tell me again why we're aiming for the library at Vae Arahi?" Gannara leaned back against our packs.

"Well. I had an idea for a story that the Yeoli National Library might have records for. It's something specifically about Yeoli/Arkan relations and... with Chevenga on Haiu Menshir, after he was stripped of his rightful place by my *stupid, blind* people, according to the Pages, it's the last place anyone would expect me to go!"

Gan nudged me, jerked his thumb at the *kaeryal* looking at us... at me. I dropped my voice some. "I wanted to see it, too. His home..." I shrugged. "I couldn't think of a better place to hide from Mahid either."

"Right. So... we'll stop at Hirina, check out the library there... there's a big one. I can write my folks in Arko... or Haiu Menshir... like I did from Selina. Not letting them know where I am but still letting them know I'm safe."

"That's good. They'll have a trail of where we've been but if we can keep it random and only send from big cities... Look, Gannara. It can't be your whole life. I'm all right. Ili and I have enough funds to keep running my whole life. You shouldn't." I threw up my gloves to stop him sputtering at me. "I could do the same as you are with your folks. You have a life to go back to. I have to figure out what my life is going to be."

He took a deep breath. "All right. Not immediately, though. You're safer in Yeola-e with me around. Once you figure out what you're going to do... long term... you can 'not tell me' so when they truth-drug me, I'll go home."

"All right."

"Ili!" My little brother and animals. What was it? He and JiaKlem were sitting in the middle of the *kaeryal* and it looked like he was going to try and get up on one of them, a big piebald male who turned his head at me and belched. "Come out of there, please. I'd rather not get vomit out of my hair again, and these *kaeryal* are not yours. And I'm *not* getting you one!"

3

―――――

"DAD, LOOK OUT!"

THE HIRINA LIBRARY, LIKE ALL YEOLI LIBRARIES, HAD BEEN HIDDEN away from our invading Rejins, since one of the first things we did when we conquered was pull all information that would let us control the indigenes and burn the rest to begin eradicating the culture. As it was, the standard Arkan texts were added in when the restoration happened and with the Great Press's technology being opened up there were spawn presses springing up everywhere.

So the sheer number of books appearing now was phenomenal. People were taking old hand-copied texts and printing them and there were library caravaneers travelling all over the Yeoli-Arkan Empire and bookfairs in every market now. Gannara had to stop me from just buying too many books, since I had to carry them with us.

"Make a note of the title and just keep a list."

It was late fall in central Yeola-e and the weather was growing cold fast. We settled in for the winter here, rather than further up the north mountains. I started teaching Ili things. We would go into the big library and he would find a book that interested him. Or we would go to artists displays and the renewed collections and then we'd read about the older pieces whether they were paintings or statues.

We visited blacksmiths and coopers and hostler's, with Gannara doing the talking so people were friendly enough. The shipwrights were happy enough to teach Ili anything he wanted to know, as long as he didn't get in the way of a build, people working in the boat barns to finish before the river broke free in the spring.

The Haian in town took Gan and I both on... Ili didn't want to; and we hired someone to sit with, or teach him when we were busy, or recovering. Dirinaer was her name and I was very uncomfortable talking to her. Even though she was Haian... she was she... and I was never going to be able to talk to her about my sexual training from the fat guy and Ice Eyes.

Ili's sixth birthday was celebrated in our winter apartment, with his now traditional pan-pastry with whipped cream and fruit layers. He wore JiaKlem wrapped in a wooly red scarf because the creature was not terribly happy in cold and kept blushing from a red -- to match the scarf -- to a pale white as if to try and hide in the snow.

The domoctopus became a favourite of the fishmonger in town, given that we were his steadiest customers. Jia was also made much of by the shipwrights, even though they built river boats rather than sea-going vessels and they wondered if he might eat fresh-water boat parasites. He seemed to love freshwater clams but disliked the ice-water.

We rode north after it became possible to travel again, up the new road we invaders had begun and the Yeolis had finished. We followed the retreating snow up the mountains and by late spring we were in Vae Arahi.

The University Library at Terera was warm with the carefully tended stone stoves on every floor, and peaceful. Gannara and Ili had seen all they wanted to see the first day and left me to delve into the dustiest of tomes by myself.

One of the largest book I'd ever seen was the "Civil and Tax records" for the year I wanted, and I had four smaller but thicker books piled on top of that; with my loose notes where I'd referenced them all stacked on top. Focused on getting them back to my claimed desk and the other materials there I turned without looking up, and walked straight into someone to a cry of "Dad! Look out!"

The papers went everywhere, the top two books hit the floor and in saving the bottom three, most valuable and fragile, my spectacles were knocked askew. Even clear glass before one's eyes distorts, the frame blocks and my hair was everywhere of course.

"Ker! Oh, aym sorry Ser! Ay din't see ya Ker," My apology was a bizarre mix of Yeoli and my *fessas* Arkan.

"It's all right, lad. I didn't see you either." My heart nearly stopped. It was Chevenga. I'd run straight into Chevenga. I knew his voice and it hadn't changed at all. *Oh my great... um... Oh my goodness. What am I going to do?*

4

———

A SCHOLARLY CONVERSATION

What kind of politician EVER enters a library? Without formally unlocking its doors for the first time with a crowd of Pages Reporters to write it up?

I'd dropped to my knees which helped hide my shock and looked down at the papers and books, scrambling them together. *I desperately want to fling myself on my face, grab his feet and confess. Ask forgiveness. I want to vomit. I want to pass out. Oh, Sinimas, Ancestors help me!*

There was a boy with Chevenga, helping me collect myself. *Oh Gods.* I blinked at Chevenga, down on one knee, gathering up scattered scraps of paper. I thought my heart might fall out of my chest. He looked all right. The last time I'd seen him was... that night. I nodded and looked down again, struggling to swallow the lump in my throat. I hoped he would take my tongue-tied silence as awe.

He looked so much better than the last time I'd seen him. *The heliotrope stinking golden bedchamber...* I cut that thought off at the roots because I couldn't bear it. It would put me on my face... oh, as Imperator I should... Even as former Imperator...

I made to lie down in the mess and he caught me by the shoulder, *his touch was the same,* and pulled me up again. "No, no, lad, I'm not your Imperator any more."

I nodded, jerkily, answering in Yeoli. He always wanted people to speak to him equal to equal. "Nooo... kere..." I flashed a glance at the boy, who was obviously his. He looked like him with lighter eyes, perhaps a bit more round of the face, but only a bit. *What am I to do?*

The answer floated up, too slowly. *Act.*

"F...f...f..ourth... um Imp.... um... Ser???"

He smiled. "Chevenga. You may call me that. This is my son, Fifth Chevenga, better known as Tawaen."

"Pleased to meet you," he said formally. I flashed a glance at the boy, then down again as if I didn't know what to do.

"Are you here as a visiting student?" Chevenga gave me a quizzical look as though trying to remember me. My guts clenched."You look familiar; do I know you from somewhere?"

"Ay... ay shouldn't think yeh'd know me, ser -- Ch... Ch...Chevenga. Um... Aym visitin', surely, yes." Oh good, I did sound like a terrified young scholar. Of course, I wasn't faking the terror part. *Would he recognize me?* Tawaen handed me the last piece of paper he'd retrieved from under a table.

"Did you ever go to the Mezem when I was a ring-fighter? I might have seen you in the crowd."

"S...s... m' father was a ringman... a fan... Ay did see yeh f...f...fight when I was a youngker."

"That explains it. What are you studying? Looks like something political."

"Oh, ay ser... um.. Chevenga." Let the really broad accent fade a little, as I go to the more scholarly, less the panicked student. "'T time of Notyere. M' theory is thet he n' t' Heir, Tatthanas Aan, at the time were friends. Notyere came ta Arko then... f'r a month away. I hev a paper I'm writin' about the massacre t' new Imperator did and how much it influenced yer *semanakraseye* who'd be a king." Tawaen was watching quietly, apparently as interested as his father. It was unnerving having both sets of intense eyes on me like that. I swallowed hard.

"Really?" Chevenga said. "I didn't know he went to Arko. Is there much information on it? What did he come away with? Was he quoted saying anything about it?"

"Ay hed access to t'Imperial Archive, ser... Chevenga... and ay only found some of t' letters from Notyere tah Tatthanas... t' Imperator kept 'em on his side an' I only could read one or two in the time I had."

Thank the Gods he'd never heard me speak Yeoli... and with an Asinanai accent as well. "So I thought ay'd come 'n see if there were anythin' preserved on this end." I shifted the books in my grip, moving them to a little more stable tower. ”T' high editor though 'e'd like to publish m' idea if I wrote it... 'n I'd do a short piece fer the Pages, ser... Chevenga... oh, I'm sorry. My name is Minakas Akam, ser.”

I had to swallow again when I saw him just lay a loving hand on his son's shoulder. *You, boy, are loved.*

“I'm sorry, we're keeping you standing here with all that... lead on to your space and we'll come with--wait... did you say Minakas Akam?” I'd begun to turn, checked when he said wait and ducked my head yes.

”Yes, s.. Chevenga.”

“Who wrote 'Definition of a Great Man,' and the piece about the additives affecting Imperators? Tawaen this fellow wrote that story arguing that only the weak feel the need to be cruel and the other pieces in support of freer Arkan women!”

He'd read them? He remembered them? I couldn't help smiling. “Yes, I did, that. Um... those...” *Maybe he'd hated them.* My smile faded at little.

“I'm stunned,” he said, with an amazed smile. “I thought you must be in your thirties at least, and you're what... seventeen maybe? It's excellent work; you have a very impressive future ahead of you.”

I could feel myself blushing. “Just third threshold, ser. Thank yeh. We never had a parti-coloured cat in the house. Always a solid colour.” *Go to the most innocuous part of that list, the law against striped cats...*

“Not mottled or hooped? Sorry, love,” he said to his son, “that's an Arkan inside joke.”

“I know about that, Dad,” Fifth said. “I read about that law.”

“You did? Pardon me, then. You're in the presence of an Arkan celebrity; this young man writes for the Pages.” *Celebrity? I just... I couldn't... ahhh. Just as polite as if the boy were older. Just as polite as you were to me, at that age... or thereabouts. Asking his pardon.*

Tawaen's eyes grew wide and round. *“Really? Wow.”*

“Oh, no, not a celebrity, surely. I've written some, yes. I've been lucky they've been wanted. Anything ta give Arko some p'rspective, se... Chevenga.”

“Future celebrity then. You're doing good work to bring perspective, always a good thing. So... Notyere and Tatthanas... interesting. What have you found so far?”

“Nothin' pers'nal, I expected most of it to 've been destroyed.... but there's the approval fer him goin' ta Arko in the Assembly records... ay'm just checking the funds and taxes. And lookin' for more evidence... lots of Assembly sessions.”

"Not that the news that Notyere had Arkan influence will help ease animosities against Arko here... but then, you're writing for Arkans, and most Yeolis won't see it."

"Ay ser. P'raps I should look ta see what good influence the Yeolis had on Arko if any. Sorry, Chevenga, rather than the bad. More stories there."

"Well, I doubt any good came through Notyere. The idea that they had a relationship... how much did they write each other?"

"T letters in thet archive were, p'raps, thirty or so?"

"The Imperial archive? So, there are letters there from Notyere? And... how did you manage getting into the Imperial archive? That's not something just anyone can do."

I let myself smile shyly. ""Chevenga... my tutor... hed some pull." *All true.* "I only saw them once." *Also true, but not for the reason you would think. I wish I'd cared when I found them. I wish I had been interested then.*

"Had? It sounds like you no longer have this arrangement... lost it in the sack? But that doesn't make sense; you'd only have been fourteen then, much too young to be let in there even with pull. You must have been there when *I* was Imperator." His eyes took on the look of trying to figure something out. *Oh Gods, he'll figure it out if I'm not careful.*

"I din't aquire my tutor till just last year. So I got let in on his recommendation, ser, but t' gratuity asked... sorry tah be blunt. I couldn't afford it when more was asked."

"You lost me, but I guess it doesn't matter. Thirty letters? That is a find of great historical significance to Yeola-e; the scholars will be drooling over it. Oh, here..." He sat down at the table, ripped a page from a notebook that he was carrying, wrote something in Yeoli in his fast hand and signed it. "There. When you go back to Arko, go to the chamberlain of the Marble Palace and have him show this to my sister."

I took it and read it. My hands started shaking. *Would I have the nerve?* It requested the Imperator's signature giving me access, as Minakas of course, to the Imperial Archives. In the Marble Palace. *Would I have the nerve?* "Thank you! Oh, that will be wonderful, Chevenga!"

He looked good. He looked better than I had ever seen him. Hale. Free. It was enough to choke me up.

I turned my thoughts resolutely to what I, as a scholar should be intensely interested in. Archive access. There was a whole box as I recalled, of things packed away from that year. What else might there be that I hadn't bothered to look at? If I had the nerve.

Tawaen sat, listening intently. For a ten year old he seemed very quiet, watching everything carefully. He seemed so calm for a child. Was that because he was Chevenga's, or because he was secure, having been loved. Of course, he was in a library and required to be quiet.

"Did you actually read them?" His gaze was intent on me, absolutely fascinated with what I was telling him. "What sorts of things do they say? Are they well-preserved?"

"Ay didn't read them all, just two or three. And yes they've been bundled together in a box inside another, bigger box. He talks about the animals he was gifted while visiting, reminds the Heir of some escapade they did that he does not detail. Um... sexual reminiscence about the main House of Masks... makes reference to something political and thanks Tatthanas for the offer of chains, but thought he might be able to do something on his own."

"Chains! Tatthanas offered Notyere *money?* All-Spirit!"

"Em... ahem..." The librarian, Korana by name as I recall, had a cough remarkably like Ailadas's. "*Semanakraseye,* if you don't mind, please don't disturb the other patrons."

"I'm sorry!" he said, in a whisper. Tawaen giggled. "But I'm not *semanakraseye* any more... except when I'm misbehaving, I suppose. Korana, do you know who this is?"

"Of course I do. He is here very frequently this past moon. Minakas Akam. An admirably studious youth."

"And he writes for the Pages, and you won't *believe* what he just told me."

"I need not believe it, Chevenga. I heard it quite clearly."

I thought I'd set my hair on fire, blushing. I hunched my shoulders in a Minakas way. Tawaen giggled again and I looked at him, and then down. *What is this anger? That he's free enough to laugh like that, at his father being embarrassed?*

"Well, then, you understand the significance. I will rein in my excitement and keep it to a whisper. Anything else interesting you read, Minakas?"

"That was the most of it. But as ay've said. Ay only read two or three... and not in any kind of order. Is there a Yeoli scholar ay should bring this ta' the attention to? It'd be best to hand it off to someone specializing in that study." *It's what a self-effacing fessas would do.*

"I'm more familiar with the political and military scholars than the historians," he said. "You might be best to ask Korana or one of the others, or go down to the history department and ask around."

"Thenk yah fer the advice, Chevenga." *And how much do I wish to make my name as a scholar, since I will never be Minis Aan again? Should I keep this for my own publishing?*

"You're welcome. I want to see this bear fruit." I nodded and signed chalk.

"Ay could surrender my notes if that'd serve."

"Surrender your notes? Hardly. Two scholars can look at one set of letters, and each have his own thoughts. But you should get the credit for finding them and bringing them to light."

"Ser... Chevenga... there's mah youth ta consider. Ay'd but be the student assistin' th true scholar. Thet'd be the correct thing ta do." *I'd pull my own teeth out before I was willing to give up credit.* I was surprised at the ferocity of my own thought.

"And very Arkan. Up to you, Mini—I should say, Minakas, sorry. Don't undersell yourself because of your youth, though. You recognized those letters as significant enough to study the time and the events they concern."

My heart froze as he stumbled over my name. "Ay sor... Ay'll take yer advice tah heart, Chevenga."

"If I weren't going to be *semanakraseye* when I grow up," said Tawaen, "I might like to be a scholar. Maybe a historian. I like learning things."

"You'd be a good one," said his father. "But you'll have to settle for *semanakraseye*... sorry, love, but that's how it goes."

Think fessas *to a superior's child. Defer, defer.* "But somet'in tah consider fer when ye retire, young ser." *Semanakraseyel could retire. Not by assassination, either. I was never where you were, boy, however much I longed to be. I was a brat, an unloved prince. You... have always had him.* I blinked at him as mildly as I could. He was looking at me... could he tell?

"I could do that. As long as I don't get killed in a war or something."

"Minakas," said his father, "might you like to come up to the Hearthstone Independent and join us for dinner some time while you're in Vae Arahi? That would be a great pleasure for us."

"Ay...d l...l... like thet a great deal..." *And don't dare take him up on it. I'll have to leave... soon. I've pushed my disguise as far as it will go. He already knows me, on some level or he wouldn't have almost called me 'Minis'. I'll send a note.* My heart was banging in my throat but I managed to smile. "Thenk yah, s...Chevenga, fer yer 'tention today, and yer fine son." I mustn't dislike him any more than I disliked my own brother. He couldn't help who he was. I just felt very sad, for some reason, and couldn't fathom quite why.

But. If he hadn't recognized me yet, what harm could one dinner do?

No, it's too risky.

Still…

5

DINNER

I made it to our rooms in Terera and collapsed backward on the bed with my arms over my head, wondering what I should do.

I had felt completely safe in the library thinking... for some odd reason... that Chevenga would never go into it. But of course that was stupid. That was foolishly reacting as if he was like my father... who wouldn't have been caught in a library unless forced into one.

Gannara came in. "Hello Min, Ili's downstairs--" He cut himself off. "What's wrong?"

"We have to go." I'll admit I whined.

"Oh, *shen*, did Joras follow us *here*?" He sat down abruptly on the end of the bed. "Oh, *kyash*, how—"

I cut him off. "No... worse."

He went silent before whispering, "Second Amitzas? What are we—"

"Even worse."

Now he was puzzled. "Worse? What in *kevyalin Hayel* can *possibly* be worse than Second Amitzas!?"

"Your mother's shade isn't going to like me teaching you to talk like that."

"*Fik* that! *What's worse than Second Amitzas and where do we run?*"

"I..." I flung my hands over my face.

"*Will you just spit it out?!*"

"I ran into Chevenga in the library and he invited me to dinner."

There was profound silence for a moment on the other side of the wall of my fingers. "You... ran... into... Chevenga... in the library... and he invited you... to *dinner!?*"

"Yeha, as Minakas Akam, the writer whose work he likes in the Pages..." I said, a bit muffled.

"That's not worse than Second Amitzas! That's not bad at all!"

"I... it's probably just for politeness. And how likely is it that he's going to be in the library again? It was probably for form's sake. He left it vague."

"So you didn't settle a date." He looked distinctly disappointed.

"No, he just said 'sometime'. Gannara... if anyone should go to dinner it should be you... He'd be concerned to find out about you. As long as you and I weren't together, your looking like him wouldn't give me away."

"He doesn't know I'm here. And it would be too risky for me to go-- we'll end up apart." He looked even more disappointed.

"Gan, I'm sorry."

"So you go... I mean... that's risky too, he might recognize you. But then... if he didn't already..." This was a good time not to mention how Chevenga had felt he knew me, if I didn't want Gannara giving me grief for going.

"He was probably just offering to be polite in front of his son..."

"His son was there? The oldest one, the *anaraseye?*"

"Tawaen, yes. He's a very polite boy which is no surprise seeing who his father is. I mean... when I said run into him... I did... with a pile of books..." *his hands had steadied me before I went down on my knees...* I remembered that touch all over again. I'd recognized him the moment he touched me, even before his voice. "Talk about the spreading of literature..."

Gan didn't answer me.

"I... There's one more set of records I really want to delve into... I should be safe enough doing that tomorrow. Then the sensible thing to do would be to leave."

~

I was just pulling my glasses off and rubbing my eyes next day, from squinting at the ancient, faded text, when Chevenga's voice said

"*N'yingi,* Minakas," next to me, freezing me in place yet again. *Now why did I think he wouldn't come back into the library?*

I gulped again. "N'yingi...s.sss.sssemana... Chevenga," I managed, and put my glasses back on to look at him, as if I needed to.

"We forgot to set a date for dinner yesterday; when is good for you? And do you have anyone with you who should come as well?"

"Ah... ah... date... oh..."

"You needn't be shy." He had his grin back. The last time I'd seen him smile so light and fast was years ago, in the Mezem before things went completely to *Hayel* for him. "I know I'm famous, but so are *you.*"

Gannara, I'm sorry. "Any day. This 'un's time... is this 'un's own... oh, *I* should be speaking equal to equal... I... can.. but forgot."

"We can speak in Enchian, if you prefer," he said, in that language.

"Oh... I'm sorry, no I should speak Yeoli, I suppose, if I'm doing the research in it... sorry." I said, in my Asinanai-accented Yeoli.

"You speak Yeoli? I gathered you must read it, but reading and speaking are two different things..." I was so happy to hear him speak his own tongue and glad I could understand him in it. It changed how he seemed to me in a strange way. The soft, almost rolling inland accent compared to how Gannara spoke, made him seem more complete, of a piece, rather than ripped out of his context. Though I had met him so displaced.

"Where'd you learn to speak it?" he added. "Asinanai?"

"Yes, *kere* Chevenga." It was easier to speak equal to equal in a language that didn't have a lot of caste separations. It felt less disrespectful somehow.

"You did well... no surprise for one of your intelligence. Let me think... I don't have anyone else coming the night after tomorrow."

"Ni...night after tomorrow... um what bead should I come?"

"It's usually fairly late these days, with the decadent, easy life I'm living. Say around six and a half. Just come to the door and say to whoever opens it that I invited you."

"Thank you for the invitation, *kere.*" *He'll be less likely to recognize me speaking Yeoli. Stick to Yeoli.*

"You know I was thinking," said Gannara, when I got back to our rooms. "Going to dinner with Chevenga... would be *really* risky... I don't think you should do it."

"You're right. It's risky. But I feel better about it... especially if I stick to speaking Yeoli. He *never* heard me speak it when I was a kid."

"But you speak it like me, and he knows that I'm from Asinanai and he... well, I don't know if he'd figure all that out... but he's *really* smart, so he might."

"Asinanai is a big city and has a lot of people coming and going. There's no reason for him to put those particular two things together."

"You sound like you... *are* going..." His big dark eyes were so worried.

"Well... since he actually asked me today.. He invited me for night after tomorrow at six and a half beads..."

Gan threw his hands over his face. *"Kahara... mamaiyana...* I can't believe you sometimes, first saying he's worse than Second Amitzas then going to *dinner* with him. Fine, if you don't come back, I'll know why."

"Gan! HE's not worse than Second Amitzas! I don't think anybody alive is worse than Ice Eyes. If I don't come back would you look after Ili for me?"

"I'm kidding, you're going to fikken *come back!* But you know, of course I'll look after him, if anything happens to you." He looked at me under his brows. *"Fikker."*

"Yeha. I am sometimes." But I grinned at him while I said it. Suddenly I felt full of wild recklessness. This was going to be fun, even if it was dangerous. Even if he did find or figure me out, he probably wouldn't drag me off to his sister in Arko. Probably. He might throttle me himself but that wasn't... well... I'd just have to be careful to be Minakas through and through. And not get found out.

The Hearthstone Independent was the newest building in... or rather just outside Vae Arahi, uphill. The Assembly had gifted Chevenga's family with the use of the land to build on and it had been built by donations of Yeolis and others all over the known world.

An Arkan would call it a middling to large *Aitzas* manor house, built Yeoli style with the steep pitched roofs to throw off snow over the edges of deep porches all around, not only the first floor but the second. There were arched windows set in the roof all along for the third floor, giving what would have been a severe cedar shingled expanse a whimsical, inquisitive look, almost like Chevenga's arched brows when he was curious. And all Arkan glass.

I could see a glass room off the south side second floor as I came up the path, which was curved completely naturally into the mountain, though it had been carefully laid out, I could see. An Arkan architect would just have rammed it straight from town to house. The house had no 'wings' coming off the sides, but a series of terraces and gardens curved around it and up the mountain behind.

The front doors were a fantasy of dark wood and light glass where Yeolis would have had shutters before, or perhaps a green pieced-glass window instead of the clear, see-through panes.

I was met at the door by someone I recognized and I ducked my head, hoping beyond hope that he would not recognize me. Skorsas Trinisas. Of course. He was a grown man now. And a devastatingly beautiful man, perfectly turned out. Now his beautiful clear blue-with just a hint of turquoise-eyes were set into the fine lines of a man, his hair my shade and cascading down past his knees. "Ser," I said in my best *fessas.* "This abject one's bin bidden here by the exalted owner."

"Shefen-kas, it means?" he said, two-down as was appropriate to his current station. "Name?"

"Ay, exalted ser. This un's name's Minakas Akam *fessas,* ser."

"Minakas Akam? That name sounds familiar... it looks familiar, too, I'm sure I've seen that face. Oh..." His perfect brows rose. *Oh, no.* "I know who you are!"

6

____

I WISH I HAD FAMILY

I HELD MY BREATH SO HARD I SAW SPOTS. *THIS WAS SUCH A BAD idea.* "The exalted ser knows this 'un?" I managed to squeeze out.

"Yes... Minakas Akam, the writer, right? That's why he invited it... he was talking about it the other day, how it's only twenty-one when he thought thirties or forties for sure. Come on in."

"Writer, ay ser..." *Breathe! Breathe!* "Thenk the gracious ser fer his rememb'rence of this 'un, ser." He showed me in while I yanked my heart back down out of my throat. A number of the house dogs came barking up to greet whoever was at the door and a lovely brindle hound sat politely behind the pack, waiting its turn to be petted.

Once we were out of the entry hall with its cleverly disappearing closet doors, he lead me around to a very nice little dining room... well. Little if one were used to the Marble Palace. One of the walls was mostly glass doors open to the roofed-in central garden with potted *paila* trees almost brushing the glass ceiling. Two parrots... one scarlet, one blue and gold, obviously not allowed into the room while food was being brought in, pacing sentry back and forth along the door-sills.

The dogs found their way through from somewhere else and lined up behind the parrots, gazing hopefully into the room with the food. A blue-pointed wing cat, hung from his tail from one of the potted trees, pretending he was not coming in just because he chose not to, licking his belly fur.

The chandeliers above were partly lit and above them, drifting in the rising heat from the candles, was the ceiling hung moyawa that he entered Arko with to conquer it. It was the Banner of Yeola-e in wing-form, the blue and green with the seven white stars... scorched here and there where an ember had caught it from the burning city. I dropped my eyes to the chaos around the table, which was round and could easily seat more than a dozen with an odd circle of miniature wheeled carts set up in the centre. Everyone was coming in from a door at the back, obviously a kitchen, with things in their hands, the children trotting back and forth with eating utensils of all sorts.

The youngest little boy walked in, carrying only an eating pick but was directed by Skorsas as we came in. "Set that on this side, Roshten," he said and the toddler did his work proudly before scrambling up into a children's chair already set up for him. The muscular dark-skinned woman was his wife, Niku, very different from when she was the wild-woman fighting in the Mezem.

She wore an eye-burning pink pareo over black trousers and a black sweater tight to her chin and wrists. Her wavy hair was almost shoulder length now and held in place, apparently by a flower that matched the hip-cloth. She placed a glass dish with a cover into one of the little carts upon the table and settled Roshten into his chair with a tray clipped before him.

The other Arkan in the room must be Kallijas. I had never seen the man up close in Arko, though I had heard of him. I had a Hero card... had a Hero card when I was still Minis. His hair was tied back and loosely clubbed up so it was impossible to see the length. He stood and marshalled the older children at what had to be the kitchen door, blocking the red parrot's sneak attempts to walk in, with his foot. "No, Pitpit. I see you there, stay out."

Tawaen and a girl who must be a near-age sister were filling the animal's bowls along one wall and a dark-skinned - but with *Aitzas* blond hair -- little girl poured water into holders on perches for the birds. Each bird had several pieces of fruit and what looked like whole nuts the size of my head... like the Haian's tree nuts... apparently nailed for them to gnaw upon. Chevenga himself came out with a glass pan balanced on each hand... on a hot pad, with a blond Arkan boy about Tawaen's age following him... he had the look of Kallijas about him.

"Minakas! Welcome!"

It was like a shock every time I saw him. Each time reminding myself that he was no longer that flesh puppet the fat guy had made. I ducked my head. "Kere Chevenga, hello." I reminded myself to speak Yeoli. Nothing but Yeoli, he never heard me speak it... I didn't know it then. I'm safe from any recognition as long as I spoke it.

He set his glass bowls into two more little carts and pointed at one of the seats. "Have a seat - say - this one."

"Should I help?" *A fessas would help.*

"Sure, if you like. Come with me." He led me into the kitchen, much smaller than the ones in the Marble Palace but big enough to easily feed a ball or large party. Only one of the four stoves was lit and glowing. Two other Yeolis, a woman and a man split around us with baskets of bread in their hands. "We're almost set, Chevenga, not much left to carry," the man said.

"Thanks Etana." I was handed a cool, clear glass bowl of butter and a stack of face towels and a pepper mill, while Chevenga scooped up a lone tray of full glasses of water and juice of various colours. A Haian just entered, drying his hands, from another door. "I'm here Chivinga. My last patient just left."

"Good, Kaninjer can you please bring the salt cellar?"

From the dining room there was a general cry of 'Begone Bird!" echoed by a squawk and a bird-voiced repeat. "Rawk, Begone, Begone, Begone."

"Your Yeoli's very good for an Arkan your age."

"Thank you, ke... Chevenga. I had friends in Asinanai who taught me." It smelled so good in the kitchen, my stomach rumbled loudly enough to make me blush. "It smells so good."

"Krisinga here..." his hands full, he nodded at the man untying an apron and apparently preparing to join the family at table. ".. has his work cut out for him, trying to satisfy all these different tastes."

"Oh, Krisinga, can you bring a set of Arkan eating tools for our guest?" His and my hands were both full.

"Certainly, Chevenga."

It was a little overwhelming, all the people and the friendly, happy noise and the smell of food. It all mixed together as things were rapidly sorted out at the table, minor squabbling among the children whose turn it was to call the animals in to eat.

"You called them in yesterday!" "I did NOT! That was Vitara!" "Did not! That was Vriah!" "No, it was you."

Vriah appealed to her father. "Aba, tell them to stop. It's hurting my heart."

"Ah ah ah - it was Vitara yesterday, Vriah the day before - it's Kila's turn."

"Thanks Aba."

"You're welcome love."

The girl stood up and whistled. "COME COME COME EEEEEEEEAT!" And there was a muffled thunder of furred feet, a whirr of wings, a whine or a bark or two and then the sound of a slobbing lot of high-speed eating from all corners of the room.

"Who's leading the Haian prayer tonight?" Chevenga continued.

"Too much praying, not enough eating!" I was amazed that Roshten would speak up like that.

"Shush!" One of the girls... Kima I think, said. "It's how you learn to be MINDful, stupid."

"I will Aba," Vriah said. And I watched Skorsas just take Chevenga's hands on one side and a child's on the other, but Kallijas and his son both raised their hands to pray and people took hold of their elbows. There was a short round of a prayer in Haian, Niah, Arkan and Yeoli expressing thanks for the food. Then I found why the food dishes all had wheels. The lids were clipped down and people would wheel them across the table to the person requesting it, but the person on one side or the other would stop the dish -"more gently, please, Kila-" and serve the person asking, so no one ever had to serve themselves.

Kaninjer, on my left, offered something I did not catch to Tawaen who offered it to me and I recognized a braised vegetable seaweed I'd eaten on Haiu Menshir. "Thank you, yes. I like that."

Two dogs circled Roshten's seat and I could see why. He kept leaning over to drop food down to them. "Roshten, you keep your food on your tray," his mother said to him.

"But I like feeding dogs!"

"Feed yourself first," she said. "Here, taste this."

"Give them the parts you can't eat - the gristle, the bones. That's the parts they like the most." Chevenga saw me looking at the odd serving dishes... the one in front of me was a miniature copy of an Arkan brewer's cart and had some kind of creamy coloured bean dish in it. "I got the idea of rolling dishes from Arkan *faib* skates."

"That's a wonderful idea for a big table," I said.

"It's a test of skill. If someone doesn't pass it with enough strength and it stops in the middle of a really big meal, someone has to fetch a broomhandle or quarterstaff to liberate it. But you don't want to push hard enough to splash the soup even with the lid clipped on!"

"Or bash two together if you didn't hear someone call at the same time," the Yeoli woman said.

"That's how the asparagus mango dish was invented!" Chevenga was smiling.

"Two dishes collided on the table," Niku said. "What a mess! Pitpit thought that was permission to land upon the table and help us clean up."

"We should introduce ourselves to our guest," Chevenga said turning to his right. "Skorsas, why don't you start?"

7

STARVING IN THE MIDST OF PLENTY

HE DIDN'T EVEN STUMBLE AT REFERRING TO HIMSELF AS *AITZAS*. BUT that would have been less than smooth or polished and he would never be either.

Beside him as Chevenga's oldest girl, Kima, and then her shadow sister Kila, oldest child of the couple who where the other half of Chevenga and Niku's four, Shaina and Etana. They were full Yeolis, bureaucrats, he'd married before he found his love match. Because of the debate in the Assembly over him marrying Niku, anyone who followed Chevenga's life knew he'd married them, and they him, for convenience.

Another child of theirs was on the other side, a boy named Vitara. Then came Kallijas, the Younger next to his father Kallijas. No one mentioned the scandal there any longer because the elder Kallijas had made the woman who bore the boy his 'year wife' and made it all right with the Gods, so his son could not be called a bastard.

Then came Roshten who ceased beating upon the tray of his chair with a fork and announced, mushily but perfect in its particulars, ""My name is Woshai Tennunga Shae-Awano-e aht Niku nar sept Taekun called Woshten. My blood-daddy is Iwaen Shewenga Shae-Awano-e and my shadow-mama is Shainano-e Anataeya and my shadow-daddy is Etana Shae-Sai."

"I'm pleased to meet you, Roshten," I said to him as carefully as if he were an adult.

"I'm pleaztoomeetyou too." He said, grinning and almost knocked over his juice cup which was caught by his mother Niku next to him.

"I'm Niku aht Tanra nar sept Taekun, sometimes called Wahunai." I nodded at her. Next to her was Krisinga, the cook for the family, Tawaen, then Kaninjer, then it was my turn.

I took a sip of water to moisten my throat a bit. "I'm Minakas Akam, *fessas*." *Good I didn't stumble on that one.* "I write freelance for the Pages and I'm studying Arkan Political History. I'm very glad to have been invited tonight. Thank you.

And then every eye wasn't on me any longer which was a relief. I was quivering inside and even though I was hungry I was starting to get the nervous signs that I shouldn't keep trying to force things down. I sipped my water more and sat back, trying to draw into the background and watch the magnificent chaos all around me.

Chevenga kept telling me what was this, or that. I had to demure at the *kri* though.

"I cannot eat spicy foods. I'll eat anything else, thank you."

"All right," Chevenga said. "Try some of... Kall, can you roll the spinach rice over here please?" The little cart carved to look like a chariot, skittered across the table as if coming to his hand. "Thanks, love. Here, Minakas, try some." That was nice and I ended up being able to eat more than I thought, even just a spoonful here and there.

"The food is all wonderful!" I exclaimed at one point and Chevenga turned to the cook. "Did you hear that, Krisinga?"

He leaned back to address me behind Kaninjer and Tawaen. "Thank you, Minaka."

"Oh you're welcome... you are amazing." I was impressed because this food was as remarkable as any I'd eaten elsewhere, even in the Marble Palace where too much ostentation and over-treatment ruined a lot.

"Well, I did not do it without help," he said. "To cook all these people's dishes." I noticed a number of the older children smiling at that.

"I don't have an occupation now so I spend a fair amount of time in the kitchen," Chevenga said quietly. *He is doing some of the cooking?* I nearly fell out of my chair and tried to hide it. *The one time Imperator of Arko might have cooked this food?*

I sipped more water and managed to come up with a fib to offer the table. "I was in a boarding school where the food was awful." *A Mahid boarding school, in the woods.*

"They are as a rule, as I understand," Kallijas said.

Skorsas spoke up. "What would they serve you?" *He'd been a Mezem boy and never had the opportunity to go to a boarding school, even a fessas one.*

I noticed that in Chevenga's presence the two Arkans spoke Arkan, though equal to equal. I stuck to Yeoli. "The meat was always tough if there was any. There was one cook who alus scorched the eight-day roast..." *-- That had been Tathanas Mahid –*I thought.

"I never do that," Krisinga said, to a chorus of agreement.

"And barley porridge fer breakfast, cold barley soup for lunch and barley soup for supper. Oh, and for a treat -- barley and pea soup."

"Not as bad as army food, I'll bet," Chevenga said.

"Oh dad, quit complaining." It was odd to hear an Heir chastising his father.

"You haven't been there yet, my child." Chevenga grinned at him. "You have no idea what our souls... and our tongues... suffered."

Niku said, thoughtfully, "Niah army food is a lot of roast pork... but then we always were close to home," she caught herself. "Usually close to home."

Chevenga turned to me. "They roast it buried in the beach." I couldn't imagine how that was possible. "With giant cormorant eggs and mangos and earth apples."

"Doesn't it get covered in sand?"

"It's wrapped in *paila* and yellow-fruit leaves." He sipped his own juice. "All armies should eat like that. Unless I'm fighting them."

"Aba, didn't you say that you could use the hardtack as a weapon?" That was Vriah. Tawaen laughed and cut in.

Yeah, put it in a slingshot!"

"Yes, love, we were considering that when I was fighting the Lakan war. Shooting our hardtack into the enemy camp. They were *doomed."*

That summoned up giggles from the children all around. "But then, the first night,when I went up on the mountain to think, this little girl came and offered to show me the Lakan camp for a piece of hardtack. She ate it so desperately..." His gaze looked into the past, even as his fingers absently rolled another dish expertly across to Kaninjer who had quietly asked for it. "I realized how lucky, in truth, I was." His eyes came back to the now. "So, you're right, Tawaen, I shouldn't complain. If you're hungry, worms'll taste good."

There was a resounding chorus of "EEWWWWWWWWWWW" from the children and round of smiles from the adults.

An impulse I didn't understand, truly, as if I were teasing Ili prompted me to add "You have to squish the dirt out of them first."

Chevenga grinned at that. "The voice of experience." Even as the children squirmed or cried 'eww' again.

"No, no I just interviewed someone!" I was smiling. "Honestly!"

Vitara said "You... ate WORMS?"

"No, no, Vita, they're just kidding."

"I figured one day I should try it." I said, even as Chevenga said "Again."

"I haven't yet." Some of the children actually looked disappointed that I, the exotic guest, hadn't actually eaten worms. "But crickets are very crunchy."

"EWWWWWWW."

"So when you do the grand experiment of worm-eating, you are going to write it up for the Pages?" Chevenga winked at me. "In the form of a restaurant review, perhaps?"

"That would be good idea." *Better than anything a Mahid could cook.* "One thing I cannot eat. Akopo-e Asinanai style any longer. A... friend of mine has a domoctopus and it would be too much like eating a friend."

"We have a domoctopus!" Kila said. Her sister chimed in with "She's in her aquarium right now."

Kaninjer tore a piece of bread in half. "I recall someone trying chocolate in kri sauce, once."

"So," Chevenga said, loftily ignoring his healer. "...before we make each other throw up, let's change the subject: Mini--I mean Minakas, what are you researching?"

That stumble again. My throat and stomach closed up tight. I wasn't as safe as I had started to imagine myself.

I couldn't help it, my voice dropped. "I'm researching Yeoli/Arkan relations during the war of the travesty."

"There were some?" Tawaen asked me.

I answered the girls in an aside. "Really? I'd love to see it later if she wants to come out," and turned to the Heir. "Yes, actually. Notyere and the Imperator Tathanas were apparently friends."

"We can show you the whole menagerie!" That was Vriah. I partly heard her even as her father said, "Well, you found some evidence that there was Arkan encouragement for Notyere to do what he did," Chevenga said.

"I'd love to meet them all," I said to the little girl. I was suddenly overwhelmed with the conversations I was trying to keep track of and the questions and the disguise and the fact that all of this love and camaraderie and inclusion was all illusory. It was all a fairy story. It wasn't for me. It was never going to be for me. I could not imagine myself the patriarch of such a table, of such a place. I could only see myself alone in my rooms, like an elderly Ailadas, with not even a sister to keep house for him. Alone.

I couldn't bear any more food, the words were almost too much as it was. I pushed my plate away slightly. "Yes... apparently there were a number of times that Yeolis allied or at least met with the leaders of other sea powers, usually to get around trade embargos and trade route monopolies on land... that long coast...one reason I was in Asinanai." I took a deep breath and managed to keep my dinner in place. "...looking at their records."

"The animals records?" That was little Vitara, looking confused. I blessed him for taking their attention, the pressure of their regard, off me. Several of the children laughed.

"No, no, silly!" Kima said.

He isn't either silly or stupid. I turned to him and answered. "No, the Asinanai's tax records, Fitara."

His father chided her gently. "Kima, that's how he heard it."

"I sorry I wasn't being clear," I said. My own voice sounded thin in my ears and I was overwhelmed suddenly with a wave of sadness. It was too much. I couldn't bear it.

Chevenga leaned over and murmured in my ear. "Are you all right, lad?"

I jumped, a little. "Oh! Oh yes, ser... I mean kere..." I choked my feeling down again. "You have a big family."

Vriah, across the table, was looking at me with sympathetic eyes as if she understood and I looked down.

"Tonight you are part of it," he continued. I nodded and signed chalk. "We had a very small family, for our caste, Chevenga." He reached to put an arm around me, holding me together. It was so much like how he used to hug me. Just me. Not who someone thought I was. Just me. It was almost enough to undo me entirely. I held very, very still.

"Thank you, kere," I managed to whisper.

"Chevenga."

"Yes, sorry, Chevenga."

"Aren't you hungry any more? Would you like something more, lad?"

"Oh. Um. No, thank you. Just some more water or juice will suffice me."

"Whatever you need."

Oh, how I wished you knew what I needed. How I wished I could just go back in time and be your son instead of the fat guy's. Why? Gods why did I have a father, as family, who did not know how to love? I'm sorry... Ancestors, could you ask the Gods that for me? Why was I raised starved for what flows so freely around this table?

I straightened and he let me go. *Such easy hugs.* I pointed at a dish I hadn't tried. "What's this?"

Tawaen said "It's good for you. Eat it and I'll tell you!" I had to laugh at the obvious parental voice in his mouth.

"All right."

Kima chimed from across the table. "It's not worms, we promise."

"Or eyeball soup," Chevenga said.

"EEWWWWWWWWWW! DADDY!!!!" Came the chorus of children again.

"And you wonder why your kids are considered unusual," Kallijas said dryly.

I swallowed and tried to join in again. "Or domoctopus in aspic."

"I *like* domoctopus in aspic," Skorsas said. *Oh dear.*

Vitara exclaimed in absolute horror. "You'd EAT Kinarina?" His face was a study of total shock the way Ili did just before opening his mouth to do a major wail. As if someone had just offered to eat his Jia Klem.

"No no no no no! Never mind..." Skorsas backpeddled rapidly. "Can't stand it."

"Shefen-ka, what's eyeball stew?" Little Kallijas said, pulling on Vitara's elbow to distract him.

"Stew with eyeballs in it," Chevenga said without a pause.

"He first saw it up at Sukala's!"

"That's the only place I've ever seen it," Chevenga said.

My stomach and guts had settled down somewhat. "I saw some once in the city," just as Chevenga said. "Oh I forgot, Feliras's Glory, too. Sheep eyeball on a bed of rice..."

"That place... was unbelievable," Skorsas said, reminiscently.

8

PEOPLE PROTEST AS THEY CAN

I clamped my lips shut as I realized I had almost slipped up, opening my mouth to speak. The *fessas* boy I was would never have gotten past the *laefetas* doors. I sipped more juice. "Really?" I tried to ask as innocently as I could. "What was it like inside? I heard it was very different before the… ummm." I sputtered to a stop, not wanting to mention the sack at all. "Never mind."

Skorsas looked at me indulgently. "Well, let's start with this – if you had to ask the price, you just couldn't afford to eat there. It was unbelievably ornate inside, all gold and glass… just glistening. Waiters who could have been assassins so quick and quiet and unobtrusive they were." That made me laugh because it was true. "You tucked the tablecloth into your collar."

"Before the sack?" Chevenga said quietly. "We're describing it before the sack. It's not the same. Which I regret." I could feel the weight of his gaze on me. "You're from the city, aren't you, Minakas?"

"Yes, Chevenga." I turned to look at him, thought I didn't want to. He was going to apologize and I didn't think he should. The chatter and clatter around the table had stopped, everyone listening. *Why do you have to do this?*

"Did you lose anyone?" His tone was perfectly even. Even Roshten looked a little somber.

I took a deep breath. I'd thought about the answer beforehand. "My father was killed." *Absolutely true.* "My mother and I..." *If you count Binshala as my mother...* "we were out of the city then."

"I am sorry."

I didn't want him sorrowing for that piece of shen who started the whole war that took the Empire down and tortured, raped and murdered far more than Chevenga ever did. "Chevenga... you read my piece about how we Arkans feel the need for atonement? As if we could have taken the sins of the old Imperial line and made it right by suffering? Your sorrow for our losses is *wrong!* But if you need to hear it –" I could almost hear Zinchaer and perhaps Misahis distantly – "I certainly forgive you with my whole heart."

"Yes, I did read that." The old black dog padded over and thrust his head into Chevenga's lap, not searching for food but giving what comfort he could. "It was very interesting."

"We as a nation needed to be removed from our own power!"

"Thank you," he said softly. "The sack was not necessary for that." He carried pain for that still, you could see it in the drawn lines of his face. After all we did to him and he STILL cared that much for Arko. *Oh you fools who voted such a man out of his office.* "But thank you."

"You did us good, Chevenga." *Why could he not see that? Both Skorsas and Kallijas are nodding, they know.* "Don't *ever* forget that you set us free. You did us good. We needed surgery." *I remembered a half a dozen dreams of drowning in corruption.*

"I think that remains to be seen."

He's not paying attention. I sat back abruptly and then ducked as the red parrot decided she liked me and flapped over to land on the back of my chair. "Pitpit!" Niku called sternly and the parrot turned her head upside down at her.

"Don't try and eat his hair. It's like Skorsas and Kallijas's. It's attached."

Chevenga ran one finger around the rim of his glass, looking at it. "I think it's too early to truly say."

For some reason I needed to argue with him. "But we are are a voting people now, because of you. Or a voting people again, perhaps."

"I am just hoping that sticks." He tilted his head at me. "Again? Well, that's what I find most interesting about your work. More humane customs buried in Arko's history. It takes away from the claim that anti-voting people make, that it's a Yeoli thing. It isn't."

People were mostly picking at favourite dishes by now and eating utensils more often than not were down rather than in use.

Skorsas got up and fetched a decanter, waiting on a sideboard, with glasses for all the adults and poured for everyone as deftly as a waiter at the Fig or the much reminisced about Feliras's. While he did that the table was cleared of things not wanted in a swift chain of hand-to-hand children, giggling and teasing that no one got gravy or sauce on themselves.

Just as swiftly a round of small bowls came out with various flavours of iced creams in them and a serving tray of frozen fruit and hot sauces. It was better than some of my celebration cakes.

"We not the only people who have voted," Chevenga said to me under the cheerful clatter of desert and wine. "We never were."

I signed chalk at him. "Here, Minakas, try some of the chocolate iced cream with frozen pink grapes."

"Thank you."

Kila chimed into our conversation. "People who say that are just stupid!"

Shaina looked at her and said quietly while people laughed. "Perhaps a little severe to say they are stupid; more likely unknowing."

"Or just seeing it differently, love," Chevenga said.

Why could I not keep my mouth shut? "Or deliberately destroyed, in some cases. Tyrants hate free people who insist on speaking what they feel." *Even under truth-drug,* I thought, thinking of Joras Mahid, dying under the fat guy's feet because he told the truth.

"Yes," Chevenga said. "To preserve power... But when it is within living memory, it is much more powerful. And I did want to give Arko that."

"I should tell you about the Jitzmithra protests –" I almost said, 'my father' but managed to choke that back. *Minakas Akam, fessas. Remember that for the rest of your life or you'll be dragged out into the square and beheaded because they fear you are like your father.* I was not safe here, for all that I felt so. "That Sixteenth Kurkas put down, fourteen years into his reign. No matter how helpless, people will push their protests as far as they can."

9

GIVING UP POWER

"I DON'T KNOW IF YOU EVER READ MY PIECE ABOUT THAT. IT WAS called 'Protests and Massacres' and was about why you almost never see horse costumes during Jitzmitthra."

"Yes, I did. You might not believe this Minakas but I look for your stories." Chevenga's eyes were intent on me and I suddenly wanted to sink into the floor for very different reasons. It was almost too much attention. When I wrote the political stories for the Pages I had originally begun writing them as if to him. Now finding out that I had succeeded was almost embarrassing.

"I will tell you... to be absolutely honest? Oh... and off the record...!" Of course he had to say that... as far as he was concerned I was a journalist. I could feel my face heating because I didn't think of myself that way, truly. I just wrote things. "Giving up power was very, very hard."

That surprised me. "Truly?" Tawaen was listening very carefully, I noticed, and Kima and Vriah both. It was unlikely that the girls would need to know such things but they were in line of succession.

Chevenga's voice was very soft. "I kept thinking, 'But what if I give it to someone else and they screw up?' As if I am perfect. But it's almost as if you think, sure, I can make mistakes... but at least they'll be my mistakes." He sipped at his water rather than his wineglass. "Ones I don't mind so much... It was very very hard. It would be hard for anyone... One reason why you so rarely see it."

"Yes," I said softly to not break too much into his thought, just encouraging him to go on.

"I look back sometimes and think, 'What have I done?'" He continued. "Throwing Arko into uncertainty again..."

I couldn't help it, I needed to argue that. "No. No you did the right thing. It is our uncertainty now, because of the vote. We chose, because you had the courage to give us the choice."

His eyes came back from the middle distance to settle on me and he smiled just a little. "I know. All these things are fear talking. You should never listen to fear as a counsellor. Fear or conceit."

"Chevenga... this is off the record... but may I take my starting point for a story, that line? Fear is a bad Counsellor?"

"Sure. It's not even mine."

"Thank you."

His grin grew a touch shy as if he were confessing a minor misdeed. "I don't own it. I actually wrote about it in one of my columns... at least one..."

"Yes, you have. I've read every one."

That had been Intharas's inspired idea to ask the former Imperator to write columns for the Pages. There were always a lot of letters in response.

"But as I was saying, you'll have your take on it, which will be different. A decision based all or even mostly on fear will be a bad decision, every time. Unless it is a decision of the body, such as, "A mamoka is charging me, I'd better get out of his way.'" The older children laughed, and Vriah smiled, obviously having heard such things before. They were not being dismissed from the table to let the adults talk, but were part of it, if they chose.

The youngest were still making puddles in the iced creams with their spoons but the older children were all there. They were interested. My throat almost closed up with longing that I couldn't express. Considering all the bad decisions the fat guy made that he decided based on both fear AND conceit, I could see his point. For some reason Vriah was looking at me again, with more compassion and understanding than a child so young would have, normally. More like a much older child.

"Those situations are pretty simple!" Tawaen said.

Kila chimed in. "Yeah. You just get out of the way."

"Or get squished," Vriah said and Vitara protested, "You could throw a spear at him instead."

"Or fire arrows," young Kallijas chimed in.

"They're very effective against mamokal," Kima said, apparently quoting a lesson of hers.

"Unless they're soaked with water first," Tawaen said, sticking his tongue out at her.

"…even so, they're scared of them," Chevenga said, raising an eyebrow at his son, who blushed.

"—sorry, Kima," he said quietly to the approving nods of the adults.

"If it's a decision of the mind, you make it by thinking it through and not letting fear distort your thinking."

"Hmm… see an avalanche coming… run?" I offered to the table.

Tawaen took me up on it. "Not straight away from it, because it'll catch you. Try to get off to the side. –" even as Vriah said "Or hide behind something really really big like a big rock or cliff."

I grinned at them. "Just don't get so scared you freeze."

"Bad decision," Chevenga said.

"Chevenga, may I ask you… would you say for most things, the worse decision is to 'not' move?

He thought for a moment, even as Kall said. "It depends." And Niku said "If you're flying it is indecision that kills."

"Most things?" Chevenga smiled at his spouses. "That's a question of how many. Hard to say. Sometimes it's absolutely the best decision."

"Yes," I said. I hadn't asked it clearly enough. "But that is an active decision to 'not move' rather than passive one. Deciding by not deciding."

"Deciding by not deciding is a bad move. If it turns out good, that is only by chance. The best decisions come out of deciding."

"It is an active thing, not a passive one, even if the decision is to sit still," the elder Kallijas said.

"General Pasen said that once." I remembered him sitting out of sight of my Mahid, behind a screen, teaching from the shadows.

"If you look away -- you interviewed him?" Chevenga looked intrigued.

"Oh, no" My heart was in my throat suddenly and I was glad to seize on the excuse he offered me. "I didn't. I read it in the military library at the University." I couldn't say which piece I would have interviewed him for… I had no reason…

"Ah. Interesting person. I like him a lot."

Roshten asked to be let down and Niku wiped his face and hands with a wet cloth and unlocked the tray for him. Vitara and Vriah and he exused themselves and made me promise I would come see the domoctopus later. The brindle hound came and put her head on Kaninjer's lap as he sat and listened to the table talk.

"I studied General Mud's plans when I was in the Mezem," Chevenga continued after the children and a goodly number of pets had clattered off. "Then got to talk to him once I was Imperator. Rehired him. He was yet another good mind driven away by Kurkas." *Didn't I know it.*

Chevenga nodded at the glass of wine I had barely sipped. "Why don't we clear the dishes and then we can sit in the garden so you can finish that in peace? The children will want to show off their menagerie soon enough."

"Oh, certainly, kere Chevenga."

Niku said "Kallijas," – obviously addressing the boy not the man – "run and fetch Vitara would you? It's our turn to wash dishes tonight."

"Yeah, Kall, if he doesn't come he'll owe us one," Kima said, gathering up bowls and spoons.

10

I NEVER WANT TO LEAVE

The cheerful clatter and pretend protests of the children that they had to work soooo hard, was like music, though music I had only heard a faint echo of in the Marble Palace, when I was pretending to be a servant boy. The servants and slaves there, in the vast kitchens, had been making the work as cheerful as they could rather than expressing true happiness.

It was also done very quickly with everyone knowing the routine. I helped carry, but as a guest was settled to one side where the stove still radiated a lovely heat. I hadn't noticed any of the traditional Yeoli stoves anywhere but the house was warm. The kitchen stove was the first heater I had seen. It was something innovative, I was certain, but put it aside to ask about later.

I sipped my wine and watched and listened. "I like big families," I found myself saying suddenly. "Since mine was so small." *And so mad, bad, and corrupt.* That, of course, I didn't say.

"You'll fit right in here, then," the adult Kallijas said to me, with a smile, passing by with a stack of cleaned plates to put away in the butlery.

"You wrote about horse costumes being a form of protest that Kurkas hadn't liked?" Chevenga came back to that, sitting down next to me with a cup of *ezethra*, his clean-up work apparently finished. "But you didn't write precisely why he arrested and jailed people during *Jitzmitthra*."

"Oh, that form of protest was linked to a massacre in Tatthanas – and incidentally Notyere's – time. Tatthanas used cavalry to put down a mob in Presentation Square. I'm still researching what that was all about, because the histories all say the mob was rebelling and calling for his downfall and that he was justified in what he did."

"I see. So people wearing horse costumes are in a very subtle way… referring to the Imperator as illegitimate?"

"It can be seen so. No one would ever say the word 'tyrant' out loud."

"Very Arkan. I'll be interested in seeing what you find. Especially with the links with Notyere."

"I'd be pleased to send you a copy once I'm done, *kere* Chevenga."

"Just Chevenga, please."

"Chevenga. May I ask you…how was it… working with generals either disgraced or who had fought you?"

"Two very different questions, Minakas. I generally found that it was easy to work with generals like Dafidas Pasen… and even with his brother, since men Kurkas didn't like most often turned out to be very sensible, practical men." There was a quirk of a grin. "One might say even smart." I had to smile at that. "When I was Imperator I was very happy to find that General Perisalas wasn't dead, merely exiled."

"You – um – called him back from some hinterland where the old Imperator had stuck him… possibly to either get killed or die of some obscure illness?"

"Exactly. I wish I hadn't had to kill Triadas Teleken."

"Is there still a petition to have a statue to him added to the 'Solas Muster?" His gaze was steady on me but the red came up on his cheeks. I hadn't meant to embarrass him. The general's lover hadn't attempted the memorial until after the Impeachment vote.

"Yes. People didn't understand that I would have supported that while I was Imperator. I asked Skorsas…" there he did stumble a little, probably over the idea of having control of his own money… "I donated to the statue trust."

"Chevenga, we Arkans haven't been free long enough yet to under-stand that kind of thing." I tried to tell him that gently. "People still think the Imperator is above the law and a vindictive person." I caught myself again from saying 'my father'. "Kurkas was in power for more than thirty years and his sire was like him, apparently. Bad enough for people to look to Kurkas to save them."

He sighed. "I do think people will change faster than I think they expect. Most people will change lightning fast given the opportunity.

Others, I know, would rather die than change." How odd. He was thinking better of my people than I did.

"You were saying how hard it was to give up power," I reminded him so we could veer away from this topic. "You were surprised?"

"Yes and no. On one level I was relieved. It was an enormous amount of responsibility." For a moment there was a flash of tiredness on his face that was far deeper a kind of fatigue that could be fixed by a few days of rest.

Pitpit flew into the kitchen and straight toward her perch and then at the last moment veered over to land right on my head even though I ducked. I managed not to spill my wine. She seized a hank of my hair and pulled hard even as Chevenga said "Pitpit! NO!" He seized the bird in one hand and held her still so as to not pull my hair, apologizing as he set his tea down and cupped the bird in both hands. "Mini... sorry. I don't know why I keep doing that, sorry again. Sorry, Minakas, Pitpit, let go! Let go right now!"

The bird gave a hair-muffled squawk but did not let go until I put a hand up as well. She grabbed the tip of my gloves, two or three fingers as Chevenga lifted her up and dragged the glove half off that hand. "I'm sorry, Minakas... Pitpit..."

"It's all right, Chevenga. Don't worry..." He set the bird down on the counter between us and she refused to give up the glove. Since she couldn't use her wings held by Chevenga's hands she scrambled on the counter top with her claws trying to walk backwards, still pulling.

"Sorry shadow-daddy. Sorry, Minakas. I let her in." Kila came and held a piece of apple under Pitpit's beak. The pupil of the birds's uncanny eye expanded till it was almost black then contracted to a pinpoint. She dropped my glove fingers and snatched the apple piece then tried to grab my glove again. But I had already drawn my hand back out of reach.

"Thanks, Kila." Chevenga said and carried the bird over to sit it on the perch. "Bad bird. No snatching hair!" He set her on the perch with her apple and tied a ceremonial ribbon around one leg. "You're confined to your perch for a full tenth!"

Pitpit, who could have bitten through the ribbon in a heartbeat sidled over to Chevenga and tried to lay her head against his chest, whining mushily around her apple. "Poor bird! Bad bird! AWWWW! Noooo! Sorry bird!"

"You will be a sorry bird if you get off the perch. No, don't try that."

"I'll come get her when her time's up, Shadow-daddy."

"Thanks, Kila."

"Minakas," she said. "You wanted to see our domoctopus? Shadow-daddy, let's show him!"

Chevenga hugged her and laid a kiss on the top of her head as they turned back to me. My heart was a roil in my chest but I smiled. *Gods, why? Why did I have to be born with a rotten soul and bad blood?* As long as I was a guest here I was part of it and I never wanted to leave. "I'd love to see her? It was a her wasn't it? And any other creature you happen to want to show me."

"Oh, good. Vita has a scarf-snake that just had babies... they're so cute because they want to keep coiling around your fingers but they're almost too little," she said.

"It's too bad they don't live very long..." Chevenga said quietly in my ear. "There are tears every few years because of that. And tiny funeral pyres on the mountain."

She led the way out into the garden from the kitchen and Chevenga caught up my wineglass and handed it to me as we went. Just thought-lessly polite. I might want it. I smiled at him and tried to pour a little wine on the fire in my throat.

"It sounds like you're researching a whole era of a lot more turmoil than was written."

"Well, by all Arkan accounts, Tatthanas's reign was quiet. Not a lot of wars, but that was because he was building up the rejins quietly -- leading to a whole generation of aggression. Of course Arkan historians see this as a good thing. To get a better picture you have to go to other countries and find out their perspective."

"A lot more books are being circulated in a lot more languages." Chevenga said. Totally matter-of-fact when he had every right to be proud.

"And Presses being built in almost every major city in this part of the world," I said, reminding him.

The glassed-in garden was lush and redolent as if it had been growing here for years, the big *pailas* trees in their pots, along with raised beds of flowers as red as the one parrot, and some as blue and gold as the other. There were white flowers cascading down from a balcony all the way around, since the second floor hallway was also open to the garden.

It's impressive, if you've never seen the Marble Palace. Or only once or twice. "You have an amazing manor house, Chevenga!"

To my surprise he blushed red again. "It's not really mine. It belongs to all the people who donated to build it. Mostly Skorsas... but people want it to be mine."

"Probably because they love you," that was... what was her name? Shaina... yes. She sat near a small fountain by a staircase leading up to the second floor.

"Yes, Shaina," he said quietly, "I know."

To me, once we were well up the half-spiral behind his daughter leading the way, he said. "I find it difficult to accept that people want me to have things... especially things like this." I nodded at him. "I've been taught all my life that wealth, an abundance of accumulation, is suspicious," he continued. "Yeolis tend to think of Notyere immediately."

"When they're talking about a man who had the whole Empire of Arko on his hands and gave it up?" I stopped at the top of the stairs. "Even if you said it was hard, giving up that kind of power, you still did it. As always you choose and you show who you are by your choices."

He smiled at me, gold teeth flashing. "Now you're quoting me back to me, lad."

"Yes, I am," I said. "I did say I read all your columns." He laughed.

Kila showed me a room with a number of glass tanks, lit with tiny *kraumaks* in them, some floating, some sitting on the bottoms. The domoctopus was playing with the glittering little balls, arranging them around the bottom of her aquarium.

She came out waving two tentacles when we came in, insisting on being petted, slime and all, before she went back to her toys.

Chevenga offered his daughter a towel, since I had not wanted to get my gloves wet.

There were three bowls with different colours of fish, swimming. Apparently they belonged to Kall the younger, who also had a bowl of frogs, with eyes that shone gold, almost as bright as the lights in their bowl.

"We have a lot of animals in the house." Chevenga said, "The children love them." He was ignoring the big black dog pacing with us, apparently to keep him company, the little black dog alternated between him and Kila.

In this room there were a number of clusters of ribbons hanging from a rack on the door and Kila picked out two. "I want to make Pitpit wear ribbons along with Kvas tonight," she said firmly. "Because she needs to learn manners with guests."

We followed her back towards the stairs and along the corridor met with Etana and Vriah and Kima and Vitara all carrying drums. "We thought they might come in handy later tonight," the man said.

This is turning into a party. "Has everyone finished their schoolwork?" Chevenga took the big drum from his littlest daughter who giggled and said 'I'll get another, Aba," even as Etana signed chalk.

"I think I would like a soak before everyone gets into the instruments," Chevenga said. "No drumheads in the pool room."

"We know, Shadow-daddy," the boy said. "The heads get soggy."

"Would you care to join me in the hot pool?" Chevenga addressed me. "It's shallow, to sit. You needn't worry about swimming."

I hesitated and then thought, *why not?* "Thank you for the invitation. Like the grand-old fashioned baths that were popular in Arko a hundred years ago?"

"I'm told they are like that."

Can I pretend I'm your oldest and just move in? No. I'm your hated enemys' son, who raped you when you were mind-broken. This is just a dream a longing, something impossible. But I can feel it and long for it and want it with all my heart.

"On second thought, Chevenga, perhaps I've imposed on your hospitality enough and should wish you all a wonderful evening."

11

HOW DO I GET INTO THESE SITUATIONS?

HE LOOKED AT ME QUIZZICALLY. "YOU'VE HARDLY IMPOSED. IF YOU wish, of course, but you're welcome to stay."

It had taken all I could muster to say that I should leave, so I smiled at him. "Thank you, Chevenga. I was... nervous I was imposing. I'd like to stay a little longer, if I may." *What are you doing?* It was as if I had a terrified voice inside screeching things at me. *You said you should go. He's already almost called you Minis TWICE, or was it three times?* I told the voice to shut up and followed him down the stairs.

The moon was at the wrong angle to shine in the glass roof but there were kraumaks and wonderful smelling beeswax candles everywhere so we could see easily as we crossed the garden to the side opposite the dining hall. The glass doors there were all shut to keep the moisture in, water condensing down the big sheet doors making them easy to see so no one would walk into them. It was like stepping into my own baths years ago.

There was a lovely, natural looking waterfall pouring down into what I could see was the hot pool from the tendrils of steam rising. There were plants up and down it and channels that could be adjusted so that it could be a rushing stream, churning the pool below, or a mere trickle. The hot pool butted up against and overflowed into what must be the cool pool, big enough and deep enough to swim. Next to the hot pool, so one could walk in, were a graceful arc of steps. The windows looked right out onto the mountain as far as I could tell, the gound falling away on that side but it was dark enough I couldn't see out.

There was a cascade to one side, shut off and racks and cubbies so people could leave their clothing to stay dry. A cabinet to one side held Arkan and Enchian swimming costumes I could see.

"Do you need one?" Skorsas, who was already in the room, tilted his head at the costumes and I shook my head no.

"Thank you. I'm all right."

There were cushions and chairs and padded places to sit, made to look like part of the walls in places, or a glass table by the chairs, should someone wish to sit but not become wet.

I hung up my clothing and loosened my loin wrappings before pushing them down my legs with my scholar's kilt. *There is nothing on my bare body that will give me away. No one will ask about any scars, you won't have to lie about anything... and if you pretend you cannot swim, so much the better, since Chevenga knows he taught Minis how.*

I pulled off my parrot-nibbled glove and the other one, left my spectacles on, however as if I needed them to see with. *Am I dreaming? I'm going to go into a hot pool with Chevenga and we're probably going to talk politics.*

Most of the rest of the family came in to join us, even Pitpit, released from her bondage. Both parrots now sported a ribbon hat placed on them by Kila and looked disgusted with life. The wing cat was at the top of the waterfall, trying to catch drops from a trickle. Then the children hit the water with screeches and yells as they jumped in.

I settled gingerly into the hot pool, as if a little nervous, glad to hide my cringing skin under the froth. It was so hot and felt so good. It was as if I peeled off a layer of rotten just by sinking into it. I couldn't help it, I leaned my head back and closed my eyes, just listening.

The children teasing each other, though it grew a little heated now and again, was truly loving. You could hear it. It reminded me a little of how Gan and I teased each other and how sometimes, Ili was starting to get old enough to try.

The murmur of the adults voices undercut the children's louder, more profligate shrieks. Steady. Interlocking as they spoke back and forth. You could hear they'd rubbed their conversation smooth against each other over years.

"Kall! Kall! Daddy, throw me! Mummy, throw me!" Kallijas and Chevenga and Niku ended up at the deepest part of the cool pool, with apparently murderous intent, flinging their innocent children repeatedly into the water to laughter and giggles and cries of 'more' and 'do it again, please.'

When the adults were tired they came into the hot water, with Skorsas and me. "Too soon after food, to do that," Kallijas said. "They'll all cramp and drown."

"You are teasing, Kallijas," Kaninjer said. He had joined the rest of the family only a few moments ago. "Eating before swimming does not cause cramp."

"Yes, Kaninjer. I am teasing. And you are being serious. Terrible. Just terrible that a man cannot be taken foolishly around here."

A man known to be as lethal with a sword and other weapons as Chevenga. Arkan. And he is teasing a Haian in the gentlest of ways. I don't truly understand how. Chevenga is odd that way because he's Yeoli, but Arkans? The faces of the Mahid who had been all around me in my life marched through my memory, hard as marble. But I was reminded of the *solas* courier I had hired, ruined by his commander over a girl. I had liked his face and manner, soft spoken as Chevenga and now, I found, as Kallijas. I didn't know how good a warrior Tzanas was so I couldn't correlate soft-spokenness and excellence as a warrior.

"Minakas," Chevenga said. "Where did you find out about the unacknowledged graveyard in the Marble Palace?"

I was deep enough into my thoughts that I was startled a little, slipped and coughed up some water. My eyes popped open. "Oh... that..." *How in Hayel was I supposed to explain that one?* Chevenga had slid into the foam a few seats down, Kaninjer was almost across from me, the adult Kallijas on one side of Chevenga, Skorsas on the other. I was next to Skorsas and the rushing waterfall was next to me. "I suppose I could be coy and say a writer never betrays an informant, but really..." *think, you idiot, think...* "A bureaucrat was sloppy about erasing Seventeenth Kurkas's existance...an old bill to the household of the Spark of the Sun's Ray and I realized there was a discrepancy and started digging around."

"So you must have come in and looked at it... after I read that, I went to look at it myself, and it's just as you described."

"Oh it was total chance... a friend of mine... his father was a harness maker and when we boys helped clear out *his* old records, there was an undelivered bill and a letter to Seventheenth Kurkas. The family had hoped to gain the Spark of the Sun's Ray's permanent patronage... and apparently when the order came down that there was no such named

Spark... they never sent the letter, though they should have burned it." *That's plausible enough.*

The sadness in his face made me want to hug him. *He'd* hate *the idea of people vanishing like that.* "I see. You always wonder, when that happens, what sort of person he was, what sort of Imperator he would have been, what he would have done in the circumstances as they were... ah well. How old would Minis have been when he was killed?"

"He would have been in his second year."

Chevenga shook his head, still sad. "I wonder if he has any dreamlike memory of having a brother. I knew Minis... when I was in the Mezem."

"You did?" *Oh my... Sinimas how did we get* here?

"Yes. He declared himself my first fan. He came to all my fights, when he could. And we spoke, several times."

Don't swallow obviously... "I'd heard that he named you. And that he was a little rotter, like his father. I heard stories that he could have you killed, just if he felt like it." *I am going to die and sink into this hot pool, melting away into the drains, never to be seen again, right here as we sit.*

"Yes, Karas Raikas was his idea. He wasn't as bad as his reputation, in truth. He was just being raised without enough love, and he was angry about it, as a child has every right to be.

Why I do some things I have no idea, like worrying at an itchy cut. "Do you ever worry, Chevenga, that he might try and avenge his father on you?" *Knowing myself that's about the stupidest question I could ask. But it would seem like I not know me very well, and it would be the right question for your average Arkan man to ask.* "Whether you are Imperator or not?" *I feel a little like a cat chasing his own tail. What am I truly chasing and what will I do with it if I manage to catch it?*

"I could be wrong, but I don't think so. He and his father... didn't entirely get along."

12

IN ANOTHER LIFE

Minis was just being such a moron. It was too early spring in the mountains to sit outside, but not to go for a walk in the evening after dinner, so Ili and I did. We walked over to the Hearthstone Dependent, to where they'd closed up the new cold-frames over the public gardens for the night, against the chill. All Arkan glass.

I couldn't help but look across the valley to the Hearthstone Independent, lit-up against the dark mass of the mountain. There didn't seem to be any alarms being yelled. So no one had recognized Minis. Yet.

You idiot. You just had *to go to dinner in disguise. You just had to. I could just kick you. You're a wanted fugitive and what do you do, walk into the semana-- the* former *semanakraseye's house right under his and all his guards noses. Minis Kurkas Joras Amitzas Aan, if you get yourself caught and killed because you want to talk to Ch'venga over dinner, I am going to--*
- THWAPSlffff. I staggered a little sideways as something hit the side of my head and latched on.

"Hey!" Jia, cheeping, as loud as he ever got, clung to the side of my head where Ili had thrown him. "That's not nice, kid! Do you think he liked being thrown? You could have hurt him!" I put my hands up and the tentacle he had clinging to my face under my nose let go.

"You weren't listening to me. Jia's all right and so's Minakas. Don't worry, Uncle Gan. He'll be all right. That's what I said and you didn't hear me."

Jiaklem, pulsing between pink and the colour of my shirt, a pale green, crawled down to my shoulder, quiet again. "I suppose. I'm sorry I wasn't paying attention to you Ili, but you've got to promise not to throw him at people it's not polite to him or the person who's got hit."

"It worked!"

"But it still wasn't polite. You cuddle him and say sorry." I held out the pulsing creature to Ili.

"Sorry, Gan." He took his pet and tucked him in a writhing ball into his coat. "Sorry, Jiaklem."

The adults had tired of the water before the children and had all gotten dry. We were out in the garden again, all with fresh glasses. I sat near Kallijas the elder and chatted with him, in my *fessas* accent. Across a raised bed of jasmine vines I could see Skorsas talking quietly in Chevenga's ear. I wasn't worried at first, but then caught Skorsas looking across at me and then back to Chevenga, saying something else.

They're talking about me. My heart contracted. I had to leave, if the real one-time *fessas* suspected me. I watched without watching, my eyes apparently fixed on my wine glass. "Living with Shevenga," Kallijas was saying. "I do have the occasional alcohol, now. I've learned it isn't all or nothing."

"T' honoured *solas* must find it easier," I said trying to be polite while I wondered if I could run straight out the pool room window if I had to. I hadn't seen how far down the ground was on that side of the house. My heart started pounding hard.

Chevenga looked at me, looking quizzically over, then his brow cleared and he signed charcoal at Skorsas, saying something that made the *Aitzas* shrug, glance at me, shake his head as if to illustrate a hair-law... an Arkan still gestures somewhat, even without using hands.

Chevenga held out a hand and he took it. They both laughed and then it wasn't about me anymore. It was about the held hands. I took a deeper breath.

"'m sorry, kere Kallijas." I said in a mix of *fessas* and Yeoli. "I was inattentive, what was that you just said?"

I needed to stop pretending and get out of here so I had to make my goodbyes to my host and I *had* to ask him one more question. I had sent the letter, I had confessed to what I did to him. I had to know.

I excused myself from the conversation and went over to where Chevenga was, seizing on a rare instant when he was by himself, except for the dogs and the wing-cat draped over his shoulder.

"Ch'venga," I said, realizing I was saying his name the way Gannara did... "I had one question I couldn't really ask in the pool, may I ask it now?"

"Certainly, Minakas." He clicked his fingers at the big dog sprawled in front of the bench next to him and pointed. "Shoo, dog, you're always in the way and underfoot." The big dog sighed but got up, slouched over and sprawled again a few feet away.

I sat down and drew my courage in with my breath. I'd never get a chance like this again. "You were talking about Minis Aan earlier. Just between you, me, and this dog... oh, and off the record... it sounded like you truly liked him. Did you?"

I had sent my letter of confession to him when we left Haiu Menshir. He would have gotten it by now. I held my breath.

He looked thoughtful, his one hand petting the wing-cat purring on his shoulder idly. "Yes. Yes, I did."

"What did you really think of him?"

Chevenga smiled a little, in a reminiscent way. "He was very smart for his age. In that way he reminds me of you."

I nearly choked. "Thank you. Um... thank you." I could squirm in my chair, embarrassed, naturally enough. "I'll take that as a compliment."

"You should. In some ways he was older than his years, than he should have been. I only knew him as a child. He had an absolute, unshakeable sense of entitlement. What he wanted, he saw as his by right. But all children have a little of that. He had a good heart, though. As I said, he craved what everyone craves, someone to give him their whole-hearted attention and love and his father was, to put it politely, indifferent to him." *And you are being so careful of my confidences, to a stranger, thank you. Thank you, Chevenga. But I know you are not going to say anything evil about anyone usually, not even the fat guy. That's just you.*

He scratched under the cat's chin and it began purring loud enough that I could hear it where I sat.

"So you consider him... or did consider him a friend?"

"Yes." *Had he somehow not gotten my letter? Were the Gods so merciful? Or did he only mean he considered me a friend in the past?*

"Was it hard to be enemies with the father while friends with the son?" I was craving every word. *He liked me then and, somehow, still did now.*

"Harder on him, actually. He wanted to set me free, for one thing." I could feel my cheeks heating a little and buried my face in my *kaf* cup so I could blame the fragrant steam if he asked.

"Truly." I should sound amazed.

"Yes," he said, making the chalk sign at the same time, for emphasis. "He couldn't do it, though." Roshten came out of the water room and trotted over to his mother for help getting his head towelled dry. "So, why are you so interested in Minis?" Chevenga wasn't looking at me when he asked that, his glance going across to Niku and Roshten. It gave me time to gulp and say,

"Oh, I'm interested in all the political figures through the whole transition... and I mean, the war, conquest, your retirement."

He laughed at my prevarication. "Such a polite way of putting my impeachment."

Oh dear... I hadn't wanted to bring that up, that way. "I'm sorry," I started to say and of course he said "no, no, lad, not at all."

"So, I thought you were more interested in the historical things, the Notyere and Tatthanas era," he continued. "Rather than modern politics?"

"I have that paper to finish researching but it's Yeoli/Arkan relations past and present that interest me."

"Of course finish the historical piece but I have a big library of contemporary political books and papers. If you are going to be in Vae Arahi you could always come back and we could talk about it."

"Oh, I would love that," I said. *Oh how I long to do that and am terrified of it all at the same time.* No, I had to leave tonight.

"We could arrange it then, if you like." I definitely had to leave tonight. "Why don't you let me know once you're done your historical research?"

"Oh, I will, thank you." I wanted so much to fling myself into his arms. I could see the rest of the children in the pool room. Kima and Vriah were rubbing the water off the glass to look into the enclosed garden. They would be out soon and then the music and drumming would begin and I'd not be able to tear myself away.

"Ch'venga, I am so happy to have been invited to your lovely house and to such a good dinner and good company. It has been a wonderful evening."

"Well, you're welcome. I've had a good time talking to you. Perhaps next time we'll be able to get into a more intense discussion, hmmm?"

You have no idea how intense this whole evening has been for me. "I'm always glad to have a good political, or historical, or philosophical discussion, thank you."

He grinned at me and rose. "Let me walk you to the door, Minakas."

"Thank you, Ch'venga."

"If you keep coming back maybe I'll be able to figure out why you are so familiar to me." He was turning to lead the way fortunately so he didn't see my face. I managed to swallow and tried to keep my answer as light as if I were lying to 2nd Amitzas.

"Like you said. Lakans would say you and I knew each other in another life, Ch'venga." *Another life where I was a fat, spoiled rotten child, longing to be loved and you a gladiator all alone, enslaved and imprisoned.*

13

___

A KYASH-SUCKING KEVYALASEYE

Dear Chevenga,

I'm so sorry to have to cancel any other meetings we might have, I have been suddenly called away on an urgent matter of family. My sincere apologies and hope that I might one day be again in Vae Arahi and call upon you and your gracious family once more.

Minakas Akam, fessas.

We reversed our progress down to Hirina but this time, at the crossroads, we headed up river to Tinga-e rather than down to Selina on the sea. We had no destination specifically in mind, so I thought I would perhaps find some interesting books and research materials in the Plains Library.

We took our time and toured sites of the battlefields and memorials along the route where the Yeolis had won their country back.

What was I going to do with my life? And how could I convince Gannara that he should take up his own again? And I couldn't take Ili back to Ailadas, simply because if I were an investigator I would periodically check to see if I had had any contact with him since the last time.

And Ili... I was seeing myself as a crabbed old scholar but I could hardly as him to share my life or try and make him into something he was not. He was smart but his strength was... literally his strength.

What was he to do? Follow me vaguely about the earthsphere playing with Jiaklem? I needed to settle down somewhere, and permanent residency on Haiu Menshir was discouraged or half the world would try to move there.

I wanted desperately to live in the city itself if I could establish my persona as a *fessas* well enough. But Joras showing up on Haiu Menshir showed me that as long as the Mahid were out there, searching for me, I couldn't stay in one place for very long. I had no idea how they were finding me.

It was evening in Tinga-e and I had presented my credentials to the librarians there and already found some interesting articles and correspondences around the time of Notyere... actually his sister Denaina.

Gannara and Ili and I had taken some time to tour the new Tinga-e paperworks. With all the new presses there was an enormous demand for paper and the trees quilted the land in their thickness from Tinga-e up into the mountains right up to where they gave way to the lichens and mosses. It was in Tinga-e that they were growing a kind of rope-weed that made better paper than wood pulp and cheaper than linen ragstock.

The paper works were the most advanced I had ever seen, built by Arkan craftsmen. Likely with loot from Arko as well but I was just as pleased to see it used so. It was big and new and for a small fee they would tour you through the whole process of how some papers were made. I thought it fascinating and Ili seemed to, Gan was almost more humouring us but got caught up when they showed him papers that could be written upon but were water and salt resistant for use at sea.

There were paper masters who made great single sheets of paper with flowers and grasses pressed into them, meant for shade windows and art works, or to be cut into the finest of writing papers.

I bought eight varieties and had them wrapped and sent to Arko for Kyriala and for Ailadas, along with a gold and rosewood pen for her and an inkwood and silver for Ailadas, each in their own presentation boxes.

But it had been a long, full day and Gan and Ili and I had all lain down with the intention of sleeping in the next day, but I found with all I had to think about, I couldn't sleep.

There were torches all along the river and this series of four shallow locks, the thick stone blocks glittering almost white in the moonlight. A rush of water and a distant group of singers made things seem both less lonely and more lonely, both at the same time.

There were gardens all along this walk, with the torches becoming lamps as they proceeded closer to the market place, deserted this time of evening. The only thing open now would be the inns and drinking houses and perhaps a late eating place. Up ahead, the rounded bump of a bridge crossed this canal here below the locks, leading back to our inn. It would offer me a good view and a place to stand and think a while.

I climbed up the steps between two enormous rose bushes, thinking of Ky as I did so, even though it was just past their blooming time. It was too dark to see if they were blue roses.

Where could I settle Ili and I and be safe? A hand came out of the dark and smacked against the middle of my chest stopping me where I walked. I had my hand on it and was going to fight back when the fellow who'd stopped me pushed me back… staggering against someone else's hands. I'd walked right into the middle of a group of Yeolis. Young men surrounding me. In the light of the torch behind the one who'd pushed me I could see five, or perhaps six of them. I sucked air.

"Well, well, well. Hey, Sal, would you look at this? An Arkan *kyash-sucking kevyalaseye*, walking around our country, all by his lonesome, like he owns it."

14

OUCHIE, CALL AND ADVOCATE!

 if they stung. It was so hard to just write as if to another person at home rather than an official report. Reports were so easy. You just took the required words, slotted the new information around them and then signed one's name. There was none of this 'friendliness' nonsense to hide code in.

He burned the first page and took up his pen once more.

Dear Cousin Amitzas,

I'm going to be coming home soon because our dear friend is all healed up and has left Haiu Menshir.

I would have been most diligent in passing on your felicitations to him, had I seen him, but he was healed and had left before I arrived.

I've consulted with the medical glassworkers here and they tell me that glass needles, while a good idea, are unlikely since they are so brittle and are likely to cause more harm than good if used.

I send this letter on ahead to herald my coming and hope to see everyone hale and whole soon.

My best regards,

Joras

~

"What the *kyash* are you doing here, Arkan?" They were swigging out of flasks in their hands, the stenches of alcohol on their breath. "Who do you think wants to see your ugly slab face?" It was all confusion, my hair in my face, my scholar's robe tangling around my limbs as they pushed me. I took a deep breath. *Idiots.* I was starting to be afraid because Mahid are Mahid even if they aren't trained.

"Go back to *kyashin* Arko where you belong!"

"There were enough of you ass-suckers here long enough!"

They were shoving me back and forth between them, too many to fight. I was unarmed and if I killed someone I'd be discovered. I had that flash of thought as my glasses hit the ground and crunched underfoot. I struggled upright and snarled at these young thugs. " War's over! You won. I can walk where I like!"

"No." The next shove half threw me into the arms of two behind. "You can't, you straw-haired piece of *kyash*!"

I cried out "Hey!" even as they thrust me upright and forward, hard and I took advantage of their pushing me, dove under the outstretched arm of the ring-leader and ran like a rabbit.

I heard a flask smash as it was dropped, and cursing. The deep shadows around the rose-bushes gave me a head start and they were after me like a pack of hounds, baying human sounds.

"There he goes! Get him Fin! No, cut him off! Ouch! That was me! There, look there!"

I ran for the bridge thinking that if I could get to the other side, it was that much closer to people, to an inn or something... I tried to dodge, hearing their panting breaths come up faster than mine, they knew the ground better and one flung himself at my heels and both of us landed hard, my chin hitting the grass on the edge of the pavement just at the bridge, with a smack that had me seeing stars.

My breath was knocked out of me and they hauled me upright as they all came up again. They were mostly shaking me around as they spoke.

"What shall we do with you?"

My breath came back with a half-sob and I heaved my chest open enough to snap back "Nothing, *shen* you! Leave me alone! I'm no warrior! I'm just a scholar!"

"Hmm." One of them said. "We hurt you, kill you... a jury would take one look and go, "Oh, an Arkan!" They won't give a flying *kyash* about what we did."

I started struggling harder. One of them cuffed me in the back of the head, another jabbed me in the kidneys, though fairly lightly. They were working themselves up to it. "Let go of me! I never fought! I never hurt a Yeoli!" *That was a lie.*

They were ignoring me, egging each other on. "We could… strangle you…" one of them said, thoughtfully.

"Or smother him," said another. I got an elbow into one gut and he grunted. I could hear bracelets rattle.

"I think we should beat the *kyash* out of you before we decide what else to do to you," he said. The edge of my hand cracked into someone's temple but I was held hard enough it only staggered him.

A fist drove into my gut and I snapped forward around it, vaguely grateful it was only a fist and didn't have a knife in it. Yet. It was getting more vague as another fist glanced off the top of my head. They were getting in each other's way.

"How about flog the *kevyalaseye* to death?"

"Fik you, you dirty wool-heads!"

They were laughing. "Ooooh! Tough Talk! I feel soooo mortified." "Ouchie, Ouchie, call an advocate!" "Whooo! The boy has words! Got any more for us, bumboy?"

"Filthy beasts!" I was on one knee and struggled up to standing, my arms over my head. *Don't go down unless you want to get kicked to death. I hurt.*

"That's what we should do!" One of them exclaimed as I tried to kick, with my robe binding around that leg and one kicked back, hitting my calf. "The Arkan thing!"

"That's *kyashin'* perfect!"

"*Shen, shen, shen!*" I was yelling now as much as I had breath for, one backhanded me across the face and I tasted blood. A hand slapped itself over my mouth.

"Where do we take him? We can't do it here by the bridge, my mother might see."

I bit the hand over my mouth and he yanked the hand away. "*Kyash*! I'm gonna get a disease!"

"Take him into the woods, rape out his brains there." A knee slammed between my legs, doubling me over, gasping, making me sag for a moment in their hands. "I don't know how." "Now's your chance to learn, Kam. If you don't do it with your dick, cause you're too drunk, you can get a tree-branch."

I have to do something to get them off this. I don't want to die, Sinimas,

Ancestors… I surged upright, struggling hard enough that the robe tore, leaving me with my shirt and kilt, the one sleeve of the shirt already ripping. *Can I convince them…?* I thrashed and smashed my toe into one gut and half freed myself, but shied away from the bridge. "Gods! Oh Gods!" I started screaming, as the knot of us lurched toward the canal. "Not the water!"

One of the younger ones sounded uncertain and a little sick. "I don't want to do this."

"You can stand guard, then…and watch our flasks," and to me, "Shut the *kyash* up!" And his fist hit my face hard enough to almost stun me. I sagged a moment then scrambled up, trying to thrash away from the water again.

"Not the water… Gods, no, no, no… oh Gods… anything but the water…"

"The little *kyashaseye* is afraid of water, just like his *fikken* Imperator… Shut the *kyash* up or we'll throw you in!"

"Hey, Fil let's show him the deep part!"

"AHHHHHHH!" I screamed as if completely terrified. *Oh Gods yes, let them try to drown me. "Shen you, shen you, you kaina…"*

They dragged me, struggling, screaming almost as high as Kyriala, to the middle of the stone bridge and heaved me up slamming my gut into the stone rail so I was looking down into the black water. "Shut up or we'll throw you in!"

"HEEEEEELLL—" I got hauled back and struck again, open handed across the mouth, by the leader, I could see the mole on his chin in the lamplight. "Yeola-e doesn't want you, you *kevyalin* ass sucker… I wouldn't soil my dick with you. Shut up or you go swimming."

I managed a sniveling, half scream… "I *can't swim!!!!!! Hellllllp! Assssakkkkkkoooooo.*"

"Then it's straight to the bottom of the canal you little asshole…"

"Throw him over! Throw him over!" I managed to let go enough to piss myself as if I were that afraid of the water. "Eww! Throw him over!"

I was screaming again as they hoisted me up in their grip, struggling… "We'll say we were just joking around and he slipped… oops…" They heaved me back and swung me forward hard, arcing up and I caught a glimpse of the stone flying under me and the black water below before I hit with a huge splash, flailing.

My belly hurt where I'd hit. I thrashed as though struggling, flailing the water up all around me, gurgling and coughing. I went under once, struggled up, splashing, screaming for my mama. I kicked with the current as much as I could and though it was hard, through the flying water, I thought I could see pale faces along the rail of the bridge watching me. "Mikas help m-glgleleph."

I flailed and splashed and went under again. "I'm too yo- cough-ng to die! I –akkkaffspcoug—never fought—" I gagged and made retching noises. *I hope you feel guilty you fikken wretches.* I was trying to give them enough of a show of drowning I caught a breath of water and coughed and choked for real for a bit, slowed my thrashing, gulped a lung full of air and made myself drop under, pulling myself down hard with the one arm, reaching up with the other, till the water closed over my fingertips.

Then I turned and swam as hard as I could underwater in the direction of the trickle of current. My sandals dragged but weren't as bad as boots. *Thank the Gods the robe was torn off. I have to get as far away as I can, underwater.*

It's black as a Srian's armpit I can't see anything how far? OUCH. The current had banged me into something a rock or a log, I was lower than I thought. I was running out of air… I struck for the surface and tried to come up quietly.

Thank my Ancestors the water is cool. Sinimas pass on a thank you to the Gods, please. I'd be hurting a lot more if I weren't in the water. I struggled not to gasp in a lung-full but it was so sweet. I was perhaps ten manheights down the canal, clinging to a set of steps leading into the water for harnessing the tow-animals.

There were no more heads fringed along the bridge and I could hear fast fading feet. However much I wanted to, I wasn't going to complain to the authorities... or show up as a bloated corpse, so my torn-off robe probably wouldn't cause anyone to raise any kind of questions. I heard someone in the distance, but I couldn't make out the words. Probably coming up with a story of some kind. I stayed still and was so glad it was summer so the water was just cool, hanging on to the edge of the steps in the dark and enjoyed breathing.

15

THE STATUE SEEMS EXCESSIVE

Dear M,

The papers and the pen were absolutely beautiful! I particularly loved the paper with rose-petals.

I wonder if you picked this out, and when? And where are you now? The serina from the Marble Palace came and asked me in for another follow up session of questioning. Have I heard from you? Have you written me. I was pleased to be able to tell them no with a clear conscience because I know I have a mysterious admirer but I don't know for sure it is you. I can say I have never received a package from Minis Aan.

This note will, of course, end up in the fire.

I'm afraid Mama is starting to invite eligible young men to our salons, to hear us read and to read in their turn. It is her way of winnowing out any men who would take exception to our reading skill. And I know she hopes I will express my preference for one soon. Unfortunately a lot of these young men… I find rather shallow and feckless. Mama tells me that I should be careful not to let myself get too old to be eligible, though since the war

women are making matches where before they would have been
considered to 'long in the tooth' to be seen as valuable as a wife.

I am starting to question that. I might even allow myself to
become upset by the idea. Such ideas. The new 'Fenjitza' is still a
scandal to half the city and a lot of people have been waiting for
the Gods to strike her down, but she walks in the Temple before
the Goddesses without harm. Personally, I find her sermons to us
women much more… how do I put it… real and practical. Very
enlightening and uplifting, appropriate for a people supposed to
be sprung from the stars.

Mama nearly fainted the first time I invited her and some of her
newly ordained priestesses for afternoon kaf but now finds her
very personable. The mask is a little disconcerting at first, since
everyone had it associated with something supposedly so low as…
dare I even write the words? Yes. Prostitution and midwifery.

This letter is definitely going into the flames. I could share such
scandalous words and thoughts with you M, but I would never
allow anyone else to see them. There are writers who are writing
such radical things in the Pages that a lot of women are talking
about them and their ideas. They are writing about how women
have been gradually demonized in our culture, by fearful Imperators past. A number of people are following their lead and the
Pages are actually printing their writings. Fascinating really.

Did you hear about the new initiative to raise a statue to the
former Imperator, Shefen-kas? They would have to remove most
of 'Solas Muster' on the avenue of statues and perhaps one of the
university buildings to make space for it. There are protests being
staged, the women and children of some of the *solas* honoured
there, even though they have been reassured that the statues
would be removed, with honour to another location, yet unnamed. To my mind the statue to Shefen-kas seems a bit excessive,
even for someone that people are now beginning to revere. It is to
be ten manheights high, seven of which will be the bronze figure
itself.

There is a slow roil of unrest in the city, since people are becoming used to being allowed to express themselves more freely. The Imperatrix, She Who is The Reflection of Holy Light is not hated really, more distrusted, and people are unhappy having an Imperatrix on the Crystal Throne. Especially one who has never done the Ritual of Ascension.

My prayers go with you as you wander, and I wait with breathless anticipation for the next clue to your continued well being.

~

I MANAGED TO CRAWL UP THE STONE STEPS AND STAGGER OUT OF the water. My testicles hurt. My head hurt, my gut hurt, my one knee was strained and my hands and arms and ribs all hurt. They hadn't hit as hard as they thought. For all their talk of rape and their willingness to murder me they hadn't struck with as much intent as Mahid did.

I felt a couple of my teeth where loose and I took good care not to push them free with my tongue. I'd bitten the insides of my mouth. My lips were split and I'd have a black eye in the morning. My nose was probably broken. But I could move.

I burned, wanting to have fought back. I'd won by convincing them to throw me in the river but I still felt shamed. I'd done what I should but I felt like a coward for not having done the heroic thing and fought back with deadly intent immediately. They might have backed off if I'd killed or maimed one or two... but that would have brought the Yeoli authority down on me and Ili and Gannara.

I spat a little blood into the gutter, carefully so as not to send my poor teeth after it. The clerk at the front desk was dozing when I came in so I slipped quietly upstairs. I so wanted to lie down on the bed and wrap my aching arms around my heart's brother but if I did that I'd fall asleep. There were a group of murderous young louts in the city who thought they'd killed someone and I didn't want to disabuse them of that.

I pulled out our packs and began packing by feel. Gannara sat up in the bed. "Brother, what's wrong? What are you doing?"

"I'm packing, heart's brother." I said, a little mushy because of the damage to my mouth. "There's a bunch of kids...young thugs who think they've killed me. They beat me up and threw me off a bridge. I pretended to drown and they scattered. I think we need to leave."

"What?" He climbed out of the bed, quietly so as not to disturb Ili, on his truckle bed, with Jia wrapped around his ears.

"If I try to report them, or they see me and realize they didn't succeed… It'll be a problem all around. The truth-drug will come out… Can we just leave? Please?" I put my sore head down on the pack I was kneeling in front of.

"They think they KILLED you? Are you all right?"

"Yeha, I'm all right. They were going to rape and beat me to death in the woods but I pretended to be so scared of the canal that they threw me in, instead. I pretended to drown." I felt sick and shaking now, light-headed, trembling all over and cold. "Please don't light the lamp… I'll bet I look like *Hayel* on sliced bread right n… n… n…ow."

"Those *kyashin kevyalin kaina mariugh meniren, fikkers*." Gannara hissed as he got up and lit the lamp anyway and saw me kneeling next to our packs, shivering. "Get those wet clothes off, right now, Min. No arguments." His hands on my shoulders felt so good. "Here… I have some remedies from Haiu Menshir that might help." He rummaged and drew out the vials from his bag by the bed.

"I'll get sleepy, Gan and then I'll want to stop moving and if they see us…"

"Shut up. You're going nowhere tonight. You're going straight to bed and you're staying in bed until you feel better. We don't have to run off like thieves in the night. Stay in, don't let the *fikkers* see you." He looked angry.

"If I thought I could get away with it, I'd report you missing…" He turned my head with his hand under my chin to check my eye. "…but I won't. But there's no way you are going running off in the night, looking like you've been stomped by a mamoka. When you're healed up… and I'll look after you… we'll leave like civilized people. We'll just darken your hair a bit for now. Your glasses…"

"They got stepped on." I let him help me up and take off my wet clothes and wrappings. I hurt so bad now all I wanted to do was lie down. I couldn't argue with him. Ili, on his bed, on the other side, sighed and turned over clutching stuffed animals to him, and Jiaklem on our bedpost cheeped sleepily.

The remedies were bringing my hurts up sharp and I just wanted to lie down until the healing part happened. I made myself hestitate a moment more, sighed and lay down the way I wanted to and Gan tucked me in. "Don't worry, heart's brother," he said. "We'll make sure this gets covered up and we don't have to run."

I loved him so much. He blew out the light and climbed in next to me, hugging me carefully. He was warm against my chills and the feather pillow under my head felt like Selestialis itself. I was shaking and cold and he was so warm. A vagrant tear or two forced its way out of my swollen-shut eye. "Thanks, Gan. I'm sorry. I'm sorry."

"What are you sorry about?" He gathered me onto his shoulder. "You didn't get killed and didn't kill anybody or draw authorities or writers down on us."

"I should have paid attention. I shouldn't have been walking alone like that."

"Shut up, heart's brother. You won't do it again. So stop beating up on yourself for not coming across all heroic and stupid. What? You wanted to be all mythic and calling lightning and fire from heaven down on a bunch of stupid, vile boys who mobbed you?"

"You're right, Gan. I'll shut up now."

16

———————

ADIEU OH LIGHT OF STARS

Gannara made me stay in bed and left Ili with me the first day with orders to sit on me if I tried to get up. He brought a Haian trained Yeoli-medic in to see me, telling inn staff I had contracted a chill, having been silly enough to get my feet wet.

She asked me what had happened and sniffed when I told her I'd fallen off a bridge into the canal. "And you are not going to say who helped you fall off the bridge. I understand," she said. "You are lucky I was able to straighten your nose somewhat and needn't worry about having any difficulty breathing through it, once I take the packing gauze out of it."

Gan sniffed. He had Ili and Jiaklem both on his lap. "Thank you, *kere*. Minakas, you listen to her!"

"I always listen to a healer!" I said a little nasally. Ili giggled at my packed-nose tone.

There were no questions asked about my smashed glasses and torn robe by the lock bridge, or perhaps one of the young hooligans came back later and threw them after what they thought was my corpse. My teeth settled back into their places in my mouth and I stayed out of sight the rest of the eight-day.

Gannara bought me another pair of glasses with the same subterfuge we'd done to get them in the first place… then went back a few days later to get a second 'clear glass' lens to 'replace' the broken one.

I didn't replace the scholar's robe and considered digging the Hyerne men's veil out of the bottom of my pack but decided against, since it would be even more striking and out of place in Yeola-e than my slightly dirty blond head once I went out again. I told Ili I'd had an accident, the same story I had told the medic, so as not to upset him.

I kept telling Gan it was like a bad training session with Ice Eyes, but he kept not believing me, making me convalesce a lot longer than I wanted to.

~

"I am very, very displeased with you, young man!" The voice I hear is female. "My Superior is upset with you as well."

"Your Superior? Why can't I see you? Who are you?"

"Terribly unscientific thinking. Sloppy. Adolescent nonsense." The voice sounded annoyed and precise and just a trifle petulant. "Young man. You have not been using the brain given you. Inexcusable! It is a good one, if I do say so myself. And you have not noticed more gentle hints, so I shall have to be crude."

"What? I don't understand. Who are you?"

A heavy sigh as if She were frustrated. "Take a look at what could happen if you continue to indulge in your pubescent fantasies and continue to send supposedly anonymous gifts to Kyriala Liren."

The haze in front of my face fades and I am looking at the Hall of Serene Justice. An Arkan… a solas but not a mere sereniteer grandly gestures Kyriala to a seat. Her face is a mask, showing nothing, as if she faced the fat guy.

"Serina. You lied to us, telling us you had had no contact with the former Spark of the Sun's Ray, as evidenced by our most recent session, which included truth-drug as per the Imperatrix's policy. You will be charged with the obstruction of Imperial justice, your sentence to be decided by the person wronged, the Imperatrix herself. This could be as lenient as thirty lashes or as severe as death, at her discretion."

"As She Who is the World's Intelligence demands, Ser," Ky said quietly, elegantly and with poise as she did everything. "Surely She will understand I have not encourage the Spark —"

"—former Spark," he corrected her and she inclined her head gracefully acknowledging the correction.

"Former Spark of the Sun's Ray's continued attention."

"That will be up to She Whose Choice is Universal."

And the haze shifted to show a whole waterfall of things that could happen, everything, all jumbled together. Ky stripped and flogged, publicly. Ky displayed in a kind of pillory, under public eyes. Ky impaled in Presentation Square. Ky on a table. Ky stripped of her citizenship and sent out of the city. Ky made okas. Ky sent in disgrace out of the city to a distant province...

"No! No!" I yelled. "None of that is fair! I've been sending her presents, yes but she doesn't know where I am, she's not obstructing them looking for me! Not really..." I subsided. She was holding secret that I was sending her gifts.

I was putting her in danger.

"Now you see, foolish boy."

"I have to stop."

"If that will be enough."

"Yes. I have to convince her that KB is someone else, not Kefas Bear."

"If you can. Her mind is a good one as well. One I am very proud of."

"You're not her mother."

"No. But I am part of what makes her. The stuff of life that I make is intricate and delicate and stronger than steel in its way. Life is a more worthy substance to create with than stone and metal and bone and wood. Or even the chemical changes to dead things that create other things."

I don't know what reminded me of Ailadas's drunken soliloquy but I said, hesitantly, "You mean like wine?"

"Enough of that!" The Voice sounded miffed... I'd guessed right, I felt. "You, young man, have got to start paying attention! How Many have to strike you on the head to knock the incorrect theorems you carry so carefully, out of them? How many mortals?

"Wait... wait... you're.... You're a..."

I reached up to feel if my eyes were open in this fuzzy dream of faces and whiteness and sharp smells. "Heal up, boy. If you... as I said before, I shall be crude... get your head out of your ass, you will see Me again."

I snapped awake, drenched in sweat that smelled of all kinds of strangeness and my swollen eye opened all the way since it had squeezed shut, just in time to see a white rat upon the window sill of the inn.

It stood up upon its hind legs, pink eyes gleaming in the moonlight... wait, it was dark of the moon. I blinked and looked again, there was no rat upon the sill.

~

"Dearest, most beautiful Serina,

I must, in sorrow, reveal myself and bid you adieu without ever having spoken to you. I am Kerias Burien and I saw you from afar at your re-coming out fete." I read this out loud. Mama said "Oh! The admirer, sweetheart… but why must he bid you adieu?"

"I'm just getting to that, mama."

"I saw you, radiantly beautiful and could not make myself approach you, and had to express my admiration for you some-how. Alas, my esteemed father has found out why my allowance has been so early spent and has forbidden any more such unseemly and forward gifts, since I am a betrothed man; to the daughter of his dear friend, almost since early childhood, so there is no question that I should even think of addressing another lady, however smitten I have been."

"How tragic!" Kara cried. "How noble!" Personally I thought it sounded like he was reading too much of Shirmiras's Classical Love Advice for Young Men, larding his words with sentiment. *I think I know why you are doing this.*

"How unfortunate," mama said. "He might have otherwise offered for you, dear. However obscure an *Aitzas* family, he certainly had an abundance of gifts to offer you." *You're getting older and need to think of someone's wealth, in other words.*

"And because of my profligate and public gifting, father had decreed I must return to our estates in Irinina…"

"That's almost as far away and wild as Outer Kurkania!"

"There to reside until my planned wedding day. Adieu, oh Light of Stars! I shall cherish a chaste and pure image of you in my heart!"

Sincerely,

Kerias Burien, *Aitzas*

P.S. Enjoy the gifts, I'll make good with father and needn't ask for them back…

K.B.

That… could it be Kerias Burien really? Instead of Kefas Bear? That… last line. I was so sure it was M. But he is devious. Oh Minis, you try to make me doubt you.

17

ARKO SURELY REJOICES

STATUE APPROVED

The Marble Palace is pleased to announce the funding approval for the statue of the former Imperator, then Fourth Shefenkas Shaeranoias, now Shefenkas Aisheresas, to be erected at the head of the Avenue of Statuary. The proposed plaza surrounding it will become part of Presentation Square, once the University Buildings "Philosophical Arts" and "Religious Studies" are removed, and the first third of the statues of '*Solas* Muster' are moved, to an, as yet, undecided location.

All protesters and sundry citizenry concerned about the eventual relocation of the Muster needn't be. A proposed location has been suggested and feasibility studies should begin shortly about making the boardwalk along the lake the revised location for the various *solas* statues.

Feliras's Glory, a once fine dining location of the city, is considering new locations and options, the owner considering retirement. "The location of the new statue would have the restaurant's view largely obstructed by the rear of the statue, and thus one of the fine cachets of the establishment would be lost," the manager has said.

The incredible statue proposed will be twenty paces from base to highest point of the head, with the raised arm and sword rising another six, and entirely of bronze upon a marble plinth, of rare Nirisian blue and green marble. It will show Shefenkas in the victory position, arms upraised, with an actual steel copy, in large, of the famous Yeoli sword in his one hand. Though the statue will be bronze, the wristlets upon the figure will be palladium and it will have gilded leaves in the hair. All harness fittings shall also be gilded with gold, the loincloth, the softer Yeoli style, depicted flowing in the wind, will be palladium. The top filial of the column under the sandaled bronze feet will be glass and gold.

The artist, Tujiras Oren, is very proud of being commissioned to do the work and speaks glowingly of how magnificent it will be, how imposing against the white buildings of the core of the city. "It will be an astonishing presence in the city itself and spoken of for hundreds, if not thousands of years to come!"

The head of the 'Commemorative Statue Committee' Inatalla Shae-Krisa is quoted as saying "We are very proud of this design. It properly reflects the significance and stature of our beloved and often revered former Imperator and *chiranyerai* and ensures that his place in Arkan history will never be forgotten!"

The Imperatrix has not commented upon the proposed statue save to say that "My brother deserves his credit and his due."

Construction on the bronze figure is expected to begin in the foundry Faraiksas in the fall and is expected to be finished two years hence. Demolition of the University Buildings is to begin after the summer term, Anae 30, 51st year of the Present Age.

It will be a statue to rival the greatest ever conceived or made and will surely become one of the wonders of the art world. The miniature model produced by Oren to win his commission is available for viewing in the Golden Gallery of the Marble Palace, daily from rim sunrise to rim sunset.

All Arko surely rejoices at this magnificent example of artwork about to grace our city, as much as we do, a masterpiece equal to, or beyond any other artwork upon the Avenue. We look forward with anticipation to the beginning of construction.

~

I laid the Pages down and stared blindly out of the inn window. Gannara was letting me up and the medic was telling me she would remove the packing from my nose tomorrow. I had joked to Ili that all I wanted for my eighteenth birthday was the ability to breathe through my nose.

That statue was not Chevenga's idea. I was sure of that. It was the sort of thing that self-aggrandizing, insecure kings and Imperators did, not him. The idea of some kind of looming behemoth of a bronze statue, towering higher than the glass eagle, as high as Feliras's Glory… which-- was implied--would have had the statue's ass right outside the main window… I rubbed my almost healed up face with my hands, gently. Oh, whose brilliant idea was that?

I leafed through the Pages and read little stories here and there about protestors sitting all along the edges of the proposed new plaza and at the feet of the *solas* statues to be moved. The women. Mothers and Grand-mothers and little girls, all sitting. And if anyone asked they would answer they were keeping their son or grandson or father, or their brother company. Many were completely silent and could not be said to be 'making a disturbance'. Others talked to and fussed over the statues as if they were living men. People were saying they couldn't be touched because they were obviously crazed.

In a supposedly unrelated story, a rash of vandalism was sweeping the city Itself, horses being painted upon the homes and businesses of the Yeoli hawks and *Aitzas* seen to be collaborating with them in any way.

*Chevenga, I understand why you gave us the vote. Did you have to
do it this way? In such a way that we lost you, who understood us?
'You set us free'. Your sister does not know us at all. She is listening to
the Hawks and they want to crush us all under their sandals to their
profit. The foundry listed as getting the work for that damned statue is
owned by a Hawk, Faraiko Terero, as if no one is going to notice that.
The protesters had begun with solas only. Now there
were Aitza also 'sitting with the dead'. Sinimas. Please ask the
Gods for me if you would… Chevenga, who did the Ten Tens, who
gave Arkan women this sense of power… how could he walk away
from this job half done? How could we have voted him out? How?
It was unlikely that his sister, Artira would put down the protesters
but the Hawks wouldn't care if they arrested every woman out there,
filled the dungeons to bursting, for fear their crazed disobedience
would spread to the rest of society.
We have enough freedom to cause a lot of chaos, but haven't learned
yet how to judge our own limits of that freedom. We don't know how
to choose effectively yet.*

I picked up the Pages again and turned to yet another story about the breaking down of my society. Gangs of young people... barely children... hanging about in kaf houses and smoking herb, adopting the savage drums of other cultures, the man-high ones of the Srians that could, en- mass, apparently shake houses, the hand-drums of the Hyerne high and sharp as a scream, the two-note A-Niah drums and the mid-bass rumble of Haian beach drums... And sporting hair dyed any colour BUT blond, as if they were Mezem fans or even gladiators, denying their Arkaness. They declaim their subversive poetry, or sang their subversive songs or danced their lewd dances on street corners, outside *Jitzmitthra,* and vanished before they could be arrested by the Sereniteers.

The Pages were calling them 'Dyers' and saying they were an Anti-Arkan cult out to destroy society, with their declaiming of subversion on the streets, their encouraging of unsupervised association of young men and young women.

This latest article was ranting about how they were starting to include body jewelry pierced into their ears and noses and cheeks and tongues as if they were slave gladiators. "How is a young girl, properly raised and betrothed, who runs out with these Dyers and comes home with a glass ornament hanging from a bloody lip, *ever* going to marry her affianced? He would reject her in an instant for having so defaced herself!"

For an instant I imagined Kyriala with a sapphire in her perfect nose, or a fringe of bells on one ear. I cringed, thinking of how much that would hurt her, then thought... *I'd marry her in an instant, nose-ring like a savage or not.* Then I found myself hoping she actually would do such a thing, if for no other reason than to discourage a proper *Aitzas* suitor. *What am I thinking? I released her! I will never, ever be able to approach her as a suitable candidate for husband... oh how I wished I could have talked her into running away with me, however wrong that would have been. I couldn't give her children anyway, only if they were raised as 'Akam' and never know who I was.*

Who was I fooling? I wasn't even physically capable of engendering children. I no longer tied my genitals down so hard because I seldom rose at all and my perversion was confined to my dreams. Even if I dampened my sleeping shirt occasionally, that was fairly safe. Neither Gannara nor Ili were threatened by that.

These were all madness. She was safest if she married someone else as quickly as possible. I flipped to the Pages of betrothal announcements, suddenly convinced I'd see the notice.   My eye snagged on the name Liren and I almost crushed the Page in my hand before I realized it was a cousin of hers, not her.

I wanted to go home so desperately I could taste it. But it would be best if I never did.

18

A PIECE OF MINE THAT WOULD NOT SELL

The Stone Hammer Riots

Statues are something that people erect to those they wish to revere and a culture's attitudes, morals and government can be read in the countries presentation art. Statues have, not only a monetary cost, but a moral and ethical cost as well.

One must consider who pays for its initial construction, and why – both official and unofficially. Who pays to have it maintained. Who or what is chosen to be depicted. How they are depicted. Who protests it. Who vandalizes it. Is it a focus for controversy, or even riot?

For instance, during the reign of Boras the Terrible, 132 Last Age, toward what would prove to be the end of his reign, though he had truly not won any battles at the head of any *rejin* of Arko, he had a statue commissioned showing him and his immediate body-guards, all on the back of Griffons, rampant upon the bodies of Arkan enemies.

To fund the statue, Boras Aan plundered the temples of the *fessas* Gods in the outlying provinces, and the major road

construction and repair budget was cut to the bone. The immediate results were that goods and services coming into the city
either slowed to a trickle or what goods did come were inferior, as
the *fessas* dispayed their displeasure in the only way they could.

There are records of letters of protest and objection from nearly
every fielded general, complaining of the difficulty of moving
troops on deteriorating roads, and complaints from the Drovers,
the Couriers, in fact all of those dependent upon the roads to
move their goods. Despite all protest, the statue continued being
built but because the artisans were *fessas* the work proceeded
slowly and the site, near Sword Road on the Avenue of Statues
was for some reason,, the most disaster prone in the city. Ship-
ments of stone did not arrive to the carvers, blocks were dropped
and cracked, someone 'accidentally' left the barrier gate open so
that when the streets were washed, the site was flooded, scaf-
folding pieces went missing, and myriad other, smaller
annoyances.

Ultimately Boras attempted to put *solas* overseers to watch over
the work that the *fessas* did and the work quickly degenerated into
a confrontation between the *fessas* marble workers and *solas* of the
First Sun Rise *Rejin* and Sereniteers, becoming the first of the
'Stone-Hammer riots'.

The Stone Hammer generals, whom the *fessas* saw as being on
their side, ultimately overthrew Boras, before the statue could be
completed and General Orthas Liren became regent for the Spark
of the Sun's Ray until he successfully attained his majority ten
years later and was accepted by the Gods as rightful Imperator.

The remnants of the ill-fated statue are still extant in modern
Arko, four of the lesser Griffons tucked away on the Lake Board
walk, where the current government is proposing to set 'Solas
Muster', albeit without riders or any other sign that they were
once part of a greater work. The rest was pulled to bits and used
as rubble in other building projects around the city.

A statue cannot truly be forced on a people, if they truly do not

want it, even if they live in a tyranny and are not allowed
their *vodae*. No power on earth can protect a hated image that is
meant to symbolize oppression. If they cannot pull it down
openly, people will often worry it to bits over the years, requiring
that it be guarded, repaired, cleaned, or even repeatedly replaced,
adding to the initial expense of its construction and thus the
resentment accruing around it.

A statue has not only a cost in chains, but in emotion and any
government is wise to take the people's wishes into account for its
public art works.

I WROTE THAT IN A SINGLE EVENING, GOING ON MY MEMORY OF
Ailadas's lectures on those riots and when Gannara and Ili came back
from their mysterious shopping trip, I showed it to him.
"Terren will never publish it," he said, looking up at me.
"Probably not, but I needed to write it. And I might send it anyway."
"So that Imperator got deposed because of a statue."
"Oh, there was lots more than just that statue. There was a reason he
was called "The Terrible".

~

--in a post office box, Number 4589—

Dear Contributor;

We regret to inform you that your most interesting article does,
unfortunately not meet our current requirements. Thank you for
submitting, and please try again!

———

Dear Author;

While your bedtime tales for children titled Ili and His Magic
Donkey, are both well written and entertaining, we regret to
inform you that they are, perhaps, somewhat gruesome for the age
range you submitted.

We will be pleased to reconsider this manuscript, should you decide to rework it and 'lighten it up' somewhat.

Sincerely…

———

Dear Writer,

Your horror story 'Going to the Lock' is certainly visceral! Unfortunately our line-up does not include space for a story of this type.

Have you considered turning this into a play?

Regards…

~

"Happy Birthday, Min! Happy Day!" I woke up with a start, mid-morning, as Ili squealed in my ear. The medic had had mercy on me and freed my nose the evening before. I'd gone to sleep forgetting completely it was my birthday next day, both because I was just enjoying having my nose clear and from lack of *Jitzmitthra* clues. Even while I'd been with the Mahid they'd had *Jitz,* so I had nothing but the date to remind me, and I had lost track.

I sat up to see Gannara and Ili grinning at me, with a stack of pancakes and whipped cream and fruit on a plate in Gan's hands. Ili was holding two wrapped packages.

"What? No, my birthday isn't till tomorrow or next day, isn't it?"

"It's today, Min! It's today!" Ili handed one of his parcels up to Jiaklem on his head and the domoctopus wrapped his tentacles around it and flushed orange like the paper wrapping it. "Open my present first!"

Of course. That was why they'd 'gone shopping'. *Honestly, sometimes you're an idiot, Min.* I thought to myself. Gannara put my cake down on the night table and settled on the end of the bed. "It's just a little token from each of us,"

"No. No, it's wonderful, thank you! And whipped cream pancake cake! Thank you both! I just wasn't expecting anything!" Gannara's birthday was coming up soon. He didn't know I'd asked his Haian before we left Haiu Menshir. I was going to have to surprise him, in turn.

"Open my present!"

"You wrapped it yourself?" I asked him. "I couldn't tell if you'd gotten the vendor to wrap it, it's so nice! I almost don't want to ruin it…"

"OOOooohhh! Open it!" He didn't try to smack me when I teased him but danced on the spot in sheer frustration, Jia bouncing and wobbling on his head, the second package waving up and down.

"All right, all right!" I ripped open the package and opened the little box and found a charm in the shape of a dagger lying in the packing paper. "Oh my."

"'Cause what happened in Hyerne!" and there's a ship too… all the travelling! You can put them on the chain with your donkey!"

"I will. Though if you keep doing this one day I won't be able to swim because of the weight of birthday charms from my little brother!"

"Silly! You're just being silly!"

"I got you something for that necklace as well," Gannara said quietly. "You'll have a whole rack of them from both of us!" It was a silver flower that grew only on Haiu Menshir. "So you don't forget that you didn't finish healing, got it?"

"I got that brother. Thank you." I threw my arms around both of them and Jia slapped a couple of tentacles over my head. "Thank you. They're the best birthday presents ever!"

～

"What do you mean I need to be a Dyer for a while?"

"Those thugs thought they murdered a scholar, right?"

"Yes…"

"So let's turn your oh so pale hair bright, bright blue. They'll never look twice at you as if you're the kid they threw off a bridge. I got a fake nose-ring for you as well."

"A FAKE NOSE RING?" My hands flew up protectively over my nose. "The packing just came out! The swelling is just down!"

"Yeah," he said calmly. "Instead of a real one which would hurt more."

"But once we're out of here the bright blue will wash out, won't it?"

"I think so." Now he's teasing me. Ili is reading over in the window seat and looking up every time I raise my voice. "If not, when we change my hair colour again, we can bleach it out."

"Wonderful. It's brilliant. Just a little startling. It will make us all safer. No glasses for now and a poet/drummer/Dyer rebel!" I started laughing. "Ice Eyes would have an apoplectic attack and expire on the spot!"

"Now you're starting to sound right. The Dyers declaim stuff like that sometimes, pull up a hood to hide the hair and vanish into the crowd. People supporting them are starting to make hoods a popular fashion statement so the Sereniteers can't tell."

I stood up, testing for twinges that thankfully didn't come, threw my arms wide. "Authority! Authority! Where everybody wants to be! Power! Power! The flavor of the hour! The ring in the bell tower! The sting in a poison shower!--" He threw a pillow that hit me in the middle and my hands snapped down around it.

"Yeah, you can do it. Get your shirt off and your head over here. I ordered up some hot water for 'washing'."

19

———————

PATA PATA PAT BOOM SWISH BOOM

Dear Shadow Mama and Shadow Papa,

I am still doing all right and I'm safe, that's all I can tell you right now. I hope the family is all alright. You can come back to Asinanai if you like because when I come home I'd like to come there instead of Arko. You don't need to stay in Arko to find me. I'm sorry I missed you on Haiu Menshir. I'm really sorry, but there was a Mahid there that I recognized and we had to run.

I realize this must be very frustrating for you, but the best I can do right now is to keep writing you regularly so you know I'm all right.
All my love and hugs,

Gannara

~

"GANNARA. THIS IS GOING TO SOUND DUMB BUT I WANT TO HEAD back to the city Itself." I had my gloves off and was helping Gan give Ili a bath. Somehow the kid managed to find dirt in a completely bare room, so if we went out at all during the day he'd wind up needing to be washed at least.

But he was perfectly happy in the sit-bath the inn brought up and the four buckets of warm water we carted up for the job. Hardly a Great Bath, but he played with the round cakes of soap and sang while we scrubbed his hair. Jiaklem had tasted the soap once and hidden under the bed thereafter, during bathtime.

Gan looked at me seriously. "You haven't seen a scrap of hide of a Mahid, have you?" He rinsed his hands and said to Ili, "Stand up and I'll rinse your head. You're almost done!"

"No, I've mostly been in this room being turned into a Dyer!" The hair felt odd, a little stiff, and the nose-ring, sitting oh so shockingly in the corner of nose and face, sometimes itched. No one had commented on the scholar taking to his bed and coming out a Dyer. I changed my hair color, to a Yeoli it was a shrugging matter.

He thought about it a moment longer, pouring, bubbles and soap swirling down Ili's back into the sit-bath, while I got the towels from the windowsill where they'd been warming in the sun.

"All right. We should keep moving anyway."

"I want to stop moving someday."

"I'm not sure you ever will be able to stop, Min.

I closed my eyes for a moment. With both Marble Palace and former Mahid after me that was probably true. "Yeah. Maybe not."

"So we're going back to the city?" Ili jumped and splashed.

"Hey! Stop that or I'll use the towels to mop up the mess instead of drying you! Yes. We're going back to the city."

I didn't send my 'Stone Hammer Riots' piece to the Pages. The mood had changed since it was Artira on the Crystal Throne. But there were lots of less-than mainstream spawn presses and I sent it off to Madajanas Press. I'd be able to pick up the mail I'd been paying that *fessas* fellow to hold for me and perhaps I would find either an acceptance or rejection by the time we got to the city.

By the time we got downriver, to Selina, the Pages had huge headlines 'CHEVENGA SEEKS REINSTATEMENT!!!' *Good for you, Chevenga. You should never have been forced to give it all up.* Then I realized he was going for more than just *semanakraseye* again. Since the conquest Arko and Yeoli had been, in effect, one country. He stated in the papers that he believed they should once more be two separate countries and hoped to see that accomplished. Unspoken was the implication – vote me back and I'll separate the countries…

The posters sprang up almost overnight. The wild blue and green printed "YES! BRING BACK CHEVENGA!" were everywhere. In Yeola-e they were all but unopposed; not surprisingly. This time the lurid red ones screaming NO! to Chevenga again, were few. What I saw with a certain deep satisfaction was that the pattern held in Arko, even though there were a few more red ones.

This time I liked hearing the orators on the edges of the horse-troughs. Even though my own head was the blue of a parrot's back feathers and I sported a nose ring, I hadn't actually *seen* a Dyer until we put in at Fispur.

There was an anti-Chevenga orator up at the dock and he was being bellowed at by people, with Sereniteers pushing people on with their black and white sticks. Once the black n' whites were down the street, further along their patrol, a young man sitting quietly to one side of the ranter on the horsetrough began beating on a pair of drums he had on his lap. People stopped to listen and he flipped back his hood to show an astonishing iridescent pattern of dye in his hair, cut on a five-step angle up his head, all five caste levels including a short plush around one ear that had a fringe of silver and glass bells ringing and chiming as he moved his head to his own beat.

pat pat patapon pata pata chaka don
Sister, or brother, or sister, or brother
jingle jangle patadon chaka jangle jingle pon
We've had both now what the bother?
pat pat patapon jingle swish boom boom
We can choose, come here, go there
jingle jangle patadon chaka swish boom boom
As plain to see as my rainbow hair!
Pat pat patapon jingle pat patpon
We're under the wing of Hawks not
Patapapapapapata pata pata pon
Eagles. They have a claw in every pot!
Pat patapon patapon patapon

His fingers flew over the drums and the chiming from his earbells counterpointing the hoarse, unsophisticated shouts of the orator, making them crude by comparison.

"Stamp and jump and scream with joy!
This is freedom! Relish it, boy!
Somewhere in between toe and heel
You'll find out how you really feel!
Passionate brave hearts, come to me!
Come be a Dyer, wild and free!
Sing out your truth to all in sight!
Make the Hawks wet their kilts with fright!"

A shout from down the street and the man flipped his hood back up, rose gracefully, bagged his drum and vanished in the crowd just as the Sereniteers came pounding back, looking for him.

I kept my own hood up. I reached up and tugged off the nose-ring and tucked it away in my pouch. I agreed with the man, but I certainly didn't want to be arrested on suspicion of illegal oration. Chevenga wouldn't have cared what orators on the street said. There were hoods everywhere, a number of dyed heads openly sported by people in the street, young women, young men. The Sereniteers couldn't stop everyone with a dyed head, especially since most bards and street theatre folks were not doing anything illegal.

Time to bleach my head, perhaps.

20

FIGGISH BIRTHDAY TO YOU

Dorn was shutting down his kitchen and Iliakaj, Enchian barbarian that he is, leaned over and actually kissed his wife in public. They'd come in for a late dinner without the kids. These foreigners. I swear to the Gods, what is Arko coming to, with people actually showing affection for a woman where everyone can see!

He picked up his glass and came strolling through to my Fig with a few other late diners, stragglers who decided they wanted to keep drinking after eating. Dorn finished up, the sweeping up and locking up and blowing out the lamps.

He didn't wear *faib* skates like his waiters so he just walked over. The last thing his kitchen always produced on these long, slow summer evenings after rim sunset when the light faded slow, was a table load of cold foods, things to be eaten bite sized. I'd sell them to customers, flat fee, let us serve you…

People sometimes came for a simple beer and a plate of bites… Not my best wine customers but 'f you get enough people coming back then your business will thank you. My da wouldn't recognize the place.

It was a lot quieter than we'd got used to, after the sack, since the barbarian Imperator himself let us stupidly vote him out of office. I still had my 'no politics' signs up but it hadn't really been necessary since the Imperatrix expressed her discomfort with Arkans arguing with each other like Yeolis. The political arguments moved out into the hands of these young people with holes in their faces and boom-bang-boom drums. Everyone looking as though they are *Mezem* people, the way the *Mezem* used to be.

I nearly threw my youngest son Janafas out of the house for coming home with his hair dyed in tiger stripes. Tiger stripes! How is he to learn a service business in tiger stripes? And a bell in his nose. Young people. At least he keeps it silenced while serving customers... Dorn doesn't mind it.

Everything is working smoothly and I can sit back and enjoy myself for once. Nena... with no odd jewelry hanging from her face smiled at me as she went off into the darkened Figgish Gourmand. "Don't fall down those steps, lovey!" I called. It was my birthday and things were quiet enough that Tila and Isha and Dorn, all three had set up a surprise for me on the back shelf of the wine safe. They'd lined up a neat little march of glasses, from small to large, each filled with a precise amount of Iron Fist... um... Silken Gloves... the total of all the glasses were the same as years I have and I don't care to tell say. I'm doing well for my age. Let us let it go at that.

This late in Muunas, before the heat makes people crazy and just mellows them out, I could afford to indulge myself. I checked my makeup in the mirror wall behind the shelf. Not bad for a hot day... and picked up the next to last cup. I'll save the last one... the big one... for after we close.

Kaj and Riji have things well in hand and even my bouncers are drowsy, at their posts. There's a lineup of people waiting to be served their plates of little bites and beer at the patio table and Jan's there wielding my second best carving knife, his outrageous hair tucked into a kerchief. He's going well for a boy his age. And Tila is now pouring the beer. I would never have had my wife in public like that, but we needed the help. Under Shefenkas we were so busy we needed every hand, especially ones I didn't have to pay. She says she likes it. Who am I to argue?

Speaking of hair there's the Rainbow Head over there. Haras Terren, *Aitzas*, his proper name is. He respects my sign... after all my bouncers would just throw him in the horse trough if he got his bitsy-bangy drums out. He's a good young man. I've known him for years... his da brought him here after fights when he was just a young tad and before he got the stepped haircut and the earbells.

He has a right to be angry in a way... his family lost everything in the sack and then gained some of it back through the courts... under the rule of Shefenkas's law -- that his sister seems to be eroding back to the acid nonsense of the Aans.

I lift an eyebrow at Kaj and he nodded at me. *All is well, we're winding down to closing, boss.* Good. I could indulge myself for my cough-te-eth birthday. I took my glass over to Haras. "How are you lad?"

"Good evening, Ienas." He might look like a throwback to Mezem meat but he was still a polite young man. "I'm well. You look like you're doing all right."

"I am. I am. Not bad for a man my age…" for some reason that freakish band of glass bells inspired me. "… not bad for a man full of rage…"

Both his eyebrows flew up. "Ienas, I had no idea you were a Dyer like me."

"I'm not, Haras. Drink up. It's possible that Shefenkas might be *vodaied* back in."

He sipped his drink, a tall, fruity, sugary froufy conconction. "And this fills you with rage?"

"Not that. All the rest of it… all of it, my friend. The Gods gave us… Ten Tens gave us… a good Imperator…"

"I remember," he said, fiddling with the glass and making rings on the tabletop with the condensing water off his drink. "I was there. Not close enough to touch him when he flung himself onto his new people, but there. I recall him in here a few times, as well, which must have helped business." I could see his eyes flip up to Shak, my new bouncer, then back down to his drink.

I smacked my hand on the table. If anyone in this *fikken* bar was going to understand it was Haras Terren, *Aitzas*, Dyer, weird politico.

"…right from the start when he was *daifikas* and *Mezem* and Spark's new toy!… and after the sacks…" My drink… second to last for my cough-birthday was all but done. "He had not time, of course… and we were a humble place for so exalted a man. Dog mother of the Ten! Why are people so stupid?"

He smiled and pulled out that golden tongue of his. "Say not so, ser! The Gods smiled upon you so in the sack; your establishment *earned* the exalted tread of He Whose Arms Embraced the World!" He tapped on the table as if it were one of his bangity drums. "People, I find in my new line of work, are not so much stupid as creatures of habit. But their hearts can be appealed to! The difficult bit is appealing to their nobler virtues."

"Line of work?" I said. I was a bit more bleary than I thought. Of course Silken Gloves sneaks up behind you and smashes you in the back of the head with that hidden iron fist... "I suppose... I thought your mother, your sister and you got most of it back?"

"Most of it. But you can't buy a father. At least not one worth having. And it's not as though there's any money in *this.*" He swung the long *Aitzas* strand of hair back and his earbells chimed sweetly counterpoint to his deep voice.

"Ah, lad. If you need, you could always talk to my partner Dorn...or me. We know you."

"You do. And I am talking to you. But one who has lost something cannot help but long for it. I believe you were remarking along that line yourself, just now?"

"What? Lost He Whose Sword was writ large upon Arko? Yeha." Oh, I was drunk enough to be maudlin. I was so glad Kaj had things well in hand.

Iliakaj stood at my shoulder, drink in his hand, listening to us. Shak got up for some reason then settled back into his spot by the door. Why was the man grinning like that?

"He did his best... for his people, for us as His people..."

"You miss him."

"...and we..." I hiccupped a bit. I hadn't had such a drunk since my last cough-tyeth birthday.

"Yeha. I do. I'd *vodai* for him back!" I smacked the flat of my hand on the table for emphasis. Now why did Kaj have such a dog-sucking grin on his face? I was vaguely aware of Iliakaj setting his empty glass down. "*Hayel,* yes! I would! Here's to the *vodaias!*"

"So would I, Ienas. So would I." He glanced over my shoulder at Iliakaj just standing there. Now why was he nervous?

The ex gladiator put one hand on my shoulder. "Excuse me a moment, Ser Terren." Haras spread his arms wide to indicate he was not going to try and hold onto me. So many things we picked up from the Yeolis. The good ones, at least. "Ienas, would you attend me for a bit?"

I had time to say "Hmm? What?" before I was flying... at least it felt like it. Iliakaj had me up over his shoulder and out almost before my gut hit more than twice and then flying again. "HEY, YOU IMMORTAL PUT ME GLUB...."

The fikken dog-mother of the Ten Gods, dog-sucking, pig fikken son of a dog threw me in the fikken Hayel sucking horse trough!

I staggered up, clawing my hair out of my eyes and he's standing there, offering me a hand out of the water, onto the orator's step. I'm still coughing so he waits until I draw breath to blast him and he says. "Ienas. What signs do you have in your Fig?"

That surprised me enough to gape at him. "What? What signs? You know very well you Enchian barbarian! No Pol—it—ics…" I ran down to silence. I had been, hadn't I?

"I was NOT!…" I started to bluster but then stopped. I had been. He was shaking his head at me.

"Ienas, you know better. You and I are old enough friends that I realize it's not like you to be like this while the Fig is still open. But you were breaking your own rules so I thought I should help you out.

I glared at him a moment longer, then started laughing and grabbed his hand to step up onto the orator's step. Both the trough and the step were outside my patio limits so if I wanted to I could bellow politics till I was blue in the face.

I turned around just in time to catch a face full of lightly hurled flower petals and the entire staff and my family and some of the faithful customers I've had over the years, yelling 'SURPRISE!' Tila stood in the middle, holding a celebration cake in her hands and everyone else is still hurling paper confetti and flower petals and I'm standing in soaking wet clothing on the orator's step.

I consider getting angry. I consider coming across like an old fart and take offense but I can't do it. I start laughing. I have to hold myself up on the shoulder of the Immortal and laugh my ass off and right when I think I'll get my wind back, Haras pulls his bangity drums from somewhere and starts tapping them. "You're up there, Ienas, why not take advantage of it? Let people know your heart!" Bangity bangity swish pam pom!

21

———————

NO WILD BOYS

The Pages and spawn press articles were mostly more moderate than their headlines. Apparently Chevenga went to the committee who were attempting to reinstate him... but he did not seek this but rather would allow them to pursue their stated purpose.

"Chevenga Meets with Group Re Reinstatement" with the sub-head being "Ex-Imperator throws his support behind sister's deposing!"

What the story actually said was "he was persuaded to go along with the bring-back-Chevengaists because of developments in Arko that he disagrees with." *Probably that fikken statue, among other things.*

"The former Imperator says that he wishes to remain on good terms with his sister Artira and is not opposing her specifically."

I folded up the Pages and tucked them under my arm. I had my hair tied back and under a hood so none of it showed, my glasses on and scholar's robe. I had my eye on a set of rooms for rent very close to the house I'd bought for Ailadas on Bright. The rooms were actually on the next street over and two up from him. I wasn't going to endanger him by actually staying with him... since they might truth drug him any time to check and see if I'd contacted him.

I knocked on the door with the little placard advertising an apartment to let and smiled, a little nervously at the pinched-faced woman who opened the door. "Sera... ye have rooms fer let?"

I do. For yourself?"

"Nah, Nah, Sera Landlord, fer m'cousin 'n his friend and little brother. I'd be here too, Sera but m'job's called me away agin."

"I rent respectable!" She sniffed. "No wild boys!"

"I'm sure they'll be quiet'n, Sera."

"Let me show you the apartment."

It was a horrible little space, damp with a badly cracked wash-curb so that the eight-day washing no doubt poured in around the front window. "Nah, Sera, this'll not do, thenk yeh fer yer time."

I nodded at her and turned to go. "Wait a moment, young Ser," she said. "Ay have another. P'raps too big fer yer touch?"

She'd been showing me what she thought I could afford. It made me want to rip out my bright blue hair. "P'raps not with them both payin', Sera."

This one was three sleeping rooms in the attic with a huge tree so close over the back one could reach out and touch the branches and leaves, leaving no view whatsoever.

"No cookin' up here. No open fires. Th' stove niche's not safe to use. I'll see ta the ants."

"What were ye thinkin', Sera, fer this moonly?"

"Fer this, premium space it is… I'd want eight coppers per."

I made my calculations. "Give yeh five, fer no cookin' no heat."

"Seven."

"Six and a half."

"Done!" She said. "Person under yeh is a junior Sereniteer, m'own is under that, so you tell 'em no noise and no Maskers or the like brought in… an' I consider smokin' herb an 'open fire', so none o' that!"

"I'll tell im, Sera Landlord. M'names Minakas Akam, Sera."

She nodded. "I'll hev yeh sign that then and first three moons payment upfront."

So my glasses went away with the scholar's robe and the nose-ring went in again. I bought the tiny, fashionable, risqué kilts that were the stiff front in the angular patterns, and the back all but a mere loincloth drape, leaving my legs bare to the waistband. And since I was a boy I could wear all the open shouldered, short sleeved shirts.

Gannara braided up one side of my head in love-knot braids vanishing under the hair at my neck and I bought a drum and one indulgence – a new pair of flash *faib* skates and I moved into Sera Rusas's apartments, as my own cousin, Sinimas Akam.

Ili immediately lined up his stuffed animal army along the window of the room he claimed as his and began begging for another stuffie. We conveniently didn't mention Jiaklem to the landsera since the sign on her door clearly said, 'No Pets'. Considering that there was a yappy dog somewhere in the building and at least three cats in various windows, I didn't think we would have a problem.

I spent the next few days just skating, reveling in the speed again. I usually ended up going up Fast Street to the turnaround to Race Road at the beginning of the *Aitzas* quarter, across the University circle past all the supposed mad women, mad like foxes… They were there in their hundreds. One or two up on their husband's statues, declaiming one of the Mad Imperatrix's speeches… which they wouldn't have known about if they hadn't read them at one point or another, since no man would have ever read these things to them.

My wheels thrummed on the smooth race road and I heard bits and pieces as I soared by. "…we not bleed? We bleed before we birth… we bleed at birth… now we bleed…" "…My Father made me this… frail… weak… hobbled…" "… cry and scream and weep and make outraged noise against my husband…" "My son... listen... I am not mad… not overwrought…not overly emotional…"

Their words, quoted from the Imperatrix who dared say she had a mind as well as the ability to bear children, wove around my skate wheels beating against the pavement like a drumbeat. *Hayel,* I was supposed to be a Dyer… why not?

I coasted to a stop next to the board wall hiding the hole in the ground that had been the Religious studies building. I could see straight up to Feliras's from here where I never could before. I began beating my skate against the board wall, using it as a sounding board.

BOOM BOOM BOOM

My drum was a *yarbak* played under one arm. I had a faint thought that this might not be such a good idea but dismissed it.

Badda-tok! Badda-Tok!

Thoom, Thoom, Thoom!

Listen to the women! Listen to them speak!
They have tongues and hearts and will,
Enough to decry a foul reek!

No freedoms here, no *vodai* so new
Back to the old ways, slaves!
How dare you spew?

They think we're dogs
To suffer, whipp-ed curs
And they almighty, owning Gods!

Aitz-ass asses asses
Give us courts and Shefenk-ases
And kick their brasses!

The sliding shriek of a Sereniteers whistle sounded from Sword Street and was answered by another from behind me, around the boards I had kicked to get such a loud noise. Not good poetry but it was a first attempt...

Time to go. The drum went into the bag and I pushed off hard, down the hillock on Race. Then I realized with more than a little shock that the Marble Palace was putting some of their Sereniteers on skates too. The wailing whistles were moving in far too quickly for mere runners.

"There he is! That's the one! You there! Stop! Stop!"

22

STOP IN THE NAME OF THE LAW!

How in Hayel has the office of the Serenity afforded skates? I'd risked enough by having something so expensive on my feet... being mugged for my skates — if any smash and grab thief could catch me...

The drum bounced on his back as he tore down Race, the wailing whistles behind him. Children on the sides of the street squealed and waved while their parents hustled them back out of his path.

The whistles... in front of him. If he were fleeing off to the *fessas* quarter they were perfectly placed to cut him off. It wasn't being a Dyer or carrying a drum they could arrest him for, but for speaking subversion.

He crossed his feet over, wheeled sideways into an unnamed alleyway off Race that looped back up into the *Aitzas* quarter where he'd spent most of his skating time. Of course things had changed, with the conquest and sack and rebuilding but it was still more familiar than almost any other part of the city.

He heard a startled shout from behind and one of the Sereniteers, not as good on his skates, lost it and careened into a merchant's store-front stand of fine cloths and a rainbow of hand-died hanks of thread. He grinned, they'd be a while untangling him because the owner wouldn't abide cutting something worth the man's weight in silver chains.

The alley opened onto Triumphant and he tucked low over Rill Bridge, moving fast enough that his feet left the ground, even though it was only a little bridge. Market crowds weren't as thick here, mostly servants and carry chairs and… a Sereniteer scrambled off Egg and Bacon Street right on his heels, wheels squealing – *you need to get those fixed, Ser…* An express chair screamed by and he dodged into the chair lane going the wrong way, forcing the Sereniteer to wait for its passing. He caught an approaching whistle and was close enough to see the widening eyes of the lead bearer as he threw on the chair brakes, raising sparks from the stone as they jerked to a wild halt.

"If you Sereniteers did your JOBS we wouldn't have near-collisions with such miscreants!" The old man… the old *Aitzas* in the chair was bellowing at the Sereniteer with the bad skates. None of them had as good skates as his.

"If you'd let us DO our *fikken* job maybe we'd catch the *fikker*!" Minis had to grin again as the argument faded behind. He was smaller than all the skate Sereniteers--were they called Skateers?—It meant he could turn faster. A good thing he hadn't filled out yet and was slight and slender. The Black n'Whites were, to a man, built heavy.

He hopped out and ducked under a shoulder litter and they stopped in confusion, one corner tipping down and the two women inside shrilling as they started to slide. "He's there! There! You there!"

Right outside the Royal Ancients Theatre a foot patrolman flung his stick in front of him to try and trip him up. He jumped that one, swerved around his partner's black and white thrust out, waist high. A group of young people… other Dyers, milled to one side. "Skate, brother, skate!" One of them yelled after him and someone pulled out a drum. He heard it fading behind and risked a quick glance. He saw them, in the guise of helping, getting in the Sereniteers' way. He had to grin… they were being so helpful!

There were too many Sereniteers in this quarter, even if he knew it. A horse kicked at him as he flew by, rider almost unseated, it reared as he used too much bit, the noise fading as Minis dodged past Our Tiny Enlightened Temple, with its white oval shrine and either a badly painted Goddess or an angel in it, arms open, heart bleeding all over its robe. *"You there!"*

It's like skating with my companions, or with my Mahid, all through here. I didn't have to pull any of the really wild stuff that Ailadas did to force me to chase him through the Marble Palace to get my lesson. He thought his grin would split his face, even as his heart raced, thinking what would happen if they caught him.

"Hey, kid! Want a real job? Skate courier? You're good enough." That was a fellow waving from the Half-Down bridge where he must have had a good view. People leaned from higher windows now, some shouting direction or misdirection from their higher vantage point. He was surprised how many were cheering him on.

Three Black n'Whites burst out of Temple Lane almost on him, he shied sideways, was forced to jump the wash curb and go tearing down the dry water channel along Ripple Street. One of the Sereniteers tried following him straight and managed to swoop into the same channel. He came sweeping down the other side and tried to check him as if this was a *faib* game.

His stick came up as he prepared to either catch Minis with it or shove him off balance, eyes focused, when he braked completely and the Sereniteer went howling past, his skates catching in a trickle of water from the street above. He went careening into the raised wall of the channel. *I should start keeping count!* He was laughing now, as much as he had air to laugh with.

Giggling breathless, Minis whirled in place and tore off, back the way he'd come, across the dry centre up the wall on the other side, slap his hand onto the edge of the wash-curb and yanked his skates down onto Golden Alley. His two partners who'd been keeping pace on the street shouted behind him. One stayed to check the downed Sereniteer, the other whirled as Minis did and struggled to catch up, but he was on the other side of the channel now, still on Ripple. *My lungs are starting to burn.*

Gold Alley was all the shops of the goldsmiths. Though they might live in the *fessas* part of town they had their shops here if they were good enough to attract the eyes of *Aitzas*. Not so many crowds. The wail of the Sereniteers whistles just refused to fade behind him. Now they were ahead of him again. *Skate, boy, skate faster.*

Even in good training he was getting tired. Minis almost stumbled the turn onto Chain Row. A *solas* bodyguard, probably at his employer's urging, flung a café-table and a chair, bouncing into the street and he jumped, fumbled the landing as a spinning chairleg clipped one foot, but kept his feet, barely. His back was going to be black and blue from the stinkin' drum's bounce. He needed to lose them but couldn't pull off the skates easily. They took time to unlace.

Chain ended at the Boardwalk and suddenly he was rapping out a beat with his wheels. *Another moment and those whistles will be on top of me again. Oh… is it big enough? I'm bigger than I used to be…*

He could only try. His breath came hard now and his mouth was dry, the drum had to come to one side so it didn't stop him…

Rapapapraprarparaprarparaprarapa my wheels are like a herd of stampeding horses. The Griffon statue was just ahead. He'd have to hit it exactly right.

"Stop in the name of the law!" Someone bellowed from Chain… another moment and they'd turn onto the walk, see and he'd be arrested… dead dead dead.

He vaguely noticed there weren't many people about. Instead of walking their dogs and cats on leashes they'd faded away from the approaching noise of the chase… the wheels and the whistles…

He jumped, his right skate hit the slanted claw of the Griffon and he pushed off hard, up and tucked. He was a little low and his shoulder hit just the top of the rising wing and tumbled him in a rough roll onto his back into the hollow between the wings, the drum hitting him in the head before settling… He pulled his feet in close, tucked, put arms around his knees. Just as he heard the Skateers hit the boards of the walk.

RAPPARAPPARAPPARAPPA, the sharp, high sound of the wheels dropping to a rumble as they slowed.

From both directions. He lay still, panting, listening. He could only see the branches of the tree above.

"Did you get him?" "Waddaya mean, did *we* get him? Does it look like we got him?" "He was between us… I swear." "You let him slip past you!" "No, you let him slip past you! We never saw him!" "We would have heard him roll by on the boards!"

The breeze off the lake was Selestialis. He just lay and panted quietly, mouth hanging open so he didn't gasp and listened to them argue. The niche in the statue was a tighter fit than when he'd hidden here to wait for Chevenga, but was still barely big enough. It had been built for a heroic rendition of an Imperator or a guard so let him tuck in all his bits behind half-raised wings. The statue was cool from being under the shade of the tree.

"Sera?" One of the Sereniteers was speaking to someone. *OH SHEN. SOMEONE SAW ME.* He clenched his eyes and mouth shut and waited for it all to be over.

(Thanks to Karen for the commentary and the job-offer guy.)

23

A MADWOMAN LIKES DOGGEREL

"Yes, young man?" An elderly woman apparently sitting on the bench around the trunk of the tree... where I'd poured my heart out to Chevenga about Ilian so long ago.

"I am Sereniteer-Kurias Ritaithas, Sera, Marble Palace. Did you see a young man skate past here? We just wish to question him about some things he said near the University, possibly seditious things."

"Oh, Honoured Sereniteer," she said, tremulously. "These eyes haven't seen Muunas's light for nearly ten years."

"Sorry, Sera, I'm sorry. I was just hoping you had..." You could almost hear him blushing at having asked a blind woman what she'd seen. He sounded only a little older than I was.

"No offense taken young man. Not at all. I did hear the sound of skates but you were all here so fast, with your wheeled boots, I could not make out where this fugitive from justice disappeared to."

"Nothing from the lakeshore wall, Kurias." A sereniteer called to his senior officer. "The lake's right to the wall." A cat began to growl and howl somewhere close.

"Shush, Ribbons. My apologies, Sereniteer Ritaithas, my cat is very protective of me."

"Not at all. Thank you for your help, Sera."

I lay there and listened to them scour the sides of the boardwalk, looking for scuffs where my wheels might have hit if I left the walk to hide. They checked for broken bushes... all mock orange, with flowers and branches undisturbed. No body in the lake. No sign that I had left the walk anywhere. I hadn't. I was still right here, torn between glee and scared shenless all at the same time. It was the worst and the best hide and seek I'd ever played.

One even diligently checked the tree trunk, as if I could have leapt all the way over the woman's head and climbed the tree. Sweat dried on me, itching, as my wind came back. I closed my mouth and swallowed, wetting my dry mouth, thirsty, and waited, hoping none of them knew about the hollow back in the statue.

Sinimas, I'm being a little crazy. A little wild. If I get out of this, I'll be diligent and stay out of trouble, I'll be honest, kind, unobtrusive, dull, boring and just scholarly. Can you pass that on to the Gods, please? I truly will.

It really wasn't very long. They couldn't waste much more time on a scruff wanted for questioning over speaking sedition and charged with minor vandalism since they'd count the damage they caused chasing me, to my charge.

"Ser! Oh, Ser!" They hailed a man down the walk. "Did you see the Dyer on skates... bright blue hair... that we were chasing?"

"Nope. Sorry I cannot help you, Sers. I was just picking up after my little Floopsy, here."

"Ahhh. Of course. Thank you."

And their voices faded. I waited. I waited. I waited some more. The only sounds were the gentle lap of the lake and the swish of the leaves above... there. A tiny sound, a single bearing clicking over as someone standing quietly on skates shifts his weight. I waited.

He sighed at last and I heard him roll off up toward the *Aitzas* part of town, *rapparapparapparappa*. Just in case, I waited some more, even if I was itchy all over from drying sweat and the blasted drum sitting against my head.

"They've gone, boy." The old woman said, equal to equal. "Ribbons was watching the last one for me."

I shifted slightly, up on one elbow then, slowly, all the way up on that arm so I could see over the stone wing. She was right. There were only people starting to come back out on the walk, with their pets.

She was still sitting quietly, with her big tiger cat on her lap, flexing curved claws that I would not want to meet with, anywhere. He stared at me and meowed. He was so big I was amazed she was able to hold him on her lap, even with his behind half on the bench. "Um. This one thank you. Sera... this one..."

"A radical like you, speaking one up? Equal to equal if you are going to rebel properly. You needn't say a thing." She held up one hand imperiously. "But... for keeping my tongue and letting you hide up in the statue –" her eyes gazed at me as if she could see, but focused past me. "—I want you to –quietly— chant to me what you declaimed. I should like to hear it."

I gulped. "This one... um...I... um... certainly... I might not remember all of it." I climbed down from the statue, absently patting its neck as I did... as I had... I straightened my disarrayed clothing and scratched all my itches as discretely as possible, patted out a very quiet version of the drumbeat I had used and told her my little bit of doggerel.

"Thank you, young man," she said. "I liked that."

"You're welcome, Sera." I said.

"If you are out playing your drums... and not getting into trouble by adding words to those drum beats... along the walk, here.... I--and Ribbons, of course, are here every day around this time, rain or shine. We would be pleased to listen."

"Um... Certainly, Sera. I'm Sinimas Akam, *fessas*"

"I'm Trathila Eren, *sola*."

"I'll see you another time, then, Sera Eren. Good day, and thank you, again."

She wants to hear the drum? Hmmm. I wonder if she's crazy. Equal to equal if you want to rebel? It makes a kind of sense. It's like Chevenga when I met him. He was afraid of nobody and spoke equal to equal all the time. Where did Sera Eren learn to not be afraid of what people think of her?

And my wheels beat out a slow rhythm on the boards as I went, slowly picking up speed. *Arap Arap Arap Arap.*

Arappa Arappa.

Rapparapparapparappa!

〜

WHO IS BANAKSIAS?
-- By Jorasas Arafen

This reporter is still asking. Banaksias is the name applied to the mysterious and elusive chalk artist whose works appear in the most odd places in the city, pointing the artistic finger at government officials and civil servants with a somewhat less than stellar reputation. He remains at large and undiscovered and as mysterious as ever.

The Minister of Serenity declines to elucidate further on his previous statement "We are doing our best to apprehend this person, though we cannot place a high priority on someone doing something equivalent to temporary vandalism. Other than trespass there truly is no law against what this public artist is doing, despite the outcry of people upset by this or that caricature. We advise a judicious application of soap and water."

The art community is outraged that such astonishing works of art are regularly and repeatedly being destroyed rather than preserved, but the officials in question are objecting to their 'portraits' in public view and the artist himself has been placing some works where regular traffic has in and of itself erased it.

The latest art work, on the wall near the Main Gate itself – and no one saw the artist at work --shows a fighting eagle chained down by hundreds of threads held by nasty little rats, all of whom have curly hair. What is truly remarkable is that iridescent chalk was used as well as regular chalk, so in different light the different parts of the piece seem to brighten or darken.

Whether one agrees or disagrees with this artist's messages, the work is still of excellent calibre and worth a look before the next rain, or over-zealous city cleaning crew erases it forever.

24

ACADEMY OF THE ILLUMINATION
OF YOUNG MINDS

The school seemed nice enough from the outside. It was on Wash-River Street, very close by. If we were going to be in the city for a few moons, Ili should get the advantage of more education.

It was easy walking distance, one reason I chose to inquire about it to see if I wished to enrol my little brother for a time. It had boys in the yard, shrieking and yelling and running around, though it did seem to be an angrier noise than the schools in Haiu Menshir or Yeola-e. The yard seemed harder too, a pounded dirt rectangle, rigidly fenced.

I let myself in and found the office immediately at the front door, with the welcomist acting as gate keeper and guard behind an intimidating slab of desk. "Excuse me," I asked him. "Who would I speak to about possibly enrolling my little brother in school here? For several moons at least."

The dragon guarding the sacred school space was an overly made up man, trying to look much younger than his age. "I'll see if Ser Farakan has a moment to speak to you..." There was a noticeable pause as he looked me up and down, his eyes catching on both the hair and the face jewelry. "If you would sit..."

I barely had time to put my posterior on the uncomfortable chair when the dragon was back. "He will see you now."

"Ser Farakan," I said and nodded politely as I came in. He did not rise to greet me. Not a good sign, I thought. He seemed an amiable sort of fellow though, with a pleasant enough round face. "My name is Sinimas Akam, and I am looking to enroll my little brother in some learning establishment."

"Good Day to you, young Ser," he replied, while sitting straighter in his desk, and lowering his hands out of sight. "Welcome to the Academy of the Illumination of Young Minds." He stood then, and began to pace and lecture; leaving me standing before his desk as though *he* had summoned *me.* "I am Ser Hikaras Farakan, owner and founder. This professional establishment offers the finest in education in academics and propriety available to the *Fessas* of the City Itself." It was amazing how I could *hear* the capital letters. He was reminding me, unfortunately, of my *dekinas*, Tobias.

"Truly? I am impressed." I managed to keep most of the sarcasm out of my tone. I shouldn't jump to conclusions, just because I took a sudden dislike to the Head Master of the School for no reason. I would have to see more. "What kind of curricula does your establishment offer for the age six to first threshold student?"

He blinked, as if mildly surprised that I would interrupt, then remembered to smile and sell. "For our smallest scholars we have a three bead program and a six bead program. My system of pedagogy for these most malleable students depends heavily upon instilling proper foundations for later accomplishments. Reading, beginning penmanship, memorization of laudable works and of course, comportment are covered in the three bead program, while the six bead day includes noon observances, a meal, another exercise break, and more comportment.

"And if the student in question can already read? He is currently reading "Tathanas's Eagles'."

"Well then surely he could use extra instruction on writing with a clear and graceful hand. Copperplate is a jewel of great worth in any field of endeavour. My calligraphy master teaches an exquisite fist."

Just what Ili needs... he'd spit in this man's eye inside a half-tenth. "Might I see your most estimable establishment, Ser?"

"But of course! Please, do follow me." He then turned to the outer office, and summoned the dragon. "Boras, take the young Ser upon a tour." He raised his hand as if to snap his fingers, but jerked to a stop and carefully clasped his hands behind his back before turning back. "I am sure that you will see that we have much to offer. My assistant will show you about and answer any....questions you might have." He began to turn away even before he finished speaking, then turned back when I spoke up again.

"Oh, Ser, I have two more questions for you, before I tour your charming school."

"Yes?"

"My brother has been attending a Haian School. What are your opinions of those? And what are your policies regarding corporal punishment?" These two would tell me more than just my vague feelings about the place.

He reared back as if someone had thrust a turd under his nose. "Haian school? A school taught by...Ahheem. Hem. Well, we usually do not do any sort of placement testing, but your little brother sounds...well you mentioned that he is reading at an advanced level, perhaps an evaluation by one of our tutors would help us place him best. Yes. An evaluation, yes. Ahem, and what was your second question?"

Hmmm. "Your policy regarding corporal punishment? Oh, and is there a different curriculum for those who can pay silver as opposed to copper?"

"We do not have a different curricula per se, but there is always more available to those who are prepared to pay extra for additional lessons, tutoring, and of course we do have several different packages for the uniforms and meal plans." His eyes skittered across my head when he mentioned uniforms, but then he resolutely tried to ignore the colour. "We have a deluxe package for those who feel that their sons deserve more refined choices of fabric and diet."

I see. Fine cotton and cheap silk if you can get it. Beef for the high paying student and who knows what meat, if any, to the others. I would lay chains on it.

"I pride myself on only hiring teachers who respond with properly gauged responses to juvenile misbehaviour and defiance. Any teacher who cannot control a class with no more than a standard yardstick has no place here, and I would never keep an instructor who loses control while administering discipline."

A Mahid corrector is smaller than a yardstick. And he is starting to sound very Mahid to me. I nodded. "Thank you for your time, Ser Farakan. You have been most gracious." *Never let a Mahid know you can see through what they've said to what they really mean. Flogging with the rod is, it seems, allowed in this school. Or encouraged.*

Boras led me through two empty classrooms, explaining that the young gentlemen were out in the yard obtaining physical exercise at the moment. The rows of desks were perfectly aligned, as were the books and papers upon them. A single pen lay just so across each desk. The drawings hung in a single line along one wall were grid-rendered copies of classic paintings, all the same.

"Our drafting teacher is excellent," my guide said when he saw me looking at them. *I think Ili would go mad here. Perhaps I should see if I could steal a word or two with one or two of the students.*

"Thank you for your time, Ser." I said to Boras. "I'll let myself out."

~

"Hey, boys." I didn't have my drum with me but I rapped my hands on the edge of one of the wooden row seats surrounding the field. Two boys sat on one row two seats up. Everyone else was out running about to the instructor's shouts. He had a yard-stick tucked under his arm like a long corrector. He used it occasionally to point, either at boys or where they were to go. "No joys? No toys?" I said, quietly. "Could you talk to me a moment?"

"Your hair is *blue*, mister, why is your hair *blue*?" That was the younger boy, who had a small wen on his face next to his left eye.

"'Cause I made it that way. I tried holding my breath long enough but that didn't work, so I dyed it."

That caught a furtive giggle from the two of them, which they hid behind behind dusty gloves, glancing at each other, then at the teacher on the field as if to make sure he hadn't noticed them not paying perfect attention.

"You like going to school here? I'm thinking of putting my little brother here."

The half-smiles cut off and they stared at me without saying anything, glanced at each other, then away. Their faces had gone still. I knew that look, that 'don't let anything slip' look. Ice Eyes would call it 'dumb insolence'.

"That good, hmmm? Thanks." I rapped out out a rhythm on the stand they were sitting on. "Hey, hey teacher, preacher, beat-cher... harsh man, old man, cold man! Keep your words within your mouth and keep your teeth... got no relief...." I stopped and nodded at them.

One reached back to scratch his back, gingerly, along a line, as if to sooth a welt. *I understand, lad.* He whispered to his best friend, then asked, "Where's your drum?"

"Wasn't going to bring it talking to a Head Master. But everything's a drum and everyone is a drummer."

They grinned at each other, then both stomped out a long drum roll, and began to shove and squirm. "Intharas! Tathanas! Attend since you cannot participate!" The instructor called them to order.

"I'd better go before I get you in trouble." I raised a finger and ran it over the faint scar on my cheek. "I had a teacher like some. Bye, boys."

"Bye, Dyer!"

"Bye-r Dyer! I'm no liar!" It got another giggle that faded behind me. *No, I don't think Ili will have his mind illuminated here.*

25

ANTI SHEFENKAS RALLIES

ANTI-SHEFEN-KAS RALLIES PAID FOR!

The Pages headline screamed it.   The story made it clear. An *Aitzas* lord who actually liked things the way they were, had been quietly funding the near riotous rallies against the former Imperator coming back into power.

The Marble Palace declined to release the name but did say that the caste of the 'person of intrest' was, indeed, *Aitzas*.

～

The pro Shefen-kas rallies had almost doubled in size since the Pages article came out. Speculation all around was that the *Aitzas* was fronted by the Yeoli Hawks, but that hadn't yet been comfirmed by truth-drug. I'd seen three other Dyers chased through the streets by Sereniteers trying to catch the seditious vandals.

"What is the world coming to, our landsera groused, when I asked her to see to a leak in the roof as well as the ants. "These young people... hardly respectable. They're probably stealing things to afford those faib-things..."

"They're probably half-broken down faib skates thrown out of the *Aitzas* league, Sera," I said quietly. "Thank you for attending to things in the apartment so promptly." I eased back a roll or two on my skates so her tom-cat wouldn't instantly spray on them.

"You're a good boy," she said. "I'll look after the roof, not to worry."

~

"Now, Ili, you have to leave Jiaklem with Gannara or I… or put him in his brand new tank while you are at school."

"I don't want to! I want to take him!"

"He'll be bored, Ili and crawl around under the teacher's desk and nibble on his toes. The teacher would end up not liking him and that wouldn't be fair to Jia. He can't read or recite with you."

"Will it be a school like Haiu Menshir?"

"No, Ili, sorry. It will be an Arkan school though I looked for one that has a lot of foreign students and different ideas. You'll have to sit and listen more than you did on the beach at Haiu Roru."

"Sounds dull."

"The teacher is very nice. He doesn't cough as much as Ailadas did… or does."

"Can we visit Ailadas?"

"No, Ili, I'm sorry. We'd be putting him in danger if we did."

Since I had rejected Ser Farakam's school out of hand I'd inquired of three others, all further from where we were lodging. I took Ili's hand in mine and we went out over the Blackstone Bridge and down the way to The Bright Sparks of Mikas's Eye School over on Tall Grass Alley.

It was interesting that in the middle of the *fessas* quarter usually straight-lined, scoured clean cobbles, this winding road had actually been turned into a forest of tall grasses and flowers with a stone path meandering through it. It was still wide enough to let people pass easily without stamping the grass down and the residents of the street kept it looking half wild, quite carefully. Instead of washing this street, the water flow watered it every week.

The school was tucked into this apparently ocean of grass, with short cut grass leading neatly up the walk. It was a plain block building with square windows and a black door. "It looks nasty." Ili said, but without nervousness. He clung to my hand and threw his shoulders back. "I can do it!"

"I know you can."

"Are there girls, like on Haiu Menshir?"

"Yes, Ili. They were particular about letting me know."

"Oh. That's all right, then."

Bright Sparks was a less rigid school than most private *fessas* schools, the best of those I had toured. I had chosen it just for that reason, since I figured Ili had enough of rigid even though he had not been taught by Mahid. Just being forced to be with Mahid must have been bad enough.

I'd remembered how I felt when Father just picked a tutor for me, though I had been lucky with Ailadas, so I asked Ili what kind of things he wanted to learn and held that in mind while I looked for a place for him. He said he liked the Haian school, or being tutored by Gan and I.

I saw him into his new class room, where ten other children – even girls -- were diligently building wooden models of various machines, including several who were working on a wooden replica of the Great Press itself. Ili immediately wanted to join them but I made him say his hellos and introductions to his new teacher, a young, dark man who introduced himself to Ili by his first name.

"Ili, my name is Gian."

"Hi, Ser Gian... can I go help those boys... um... and girls?"

"In a moment. Please sit here and you may look at these books that have the plans for all these models, while I walk your brother out."

"All right, Ser Gian."

"Just Gian, thank you, Ili."

"Gian." He already had the top book off the stack and was leafing through, looking at wooden gears and rods as we stepped out.

"I think he will do fine here, Ser Akam."

"I hope you don't mind my asking, are you Niah?"

"Ah, no Ser. My family were caravaneers. We are a nomadic people... but we brought our caravans to the city after the sack and settled ourselves in Tall Grass Alley."

"Oh. So you could have your homes roll into place and wouldn't have to build?"

"Exactly so, Ser. Though we have done our own bit of gardening to the street." *So they were the ones who had made the Alley truly Tall Grass. Interesting. Ili will like him, I think.*

～

"All right, Gan all you need to do... oh... did you ever do this on ice? Ice sliding?" Gan looked at me a little sourly.

"I don't remember, Min. And I was on board ship or in Asinanai which doesn't get a lot of snow."

He sat on the bench by the used skate merchant with a set of really decent skates on his feet, that looked terrible. Probably scratched and dinged up in a Mahid game and discarded. The merchant had smoothed the leather but dyed the leather this ugly greenish colour that had absorbed oddly. Not that I cared if they were expensive, but it would have been out of character for us to have bought him new.

Ili was already wobbling along on his new big-boy skates, remembering from a long time ago, giggling like a little devil. Gan grinned and got up, flailed and sat back down on the bench, grabbed my wrist and managed to gain his feet the second time. "These feel odd!"

"You'll get it. It's fun.. whooo ho ho woowh... hang on to me!" It was a funny, almost slow motion fall. We ended up on the pavement sprawled out like some weird Haian starfish.

Gan was laughing, his chest going up and down under my shoulder as I rolled off him to get up and help him to his wheels.

"You'll get it!" I said.

"I get why the skate seller insisted on selling me all this padding!"

"Yes, exactly. So let's go catch Ili before he makes it all the way to Holystone Footbridge into the park!"

I ended up towing him because he did manage to keep his feet pointed in the same direction and steady, even if he couldn't yet glide on them.

26

VOTING AND ONE OF THE HUNTS
FOR MINIS

The chalk spreads on the stone smoothly, making tiny squeaking noises as I draw. The Sereniteers look like black and white donkeys chasing Dyers with big butterfly nets and the Dyers flying away like birds.

The whole dry-wash will be full of my drawing until the next washing day. The line of an ass's grin, big flat white teeth... The Dyers' flapping away. The iridescent chalk that will glow so nicely, highlighting edges and shadows.

Oh, here come the lamp-tenders.

The tenders came down on either side of the wash, calling to each other. They were friends who made a little competition of who could snuff and tend all his lamps before the other. They'd been doing it for years. The one ahead called excitedly to his friend.

"Hey! Hey! Tan! Lookit! It's another Banaksias!"

"Mikas bless, that's a big one!"

"Lookit that!" They laughed at the silly faces on the Sereniteer Donkeys and then looked around but saw no one they could identify as the elusive artist -- an old man walking his two dogs, the great hound and the sleeve dog, an *okas* girl carrying a chamber pot off to the night-soil buyers, a farmer just pushing his hand-cart in toward the High market, a Masker Midwife, and themselves.

The artist smiled and kept walking.

∼

The line-ups for the *vodai* to bring Chevenga back were, if anything, longer than the lines to impeach him. Everyone knew that to bring him back would mean we would be doing this again in less than a year, when the two countries would again be separate. Chevenga would take his Yeolis home and we would vote for an Arkan Imperator to sit upon the Crystal Throne.

Everyone in the line was talking about it, wondering what family, which *Aitzas* would be competing to be the new Son of the Sun. "I'll bet the Hawks don't go home. They'll say they're Arkan citizens and maybe even put one of them forward to run for the Throne." I smiled to myself to hear such analysis from an *okas* brick layer. *"... what if an okas is born brilliant?..."*

The question echoed from years ago.

I had my hair braided back and tucked under a sun hood, my glasses firmly on my nose, since I had my identification as Minakas Akam in my pouch. As Sinimas, I was too young to vote. Gannara had been in the machine smithies quite a bit while Ili went to school. My brother liked his teacher and was coming home with new friends every day, to introduce Jiaklem to them.

I had gone back, as Sinimas, to track down the fellow who had bellowed the job offer at me, to find out if he'd been serious and he had been. I skated courier a few beads a week, as well as writing. Not that I had to but it was fun, and I did know the city, aside from the changes that the sack had wrought and those were quickly learned. If I didn't do something, I found I was bored with lazing about.

The Sereniteers were ignoring the Dyers making their music... voiceless today to not draw them, but the pounding rhythms came up, wove together before fading as they moved from place to place along the lines. They also turned a blind eye to the Dyers on *faib* skates swooping around the 'Back to Truther' protestors. *Aitzas* every one... and their children, with *okas* paid to shave their heads and pretend to be slaves – since the abolition of slavery it was fashionable in a certain crowd of *Aitzas* to hire *okas* like that. They waved their picture signs, since women and *okas* weren't supposed to be able to read; signs showing Yeolis and other foreigners stuck through with swords and spears. Two lone text signs read "Muunas hates Foreigners" and "Muunas Hates Arko! Repent! Don't vote!"

"Friend..." The voice next to me was quiet, friendly, equal to equal. "Hot today, hmmm?"

"Yes, it is."

He was a pressman, by his dress. "You bringing the wool-hair boy back?"

"I wouldn't say, ser."

"Of course, of course. You watch out for those thugs up ahead..." He nodded at the rough men standing near the door of the polling place. They looked frustrated and hot and the Sereniteer patrol, leaning on their staffs also a carefully casual distance away, smiled and chatted with the line.

"You think they were supposed to do something?" I blinked naively behind my spectacles. "Something *illegal?" And I'd bet a gold chain you know what they were supposed to do if they could. Start a fight, start a riot, disrupt the vote line and scare people away from the poll.*

"Not with the patrol right there..." he shrugged. "I'll bet they were supposed to threaten people."

I made my voice squeak as though shocked. *"Influence the vote?"*

He looked solemn. "You never know. Say friend, what say we and my friends go have a beer – I'll buy -- until the line thins out." Other people around me, who he'd been talking to before, nodded thoughtfully. "It'll be easier to wait after Rim dark."

And easier to persuade me and however many others here that we have plenty of time to vote. Plenty of time to find out if I want to vote for, or against and see if I and a dozen other people want to bring Chevenga back and get us drunk. I'd seen other men working the lines somewhat like this. Whoever thought of it was smart. "Oh, I'm sorry ser, I have to vote now. Later I must pick up dinner for my family."

He nodded genially and managed to get four other people to just step out of the line with him, just till later.

The blue/green posters were everywhere, however much the red poster people tried to pull them down or paper them over. I was happy to see the Sereniteers still blithely ignored Dyers zooming by to take another drumming pass around the protestors, keeping their attention firmly on the obvious ruffians.

I think I shall be in presentation square... as Sinimas... when the vote is announced. I would bet a gold chain that we shall have Chevenga back soon.

"Ahem, good day again, Ser Perisalas." Ailadas settled himself familiarly in the ornate little chair across from Perisalas. "I am assuming you wish to ask me, yet again, whether Minis Aan or any of his aliases had contacted me since the last time you asked. Alas, the answer is no."

"Good day, Ser Ailadas. You are quite correct. Are you certain of this?" Perisalas placed the kaf cup next to Ailadas's elbow. "Cream and two spoons of sugar, correct?"

"Yes, ahem, perfect thank you." Ailadas stirred his kaf and sipped appreciatively. "Yes. You may, ahem, of course, truth drug me to confirm this. I have no classes to, ahem, cancel this afternoon, thank you for that consideration."

"Oh, you are welcome. I shall confirm with truth-drug."

"I -ahem- quite understand."

It was the typical 'Did you tell me true," truth-drugging, though Perisalas learned about a different date in Arkan history as Ailadas succumbed to the drug. And Serina Liren's undrugged answers always corroborated the old scholar, so it seemed that the former Spark was scrupulously avoiding his one-time fellow fugitives. It was also the most frugal of ways to cross-check them against each other. He saw the old man on his way and went back to the latest raft of Minis sighting stories.

This one has him grow wings and ascend to the Moon like our esteemed ancestors. So now I am supposed to go to the Moon to find his fortress?

The Moon fortress keeps coming back lately. Lunatics.

"Ser?"

"Yes, Dagasas?

"The Melachiya boy's parents are here to see you, Ser."

27

RESULTS OF THE VODAI

Dear Elder Brother,

I have found out that our missing relative might be in Arko...
perhaps even the city itself. I will renew my search there and
report to the family shortly.

My journey from Haiu Menshir was somewhat delayed by storm,
a minor illness and pirates, however I shall be posting this letter
from Anoseth as soon as the ship docks.

In duty,

Joras Enkasas, *fessas*

2ND Amitzas crumpled the letter and tossed it in his fire.
"Wife!" He called.
   "Yes, husband?"
   "Prepared the women to move tonight."
   "Yes, husband."

~

I was in a group of Dyers in Presentation Square, with Ili on his skates as well. Gannara was somewhere about... possibly hanging around with a girl from Tall Grass Alley, one of Gian's people. She was pretty enough in a dark way but he and I had talked about girls on our various travels and she was much more his kind of girl than mine. Even if I thought of girls at all.

I thought maybe I might be spared that nonsense any more. Gannara hadn't caught me indulging that even in my sleep lately. Though I hated getting the sheets sticky, I was at least able to keep a lot of those perverse dreams more private.

The crowd was almost as festive as a pre-*Jitz* party. Sausage sellers doing brisk business next to beer sellers and a fellow with a waist-tray and a row of wine bottles jingling. "Peanuts! Sweet wine!"

I bought Ili a paper cone of *fanilas* flavoured ice shavings and chilled melon spheres. I had my drum and we made sure that the Sera Eren and her enormous cat on his leash had a good place. "Sinimas... I hardly need to 'see'," she said snippily and I laughed. I had been to play for her on the boardwalk almost every day. "I merely need to hear well and I can do that from here."

'Here' was at the edge of the ruin made to make way for the monstrous statue. All work had been suspended on it since Chevenga's coming out against it, but the boards still stood... now covered with good, bad, indifferent drawings and Banaksias's chalkwork. People had set up informal benches before some of them and I had settled Sera Eren on one of these, Ribbons at her feet.

"And we truly have no good sight-line but the Presentation Platform offers enough of a sound-line." One of the shadefountain trees kept us cool with a light mist, paper leaves whispering, which was part of what obscured our vision though it would periodically fold shut to give people a better view of the front of the Marble Palace.

Ribbons sprawled over my skates and growled and clawed at Ili's. He giggled and dropped JiaKlem on the cat. Everyone froze and Jia nibbled on Ribbons and the cat pretended to shred Jia into seafood.

"ARKO! ARKO! ARKO! HEAR THE RESULTS OF YOUR VODAI!"

The whole crowd quieted and turned our attention to the herald on the platform.

〜

"They are being very even-handed," Sera Eren said quietly as everyone stilled to hear the count in Arko. She opened her lace sun shade and people all around shuffled a bit to accommodate her. "I thought there would be a bigger will to vote him back in but they like the Imperatrix's work for them."

"They aren't upset by her being a woman," Gannara said as he wobbled up to be with our group. He was still a little unsteady on his skates but that was going away fast. A Dyer girl with a butterfly dyed into the back of her head sent a ripple of sound around us with her Jang drum as the herald held up his hand.

"THE TOTAL VODAI COUNT REGISTERED IN ARKO WAS TWO MILLION EIGHT HUNDRED NINETEEN!" We were so unused to the idea of our power, in our numbers, that the announcement of the number of us who voted raised a cheer in the square. *Please Gods let us be sensible and vote the Imperator who really knows Arko back onto the Crystal Throne.* A huge arguing point during the pre-vote campaign was the fact that Artira Shae-Arano-e had never learned Arkan of any stripe.

"SPOILED BALLOTS, SIXTY ONE THOUSAND, TWELVE." *Of course they're going to drag it out. The crowd is going mad with noise.* "THE VOTE AGAINST SHEFENKAS RETURNING TO THE CRYSTAL THRONE—" *Get on with it, man! Do all heralds have to drag it out like this? Are you paid by the word?* "FOUR HUNDRED THOUSAND EIGHTY SEVEN!" The roar as people figured out what that meant submerged his final bellow of "THE VOTE FOR SHEFENKAS, TWO MILLION, THREE HUNDRED THIRTY-EIGHT THOUSAND, NINE HUNDRED TWENTY!" under a wave of sound, cheering, screaming, chanting and many of the women present weeping, for joy I believe.

I had both hands in the air over my head... most of the crowd did as well, the expansive prayer gesture that dared to reach up to sky as opposed to just stopping at one's head. My throat hurt and I realized I was adding to the noise as much as anyone, though I couldn't hear myself.

Sera Eren had both hands clapped over her ears and Ribbons had his ears pressed flat against his skull as the thundering boom of fifty thousand people in the square, rolled on. They looked equally overwhelmed by the sheer amount of sound. Ili was jumping up and down on his skates even, Jia locked around his wrist, clinging for dear life. Gan's grin split his face and I realized I was grinning just as wide. *Chevenga, at least, understands us,* I thought and then bellowed it. Why not? Why not say that out loud?

The noise ebbed back a bit into people's throats and actually faded to startled silence when the two gongs at the top of the Temple steps, behind us, began sounding. It was the beat that the city had heard once before in this generation, when Chevenga had done the Rite of Ascension. The Ten Tens.

The two priests who alternated so there was an unbroken ringing, wore the black robes of cleansing, as did the two rows of *dekinas* filing out of the great golden doors, half of them now female... Maskers... so they would be *dekina.* They carried the great books of the Ten, that normally were open on altars before each God or Goddess in their hands, all bound in silver metal cloth... just the same as I had the Imperial Book and Ilesias the Great's book wrapped in, at home on the bottom of my closet with the Imperial Sword. That wrapping I knew in my bones now, was impervious to water, never snagged and was impossible to tear, perfect to protect the God's Books.

The shadefountain tree folded its paper leaves as the water pressure shut off, leaving us under the eye of the Sun.

The Fenjitzas, and now the Fenjitza as well, came forward out from under the shadow of the portico into the sunlight on the top step and raised their arms to the sky. The gongs faded and everyone's attention locked on the High Priest and Priestess in complete, befuddled silence.

The two turned to face the now-empty Temple, her raised right arm crossing his raised left so they looked like one creature. "Ergas. Rabi. Difment. Rogran."

I found myself staring with everyone else. The Ten Tens was being called for. The Ten Tens. Again. In response to the sacred words, the massive golden doors began to close without being touched by any hand but the Gods. They shut with a BOOM that I felt through my feet and made my chest quiver. "My most high Goddess." It was quiet enough, the crowd stunned silent, that I heard Sera Eren whisper behind me. "He is going to do the Ten Tens. Again." The sun shining on all our heads seemed more intense, more real, pouring down over our heads.

I swallowed, realized my mouth was dry, raised our water jug from the bench next to Ribbons and drank without taking my eyes off the Temple.

As the Temple door sealed with a sound I had never heard before, as if they kissed each other, an almost moist noise, from the roof the *okas,*--not slaves—tipped the massive vessels, built into the edges of the roof, over and sent the black coating sheeting down over the building. It was not tar, nor paint. It seemed alive and spread as though the building welcomed it and drew it into every crack and crevasse. The priests now ringing the building began painting the base stones. It would take them the rest of the day but by the time the sun rose tomorrow the building would be entirely covered and the ceremonial guard pacing the sacred boundary.

They were there not to protect the Temple but to protect people from coming too close as the Gods burned the dross off the outside of their House on the Earth. The Temple would be glowing with forge heat as it cleansed itself over the sixty days.

I would have seen this... if Arko hadn't been conquered... after my father died. I would have watched that from the Presentation Balcony, dressed all in black, my head dyed black, not bright blue. In sixty days, when the Temple was clean again – had cleaned itself over that time, I would have stepped up to the doors, raised my hands, newly weighed down with the Seals, to touch the hands of the pretenders who wished to attempt the Ten Tens and so, possibly, become the new Son of the Sun.

I would have opened the doors with the sacred word. I would have danced for the Gods... That was when my mind skittered to a halt. The Gods had showed me how much they did not want me. The Gods... if Father – the fat guy—was wrong and there were Gods -- *Sinimas, my ancestors, please apologize to the Ten for my blasphemous thoughts, my questioning of Their existence.*

I hiccupped to another stop. If the Gods did not exist then I was not damned. I did not have to believe myself *forzak* once I died. *I would have to cease believing in Hayel... or Selestialis for that matter. I would have to become* athye, *like a Yeoli. It would be so good to not look at the end of my life and expect nothing after death, rather than eternal punishment for having been my father's son.*

But to repudiate the idea of my damnation, I'd have to give up my Gods... I feel them. They are real to me. I dream of Them. Aside from a few lapses, much apologized for, I haven't dared pray directly to Them, since I realized how evil my soul must truly be for Them to hate me so much. I...must think on this. Gan would just say 'You're not evil, that's just crazy. Why have Gods to punish you that much, just for being born? Because you were born to a bad man? If Gods are merciful and just they wouldn't set babies up like that because it's just mad... and unjust."

All this flashed through my head, even as I stood staring at the blackening building, Ili hugging me around the waist, my arm around him. He looked at the Temple, then up into my face. *What am I showing?* I smiled at him to wipe the remnants of my thoughts away, like a napkin rubbing oil off my lips.

The trumpets from the Presentation Balcony cut through the rising, confused hubbub as people wondered aloud whether all this meant really that Chevenga, having been voted back onto the Crystal Throne, would truly be contemplating doing the Ten Tens a second time.

Our attention swivelled back to the Marble Palace and I said to Sera Eren, "It's Ch'venga. He's here, not in Yeola-e. He's here and He is going to speak."

28

AN ECLIPSED SUN, AN ECLIPSED COURT

From where we were, half way across the Square, I could see his black, curly head and the dark shirt he wore, his face a white smudge. I could imagine it though. At the family dinner I had finally been able to shake the memory of that horrible night when I looked at him, but seeing him on the Presentation Balcony, in the Marble Palace, reminded me. My guts knotted. I looked down at the toes of my skates instead, and just listened.

The Balcony was designed to throw the voice of the speaker, as long as he stood or sat in the right place, so that everyone in the square could hear him without the need for shouting. He thanked us for voting him back in. He promised that the statue would not be built and that a committee would be formed to study what should be in its place on the Square.

He announced that he would immediately begin setting up our own Assembly, with our own representatives and write a new constitution. But then he addressed our confusion directly, about him doing the Ten Tens again.

"Some might wonder why I intend to do it again when I have done it once, and other Imperators have only done it once, accepting that as proof that they have the approval of the Gods.

"It is this: the Gods approved me before as I came to the Imperatorship then; this time I ask Them whether they approve how I came to the Imperatorship this time.

"In other words, this is to ask whether They approve what *you* have done--how you have voted, and indeed the entire notion of voting.

"This is to confirm that an Imperator chosen by the people of Arko is legitimate as Imperator in the eyes of the Gods, and to sanctify--if I am successful--this vote and the act of voting itself.

Of course. I felt as though someone had snuck up behind me and smacked me in the head with a board. *That is so... perfect. Of course.*

"You know," Sera Eren said thoughtfully. "We have a truly extraordinary man as an Imperator... again."

The truth of it all had me reeling. He was talking about what he'd said to us in his campaign, that Arko needed to be returned to Arkans. An elected Arkan Imperator. We could do it. We knew how, now. We had the tools.

I thought back to the sickening feeling I lived with under the fat guy, the feeling that there was not only no direction offered the Empire but that we were all being steered toward grotesque destruction... and realized that the Gods had answered our prayers. The Gods had punished us... for allowing such a Son of the Sun that they repudiated him and raised up a foreigner to teach us.

The corruption is not gone. It is still here in the form of the Hawks now, but that is both less and more identified as corrupt. There is not a vague formless mass hovering over the city and the Empire. The mood and will of all Arko is better. It's the home I wanted when I was a child, the home I was supposed to have. That I had to pretend was perfect. I have been so much happier, so much lighter as a wild subversive Dyer rolling messages and pack-ages all over the city.

We had the tools, and the crowd knew it. His speech and His presence raised cheers and applause all over the Square. The whistles of approval came from all around the plaza, trying to make Him stay longer on the Balcony, though his speech was fairly short.

"I want to camp out here, on this spot, to make sure we see His Ten Tens." I said.

"Oh." Gan said. "Yeah. We're closer to the Temple here. It's a good spot."

"And Sera," I said to my friend. "We can hold place for you."

"Pish!" She said. "I can help us out as well. Ribbons and I can hold our ground and let you boys free for things like getting this young man to his schooling and back!"

"Aw, Grandmother Eren..." Ili whined but didn't have his whole heart in it. When I had taken Ili with me to play drum for her, or tell her what news the street had, he'd almost instantly adopted her as an unofficial Grannie.

"Not very attractive, young man," she said and he giggled.

~

So we set up camp on the Square, right where we stood, exactly in front of the great Temple doors.

Gan and I took turns staying overnight and Sera Eren often came in the mornings or evenings, to sit with Ili when he was not in school or with one of us. Ribbons decided that our spot was the exact extent of his leash all the way around.

So it was that Sera Eren came with Ili, earlier than usual this day, to relieve me of duty. Gan was back at our rooms and I scooted back to fetch new clothing before heading to the public baths. I was no longer dying my hair, letting the blue fade naturally. I wasn't sure why but it seemed right. I left the nose ring in.

I unlaced my skates and grabbed them by the laces, padding up the stairs in the boot liners, pushed the door open and froze. The bed was folded open and there were bodies on it... heaving, moaning, groaning bodies... having sex...

Gan's head, tousled and sweating jerked up from where he was kissing... a girl... they scrambled up, him jerking sheets up over themselves though not before I saw the girl's dark nipples staring at me like her eyes. She was one of Gian's people... the caravaneers... and she wasn't covering up. Gan had taken in enough Arkan propriety to want to cover them. "Min! What are you doing home early?" Then his nature as a Yeoli asserted itself and he dropped the sheet, leaving them both sitting naked to the waist.

I manage to swallow and look away, sidle over to the cubboard... "Oh, you two having a... nap? Sorry I woke you."

"No, no," she said. *What was her name again? Farish? Something like that.* "You didn't wake us, we were just having sex."

I nearly melted on the spot. *Oh, wonderful... another race with no basic decency...* I grabbed for the first set of fresh underkilts that I had and a clean shirt, babbled "Oh, well, then don't let me interrupt." I managed to squeak out a faint "have fun," before fleeing downstairs and out to the baths, away from the image of her dark breasts and his pale, tattooed chest. He'd had the *semanakraseye* brand covered with this purple bird-like thing he said was an interpretation of their Summoner to Death, and Ice Eye's initials became sails and waves. The colours inked into his skin effectively hid the scars and he would be able to take his shirt off without explaining to people that his burns were because of Mahid torture. I thought the whole scene on his chest was beautiful.

I fled their eyes, hers amused and Gan's confused at first, then – what burned me most – full of compassion. He was feeling sorry for me. *It's good. It's good. He's normal. He's healed enough. Yeolis like girls and boys both but Gan's always like the look of girls more. It's good. 'Having a nap'! Of all the dumb things to say!*

I managed to wash some of my embarrassment away under hot water in the paid cascade booth, at Rathanas's Cleanser: Hot cascades, Private Baths, and Laundry, dropping off my dirty clothes at the desk.

It's good. It's good. He's recovering fast. Maybe he'll bring home a Yeoli girl next. But I should get him to at least put something outside the door so I know not to come barging in on them. A loincloth on the latch or some-thing... When I think of it, according to all the knuckle-suckers... I'm surprised I haven't walked in on him earlier... just because I don't, doesn't mean he shouldn't. My brother is healing. This is good. My face is as hot as if I had a sunburn.

I laced my skates back on and let the wind of my going back to the Square cool my burning cheeks, just at rim sunset.

~

I sat, on our mats, all by myself for once. All by myself except for the little community of campers in the Square, all of us staking out our space for the Ten Tens. But it was late and mostly everyone was sleeping.

There was a *fessas* couple, Alasas and Trina, a few paces to the one side of us and a young *solas* boy, Idiesas, to the other, holding space for his mother and grandmother at night. A few centuries ago, there had been theft and violence done to people camping out during the cleansing time and the ceremonial guard was mandated to not just keep the people away from the Temple but to protect them from thieves and pickpockets at night as well.

I sat, with my knees hugged to my chest, my chin upon them and looked at the Temple. The darkness was evaporating off it and I could feel the heat of the building from here. The black was being eaten away somehow and one could see the glow of the white and gold exposed, cleansed, renewed.

I am still doing my Ten Tens practice. Why? It is so illegal... just as my existence is illegal. I don't want to die but as long as I am free I'm a threat to Arko. The stone under our mats is radiating the warmth of the day and is very soothing.

...Blood. The battlefield is covered with blood. It is all Arkan blood. I can see the young commander, a boy who looks vaguely like me, wearing a black suit of armour with blackened silver fittings, like a Mahid. He stands on a war tower with a banner flapping overhead, an Eclipsed Sun, the rays bloody as the battlefield.

He is on Finpollendias and the whole city is on fire, flames reaching up to tower high enough to see over the Rim, smoke billowing, blackening the sky. I see Tawaen... as an old man... his daughter... in armour...

I know the boy in black armour... He claims to be Third Minis Kurkas Joras Amitzas Aan, but he is not, truly. I had no children but who is to know that? He is about to take an Empire so ruined it will never recover.

Arkans are lying dead everywhere I can see... injured... dying... screaming as they are ridden over by other Arkans...

"This is a strong possibility, you realize." The voice I hear is full of steel. I am horrified, soaking in Arkan blood and cannot scream.

"Oh, Selestialis, no! No!" I managed to say, but I cannot look away to see who is speaking.

"It is not an honourable war. 3rd Minis truly believes himself descended from you... he's 2nd Amitzas's grandson, truly."

"No, this can't happen. It mustn't happen."

"Do you care?"

I whip around in a rage, finally able to move. "Of COURSE I..." My voice seizes solid in my throat and I fall to my knees. He is still a God and I am forzak. *"Steel Armed."*

"I'm glad you still recognize Me." I cannot say anything under that gaze. I am trained enough under His eye that I am ashamed, just kneeling before Him. "This is... as things are... what might be."

I gaze at his knees and that it almost too much. "Father of Swords, can I do anything to stop this?" I manage to whisper. "Do I have the power to stop this?" I cast my eyes down further, onto the ground. Blood flows around my knees in the mud, Arkan blood. "Let me do something, please!"

"You do have that power. And thus the responsibility. Think on it, my shadow son."

"Sh...sh..adow son?" I cannot help it, I raise my eyes to His and am shocked to see them full of tears, and His face full of compassion that strikes to my heart. He reaches His hand and I am raised to my feet. For an instant I think His eyes were brown and His hair dark. "Ch'venga? But... You are Aras..."

"Stand tall before a commander, Minis. Don't grovel." He is speaking to me equal to equal. "*Think on it.*" His voice shakes me to my bones and I open my eyes to find I have fallen asleep, lying on my side curled up, still facing the Temple. I'm soaked with sweat but I didn't wake anyone around me, it seems.

29

THAT HORRIBLE BOY

Linasika Shae-Ara stopped at a kias, one of the street vendors in Arko who had an alcohol burner grill for his sausages. "Tisha, do you want a sausage? Or some latas cakes?"

"No, no, can you just get me some juice?"

"Certainly, love. I'll be right back."

Tisha sat down in the front row of the Fire-Fountains, the one row that was never obscured by fog, and pinched the bridge of her nose with the fingers of one hand. The crowd in front of her was like a small town that had sprung up the instant Chevenga had spoken, had let the Arkans all know he was going to do that fancy ritual of theirs the second time.

Vendors set up around the presentation Square hawked sun-shades and trinkets. Artists did fast portraits in chalk or in charcoal for people. Pets ran loose around the people camped out. Musicians played in various corners of the square under fancy fountains made to provide shade, like small trees.

"Here you are Tish." He handed her the juice and sat down next to her. "The *kias* owner was glad to sell during the day. Apparently a lot of people don't eat or drink in the days leading up to this ritual of theirs."

She nodded, half absently. "Lin, we are going to find him."

"Yes, we are, Tish. I imagine the day we wrap our arms around him again. He probably looks like Sanha by now... San was shaving by the time he was fifteen." He gazed off into the middle distance, not seeing the

Arkans camping in the square in front of them. "He's just writing these 'nice nice' letters and I just imagine some Mahid asshole standing over him with a knife, telling him he has to write well of that *kevyalin kyash-eater's* son."

"Oh, love." She set her juice down and flung her arms around him. "Perisalas said they weren't with Mahid any longer. He thinks Gan might be in the city."

"He's been saying all kinds of things, for so long," he said. "We were so close on Haiu Menshir! He left the same day, just before we got there!"

"That awful boy must have persuaded him. Even though he claims the Mahid were on Haiu Menshir, I find that very hard to believe." There were children running or skating through the crowd camped in the square, Dyers pounding on their drums or ringing simals, singing. A tiger-stripe headed boy… blond and dark red almost a purple… with tattoos showing now and again as his vest gaped open, skated by. He was a little awkward on them, a little new, but since he was a Yeoli boy that was perfectly understandable.

"Look at that." Lin waved at the skater. "What are his parents thinking, letting him get so Arkanized?" Tisha signed chalk, agreeing silently.

"In the letters he's writing, Gannara sounds happy."

"They hurt him, Lin. I can hope the Haian was right in saying he was on the road to healing…"

"But then why does he keep running away from his own family and staying with that… that Aan monster?"

"I don't know, love. Perisalas is doing his best with the funding he has, but once Chevenga gets this ritual over and settles in as Imperator again, I'm going to get on that blasted audience list and *fikken* light a fire under his kilt if he doesn't do more to find Gannara!"

The Temple was almost clean. Gan, in his skates and the yellow silk boy's vest, sat next to me on the mat and we grinned at the *fessas* girls bringing their parents' water next to us, just after rim sunset. Like most people camping out, we were sharing in the Imperator's fasting during daylight, before the ritual.

"You said it was sixty days from when they closed it, right?"
"Yeah."
"We're almost there, then." Gan pulled a handful of his hair forward.

"I don't like the tiger-striped thing... I'm going to cover up the blond stripes with the red." I thought it looked spectacular on him.

"I'd be disappointed if you did."

"Maybe I should grow out a moustache..." Gan was shaving every day because he had to. I was shaving once every few days, hoping I would have to.

"You'd have to shut up long enough for me to plaster your upper lip with bleach then."

"*Fikken idiya,*" he said absently.

"*Kyashen* jerk." I answered.

The day of the ritual everyone was up at true sunrise rather than rim-dawn. People kept filtering off to the public baths because the urge to be as cleansed as the Temple, as cleansed as the Imperator was strong.

I was full of a quivering tension as the Steel Gates opened with a trumpet fanfare and a boom. We were all on our feet, and everyone was silent as the eight man carry chair with a sea of gold and silver threaded presentation sun-parasols throwing blinding light emerged from the Marble Palace. It was hard to see Chevenga in the middle of them, the Imperial robe just as blinding. I found myself squinting, trying to see his face.

30

1010.02 SUBSECTION 1

THE PALANQUIN MADE THE RITUAL CIRCUIT OF THE SQUARE AND UP the Temple steps, safely letting Chevenga's feet on the top step, nowhere near the ground. Skorsas, the Chamberlain again, rather than that Yeoli who had no idea what kind of style the Marble Palace should have, and Kallijas, in his full red armour, lifted the Imperial robe off his shoulders, spreading it back over the palanquin seat, waiting the Imperator's return. Under the robe Chevenga wore a loincloth and nothing else. He would go before the Gods wearing plain cloth, though his head-band was gold. Skorsas knelt down to remove the sandals. The Imperatrix, also in her armour, the grey sharkskin, guarded his other side.

The Fenjitzas and the Fenjitza awaited him, flanking a single Pretender. Even after he was voted back into the office there was one Arkan who had to try to prove he would be a better Imperator, more acceptable to the Gods. He was a fleshy man, with an Imperial paunch. He held out his hands, adorned with his version of new Imperial seals.

I couldn't see Chevenga's face but he moved almost as if he were already tranced. His hands came up and he touched them to the pretender's. Then he turned his back on the doors and faced outward, gazing at all of us. "He's already half in the spirit world," I said to Gan and Ili. Ili was on my shoulders, so he could see. We had a pair of little old men in front of us, as a kind of camouflage, and Sera Eren and Ribbons to my right. We must have looked like a family.

"How do you mean?"

"He's got the look in his eyes... he's looking for the Gods... can you see it?"

"Yeah, okay. He does look... yeah. Like he's seeing something that's not... or at least, that the rest of us can't see. If it were me, I'd be scared shenless."

Oh, that is something you cannot be, Gan. You face the Gods terrified and you die.

Chevenga knelt down to wait for the Pretender to try his luck at getting the Gods to hear him and open the Temple. The crowd cheered and jeered. We all had an idea of exactly how futile it was going to be. The Pretender made a credible effort, even managing a good approximation of the opening word in the language of the Gods.

But the Temple remained sublimely indifferent to him. He tried again and was greeted with... nothing. The crowd's cheers were turning derisive. He showed little likelihood of being able to become Imperator if he could not catch the God's attention.

The Fenjitzas touched his elbow after his third attempt and spoke quietly to him, obviously pulling him away from the futile effort and guided him to one side. He would be allowed to attempt the rite again, once the Temple was open.

The Fenjitza called Chevenga from his kneeling position and he rose smoothly and turned to the sealed Temple as the Fenjitzas read the warning to Imperators. Chevenga listened quietly before he raised his hands to the golden slab of doors and as he did so, something happened that hadn't in a thousand years.

All of the religious documents I had ever read, referred to 'The Temple's Voice', as if it were a true phenomenon, not a metaphoric one. But the Temple had fallen silent more than a thousand years ago and subsequent Imperators had destroyed various writings speculating how and why the Temple no longer spoke. Likely they thought it made them look bad.

The Temple said something in a voice that wasn't human. It was a voice that echoed around the whole square, rumbling deep enough to be more felt than heard. It said. "Rak Ogniz Rajisteruuzer, Renel." The whole crowd—we all fell silent. The portico that was normally in shadow began to glow a bright gold, shining down on Chevenga's head. The silence grew deeper. The rumble of the Temple voice continued... a single low note, sustaining.

The Pretender, shaking, broke and fled. He'd made four steps before Kallijas cut him down in a spray of blood and a tumble of limbs down the stairs. He'd almost decapitated the man, precise enough to not make a mess by taking the head off completely. "Kahara," Gannara whispered. "You take this pretender thing seriously, don't you?" Ili patted the top of my head.

"That warrior, who cut the pretender down, was Kallijas."

"Ohhh. He is good, isn't he? But… Chevenga, I really *do* look like him, don't I? But I thought he'd be taller."

I elbowed him in the ribs for the taller comment, not taking my eyes off Chevenga. "Nyuuzer!" He cried, and the Temple responded.

"Uuzer Rak Ogniz, Ergas Ak nallag." There was a crack that echoed again and the Temple doors broke open, down the centre and slowly, ponderously opened. *Oh Gods, You see Him. You recognize Him.*

As he stepped to the threshold he began to sing. *That's different.* He had a high tenor, strange to hear for Arkans who were so often baritone or bass. What poured out of his mouth was one of the most ancient of hymns; and the Temple… sounding like a glass instrument, joined in to sing with him. He faltered for a fraction of a moment when the sound started but picked it up again.

We were all startled dead quiet so we could hear every word, every chime. "What's he singing?" Gannara asked.

"It's old… it's "Raise High Our Banner.""

"It sounds nicer than that."

"Shh."

"Subreu teenree payyer sitm nishiey Etad, wahlk um yuuzer." The Temple intoned. "Sabsak shoan abeohon." *Oh, Gods. The Temple is changed. It's changed inside.* The Temple was open, we could follow him inside, if we dared. It was the Ten Tens, however changed. It was almost impossible to fear. We poured up the steps, skirting around the bloody mess on the steps like a river flowing around a stone, *dekinas* coming forward to remove it. Gannara and I with Ili and Sera Eren were all close enough that we could step onto the changed platform. I couldn't take my eyes off what Chevenga was doing, however. I was just aware that it had changed, that it was somehow more alive, more active.

The slave Gods were no longer enslaved. The chains were missing from their wrists and ankles and necks. The *daifikas* and *okas* Gods had marriage rings glittering upon their hands, the jewelry sparkling, somehow illuminated as if to show us. Chevenga had freed the slaves of Arko, so it seemed he had freed the slave Gods as well.

Imbas had his left hand out, over the space where one stepped in. Also different. Different from when the Temple had been sealed. No one could have gotten inside to carve or re-carve a statue like that. We had camped outside the whole sixty days. As we stood in the vestibule, the gigantic stone at Imbas's side clicked and slowly, carefully, rotated down like a tree falling in slow motion, until it lay upon the Temple floor.

Chevenga stepped under Imbas's outstretched hand, held over his head like a blessing, and faced Anae. She, too was changed. Instead of a broom in her hands, she held a cradle, as if she were a wet-nurse, preparing for a new child. Chevenga flung himself down in the full, fast prostration to the Goddess, arms outflung. He lay for a moment and then to a cue none of the rest of us could hear, he rose.

"Sinimas? Is this normal?" Gannara whispered in my ear. "Or is something going wrong?

"It's not wrong... it's something I read about years ago... my religious teacher talked about the 'Voice of the Temple' I thought it was a metaphor..."

"Why's everyone flipping out then?"

"It hasn't been really heard in centuries and no one but me would maybe know about it... Look, he's fine..."

"Sure, but he won't be, and neither will we, if the whole thing comes crashing down or something. Why hasn't it been heard in centuries? I thought it was every new Imperator?"

"It's not going to fall down... Look. No, this is different. Only one Imperator that I know of has done this more than once and he didn't say much about it."

"Oh, because it's the second time? So this happens the second time?"

"That's what I think."

31

TWO OF TEN

"He's doing this for us the way he would do the Kiss of the Lake for you," I whispered to Gannara. "But he said it was to prove the vote to us."

"Yeah. He said it out straight in that speech."

"He doesn't need to," I said.

"I wonder which is harder?" Our eyes were fixed on Chevenga, Sera Eren's ear was turned to the Temple.

"The Kiss of the Lake you only risk death once, not ten times," I said. Chevenga danced before Anae, precise and delicate, the oldest of old formal dances. The crowd had quieted again, pressing close up the steps and to the line in the stones that marked how far they could come as the ritual progressed, each step further, following the Imperator speaking to and being spoken to by the Gods. "It's really only supposed to be five risks, but the Goddesses also occasionally punish, though they don't usually kill you."

Gannara hissed an in-breath through his teeth as Chevenga finished his dance for Anae and the statue gently released the cradle into his hands. "This is so different," I whispered to Gannara. "Look!" He took the cradle up the centre and laid it gently at Selinae's feet.

"I remember you doing that dance, or something a lot like it," Gan said into my ear. But he didn't have to be that quiet because the crowd was cheering Chevenga's first success. Someone just behind me began the chant 'First Ten, First Ten." Meaning the first of Ten rites.

"Yeah. And last time he did that, Arko was swept clean. What this means I don't know." Chevenga paced solemnly back down the central aisle to kneel before the statue of Imbas. For a long moment he knelt quietly and then said 'Yes," in answer to a question none of us could hear.

He rose and laid his hands onto the massive stone lying across the Temple floor. He stopped, and the whole crowd... we all held our breath.

The Gods are with him... his shadow is multiple... "They're with him," I whispered. "...Can you see? They're right there! Oh, Ten..."

"How do you mean?"

"It's like light... like a shadow made out of light instead of dark... they're with him like that. They're there!"

Gannara squinted and peered. Ili said "I like the God, he's nice and so is the Lady Goddess." Sera Eren was praying quietly, a song of praise, Ribbons purring a loud counterpoint to her soft old voice.

"Its hard... oh, Imperator... Arko is with you," I whispered to him. *You are strong. You can do all the Gods demand.*

Without shifting his hands on the stone, Chevenga opened his mouth and a sonorous woman's voice came out of his throat. "Second Husband would you help Us?" The whole crowd gasped. It was Anae's voice.

"What's that mean?" Gannara asked. "Why did he ask that and in that voice?"

"It's the Goddess, speaking through him... very different from the first Ten Tens." It was so changed I could almost not anticipate what would happen next. It was hard to see but it looked to me as though Chevenga expanded somehow, grew larger, grew more real.

"Oh MAN." Gannara said. "Tell me he's not going to do that!"

The voice out of Chevenga's mouth became male. "Yes... none of us can do these things alone."

"Do you see someone else there? I sure as *shen* don't."

"You're *athye* don't worry about it." Then I realized. The Gods had changed because Chevenga had changed them. "Oh, that's right... They're married in a four now!"

"Who?"

"Imbas and Anae, Oas and Mella."

"Because... Ch'venga set the slaves free?"

"Yeah... The *Fenjitzas* nearly had heart failure having to do it," I hissed at him. "Look, Look!" My cry to Gan echoed all through the crowd as Chevenga strained at the stone, muscles bunching so hard we could see them clearly. With his own hands and the aid of the Gods he raised the stone from the floor. "I can't tell if they are all four there or just the two Gods," I said to Ili.

"I don't... I'm trying... all I can see is my *semanakraseye* who's going to be flatter than a bug if his arms go... *Forae, Ch'venga, forae! Forae! Kahara tenesa!*" He was holding onto my shoulder, jumping up and down as he cried encouragement. Other Yeolis in the crowd were screaming similar things.

With a grind and a thump and a click that echoed all around us the stone locked into place. It normally took twenty priests to raise that stone and he raised it with his own two hands. I heard Gan yell 'Holy *SHEN*!" and his voice was only one of thousands. I was hoarse already and this was only the first Two of the Ten. We were cheering madly, screaming, crying, praying. 'Second Ten! Second Ten!"

"Now he's going to keel over," Gannara said. "When you do shen like that, you lose all your strength at once." --even as Chevenga began Imbas's Kurain, the men's dance with the sweeping arm gestures, the wild kicks and spins I thought, *like Gan said, he should be collapsing like a burst waterbag, raising a stone like that. He's spinning and kicking like he just got out of bed!* But just ten steps. All as if he hadn't just lifted up and set into its slot, a stone that weighed more than ten men, even if it pivoted in the floor. "There's no darkness, threat or hatred in it anymore," I said to myself under the cheering, clapping crowd. "The slaves are not there to hate us." I swallowed hard. "We cannot do any of this alone." My heart was knotted tight with desperate, hopeless longing as if I could spring into Chevenga's place. I wanted it with all my heart and dreaded it just as much. I wanted to scream and sing and cry. I wanted it.

"He can't keel over... not now," I said. "See, he's shifted to the Dance before Mella and look... look at that!"

"Look at what? He's getting red but he just moved a rock ten times his size! Of course he's red!"

Chevenga knelt before Mella and one could almost see the heat pouring off him. His face and chest and abdomen and arms and legs were all hot. Sweat was pouring off his body, enough that he was glistening and the stone around him as well. His heart was beating so hard you could see him shaking with it... when he stopped in front of Her.

"Forae Ch'venga! Anseng'! Nepa tirae! Forae!"

"Come on, Chevenga.. You can do it. Calm. Calm."

We were close enough to see his face fade from the absolute ecstatic to more anxious and then on to an impassive, meditative calm. He caught hold of his breathing, standing very straight after his last step to Mella. He vibrated like a harp string for a long time and I began to be afraid his heart or brain would burst with the strain.

"*Anseng' Ch'venga... Kahara tenesa, nu tenesa...*What's happening to him? Is that from lifting the stone, did it catch up with him?"

"I don't know." But even if it was departing from the rite I knew, I knew the true answer. "No. This is Her doing. At least She isn't going to melt him."

"Melt him? She does that? A lot?"

32

MELLA AND THE MERCIFUL ONE

I glanced sideways at him. "It happened to one of the pretenders the last time Chevenga did this."

"He *melted?*"

"He slipped and laid profane hands on the Goddess."

"Ohhh, Ch'venga wouldn't do that."

"Yeah. His clothes and hair and nails all floating in this steaming mess apparently."

"Ewwwwww.... Ch'venga, Ch'venga, don't do that!"

"No, he wouldn't, She won't, She's with him... see?" She'd laid her hands on him.

"She is? That's good... Yeah, you're right, he's smarter than that!"

"And more deft. You can't be clumsy. You can only ask, from a God or Goddess, never take. The idiot tried to treat her like his woman, and this guy forgot that..."

"I guess he paid for that."

I nodded, bumping the back of my head against Ili. "Yeah." My shoulders were starting to ache with his weight but it was something so distant I only paid slight attention to it. The pressure of sun on our heads and the sound of the Temple together were like a weight on my chest. Every time the Temple spoke it was as though something tugged at my heart, pulled at the tears living behind my eyes. I wanted to feel what Chevenga was feeling, I wanted to know what He knew.

His face was full of God light. He was perceiving Selestialis; I could see it. I could feel it.

Chevenga had mastered whatever Mella had challenged Him with and the Temple said "Trn'l virom etre jess ted. T'mr sree moft." You could see Him cooling, sweat pouring.

Gannara said, "Yeah, look he's got it. What's it saying?"

"The language of the Gods. One of the old prayers. I know that one as a secondary prayer."

"What does it mean?"

I didn't want to answer him but there was no reason for me not to. "I don't know. I was taught it by rote." I remembered Tobias's drone. His teaching was as unlike this ritual as rotten meat was from gold truffles. "It was one of the set of ten for each God or Goddess."

"Third Ten! Third Ten!" People were already chanting, even before he was finished before Mella. Chevenga reached forward toward the Goddess's statue and the whole crowd gasped. He took up the cloth from Her hand and dried himself off with it, His sweat soaking it completely. The gold threaded sweatband around His brow was as sodden as the cloth and He pulled it off. Then He laid both gently into Mella's hand.

"Ayo!" Gan yelled, along with everyone else in the crowd who shrieked in startlement and amazement as the soaking wet, sweat sodden cloths burst into a gout of flame from the statue's hand leaving behind only a soot smear on the painted marble that crinkled and evaporated even as the cries died down.

And Chevenga danced for the Goddess, light and high and wild as if He hadn't just done some physically impossible things. *She accepted His offering.* Ili crowed and clapped, rapping his heels against my chest. "Please don't do that, little brother."

"*Kahara,* you just never know what's going to happen next!" People were starting to pray out loud all around us, and sing, low. Encouraging. Extorting. I wanted that. They wanted Him to do this. They showed their love by being with Him when He faced the Ten.

He was their celestial link, their Voice to Arko. *Because I am born my father's son, I may never be that. I must never want that. I must choke down the envious longing. He is the favourite Son of the Gods and that is right and just. My desperate yearning is, in and of itself, according to the Book, an affront to the Ten. Perhaps this is my Hayel, being able to see this sacredness, this glory, know I trained for it and am still going through the shadow of it every day, and see that not only should I not long for this transcendence, I dare not.*

I sacrifice my emotion to you, oh Gods. May it be pleasing to You. Chevenga's dance for Mella moved to her Husband, the twined shadows glittering around him twinned again. *Perhaps Anae's appeal to her second Husband made that possible? The Worker God is a simple God who doesn't like frills as much as His Wife.*

I had tears standing in my eyes. I was trying to be objective. Trying to be calm. But I couldn't. Then I grew more afraid for Chevenga. Risae was next and the last time She had asked Him to cut His own throat before Her. The stain was soaked into the marble and had been preserved by the priests and the *dekinas*. Would She ask the same again?

To our chant of 'Fourth Ten! Fourth Ten!' Chevenga had come to the level of the *fessas* Gods. Each level he stepped up to had the whole building somehow coming alive with Him. The loincloth was soaked a darker gold, from sweat, and new sweat shone on his skin. But as he faced Risae He stopped. I could see him tremble from where I stood.

"If I were him, I'd be scared *shenless*," Gannara whispered.

"Hush, lad," Sera Eren said. She'd stayed with us as we came into the Temple, following the rite. "Watch and listen. Can you feel the Gods— like your *kaharas* -- even if you cannot see it? This is our harmonic singer…" He signed chalk.

I saw the stain on the stone. I came looking for it, specifically. It was two paces across. How it did not kill Him, I don't know.

"This is going to be hard for him. If She asks him to cut his own throat again."

"Oh *fik*." Gannara mouthed it silently, glancing at Sera Eren but I knew exactly what he was saying even voicelessly. The differences in the rite, and in the building… all the old songs and prayers and the Voice coming back, all had the priests on their knees or their faces. Some terrified, some exhalted. Most of us, the crowd, would have been on our knees but for Chevenga's guard and the Yeoli guard around him. They were standing and if we knelt we would not be able to see. *Professional Mother God, please be easy on Him. He's suffered enough.*

"She saved Him but I'd still be scared *shenless*," I hissed in his ear.

"I don't know how he can even stand there. I don't know how he could do that in the first place."

Even as Gan said this, Chevenga knelt on the floor before the Goddess, Her table, with its strange and terrifying instruments, immediately to his sword-side, Her face looming over him, cold and forbidding; at least as far as I could see.

"How does he do the Kiss of the Lake?" I asked him. He did the expansive Yeoli shrug.

"Yeah, well, I don't know how he does that, either." We were all getting more and more quiet as He knelt before one of the most capricious of Goddesses. *Will She reject Him this time? Will She kill Him? Will She make him bleed out His life onto the floor in final sacrifice?*

I tried to point out to him, the shadows... not shadows because shadows are made of darkness, but these where rather made out of light. I had no name for what I was seeing. "There are four Gods behind him but they're just waiting. "It's his choice." My heart was in my throat as the silence spread around Him, kneeling, just kneeling.

"Times like that, I'm thinking, I'm glad you're the one stuck doing these things, and not me."

I could only sigh. I had been taught to do the rite by rote. He didn't realize that I wasn't truly 'doing these things'. I shook my head at him. "Just... just feel it, all right?" I had to swallow hard. *Was this what the fat guy meant by time taking care of Chevenga for me? Had the Gods told the old man somehow that this was where Chevenga was going to die?*

I'd not taken my eyes off Chevenga, even as I commented to Gannara and we were close enough that I could see Him pull the God light around himself like a mantle. "Risae!" He called Her name with a voice that was full of emotion, a jumble I could make no sense of. "Mother of all *fessas*. I confess my fear to you."

I caught my breath. *You can't be afraid before the Gods! Oh, ancestors save Him! You cannot show fear! Risae has no patience for fear!* By now the whole crowd, packing into the Temple behind him, the priest around him, even his *athye* guards were silent. They remembered last time, as well.

"I tell You in offering," Chevenga said. "And hope it is acceptable to You as an additional sacrifice." He tilted his chin up before her, the scar on his neck somehow gleaming in the Temple light. I'd seen it, faint as a hair or a crease on his neck, at dinner but somehow it was visible now.

He bared his neck to her and I and everyone who had voted him in cried out in fear.

"Risae! Risae! Professional Goddess! Mercy! Mercy! Risae, Merciful One! Mercy!" We… all Arkans… cried to Her who made healing by the knife a sacrament, the most cruel, the most kind, the Goddess who had, in the beginning, brought us through the pain of surgical transformation, making us into what we were now. Her statue always had only a hint of a smile, if one had a good imagination, Mahid-like in its calm as She examined Her next subject. "Risae, Good Goddess, please have mercy this once!" *Merciful One. Her title, not Her nature.*

33

SHE WILL SAVE HIM

I held my breath and somehow, half the crowd could see, or sense something was coming, even if they didn't have my centuries' old blood-connection to the Temple. The Goddess's shadow of light reached toward Chevenga and if anything He offered His throat even more to Her, tilting His head back even further, His face a mix of forced calm, ecstasy and terror. "Oh, Goddess. She is… She will…" I couldn't tell what She would do. I flung my hands over my face, then pulled them away just in time to see Chevenga gain His feet, a fine mist of blood flowing from His neck, His face glowing with joy I could only describe as divine.

"AIGH MAMAIYANA CH'VENGA! CH'VENGA! BORUUUUUUU-UU!!!!!!" Gan screamed in my ear and Ili pushed on my head as if to try and stand, everyone was screaming as Chevenga arched back in one of the classic poses for Risae, as if held standing in a lover's arms. Kaninjer… I could hear the Haian accent in the crowd noise and Kallijas caught him around the chest to keep him from plunging to Chevenga's aid, half lifting him off the ground, clamping him against his armoured chest.

The noise was so much it was like a hammer of sound spiking into my ears. "It's all right!" I yelled. "It's all RIGHT! LOOK, LOOK!" And my yell was picked up by others, including Ili.

I grabbed Gannara by one arm, shaking him slightly. "It's all right. It's all right. He'll be alright… it's not a lot! She's just taking a token!"

"*Boru! Boru! Chevenga!*"

"Gannara. He's with Her. She won't let him die!"

He'd flung his own hands up over his face and now peeked through his fingers to see Chevenga, still on his feet, no longer bleeding, even the tiny spray of blood. It just stopped. His neck wound closed before our eyes and a bare sheen of blood appeared on his brow. A lip-print, as though Risae had kissed him. He looked more than a little stunned as though hit in the head with a brick, but He was still on his feet.

This was no where near what had happened last time. There was blood, but only the amount one might get from a cut finger rather than a cut throat artery.

There were a few spots of blood on His chest and the imprint of the Goddess's lips on His forehead and… He… was erect. That showed clearly through the gold kilt. "Kahara," Gan breathed. "How he hasn't fallen on his face yet, I don't know."

What had that felt like that it would excite Him so? Bleeding? And still ecstatic. Fessas Goddess, You are brutal in Your love of excellence…

"She was with Him the whole time…" In all the crowd noise I was surprised that Sera Eren heard me.

"Yes, lad. She was."

The table before Risae had a few drops of His blood, all the sacred instruments upon it. A drop or two of scarlet on the marble floor at his feet.

"*Forae… forae Ch'venga, forae semanakraseye mya…*" Gannara was almost chanting it now, with the other Yeolis. Chevenga took several deep breaths and proffered His hands to the Goddess, as if accepting something… a bowl or cup or something from Her. I blinked, surprised to see a glittering sparkle of silver between His hands and showing around His fingers. He raised His hands exactly as if He were raising a cup and quaffing… something. I was close enough to see His throat working, the shining light back in His face, incongruous against the mark on his forehead. You could see His pallor going away as He drank.

He bowed to Risae and offered up to Her the invisible cup, making the ten steps to Her in stately slow motion as He did so. Then He turned to Mikas across the Temple. The glass instrument in the music loft above cut across the crowd's noise, the jubilation, the hysteria from some. Many people, lower caste, were crowded before their own Gods, who had approved the Imperator, on their knees, hands cupped to their temples, the bulk of the crowd on their feet flowing past them to be closer, pressing up behind us.

"Five Ten! Five Ten!"

A full ten of herald/priests at the Temple doors relayed what was happening to the crowd, still jamming the square, so that all those who had not camped had a chance to know the Gods' will. Their collective physical presence was like a gigantic animal poised. Not poised--pushing, pressuring, leaning on those in front of them, as much a part of the rite as we, the direct witnesses, were. It was hot and people held each other up and priests handed water through the crowd so that no one would be hurt in so important a rite. *Only the Imperator and His pretenders risk death here.* I was surprised by the ironic thought, and it hurt. I thought I was past the bitterness.

Mikas's statue, where He sat, was different. We were close enough to see into His niche. He wore a pressman's smock and there were different tools and animals around Him. "That's a *marya* on the back of his chair!" Gannara seemed almost indignant. "A carved stone *marya!* And there's a kind of horned sheep that you only find near Vae Arahi next to him!"

"I don't understand it, Gan. I'm as surprised as you are." Chevenga did ten slow steps across the central aisle toward Mikas… the same as in the original, the first Ten Tens. Each paced step was a classic pose of a profession. That hadn't changed. Before the God a cushion lay upon the stone with three clear glass cups full of what looked like white wine in front of it. It was ironically welcoming, as if the God were an ancient Arkan host about to greet a guest.

As Chevenga stepped across the line of gold tiles around the throne of the God a deep brass gong rang through the whole Temple and a fountain sprang up from the floor tiles. It wasn't clear as I thought it would be, nor was it the flow from the ceiling that I was expecting either. Most of the streams were clear, but not all. Some were coloured brightly, some were gold or silver and some where white. We could feel the heat of them from where we stood behind Chevenga's guard holding us back.

"Ayo! That's… not… water, is it?" Gannara swallowed hard. "What is it?"

"Glass, youngster," Sera Eren said, Ribbons coiled between and around her feet to keep from being trampled upon. "Liquid glass for the Professional God."

"Oh, *kahara.*"

Chevenga had prostrated Himself before Mikas and, to an unheard voice, risen and seated Himself upon the cushion. He appeared to be listening but it was hard to see through the shimmering, moving, flowing wall of glass, quivering with heat. He raised each wine glass and tasted what was in it, and delicately spat the last sip into His hand, then poured it upon the floor where it vanished. "This one..." He said to the statue of the God. Then He answered a question none of us could hear. "Anywhere else, I would say, probably not; here, I'd say, probably yes."

"What did that mean?" Gannara asked me.

"The God is talking to Him. Probably asking which of the wine cups is poisoned--" "—Arsenic," Chevenga said, even as I whispered it.

"Ooooh, Ch'venga, nepa vyar sa..."

Then the three glasses melted away into the floor and two took their place filled, apparently, with red wine. Chevenga picked them both up and sipped but this time did not spit. A surprisingly cool breeze wafted past my face as I watched. Cool, while liquid glass arcing from the floor and what felt like half of Arko jammed into the space. *How?*

Two ghostly images came into being between Chevenga and the God, floating in the air. People cried out in wonder and fear. The images were ghostly but not white or pale or tortured looking; rather like two paintings but more real than real. One Arkan pale child, one dark, foreign looking, appearing as though they stood between Mikas and Chevenga. One could not tell if they were male or female. "They are both equally valuable," He said to the God.

This is what Tobias meant when he talked about the 'Test of Imperators'? An Ethical test. The fat guy would never have had to do this because it is not in the first Ten Tens. Ethics. He would have failed and died.

The two children faded and were replaced by equally perfect images of a serpent and a fish and Chevenga was obviously listening very carefully. "The serpent. If refined in the Haian way, a drop of its venom can cure a million."

"My *dekinas* taught me a whole series of questions and answers by rote in the God's tongue, in case they ever came up." I said to Gan.

"What's Ch'venga using... just his wits, I guess?" I nodded and signed chalk to Gan. Nobody was listening to us whisper, even though people had quieted to watch and listen to the Imperator talk to Mikas.

Then Chevenga stood up and walked to the wall of flowing hot glass that was higher than His head, on the side toward Dimae and hesitated a

long moment. "No, he isn't going to do what I think he's going to do
—*AIGH TE FYIRERAI TEMANAE!*"

Gannara and the other Yeolis in the crowd screamed as Chevenga reached out and thrust His hands into the liquid glass.

34

———

DIMAE

I was holding my breath, even though I knew it was coming… or something like it and I grabbed Gan by the arm as he surged forward as if to stop Chevenga from doing this.

There was a puff of fine smoke around His hands and arms and the smell of burnt hair, but the molten glass did no more than evaporate the hair on His arms as it flowed over His hands and forearms, a shining casing of glass.

"Shh, shh, He's fine. This is part of it… like the first time He did this." I jerked my head toward the wall of glass hands. "His glass hands are up there with all the other Imperators."

Gan's eyes were open very wide. "*Aigh, ayo, ayo, aigh,* am I in a dream?"

"In a way. Inside the Temple is the God's dreams…" Chevenga raised His arms and began to pull coloured glass into the shape He was forming. Green and blue glass and white… it was a sphere of fine threads swirled glass perhaps the size of a person's head… was it solid? How was He holding the weight like that? Gold glass flowed onto it from His drawing finger. "Oh, Ten, it's beautiful… it's… it's an Earthsphere… seen from the stars!" *Like the painting in the Imperial Book.* I caught my breath, watching this hot, glowing ball of coloured glass form in His hands. My eyes were full of tears again. "Last time…" I swallowed hard. "Last time according to the report I read, He formed a bird in flight

"*Ayo*! Oh I wish we could have seen that! I'm glad we're here!"

My throat closed up as Chevenga held up the glowing, cooling piece of artwork in His right hand. The curtain of glass flowed down His arm and over him as he began to step through, Imperator's crystals forming in the curls of his hair. Risae's seal on his brow smoked away, leaving it clean.

"All those glass hands… they all did this."

"Yeah. There's some who failed here. It's not pretty when they do."

"Oh, yuck. I bet." *The descriptions of hands burned off was very graphic.* Chevenga stepped through the glass, parting the molten curtain with His left hand, without harm. His eyes were already fixed on the Goddess Dimae, even as He set the spun glass Earthsphere He'd made down on the Temple floor.

"Hey, he's got things like snowflakes coming off his head, how the *fik*?"

"That's The Imperator's glass, for us, the witnesses. If you can pick one up from the floor you're allowed to keep it… or if you touch His hair afterward you can get one. People are allowed."

"You mean right off his hair? I don't know if I can get that close. I don't think I dare."

"People turn them into jewellery. Take one that falls off… they'll come off Him in a shower in a minute. Those jewels they wear only to Temple after." Chevenga shook Himself and the glass snowflakes flew though not all were shaken free. Ili caught one in both hands, laughing and Gan scooped up two that fell on the floor right at our feet.

"You can't bend down and pick it up, with Ili up there. I got it for you."

"Thanks, Gan."

I almost didn't want to take it. For a moment I wondered if I had the courage to trust the God so much I would put my hands in molten glass. The tears in my eyes were making it hard to see. I couldn't let them fall. I was looking through a pool standing in my eyes. If I blinked they'd spill. I couldn't help it, and felt the hot trails of emotion down my face. *Oh, my ancestors. I was to do this. My father took this away from me. He destroyed this for me even before I was born. Because he was corrupt and evil and made me so.*

Chevenga offered his hands toward the *Solas* Goddess. "I give myself." The choir in the loft above began Dimae's Hymn and with a crack the glass encasing His left hand split perfectly in half and fell to the floor without breaking. He turned in place and then, rather than the slow, careful dances to the other Gods, He ran. He ran Dimae's pattern on the Temple floor.

He ran the Huntress's pattern on the floor… flying through the changes as though He pursued someone, or something, and the Temple called up a drum from somewhere, a massive sound like a heartbeat. I hadn't realized that the God of Dyers was Dimae but it made sense. As He leapt and spun we ended up clapping and stamping to the beat and it grew faster as He went.

His leaps seemed bigger, slower, swooping leaps that shouldn't have been possible and then He leaned as though in a hard wind, arms out and swept back and He began to smoke… as he came to the last frantic bound His hair and kilt burst into flames with a 'whuff'.

"AAAIIIIGH!!!! SOMEONE PUT HIM OUT!!!" But the Yeolis barely had time to scream before the flames whiffed out. His loincloth was gone. He stood naked and His hair was perhaps a trifle shorter… still with gleaming stars of glass in the curls.

"SEVEN TEN! SEVEN TEN!" The crowd chanted as one.

"There are three more Gods, Gannara. Take a big breath. More stuff like this is going to happen."

"Ohhhh my *kahara*, is it all, like, magic tricks? Or am I dreaming the whole thing?"

I glanced away from Chevenga for a moment, annoyed. Then I took a deep breath. How would he know? I looked back to the Imperator and tried hard to set my anger aside. He was facing Aras now, naked but for a right arm covered in glass and His hair full of glass stars.

"Sorry," he said, realizing I was truly angry.

"No, Gannara." But I couldn't help adding, "If I were at the Kiss of the Lake and kept asking it's a trick, isn't it, would you be ticked at me?

"I said I'm sorry! The Kiss of the Lake… is much more straightfor-ward than this!"

Chevenga had no kilt and as He stood between Dimae and Aras it was very obvious that He was excited. His erection was clear, standing up in the nest of black curly hair between His legs. I almost couldn't look. "I guess he's not suffering," Gannara said.

My own vile organs stirred and I caught and held my breath. *No. No. Not here. Not now. No. Sinimas Aan help me, no! This is a sacred space, don't let my evil come out here!* I clenched my eyes shut for a moment and things subsided, but I didn't want to miss a heartbeat of Chevenga's second Ten Tens, so I pried them open again and tried to ignore my subsiding ugliness.

Chevenga faced Aras, His face calm again and the glass shattered off His right hand with a ringing sound as if it were struck.

"Blade?" He was speaking to the God. "I'm unarmed." His face changed to a look of shock and He staggered. "I give You myself," He said and fell to His knees.

35

OH BRIGHT AND SHINING GOD

"The God is harsh," I said. "Chevenga, be strong." I wrapped my arms around Ili's legs and he patted me on the top of my head. Thank our ancestors I had listened to Chevenga when I'd first asked him about little brothers, else I would not have had him now, nor he, me. His weight on my shoulders was a tremendous comfort. I could hardly go into paroxysms of self-doubt or self-hatred in front of my little brother. It would not be proper. I took a deep breath. "How are you doing, Ili?"

"Oh, good! This is great!" I caught myself from tumbling straight into rage. It wasn't flippant. He hadn't been hurt the same way... he wasn't minimizing the rite. He was taking it in as good and nothing but good. So should I, but I didn't think I could. I took another deep breath and Ribbons coiled around my feet, even as Chevenga stepped up toward Aras.

I was anchored to the Temple floor by the weight of love, caught between my little brother on my shoulders and an insensate animal on my feet. Sera Eren had hold of one of my elbows... when had she taken hold of me? I couldn't remember. And Gannara had me by the other. Beyond them the press of the crowd held us all close, all of us together, watching the Gods approve of our *vodai* and re-approve our choice of Imperator.

Chevenga answered something the God said to him that we could not hear. "I accept it." He reached out to the empty air before the Steel-Armed God and accepted a weight into His hand, hefting it as if the air

He took up were a sword. That made sense. He sank into a fighting stance I recognized from years ago, in the Mezem. A stance so minimal it was hard to call it a 'stance' at all.

"Who's he fighting?" Gannara hissed in my ear.

"Aras, of course."

"Oh, *shen!*" His grip on my elbow was convulsive. "He cannot win against a GOD, if they exist!"

"Nice of you to admit that they might. He doesn't have to win. Just fight to the best of His ability." But Chevenga wasn't fighting full out. He was sparring someone we all could not see. One stroke, two... the moves were restrained, restricted. "I hope the God told him to." Aras would test him, again, somehow. "No one else can, here." Chevenga staggered sideways, jolted, his head snapping over as if he'd been struck, or slapped on the side of the face and fought back harder, but still restrained. We were close enough I could see the worried crease on his brow.

"FIGHT HIM, CHEVENGA!" I bellowed, before clapping my gloves over my mouth. He couldn't know that that was what the God wanted. For him to fight to the fullest of his ability. To fight him to the limits of glory. *I shouldn't have done that.*

But Chevenga was fighting suddenly as if He'd heard me. I kept my hands over my mouth in awe. Was this what the duel against Kallijas had looked like? Even though I could not see Aras I could see Chevenga's counters and it was as though the God's moves were images burned on the air by Chevenga's responses. Four, five strikes... I could see His golden smile... deadly in its intent. Six, seven, eight so fast I could almost not see them... they were all moves I had learned... for Aras. Formal. Slow. Presentation moves. Not this clash of wills.

It didn't matter that I could not see the God. Chevenga made me see Him. Nine, ten. Then He froze in place, the look on His face as though He'd heard something startling, surprising though not life and death. His hand opened and His sword of air vanished into the air it had been called from. The shock on His face was more... inward. He went to His knees a second time.

This is far more than for the first Rite of Ascension. This is all different. He gathered Himself and was fighting as if for His life now, the sword of air snatched up at His will, from the clearness around Him. One.. twothreefourfive... sixseven... eightnineten! "Be strong," I said. "Chevenga. He is there for you."

Gannara's fingers were so tight on my upper arm they might leave marks but I didn't shake him off. This was important. This was above mere body aches and pains. My tears had spilled over and trailed hot over my face.

The imprint of the Imperial sword in my hand itched with the memory of its weight, echoed this glory, this contest. It was the sword that would have deserved to be wielded here if any steel sword did. But Aras would not allow anything less than His own given weapons in the Temple. Both Chirel and the Imperial sword held faint echoes of the swords of air that Aras granted. I gulped and managed to swallow my tears back, to not shame the Imperator, or the God. This rite had me in tears now, twice. I would have to try harder to not shame myself before the Gods.

Chevenga stepped back and straightened and bowed to His invisible opponent. "You touched something in me that... I don't understand and that I fear," He said quietly. We were all silent enough that the whole Temple full of people could hear Him.. *He will test you hard, Chevenga.*

"Thank You," He continued. "I'll remember." *Be strong.* The Imperator reached out both of His hands to the space before the Steel-Armed God and was enfolded in invisible arms, His own arms tight around a torso we could only see by how He held onto it. "I am honoured beyond honour." Gan shot a look at me and I answered his unspoken question.

"The God is prophesying for him. I think."

"What's he saying?"

"I don't know, you'd have to ask Him that."

The God... you could see Him easing Chevenga back into the odd pose called for by the first Ten Tens, and the blades in the floor and in the walls shot out with a crack, quivering, to encase Chevenga in the same web of steel as the first ritual.

"AYAIGHGGGHHHH!!!"

The one blade over His head actually cut one of His curls off and a blade that had shot up from the floor pressed against His heel and the calf above though no blood was drawn. The other blades left enough space for a much larger man but His arms had to be high enough to allow the passage of steel. The God had set Him into place perfectly with His embrace. The roar from the watching crowd was enough to shake me to my bones, drowning out the choir and the Temple and everything but the sound of humanity. Cheering. "EIGHT TEN! EIGHT TEN EIGHT TEN!"

I desperately wanted to take the same position. I wanted it enough that I bit my lip, drawing blood. *I should cease practicing this. I profane the Gods by practicing this.*

"HOW in *FIK* can he handle this when *I* barely can!!????" I didn't even try to answer Gannara at first in all this noise. I'd barely heard him and his lips were right at my ear. I had my hands pressed together in front of my chest over my heart, Ili's legs draped over my arms rather than me holding onto them. A good thing, I think, I would have held on too hard and hurt him.

My teeth were pressed together hard enough to hurt my jaw. *He's Imperator.* I thought, but didn't say. He proves it over and over again. *That's how.* But I tried to explain a little. "He's done this once before and the Gods led him through it then. It must have been harder then, not knowing what kind of thing to expect." *There. That sounded mild enough.*

"Aigh... man... if he didn't have every bit of him in exactly the right place, right then.... some bit of him would be skewered! I remember..." his voice trailed off. He couldn't say he remembered me practicing that odd pose. Not here. He couldn't say 'I remember when 2nd Amitzas beat you into place with his corrector if you were so much as a hair off.'"

"Yeah." I answered both the spoken and unspoken words. I realized suddenly that I still had tears on my cheeks. I hadn't stopped them at all. But almost every other face around me was wet as well.

"Oh. My. The High Gods... He's coming to the High Gods and I don't know if I can bear it." The blades pulled back, vanishing into the floor and wall and pillars and Chevenga straightened, turning to face the two Highest Gods.

"Thank You, Fearless One." Chevenga said, his voice full of emotion. Was his face wet? Surely not.

"What? What? Is he *fikked?*" Gan shook my elbow a little in the urgency of his asking. I couldn't help myself. I covered my face with my hands.

36

KAHARA MYA, ARKO

OF COURSE I COULDN'T KEEP HIDING MY EYES. I HAD TO SEE. "Sin-im-as!" Even hiss/yelling at me, Gan got my alias right. Bless him.

"No, He's fine… Just… just watch, all right?"

Chevenga's chest heaved as He took a huge breath and turned toward the High Gods. Since the *Fenjitza's* re-discovery and the priestesses came back into the Temple, Selinae's statue had been moved. Even though Muunas still held highest place, She now stood at His right hand, instead of across the Temple. Strangely enough, it was obvious that She had been there originally, once you saw the arrangement.

I could still look into the Goddess's face, barely. She looked less serene now, and more sad but maybe that was just me. *I should be ashamed even to be here. How could I think I would be welcome before the Gods at all? I didn't deserve their regard. Even to witness this is a desecration of something sacred.* My chest was tight and full and I could hardly breathe. It had been hard enough to watch with the lesser Gods, but Selina… and Muunas… had been my Gods, the Gods of my own caste. I had grown up thinking They were my Selestial parents. I could not bear to raise my eyes above the tip of Muunas's beard. *They approve you, Chevenga. You just have to dance through this one.*

I bit down on the inside of my cheek. Gannara hissed "Min-- Sini-mas, are you all right?"

"I'm fine. Watch…"

Chevenga turned His face to Selinae and the look of ecstasy came back. Naked, before all Arko and no one cared. Everyone could see Him harden and soften at the God's whim, completely with no shame. His member stood firm again. He was, if anything, high as a boy. His face... it looked like the joy He felt was almost too much to bear. Someone in the crowd made a crooning noise in her throat, a loving, sensual sound, but soothing.

The murmur was picked up by some others and suddenly I couldn't help myself... my own groin tightened and I wept this time because I was hard too. It was a supportive sound, loving. I found myself sobbing because I... I'd never known... The Arkan men all around me were weeping and the women sang Chevenga on to Selinae.

Kyriala... she would be here. Her voice would be part of this... she would not hold back. I remembered her face when she held the women's part for Binshala's burial rites. Beautiful, full of sorrow and joy too. Joy like this, on Chevenga's face. I sobbed and unashamed for once, most of the men of Arko... all those in the Temple... wept with me.

"Oh..." I said though my tears. "She is coming to Him." There was light all around him, brighter than fire, brighter than the other Temple lights, silvery... I could see Him turn in place, raising his arms up as if to show Her every thumblength. As if She already didn't know Him, inside and out. It was hard to see him do the formal steps for Her, humble before Her.

Exactly between the Two, Chevenga knelt.

"What's he doing? He looks like he's making love to someone but there's no one there!"

"It's Her." My groin ached, unaccustomed. My voice full of tears, wild joy, terrible shame in my heart all jumbled together.

Then the Light descended and bright golden light merged with the silvery sheen from Selinae. Muunas came down. It was too bright to see Chevenga between the two High Gods but we could hear Him. He moaned, almost a scream. But it was ecstasy. I could vaguely make Him out in the light, blurred and quivering in my streaming vision, rocking between the Gods as They took Him, made Him the connection through which They made love to Each Other.

My mouth was open I was crying out with Him, panting, Ili was laughing, I could feel his tummy vibrating against my head and I had to keep him from drumming his heels against me. All around me, men and women both together cried out in ways one would only hear in private, in the bedroom if at all.

If this didn't stop I wouldn't be able to stop myself… I'd shame myself right here in the Temple. My vile organs… it almost hurt. It was pain, it was too much. I closed my eyes on the glory of light in the middle of the Temple and bowed my head. But I couldn't close my ears. The music from the loft and from the Temple itself grew wilder and wilder, merging with Chevenga's yells of pleasure as if He could not contain Himself. *Oh, Chevenga, be strong, don't let your heart fail you. Your body is strong enough.*

"Nine Ten! Nine Ten! Ten Ten! Ten Ten! Muunas! Shefenkas! Selinae! Oh Gods bless us! Bless us!"

I'd bitten my bottom lip bloody, but swallowed the sharp-tasting blood, and went to my knees. Ili had gotten down and we had our arms around each other, he laughed and sang in my ear. I could feel his chest vibrate but his piping voice was lost in the cacophony of joy filling the lofted hall. *This was what I was meant to do, and am too damaged.* My tears were as much full of sorrow as ecstasy and shame.

"*SHAI CH'VENGA! SHAI! SHAI! KAHARA TENESA! KAHARA KRINAE TENESA!*" Gannara was yelling with the other Yeolis. I could hear their voices mixed in, the Yeoli, in the sea of Arkan. "Joy, Chevenga! Joy! Joy! *Kahara* is with you… *Kahara* is SO with you!"

It's all right, Chevenga. Arko loves you. The Gods love you.

"I can't look, it's killing my eyes!" Gannara yelled.

They love you, Chevenga. He shrieked his pleasure when He came, flames roaring from the floor all around him.

"*OH FIK CH'VENGA CH'VENGA CH'VENGA!!! VIYA SA, CH'VENGA, SIVYA VIYA SA…*"

"Gannara, He'll live through it… They love Him."

"*KAHARA!*" Chevenga almost screamed it. "*AIIII KAHARA! KAHARA, HARA MYA!*"

Everyone was on their knees now, hands raised. The foreigners were the last to realize, the last to kneel, but even they were overwhelmed. "TEN TENS! TEN TENS!" The cry mixed with the beginning of the Temple chant "Yesterday! Today! Tomorrow!" I could even hear a Mahid voice or two adding their part of that chant "FOREVER!" The sound was too much to hear, one could only feel it.

The Temple boomed over us all. "Zyztah min ititah." Then there came a single word, solemnly intoned, out of the flames before Muunas and Selinae.

Kahhhh Haaaa Rahhhh

The Yeoli word thundered out of the Temple rolling over us. The whole building said the word *Kahara*. We were prostrate, on our faces, silenced before the Voice of the Temple.

And in the profound quiet afterward a song rose from somewhere... a Yeoli harmonic singer... mixing with the sound of Arkan glass bells. "Oh, my ancestors... that singer..." I whispered, murmuring with the rest of the crowd as we realized what it was.

A Yeoli voice, a harmonic singer... singing the names of the Ten. Chevenga stood, facing us now, in the midst of the dying flames, head flung back, arms outstretched, open to the widest he could throw himself, quivering with aftershocks of ecstasy, as the singer finished the names of the Ten... then added '*Kahara*', the rising double note fading away to a new silence.

We dared raise our heads from the floor without permission, watching Chevenga. My gloves were soaked with my tears but I, unlike a lot of people, had managed to not add my semen to the dampness.

The ending bells, light, high, and sweet, chimed ten times. Then once more. Chevenga's head tipped forward, His eyes opening to all of us on the other side of the flames and it was as if He could see us for the first time since the ritual started. He smiled and stepped through the fire as if it weren't there, past his healer and his guards and the priests, came into the midst of us – he passed in arm's length of Sera Eren -- and knelt down.

"I'm here," He said quietly, equal to equal, speaking to all of us. "It's all right."

37

———————

PLAYTIME IS OVER

THERE WAS ANOTHER HEARTBEAT OF SILENCE BEFORE THE WHOLE Temple erupted in sound and Chevenga was hoisted up on the massed shoulders of everyone around Him. Gannara stepped forward and was one of those at his back. People were singing... chanting... praising Him, praising the Gods. "HAIL, IMPERATOR! HAIL THE ONE BELOVED OF THE GODS! HAIL, ALL HAIL THE SON OF THE SUN!" and a new cry in Arko... "HAIL THE VODAI! BELOVED OF THE GODS! HAIL THE VODAI!" *Because of what You have done here today... and the years before, Chevenga... It would take war and bloodshed to destroy the vote in Arko now. It has become ours because of You.*

Chevenga threw Himself backward, trusting the crowd completely to catch Him, to carry Him and Gannara thrust out his hand and caught the back of his head, one of many. "*Aigh*, Ch'venga, *tyana* -- be careful!" I heard him clearly. "*Semanakraseye mya! Semanakraseye mya!*"

By this time I was on my feet, with Ili pressed against my legs. I wouldn't let him go for fear he would be trampled in the crowd as they, bearing Chevenga poured out of the Temple and carried Him to the people waiting outside.

They'd parade Him through the streets in His triumph, in His new cleansing and acceptance and they would bring Him back to set him on the Presentation platform, or on the Step. The open framework step that would keep His feet off the ground should he choose to move His carving station -- and He would, as He had the first time, carve some of the cattle roasted for the feast. They would have been cooking in the Marble Palace kitchens since yesterday.

A frugal feast. If the Imperator succeeded at the Ten Tens, a Joy Feast. If He did not a funeral feast but still a feast of Joy for the Successor. Either way, a feast would be eaten by the city. I had to smile at the practical irony. But the Head chef wouldn't be ripping his hair out with the logistics of what to do with all that roast meat.

"No, Ili, no! You cannot go too! You're too little and will get stepped on!" Sera Eren backed me on that and someone stepped on Ribbon's tail as if to prove our point. But even his offended screech and him rearing up to rest his paws on our shoulders though we were all too short and slight for him to climb, didn't put Ili off.

"Oh come on! I am too big enough! Look the crowd is almost all gone!"

"We'll follow along and watch from the steps. You'll be able to see and hear fine from there!"

"Ilesias, why don't you come describe the scene for me?" Sera Eren touched his shoulder.

"Aw... all right." He agreed with bad grace but we were all full of the glory we'd experienced so his pique was half-hearted at best. He had his glass star of Imperator's glass clutched in his glove... I turned to Sera Eren.

"Sera, you didn't get any Imperator's glass... even though you were so close, here... you should take mine – "

"Nonsense, lad." She opened her glove to me as we stepped out of the Temple doors and the odd light under the portico caught it so the crystal glittered like gold. "Ribbons snatched one for me... I'm sure he thought it was a good pounce."

I hadn't even noticed it. "I'll take Ilesias with me, shall I? We'll meet you later... at the feast, at the Heir's obelisk... in a bead or so?"

"Oh, all right. Thank you." I examined my own piece of Imperator's glass, finding it was made up of what looked like a handful of tiny clear quartz crystals, like an Arkan made version of the natural ones that Yeolis wore. I tucked my tiny piece of sacred beauty into my glove pocket and wiped my face with the backs of my gloves, the only part that had a chance of drying my face. My eyes were still leaking tears. Most people's faces shone wet, even as they sang and chanted and cheered.

Chevenga was half-way around the square by now being passed from hand to hand upon the raised mass hands of all the Arkans who had seen or heard this ritual and who had seen the Temple miracles that no one had ever seen before. I could still see the bright stripes of Gannara's head in the knot of people near the Imperator, behind Him.

I looked down at my feet and found I was standing on the step where Kallijas had cut down the pretender, the stone stained a ruddy, rusty colour, already fading. The step-stains were not maintained like those actually inside the Temple itself and the steps tended to fade to pure white, apparently. I shivered all over and tried to step away from the patch.

I am a pretender. In hiding, but a pretender to this glory nonetheless. How dare I be moved by this? How dare I even see this? How? The knot in my chest is so tight I almost cannot breathe and my mouth is full of the taste of my own blood where I've bitten the inside of it. Like people all around me... I fell to my knees on the wide step, raising my hands to my temples.

Ancestors... Sinimas... please intercede for me... pass along my most abject apologies to the Gods, would you? I do not wish to offend any with my presence, with my willingness to be so close to the sacred ritual in my spirit... anything that might anger the Ten... or, now, Eleven?... I shook my head, shivering all over my body. *...anything that might anger the Ten. Please and thank you.*

I rose to my feet again and looked in time to see Chevenga carried off down the Avenue of Statuary. The whole roast oxen and sheep and pigs and even spits of poultry were being wheeled out of the Marble Palace and set up in their traditional places around the square. The gigantic double spit that held two oxen roasted head to head was being placed carefully on the Presentation Platform where the Imperator would be. The feasting would go on all the rest of the day and the night... when the Imperator came back and graciously carved the first meats.

I caught a glimpse of my shadowy, blurry reflection in the polished white stone pillar next to me, the bright blue hair suddenly a mockery. It was a sham and a shame. I had been enjoying myself. Indulging myself in pretending I was no one but either Minakas or Sinimas. I was a blot and a danger to these people as long as I kept running, kept playing.

My nightmare of a ruined city, burning far worse and far longer... the uncounted dead on Finpollendias... the boy who was 2nd Amitzas's get, with the grim face and the willingness to kill Arko to inherit it swam in front of my eyes, a horrific and stinking cloud over the heads of all who danced and sang and prophesied in the Square, real enough I could almost smell it over the mouth watering aroma of the feast.

Prophecy. People were so sometimes so seized by the ritual that they would fall in convulsions, prophesying. "... *the Eaglet walks where he should fly... the chalk and the charcoal are yours now Arko! Hold tight to your freedoms!...* a boy, held by an older man, shook and grinned and spouted prophecy, his eyes rolled up into the back of his head. Priests came at a run down the steps, coming to see to him... to make him a Temple novice... *Oh... Arko! The Ten! The Ten! And the One. Are One! Oh, Arko!"* He didn't sound like he was in pain but rather joyful.

I closed my eyes as he began to sing in the language of the Gods, a hymn I didn't recognize. "Bless you!" I cried to the man who seemed to be his father rather than his lover. All around me people were blessing them. The man gave up his son to the priests' and *dekinas'* support but followed close behind as they carried the boy back into the Temple, his face a study in joy and grief, both together. *What plans did you have, that the Ten picked your boy away from?*

I couldn't stand it any longer and closing my eyes, putting my hands over my ears, but it wasn't enough. There were too many tears behind my eyes and I needed to get into private to howl them into my bedding. I could only press through the crowd so quickly and it was enough time to make me half frantic. I wouldn't be able to get out of the crowd and back again before I had to meet with Ili and Sera Eren.

Perhaps I'd be able to find a fraction of space behind the Heir's obelisk... the slab of stone before the Heir's balcony that hid the secret way in that had been covered over so long ago. It was far enough away from the Marble Palace that the public could still access it, but close enough to make most people too nervous to go in behind.

I stepped around it, set my back to it and found myself looking at a chalk drawing by Banaksias. It was the iconic drawing of Chevenga. When the Ten had chosen Him to be the new Son of the Sun. He'd dreamed that Selinae had come to him and picked Him up in Her Hair, one of the things peculiar to Her, the hair that could grasp and penetrate.

Chevenga was suspended before Her, held wrapped in and enveloped and floating before Her upheld by Her silver/gold locks of hair. The image had been picked up by those who always supported the Imperator and there were many, many variations on it, painted, drawn, sculpted.

This one was chalk, like all of Banaksias's work, and so detailed I could see that the Goddess's hair had Chevenga everywhere and that he was as naked as in the Temple. I shuddered as my groin tightened again. Was I not going to be able to get away from that vileness today?

Then I read the caption, in iridescent white and gold letters, gleaming bright as every highlight in the Goddess's and even in Chevenga's hair, making his black curls even darker. It said—

"If the Ten never forgave, then Selestialis would be empty."

38

"I'LL NEVER WASH THESE FINGERS AGAIN!"

I MANAGED TO CATCH MY BREATH IN THE SHADOW OF THE OBELISK and I couldn't tear my eyes away from the drawing of Selinae and Chevenga. *If the Ten never forgave, Selestialis would be empty.*

My mind was thrashing around, trying to think of all the scripture about forgiveness and I couldn't bring one complete to my mouth. I'd have to think about that.

I emerged from my semi-hiding place, longing to run down to the lakeshore and tuck myself between the Griffon's wings again, just to let all my unseemly emotions out, but I had agreed to meet the others here.

"Heya, Sin!" Gannara looked as though he'd touched God and in a way he had. "I bet my parents would never have let me see this if they knew what went on in that Temple!" His grin was wide.

"You should close your mouth, you're starting to catch low-flying birds," I teased.

"Idya."

"Over-sexed moron."

"Repressed self-flogger!"

"Boys! Boys! Please do stop," Sera Eren said. "After all this glory… perhaps one of you young gentlemen would bring an old woman some of the feast?" She'd found a crumb of space to sit at the obelisk and we all had our feast plates, made of wood so that we could let them hang from our belts by a strap until we needed them. Sera Eren gave us hers and the three of us went to stand in the forming lines, though not the one where Chevenga was carving and serving, talking to all who came to him.

"I touched him! Did you see? It was when he threw himself back."

"Be careful, you said?" I had to smile. "After all he just went through you were worried people wouldn't catch him? You caught his head."

"It wasn't just me telling him to be careful! But yeah! I'm never going to wash these two fingers –" he held up the third finger and smallest finger of his left hand. "—again." He kissed the two fingers he had displayed. He sniffed his fingers. "You know… he really was on fire… his hair smells burnt."

"Yes, He really was on fire." As if the Gods would pretend.

"Ch'venga's trying to touch everyone."

He was. Everyone who He served, He didn't let servants hand Him the plates either receiving them or giving them back laden. He took them Himself, and just as often returned them with a smile or a word or a touch if He let go the carving fork, stuck in the fragrant beef.

If the Ten never forgave, Selestialis would be empty.

We got our food and went back to Sera Eren and Ribbons who was graciously receiving tid-bits of meat from everyone around him, a booming purr deep in his chest as he chewed. I ended up feeding most of my meat to him when I thought no one was looking. Even though it was good, my stomach was in grinding knots.

If the Ten never forgave, Selestialis would be empty.

Ili was singing in between bites and kept getting up to see the Imperator still carving. "He looks like He's having fun!"

"Yes, He does."

Gannara leaned close to whisper in my ear, "Are you sure you're all right?

"No, I'm fine."

His brows drew together, so like Chevenga's when puzzling something out. "There's some shen you're not telling me, else you wouldn't have bit your lip." I hadn't realized he could tell. I thought I had hidden that.

"Hey, that happened during the rite... It was a little overwhelming for all of us... I don't even remember doing it," I lied.

He leaned really close, looking into my eyes searchingly and whispered, "Is it because he did this and you're not going to be able to?"

Shen. "Gannara you're too damned perceptive. I want to go home and bawl my head off in private all right? Can I meet you later?

"Are you sure you don't want me there? Oh, yeah, fik, I know. I look like him."

"No! No, it's all right. It's not that at all. It's just that I won't be able to let it all out if anyone else is there."

Gannara had grabbed my arm, staring over my shoulder looking as if someone had punched him in the guts. "It's... it's... him. It's one of *them. Shen, shen, fikken shen! It's Joras.*"

It was all I could do not to wheel around and stare. *He's not looking for a blue-headed Dyer. Nor a flame-tiger striped Yeoli.* I tipped my head forward and used my kerchief to wipe my plate and turned apparently carelessly. He was right. It was Joras.

I swallowed hard. "I'm sorry, Ili, are you done? We need to go home now."

He started whining and Gannara knelt down in front of him. "Ili, we just spotted a Mahid. Let's all go home now, all right?" He fell silent, eyes big.

"I'll pay a kid to report the sighting to the Marble Palace... all he'll be able to say is that a Dyer paid him and I'll scrub my head clear of dye tonight."

I hugged Sera Eren and her frail old arms tightened around me. "You need to run from something, boys? Never mind. Not my business. Go on. Ribbons and I will meet you tomorrow at the Gryphon."

"Take care, Sera. Until tomorrow." We moved as quickly as we could without being obvious about it. I could feel Joras's eyes travelling across the square as if he were the sight on a bow preparing to shoot me in the back; a back of the neck prickly sensation that thankfully slid off.

39

I'VE GOT YOU

"Ser!" Perisalas looked up, startled that Dagasas would burst in and -- armed in the Marble Palace? "A break in the case! There's been a Mahid sighted in the crowd! The Minister of Serenity is mustering his own Sereniteers and called me to inform you!"

"Good! Get the squad right now!"

He paused to arm himself with his kit, rather than the showier sword, and followed Dagasas at a run. *At last. One has been careless. Oh, shen is he making a try for the Imperator in the crowd?*

Outside the Minister's office there was a bustle as Sereniteers mustered and his own squad... *solas*, already half armoured. Intent and intense. He caught his breath and slowed to a brisk walk, tapped upon Rafas's door and let himself in.

The minister looked up from his conversation with... a street kid. A junior Dyer it looked like. Clean enough, intelligent enough if he could spot a Mahid.

"Ah Perisalas, I have our witness. He's pointed out the man we're interested in, in the crowd. I have someone watching discretely from a window."

"Excellent! This isn't another glass-dog chase is it? This one is concerned." It was good to work with Rafas... one of those rare men who never let his caste interfere with his job. He was one of the new guard, who'd survived and been promoted to his place after the sack.

"No. No. It looks like it's just the one. We couldn't spot his back-up and if it's just a *fessas* fellow who happens to be an incredible physical specimen we're best to check and be embarrassed if we happen to dart an innocent man from behind."

"Of course." The Minister would already have asked the boy if he were willing to be truth drugged to give his testimony… it tended to cut down on gratuitous accusations. "I'll want to speak to our informant after we've secured the suspect."

"Ser. A young man paid this 'un to point out the man… the Mahid, ser!" The boy spoke up.

"Noted, lad. Stay safe here," Rafas said and called a Sereniteer to keep an eye on the boy. It didn't hurt that it was one of the young women spreading through the city force.

It only took a moment or two for them to hurry through one of the passages in the Palace that brought them to a spy-hole just behind where their suspect was lounging, a feast-plate held in one hand, watching the crowd. "He's good, if he's not just a *fessas*," Rafas said. "He looks like an under-craftsman; a glassman."

Rafas's Sereniteers sauntered out of the Steel Gate as if they were newly off duty and going to join the city feasting. "Thank the Gods, he hasn't made a try for the Imperator!" Perisalas broke into an unaccustomed sweat thinking of his namesake so vulnerable, carried through the city, trying to touch everyone. A needle in the mob and it would be all over. But most people knew about that sense for weapons of his. A needle hidden in a glove pocket wasn't hidden to the Imperator.

Perisalas and Rafas both snapped open their blow-tubes and loaded them. Two more Sereniteers were already out in the crowd, in plain sight, leaning on their black and whites that actually had tubes built into them… an innovation from some Yeoli genius.

"Ready…" Rafas, from his own spy-hole. This would take perfect timing if they wanted the man alive… if he was a Mahid. Perisalas slid his tube through the slot and took a deep breath.

"Now!"

The man jumped as if stung, swung upright fast as a cat and crumpled with the number of darts in him.

"Now we find out if he's Mahid and if he had a poisoned tooth," Persialas said. *I will do my best to not be smug if this is, indeed a Mahid.* The Sereniteers converged on the fallen man, calling for a medic as if he were merely a man overcome with heat or sun. The darts vanished from his shoulders and back as if they'd been imaginary as he was loaded onto a litter and carried off for 'assistance'.

"This one is impressed with the Minister's people. This could have been a disaster with a fight in this crowd."

"Nicely shot, Perisalas."

"This one thanks the Minister." *And an officer not afraid to get his own hands dirty, if the case is important enough.*

By the time they got down to the cells, Dagasas was just straightening from the unconscious man, with a syringe in his hand. "He's a Mahid all right. He had a tooth, Sers. Didn't use it."

Unconcious, it was more obvious, the slack face very like the unexpressive face usually on a Mahid. Perisalas took the half-step back, letting Rafas lead, after all, he was still merely *solas* and the Minister *Aitzas*—and a competent one at that. "Secure him, make sure that empty tooth is yanked." Standard operating procedure turned the Mahid into a gagged prisoner on one of their own tables in their section of the Marble Palace, since those rooms were the least likely he would have any chance to break out of, or succeed in getting hand free to kill himself.

"Well, Perisalas." Rafas said. "Come talk to our informant while our snoozing black dog sleeps it off. I'd give him the stun drug antagonist but he has enough in him that I don't want to risk it. I am truly glad he didn't use that tooth of his."

"Of course, Minister."

And why did he not? One would think that the Mahid sent with Minis would be among the best.

"Here we are. Thank you, An-Kurias Shafa, dismissed."

"Yes ser."

"Sers," the boy spoke up even before they'd sat down. "Like this 'un tol' the High Ser here..." he nodded at Rafas. "A Dyer paid me, Ser tah make the report. Three whole coppers, ser... just ta rat on a Mahid. Arkan kid. He showed me... pointed 'im out..."

"What did this Dyer look like?"

"Blue hair, ser. Skinny kid. Really rev kilt an' a nose-ring w' a blue stone in't. Mebby tall when he's a man, ser, but not much oldern' me. Hair tied back couldn't see how long 't was." He ran out of words then.

"Was he by himself?" Perisalas prompted.

"Yesser."

"Anything else?"

"Rev eyes, ser... ta match his hair mebby." The kid was coming down off a herb high… jittering now. "He din't say how he knew the *jefalla*" – the dyer slang for a man – "was Mahid, ser but he knew." Rafas had the truth drug vial on the desk already and it was a moment's work to have the boy lie down for it.

Perisalas folded his arms, his narrow face thoughtful. He didn't really need the truth-drugged confirmation of the boy's testimony, but it would be good to have the transcript. If the blue-haired boy were Minis…and he didn't think it could be anyone else but the Aan… he was in the city, and rather than having his squad chase all over the Empire, he would be able to have a man at the Main Gate and every *laefetas* around the Rim with this description.

A slow smile spread across his face as Rafas began questioning the boy under truth-drug and getting essentially the same answers. *I've got you, you pup.*

40

THY FREEDOM'S SACRED

I'D SENT GANNARA AND ILI AHEAD OF ME, EXPLAINING THAT I didn't want to let Joras get away. Every Mahid, under 2nd Amitzas's command was a danger to all Arko as far as I was concerned.

The boy I paid off to let the Marble Palace know was herb-high but perfectly focused on both the copper links I gave him and the possibility of gaining some of the reward chains offered.

He vanished into the Black Gate to the Sereniteer's offices, as the feasting and dancing continued. Chevenga, on the Presentation Platform, carved and sang and talked with everyone He served as I waited. I tucked myself into a group of Dyers, passing a drum around, under the Lakeside Arch, waiting to see if something would come of it and so saw Joras fall and get carried off. Whoever planned that, did it well. And fast. I hoped Chevenga would commend him, or them.

Immediately after that I decamped and thanked my fellow Dyers for sharing around their instruments, since I had not brought mine. I couldn't make Gan and Ili wait so I went straight home to the apartment and reassured them I hadn't been crazy enough to try and report Joras myself.

Jiaklem crawled into my lap when I had my arm around Ili and I found myself listening to the noise we could hear all the way from the square, and thinking about the second Ten Tens.

~

*...the battle... it was no longer a battle... it was a massacre.
2nd Amitzas's grandson... the kid in the black armour was laughing as
he hacked at wounded on the ground... they couldn't get away from
him, he wasn't aiming to kill but to torture. There was blood everywhere. "I'm 3rd Minis Aan you worm-sons! You prostrate yourselves to
me! You will! I am the Blackest Sun! How dare you defy ME!?"*

*I flung my hands over my eyes and was on my knees. "Gods! Please,
no. He's doing that to Arko, to Arkans! No! Can I stop him? Can I
stop this?"*

*I'm in bright sun. Standing on the Presentation Platform. There's a
headsman's block set up, and a... a... Mahid but one dressed in dark
red, not onxyine. It's odd. He's calm but I can see traces of compassion on his face. What kind of headsman is he?*

*I look up to the Balcony and Chevenga sits on the throne there, in the
Imperial Robe. He is weeping, I can tell, though if you didn't know
him, you'd not see it. His voice in my ear... "You don't need to do this,
Minis." I consider it... and the battlefield and the screaming maniac
torturing Arkans begins to come back like a corpse floating up out of
deep water, gradually.*

*I know. I realize. I know what I must do. I don't want to die but
the power to stop that madman from torturing and murdering the
city, and the Empire does lie in my hands. I know it. I know it down
to my guts. It won't be me who tries to take the Empire back to my
father's vision, but a boy using my name. No. I am not worth more
than all the people in the Empire. My life is nothing against that
weight.*

*My responsibility. Do I have the courage to do what is the right thing?
The best thing? Ancestors help me.*

I woke in the middle of the roof garden of the apartment. I was just
sinking into the odd pose for Aras, as if I was practising the Ten Tens and
froze. It was past the middle of the night and there was no one to see me,

from the tenement windows next door. I wasn't supposed to be up here...
it was the landsera's private space. My hands... my bare hands... came up
to cover my face.

I had the power to make the future, if I believed my dreams and the
battle was all too real, too plausible for me to dismiss it as a fearful fantasy. And if I did turn myself in, Chevenga would not want to execute me.
Knowing him, section 14 compartment 8, the law that called for my
public death was probably struck from the books already. I hadn't
checked.

I knelt down, still with my hands over my face, suddenly full of
fear. *Can I do this? I must do this. I have that responsibility.* Even Ilesias
the Great had something to say about it. "Thee Imperator is nought thing
withouten thee people. A good Imperator does remembern theese fact and
is prepared to given Hymself withouten let and down to thee last drop of
blood."

"I hear, oh Ten," I whispered into my hands. I could not put off the
decision. I slid down into the full prostration to the Gods though I could
not stop a sob from pushing its way out of my mouth. It was the best I
could do for Arko. It was the correct thing to do, whatever happened to
me. It was decided. I decided. "I will obey."

In the morning I found this upon the table, in my handwriting, and had
no memory of writing it.

> *I made thee with free and wild wings and thou didst almost flutter so
> far from Me that I could not save thee, wind's kiss, soul flyer, gem of
> air and sun, and now... thou wouldst fly straight into the candle
> flame, eluding yet My love, that would snatch thee back... would
> crush thee, smear the dust from rainbow wings, destroy forever thy
> airy flight. In sorrow I must watch, and cry, for thy freedom I must
> let thee die, for all My power, or what I will, oh child. Thy freedom,
> thy choice is sacred for good, for ill.*

41

___

I AM MAHID. I THINK

I... am...Mahid... Was the first thought. The second was *What is Mahid, now?* He was restrained. There was an ache in his jaw where his poison filled tooth had sat but he was effectively gagged and could not move his tongue to probe the spot. A Mahid gag that filled the mouth with rubber that one could chew upon and never bite a piece loose to choke with. If he opened his eyes he would see the handle of it sticking out from between his lips.

A headache. He recognized it. It was residue from the most fast acting stun-drug... and from the feeling, quite a bit of it. *They would have wanted to be sure of me.*

Muunas... My most high God... my senior is incorrect. 2nd Amitzas is incorrect. Most High... you have showed me...

He shut those thoughts behind the wall in his mind. They were incorrect thoughts. But images of the Gods and the – he had to force the caveat now – *Foreign* Imperator kept burning through his mind, obliterating years of Mahid training in the conflagration.

My mind and soul are a city under siege by the Ten and by their conquering Son. He could not forget that now. The truth of what he saw... they were flames... they burned the dried-up tinder of painful learning. His mind was on fire, pain and confusion, as long-held beliefs charred and blackened, a far worse agony than a mere stun headache could give him.

I am a Mahid, trained to be fessas. Mahid is meaningless now. I have only the fessas to cling to. They will truth-drug me, and find that I have nothing to give them. I know only where to send my letters... to the postal office here... from that box they vanish and I do not know where they go or who picks them up. They might catch someone emptying my box but I do not believe they will. I have nothing to hide. Except... the worst... I am a failed Mahid of a failed Imperator. The Spark of the Son's Ray was correct to defy 2nd Amitzas.

I do not like this sensation of failure. I am used to frustration. Anger. Rage. Pain. I am not used to failing in my duty. It is correct that I be executed. I... liked... being the glassman... I had enough training in watching the glass flow from solid to liquid, transmuted by fire. I had enough apprentice burns on my hands as if through my gloves to be credible. Glasswork... is beautiful. I am like a glass rod, and the second Ten Tens is the flame applied to me.

He noted absently that the current Mahid... or Sereniteers... or Irefas... had not seen fit to use either the knife gag or the penetrating rods built into the table to immobilize him completely. They had not even fastened the head restraint. Joras Mahid lay in almost complete restraint and attempted to resist melting.

They did not wait for the enforced stillness to soften him up. They didn't need to; on several levels but they did not know this. He did not bother to open his eyes when they came... four men together who did not speak to one another.

They were not terribly rough when they pushed up his loose sleeve and inserted the needle. *What do I least want them to know? I don't even know that now. I shall be curious to find out myself when they begin.*

They removed the gag and he closed his mouth and ran his tongue around the inside of his mouth. It was a physical relief that he indulged himself in and was surprised when a glass tube was offered to his lips. "Drink," one man said. A soft *Aitzas* accent. Did he warrant attention from the Minister of Internal Serenity himself, Rafas Izan? It didn't matter. He drank. There was no reason to see the men truth-drugging him and he didn't bother to open his eyes.

There was no shame to feel as he lost his control, the *fessas* drinking song he began humming, the bawdy poetry he recited, "Finger Licking Good". It was all part of his other self... the not Mahid part that was not injured or dead yet. They listened without comment amongst themselves. He said it out loud, there was no stopping it.

"...this part of me isn't dead yet... That's funny. I've been *fessas* long enough that when the *Aitzas* dies it is keeping me breathing..." He laughed again, an almost hysterical sound, painful and long drawn out as he laughed as he hadn't for years. It was so intense he was vaguely glad he wasn't in full restraint since that would have injured him as he writhed with laughter.

"Tell us your name... lie to us."

"Tirias Firen, *fessas*."

He was, at last, far enough into the truth-drug to cease assaulting his own and everyone else's ears. They waited, and finally there was truth down to his core and no struggle any longer. This was Selestialis... no fight at all. Only *Hayel* waiting when he came out of it, but that was a distant thought.

"What is your name?"

"Joras Mahid, *Aitzas.*"

"What would you least like us to know?"

There it was. "I'm turned." Some part of him wished to weep but that was as impossible as screaming.

"You're turned? You don't want us to know that?"

"Yes."

"Why?"

"You won't kill me." An odd shift in the room.

"You want to die?"

"No."

A whisper from one man, too low for him to catch. "Do you feel you deserve death?"

"Yes."

"Why?"

"I am Mahid." It was a curious comfort to realize he still believed himself to be Mahid, even in the midst of all the confusion.

"Are you willing to swear to Ivaen Shefenkas Shae Aranoeas as rightful Imperator of Arko?"

Joras was absolutely shocked, down where he still could be shocked, to hear his own mouth open and say "Yes."

"Will you be entirely loyal, body and soul to Ivaen Shefenkas Shae Aranoeas?"

"Yes."

He almost missed the four men talking amongst themselves as his own mind flailed around inside his skull. *Yes? Yes? I'm sworn? Yes? How? Oh my great God... yes?*

"Do you know where Minis Aan is?"

"No."

"Why?"

"He left."

"He left his Mahid guard?"

"Yes."

"And you were sent after him?"

"Yes."

"Do you believe he is in the city at this time?"

"Yes."

They ferreted out every nuance of his thinking, every turn he took from Haiu Menshir to the city, one word at a time, since under truth-drug he was incapable of explaining. Then they went away. They just went away and left him and it was a mercy. They just let the drug wear off after they ran out of questions and did not take advantage of the drug to hurt him. He was faintly surprised at that but it made sense that if the Gods wanted the current Imperator... and thus by extension the men questioning him... they would do good and not ill.

Some part of him wailed and thrashed and longed for punishment to expiate his sin but that did not happen. They left him alone after they had wrung out everything they could out of his drug-lax mind.

When at last he opened his eyes on the Mahid space, ungagged this time, he found himself looking at the Imperial Pharmacist standing over him.

"You are sworn."

"Yes, Senior," he said quietly.

"You wish to die." It was not a question. He answered it anyway.

"Yes, Senior."

"It is not allowed. Your punishment is to endure and understand the current Imperator."

"I understand."

The Imperial Pharmacist unlocked him with the usual 'clack' as the restraints snapped back. "We will see to your re-training," was all that was told him.

"Thank you, Senior." And then, the most astounding, astonishing thing. The Senior answered him.

"You are welcome, Mahid."

Joras sat upright on the table, frozen in the act of rubbing his wrists, staring at the Pharmacist. *You are welcome, Mahid? I am truly going mad.*

42

———————

AFTERMATH

"Mother, you don't need to stay with me! I'm perfectly fine with the Sereniteer here, taking my report!"

"But, Kyriala! You need to be properly chaperoned!"

"Mama. She's a woman Sereniteer," Kyriala whispered in her ear but even that didn't stop her mother wringing her gloves and shawl in anxiety. And just the shame of being *here,* as well as not being entirely convinced of the... hmmm... integrity of a female Sereniteer. The Hall of Serenity was all but empty, since even the miscreants of the city seemed to all be outside for the post Ten Tens feast... when all the city was apparently full of good-fellowship and crime was something not to be considered in the wake of all that joy and sacredness pouring out of the presentation square. But it was still the main hall of Serenity where prostitutes and criminals of all stripes were brought to question and a lady was just never seen there.

Kyriala hadn't expected that she would be giving her statement in the main hall, but she didn't care about how it looked. *I saw one of the Mahid that had been with Minis, in the square. He was watching the Imperator and his eyes were looking for Minis and Gannara... why is he here? Does he think the boys are here too? They, very sensibly, haven't tried to contact me since that horribly florid goodbye letter from my 'secret admirer'.*

It was almost a relief when a *solas* she recognized, Dagasas, who acted as Ser Perisalas's second in the hunt for Minis, loomed up behind the earnest young Sereniteer. "Sharila, I have it, thank you. Serina, Sera, if you would come with me please?"

He escorted Kyriala and her mother into one of the small rooms she recognized from other questionings. "Kaf for the ladies?"

"No, Ser Dagasas, I need to make my report immediately or you might lose him! There is a Mahid out in the feasting crowd and you need to do something about it *right away!* She closed her fan with an impatient snap. "The longer you talk to me, the more time he has to move from where I saw him!"

Dagasas shook his head at her. "Serina, Serina... my superior is already preparing to scrape that man. You are correct in spotting him as a Mahid and as a threat to Arko. You have our thanks for your diligence."

"Oh." The urgency that had propelled her here collapsed. "So you caught him already?"

"Yes, Serina."

"Oh, good." *One less Mahid pursuing Minis.* The idea of using the people chasing Minis to keep him safer was peculiarly satisfying. She opened her fan more quietly and wafted the cool air of the Marble Palace into her face. Beside her she could feel Mama relax and open her fan as well.

"So, you've done your duty, my daughter," she said with considerable relief. "Ser, shall I take my daughter home safe, now?"

"In a moment, Sera. I just need to check our young Sereniteer's work, taking down the Serina's statement and then I shall escort you back out... to the feast? Or to your manor?"

Before mama could speak up and tear them both away from the square, Kyriala spoke up. "Mama, I should love to go back out to the square, please. I so rudely dragged you away from Great Uncle and Uncle and I should not wish to cut anyone's celebration short."

"Oh. If you're sure, dear."

"Yes, Mama."

"Then back out to the feast, Ser *solas,* if you please," Sera Liren said.

"Very well, ladies."

～

"Ser Ailadas?"

"Yes?" The old scholar looked up to meet his house-boy's worried eyes, and the Sereniteer behind him. One of Perisalas Shefenkas's Minis

hunters. "Sereniteer Dagasas," he said mildly. "Didn't your – ahem --
superior just truth drug me a few eight days ago?"

The big man had the grace to look a trifle embarrassed. "A break in
the case, Ser. We need to inquire again."

"Well, then-- ahem. Shall we do this like last time? Surely you have
enough witnesses here... and a vial of truth-drug with you that you might
do this in the safety of my – ahem – own home?"

"Ah... of course, ser. That makes eminent sense."

"All this fuss! Ahem. Just to find out if the former Spark of the Sun's
Ray has contacted me and for me to deny it once more. Ahem. Proceed."

43

____

ON THE LIST

I watched the last, faint vestiges of blue wash down the drain at the Bath House. The suds were mostly white and I ran my hands over my head pushing the water and soap through my hair, pressing hard down to the roots. I'd paid for double time today and gotten a mix of lime and yellowfruit juice to strip the colour out completely after I washed. Then I had a trifle of oil to ease the stiffness and chalky feeling the lime always left behind.

I was going to have to explain to the landsera that my young cousin had been called away... on family business of course... no one questioned that, and that I would be staying in the city for a time so taking over his portion of the apartment rental.

The line-up for the Marble Palace Audience list was always long and they tried to weed out people with a two-tier system. The first line got you to the Imperial Secretary and the second for Chevenga himself.

I was very properly dressed as I walked into the Black Door of the Marble Palace that led to the bureaucratic offices. I was Minakas Akam again, very firmly. My gloves were full with no odd Dyerly cut-outs, no nose, ear, eyebrow or lip-rings. No risqué kilts that were nothing but loin-cloths and my shirt had a man's full sleeves, even if thin cotton. My scholar's robe was very properly pressed and to the floor. My hair, my own blond and trimmed exactly the correct length though many people were becoming lax about cutting their hair now, particularly the younger ones. The bathhouse had a station with a razor for lower castes to cut their own hair… a fixed box that one put one's head in and it clipped everything precisely with the trimmer, once the caste was dialled in and the lever was pulled… usually a number of times to make it even but that was still better than trying to cut one's own hair with a dull edge or a glass one.

I adjusted my spectacles upon my nose and inquired at the main desk as if I'd never been there before. They directed me up three floors and down the express-chair wide gold and red tiled hallway through to the Imperial Sub-offices, rather more rarified than the Hall of Internal Serenity and the cells.

The halls up here were plainer than anywhere else *but* Serenity, and full of people. Most had papers in their hands, some had odd glasswares and at least one person I saw had a cage with something in it that I couldn't see well, but its eyes flashed red in the lamplight. Perhaps a ferret being brought in to clear out any rats the ratters could not catch. Or some odd creature as a gift intended for either Chevenga or the Imperium.

There were easily a dozen people ahead of me in the correct line, of all nationalities. I had lots of time to think as the line moved up. I knew I had to do this. I knew it as if the Gods had told me. I'd be dreaming of that asshole kid drowning Arko in blood until I did. The man in front of me was as tall as a Srian, though not as dark skinned, with a slick skull cap of jewel-like feathers. He had a box in his hands that was inlaid with chips of gold, lapis and tiger's eyes. He couldn't be one of an official entourage because that kind of thing wouldn't have gone through these channels. Most of the others were Arkan of various stripe and caste.

I looked up at the angelic frescoes on the ceiling and tried not to fidget. Or run. I wanted to run out of here so badly my calves were twitching under the proper, sober scholar's robe.

I knotted my hands together and locked them with a little Mahid exercise that stilled the muscles. Then I began the counted breathing. That way I could just step forward as if nothing were wrong, as if I signed onto the Imperial Audience list every day.

"Name?" The bureaucrat was an older *Aitzas* fellow with pinch-spectacles on his nose, but with a scar or two that a desk-driver would not normally have. Probably all the oddness in these war and post war years.

"Minakas Akam, *fessas,* sor."

"Purpose?"

"A short interview with He Whose Knowledge is the World's Treasure, sor."

"That cannot be researched without direct quotes from the Imperator?"

"No, sor. Arkan/Yeoli political history, sor." He was speaking equal to equal. He tapped his pen on his teeth, thinking.

"Would he know you? Best tell the absolute truth."

"The World's Wisdom and I discussed such topics more than once when He was between terms. He invited me to dinner... and He knows my writing; I've had pieces published in the Pages." That did the trick. It was probably overkill to mention the dinner but I wanted him to stop blocking me.

"Ah, indeed. Go up to the sentry over there and they will direct you to the Imperial offices."

"Thenk yah, sor."

The door into the *Erinkilan* level was new. It had been an open hallway before. The sentry had a servant-guide waiting to lead me through to what I knew were the lesser Scarlet rooms, not quite as over-whelming as the Highest Office, in its own cliff-perch over the Marble Palace, under the Eagle, with an enormous window and the inside--walls, floor and ceiling-- almost all gold.

Chevenga and his staff would probably want to work here more than in that grandiose space unless they specifically needed to overawe some-one. The Imperial secretary was a Yeoli fellow with kind eyes but a very precise manner. "How long do you truly need, young man?" He asked me.

The rest of my life, I bit my tongue on. "Two tenths shou'd be generous enough, sor."

He perused his book and every half-tenth of Chevenga's day, including meals, was apparently accounted for. Page after page, from early morning to late at night. He wasn't going to have time to scratch in the next year it looked like.

There were several half-tenths open but not close enough to re-arrange everyone's schedule to give me a full two tenths of a bead. The secretary's bare finger finally settled on the first open slot of the correct size. "Five moons and eighteen days from now, young man. First bead of the afternoon."

"Thank you, ker," I said in Yeoli. That fetched me a smile.

"You're welcome. Sign here." It was the final formality, to discourage anyone who truly did not need to speak with the Imperator. I took the pen with a hand that didn't seem to be mine, distant and strange, suddenly finger-sweated inside my gloves. I watched the line of black ink flow from the nib, dreamlike as I signed 'Minakas Akam'. It flowed smooth as blood and just as significant, though more controlled.

It was as though the whole world shifted as I laid the pen down gently. That was the commitment. That was it. If Perisalas Shefenkas and half the office of Internal Serenity and even Irefas were not looking for me at this moment, with a Mahid caught in the city itself, I'd eat my under-clout, raw with no sauce. I'd spend the last few moons of my freedom mostly in our apartment, writing. I wasn't sure I would have time to finish my Tathanas/Notyere piece after I turned myself in.

"Good day, ker." The secretary said. "The servant will show you out."

"Thank you." It was easier following the servant out because I wasn't really seeing the halls of my former home at all. I was going to do it.

Gannara was going to kill me. I hadn't told him that was what I would be doing today, getting on the audience list to turn myself in.

44

———————

WHY DOES IT HAVE TO BE YOU?

Kolkulas Ruren stared at me as I introduced myself as Minakas, as if I didn't know him at all. He was the owner of the courier business that I had skated for as Sinimas. "You look like your cousin. You're telling me he had to leave without notice? *Forzak.*" He was upset at all?

"M' families' apologies, sor. He were a good employee?"

"Wahl, he were a bit high in the kilt fer a *fessas* ... not good at bein' humble, but then he were a fantastic skater and very fast." *Oh. I had tried to be humble enough.* "'S good yer lettin' me know, an him not just disappearin'. I had two *fikken* couriers do that just last week, pardon me language, young scholar."

"Not atal, sor." I turned to go and he called me back.

"Oy, wait. I'll get his last paychains... ye kin send 'em on home tah tha lad."

He wasn't just going to keep them? Of course. He was a good employer.

"I'll pass all'f it along tah him. Thenk yeh, sor."

I wished I would be in a position to give him more business, but I was burning all my connections behind me.

~

Gannara, with Jia on his shoulder, since Ili was at school, just sat and stared at me when I told him.

"I thought I heard you say you did something really, really, Imperial-Statue-sized stupid. But I really can't believe you'd be that monumentally stupid, so I hope you'll tell me what you *really* said."

I sat down, closed my eyes, and said it again. "I put myself on the audience list, to turn myself in to Chevenga."

He didn't yell immediately, the way I expected. "You're turning yourself in, after all the running we've done, after all the work you did establishing yourself as this... scholar person... but... to Chevenga."

"I... Gannara..." That was when he interrupted me.

"NONONOFIKNO! BADIDEA BADIDEA REALLYREALLY BAD!" It was somewhat disconcerting to see someone who looked so much like Chevenga... or a younger relative of Chevenga... telling me it was a bad idea to turn myself in to Chevenga... I suppressed a smile. That would just set him off worse. Of course it was a smile as much against myself.

"I KNOW he's nice and he was your friend in the Mezem and blah blah blah but he lives by *semana kra* and that means he'd squish you fast as a bug under his foot if he thinks it's best for the Empire!"

He went on in that vein for a while, getting up to pace, telling me in colourful detail how dumb an idea this was. When it seemed like he might be calming down a bit I said mildly... "Then I get squished like a bug. If I don't turn myself in, Arko is going to see a lot of trouble for generations to come." He turned around and stared at me again. His mouth opened, then closed. "I can't, in good conscience after seeing the Ten Tens that Chevenga did, indulge myself in just disappearing. Gannara, if the Marble Palace... if the government doesn't know what happened to me, then anyone... anyone unscrupulous or evil enough, would be able to take my name... my supposed legacy... bloodline... whatever... claim to be a decendant of mine and rip the whole *forzak* country apart. Not just in my life-time, either. My name... my disappearance... is a threat to Arko for hundreds of years. If I do this, that threat to Arko is gone."

I hadn't realized I could argue it quite so passionately. He was just looking at me now, with his arms crossed, Jia quietly crawling down his back to go hide in his tank in Ili's room... or under the bed. He didn't like it if people shouted at one another.

"And you figure that Chevenga... being a friend... won't just kill you and be done with it."

"Yes. To Chevenga Himself. I'm not going to hand myself over to any lesser person because they might get overwrought and 'accidentally' kill me. Not that Perisalas Shefenkas seems like the kind who would try to curry favour with Chevenga by presenting Him with my head and an 'oh oops' but I want to be sure. It feels safer doing it this way, and I'd be able to give Him the Imperial Book."

I wouldn't be able to carry the Imperial sword into His presence anyway, but He'd get that from the apartment afterward. The Book was more precious, especially since He was going to need some Imperial precedents from it, if He was going to set up a whole new system of governance for Arko. The partial copy in Brahvniki was lacking in several crucial essays... and perhaps the first twelve pages would come to life for Him, the way they had for the fat guy.

"You know, you could let *me* give him the Imperial Book, if it's that important..."

"And they'd truth drug you and come and arrest me, let's save a few steps, shall we?"

"So we split up first and you don't tell me where you're going. I should go back home anyway. I've been running away from my parents too long."

"You have. But that doesn't solve the Arko problem... with some kid of 2nd Amitzas's claiming to be my grandson or some *shen* like that."

"What if he just decides to lock you up and throw away the key?"

"*Semana kra.* Then he locks me up and I get to read and write from a nice cell the rest of my life—"

"You wouldn't be happy in that!"

"-- and write letters to my friends," I plowed on, over his objection. "The Empire would be safe and my conscience would be clear."

"You..." His arms dropped and his eyes were full of tears. "Why does this all have to be up to you? What did you do to deserve all this *kyash*?"

"I did nothing, Gan, it'll be all right. I'm sorry."

"Why do you have to be the one to turn yourself in when the *fikkers* are your father and the Mahid and all those... *fikkers*....!" It only took two steps and I folded him in a hug as he choked himself silent. I could feel him shaking all over.

"It will work out for the best."

"Why should you get punished *now*? When it's all over?"

"It's all right—"

His yell in my ear nearly deafened me and I twitched but didn't let go. "NO, IT ISN'T FIKKEN ALL RIGHT DON'T GIVE ME THIS!" There was a scuffle and a splash from the bedroom as Jia hid again.

"I won't get punished... it's Chevenga. He won't want to hurt me either. He'll argue I haven't done anything wrong, and He's the Imperator."

Gan knocked his head against my forehead. He was as tall as I was even though younger. "Chains with velvet linings, then." It was only a little bitter and afraid.

"I've got him on my side." *Except for that little matter of my letter of confession about raping him. Now is not the time to mention that.*

"Why don't you just stay a *dyer* forever?" Gan sniffled and said the thing wailing around in my own heart. "You'd be happy."

"Oh... I really really would like that." Jia stretched his rubbery eyes around the corner of the bedroom door now that it had gotten quieter.

Gan drew back a bit and looked into my face. "Be a *dyer* forever and *fik* the Empire."

I had to take a deep breath and hold onto him in my turn, rather than just comforting him. I wanted so much just to do that, the rumble and click of my skates and the drums, sweet-chiming face jewelry and no care but getting across the city in record time. Another deep breath. *Goodbye, Sinimas Akam...* "But I can't Gan. I can't throw the Empire away just for me to be happy. I have that power—"

"Yeah, yeah, yeah. You follow him."

"--therefore I have that responsibility."

He turned his face way and I heard him say "*Semana kyashin kra,* muffled into my shoulder. Then he looked at me and blinked away tears, trying to draw courage. "Maybe... maybe it will all turn out okay... somehow..." I hugged him close again and he squeezed me hard enough it hurt, but I didn't say anything.

After a long moment, I said. "The day I go in... I'll put Ili with Ailadas and hope nobody asks about him. Chevenga will want to know if he's safe and that will be all."

Gan twitched in my grasp. "*FIK!*" And Jia scuttled back under the bed. "*Fik.* I forgot about Ili. But they'll scrape you! It's the same thing! If there's a danger that someone will claim to be your descendant, there's a danger that someone will claim to be his! He's still Aan blood!"

I sighed. That was the thing that hurt worst about it. I couldn't smuggle Ili out of the city with everyone and his pet ferret looking for us. I'd suggest Ailadas get him out... if he doesn't hear from me. Or more likely, the Marble Palace.

"They might not believe him to be a threat. They'll have me and I'm still technically the Heir in Exile."

"But he'd be next in line."

"And the government will know and be able to prove where he is and who his descendants are... I'll ask Chevenga."

"AAAAIIIIIGGGGGHHH!"

I heave a sigh against his hold. "If Chevenga thinks I'm innocent of any wrongdoing... he'll think that even more of Ilesias. He was the one who taught me how to love my little brother. He'll help both of us. I'm certain of it." *At least I hope so.* "You'll be able to go home to your parents as you should."

He clung to that hope. "You really think so?"

"I do." *I hope.*

"But I guess if he's taking care of you, I don't have to. But I'll miss you! *Fik. Fik. Fik. Fikkety fik.*"

Is that all this is? You're just looking after me? Oh, I am so lost, Gannara, I would rather you were my friend than caregiver.

"Gan... you need to find out what YOU need to do all your life... not just look after me, the idiot who bought two slotted spoons instead of a dipper and an extra frying pan instead of a kaf pot!" *The one who didn't know how to clean his own anus, at first...* "I'll miss you too."

45

BIG BROTHERS CAN BE STUPID

Sometimes big brothers can be so stupid. Did he think I wouldn't understand that something was going on when he stopped pretending to be my wild cousin Sinimas? When he scrubbed all the cool blue out of his hair and actually let the nose-ring hole grow shut?

It was after the Ten Tens and I figured he'd do something big. Watching it made me want to do something big myself, but I'm too little. It was the most awesome thing I'd ever seen and I asked Gian for lessons about it. Most everbody else in the class was interested too and I sat next to Ala and Tuboras while we talked about the difference between the Ten Tens we'd seen and the Ascension ritual, or the first Ten Tens. Gian had seen the first one and we wrote down all the differences.

But Minis was still having nightmares ever since Haiu Menshir and Yeoli and they'd been getting worse. Just after the feast he did something and now he was sleeping at night. I knew he had nightmares because Indispensible Bear and I would sometimes be up later than we should and hear him and Uncle Gan talking about it. I got up once, a while ago, so I wouldn't pee the bed and IB and I'd heard him. He'd been crying in his sleep.

The fat guy was a lot harder on him than he was on me and I feel guilty that I'm kind of glad I escaped. Is that bad? Anyway... he's not crying at night anymore and he's Minakas again... selling his stories to the

Pages... Even if I don't understand what he's talking about a lot of the time I try to read some of them. And I always read his stories for me, the Ili and his magic donkey stories.

I'm not a great reader. Gian sighs at me and we spend more time with the interesting books, about mechanisms or about how to actually make the swords and armour. Those make sense to me.

But Minis told me today he needed to talk to me tonight... kind of warning me that it's important.

Jiaklem cuddles me and I hold onto one of his tentacles and look around at this apartment room. It's been good to have a room all to myself and in one place for moons at a time. I liked all the travelling but it was hard making new friends all the time, and just for a bit, until we had to run away again.

This one... this change that he has to tell me about is different. He tried to leave me with Ailadas before and I changed his mind, but this time I don't think I'll be able to. Indispensible Bear's eyes twinkle in the light across the room and Kefas Bear is next to him, ready to his hand... kind of like Muunas and Aras I guess, Gian would say they were 'metaphors', something that stands for something else. But I say another prayer to Them because I'm thinking about them a lot since the Ten Tens.

Next to the bears are my *daiyanal.* I got more than one because they live in groups and one would be lonely by herself. And I kinda quit getting stuffed animals when Jiaklem wanted to come with us. I pull all the stuffed animals onto my bed and sit down with them all, Jia in the middle holding on to them at the same time. I address them all solemnly. "Troops, something is in the wind." That's the kind of thing that Mil Toras Jenas, *Aitzas*, the Bold says, in the plays and in the stories. "We have a problem. Our brother has or is going to do something stupid. So stupid that Gannara is staring after him with puppy-dog sad eyes and sniffling sometimes. He's getting rid of things and saying goodbye to people... he even pretended to be Sinimas yesterday to say goodbye to Sera Eren and she actually hugged him like she knew he wasn't just going out of the city for a visit."

Jia lets go the stuffies and comes onto my lap and I cuddle him, gently because I'm getting bigger fast and need to be careful. I can see my first threshold coming. It's a long long long way away but I can see it like a horizon when you're standing on a boat deck. "I bet... I bet he's going to talk to the Imperator. Who's a good guy but he's worried that he's going to get locked up or killed because the law says he has to. Because we're Aans and the Aans were thrown down when father... the fat guy... did everything wrong and hurt Arko."

"Ili?" It's Minis in the door. "I heard part of that... may I come in... or did you want dinner first?"

"I wanna talk and get it over with. I'm not hungry. You're gonna do something dumb aren't you?"

"Not dumb, Ili." He comes in and sits down and puts his arm around my shoulders. I like that.

"You're going to go talk to Ch'venga and fix it so we don't need to keep running and hiding anymore?" He stares at me, blinking. "I'm not stupid. But you're scared, right?"

"Yes, I'm scared," he admits at last. "I'm scared that Arko is going to want me dead and you too. I'm scared that Chevenga won't be able to save us."

"Then why do it?" I ask him. "Why risk it?"

"Well." He takes a deep breath. "You know about how to tell who as power and responsibility?"

"Yeah. Like you had Ili's Donkey say. If you can do something about a hurt or a wrong, you SHOULD. If you want the Gods to love you more, you must do the right thing, even if it hurts.... oh." He's nodding. "But you aren't doing anything wrong or making anybody hurt."

My bedroom is dim. I don't have any lamps in there usually for fear of fire. The window is open and there's a little breeze, like usual this time of day. It's warm and the air is a little thick and kinda sweet from the tree flowers and a little skunky from people's alcohol stoves.

"Suppose we stay in hiding, Ili until we are old and gray and never have children... and somebody like a kid of Ice Eyes... or a kid of his... comes and says 'I'm Third Minis! Or I'm 22nd Ilesias Aan! What would happen?"

That's easy. "There would be a lot of fighting. The Yeolis and the rest of Arko would fight back."

"So do we have the power to stop that threat?" I turn my head and hide my face in his side. I don't want to answer that.

"But you're going to go by yourself, to talk to Ch'venga." He nods. I can feel it and he signs chalk like Uncle Gan does.

"Gannara is going to come with me and wait outside. He says he can't let me go alone."

"GOOD FOR HIM!" I grab Jia and say 'sorry... sorry, Jiaklem... shh it's all right. I'm sorry I yelled. I don't think you should go alone and I'm too little. You're going to take me to Ailadas aren't you?"

"And if we're very lucky you'll be able to take his name and grow up as Ilesias Koren and no one but the Marble Palace will know that but they'll know so no one can steal your bloodline and hurt Arko with it."

I have two big fat tears roll down my cheeks but I don't want to wipe them or sniffle because then Minis, the big old poop, would know I'm crying. I take a deep Haian-type breath instead. "You're talking like I'm not going to see you again, Minis, not ever never never. I hate that."

"I have to prepare," he says, kissing the top of my head and giving me a handkerchief even if I haven't let on I was being a big baby. "I'm fairly sure everything will be all right, Ili... I just... I want to be as sure as I can be. They caught Joras Mahid, right after the Ten Tens."

"Oh *kyash*! They're still looking for us too!"

He pokes my cheek gently with one finger. "Now who has been teaching my tender little brother such language? But you're right. Even with less money and hopefully dwindling resources they are dangerous. I'll be able to help the Imperator -- the rightful Imperator of Arko catch them."

I let go Jia and fling both my arms around Minis. It's getting dark now and the lamplighters are calling from the street below. I can hear the tree outside whisper against the wall and windows. My window lets it all in. The music from the cantina on the corner is really quiet and the sound of people talking and laughing, the clinking of bottles and dishes but we can hear that too.

"The city sounds so... quiet." I say. I don't know what else to say. I don't want him to do this. I don't want to never see him again. *Hey, Ten Gods, it's Ilesias Tathanas Kurkas Joras Aan here. Can you do something to keep my brother safe? You're Gods. He's doing the right thing even if it hurts so can You reward him instead of kicking his teeth in like Rinas threatened to try and do with me last week? Please and Thank You. Since we know You're there... we saw You at the Temple. I trust You.* "It's that peace I want to help preserve Ili."

"I know. So I'll just be good tomorrow and I'm starting to pray to the Gods; since They can fix everything." He goes really really still. "This isn't goodbye or goodby forever, this is just until the Gods can fix it."

He takes a deep breath and I can't see his face in the dark. "From the lips of the innocent, shall true wisdom fall," he quotes from Selinae's Book. "And when all seems lost, the light will come again and songs of joy shall replace tears."

46

____

AUDIENCE

I looked at four campaign posters for the *Vodai* that would give Arko an Arkan Imperator again, just as Chevenga had promised. Kallijas Itrean, Mil Torii Itzan, Adamas Kallen and Kin Immen Kazien... all pinch-faced, old guard *Aitzas*, except for Kallijas who was the best of the lot, elevated and honourable. I hoped that people would have sense and vote for him rather than be conservative and vote for one of the others. The posters were all lined up outside the new Arkan Assembly Chamber; that had been the Crystal Throneroom. Gannara and I were a trifle early for my audience and I so wanted to slip into the new gallery and watch them deliberating. But that was my fear and urge to miss this audience so I turned resolutely away and went to the proper desk to begin the process of seeing Chevenga.

We were asked to wait in the Ruby waiting room. I expected the whole security searches to begin shortly, but had nothing to hide. We were with a half a hundred others in the room, two delegations and several small groups to go before my audience. Even as we stood and looked at the artworks in the room, keeping to ourselves and our own thoughts a servant brought up fresh water glasses and removed all the soiled ones onto his tray on wheels. Another servant placed a small platter of snacks on another table.

An old custom revived. Father never offered those begging audience refreshment of any kind. It cut down the number of people willing, or able, to wait beads to see him.

The first delegation was called away and several more people arrived. I stood with Gannara next to the red glass fountain and realized that the Gods had granted my wish. I had a red-haired Yeoli for a friend, like Manas the Wolf had been Chevenga's. I studied Gan as if I'd never seen him before, every line of his face, the curl in front of one ear. My friend, my brother. He'd gotten rid of the tiger stripes and his whole head was a dark mahogany red, ringlets cascading half way down his back.

He turned and caught me looking, and smiled at me. I smiled back. It was unreal. I didn't feel real inside my own skin. I had an awkward moment when I reached out and laid a hand on the gilt wood of the mantelpiece and even through my gloves my fingers recognized a chip I'd carved out of it when I lived here. In the repairs after the sack, they must have just gilded right over it, but the shape was still there, hidden under-neath. I took a deep breath and tried to steady myself, my current self overlaid over my childhood self, like a drop of water; a bubble about to burst through the skin of a bowl of water and vanish into it.

"Minakas Akam," the servant called and Gan came with me.

"M' friend'd like tah wait for me, if 's permitted..." I said to the servant.

"Of course."

Such niceties had not been 'of course' in my father's court. I can't even indulge myself putting distance between him and I any longer. My father. I am not even Minakas Akam any longer. Just as I shed Sinimas Akam so do I peel away layers of concealment to become Minis Aan once more. The masque is loosened with great difficulty. I liked being Minakas too. He could write what he wanted and the editor could tell him no, if he didn't like it or couldn't use it. Or it could be published in the Pages.

The servant led us up to the stairs to the Highest Office complex in the Marble Palace. Oh. I was going to be seen in that overwhelming little room. How appropriate. But as we were escorted up, higher and higher inside the cliff, it felt a little like a weight was coming off my shoulders.

It was all going to be out of my hands soon. I was going to do what I could, to the best of my strength, and trust that it would be enough. There was a stillness growing in me, a solid feeling of 'yes, this is correct', a vast quietness looming. After all the strain and pain and failing around and running, it was as if the High Office was the finish line in an enormous life and death game. It would be the point where, as if I had been holding my breath for something to happen, I could at long last exhale.

The vast staircase, with a spiral ramp next to it, began as plain white marble, with a line of gold along ever stair-tread, each one growing incrementally wider until the top ten appeared to be solid gold. Everything up here was either white or gold or glass. Even the white marble had gold veins running through it. Sun-slits and sun tunnels brought eye-blinding shafts of light in to illuminate gold-veined glass statues.

The desks here were spindly, light and almost vanished into the ornate backgrounds but the people working them now were dressed like Yeoli bureaucrats as well as the traditional white and gold uniforms on the Arkans.

The guards were not ornamental at all, mostly Arkans, but more Yeolis as we got higher and closer to the Imperator, the steel grey of well-used armour was more common than fancy red and gold filigree.

The other strangeness was that they didn't bother stripping me down to my skin to check for weapons and I realized it was because Chevenga would know anyway, if I were carrying something concealed. Which I wasn't. Neither of us were. A *dekinas* said the cleansing prayer over my head and touched my forehead with a dab of holy oil, scented with bitter myrrh and sweet olibanum, one used for funerals and one for weddings. One for if my audience went badly, one for if my audience went well.

They let Gannara have a seat at the Glass Bridge waiting room for me to come back and he touched my shoulder as I turned to the guard at the double, frosted glass door. I smiled at Gan and stepped out upon the Glass Bridge with a dozen other people coming and going.

The Bridge was the final step before one got to the Imperator's welcomist, right at the end, and the office itself. It was an enormous glass tube leading from the door in the cliff, to the Highest Office itself. The cliff fell away, straight down to the roof of the Marble Palace a double ten manheights below. Father had always laughed to see people struggle to cross it. To reach him they had to master their fear of falling and step out onto the clear glass, or close their eyes and be led by a slave.

Now I stood on one of a pair golden carpet runners, with a wide clear space between. People would walk to the Office on the one and from on the other, without fighting their fear of falling the whole way. A humane thing to do for people. I noticed *faib* skate marks on the path between the carpets, not yet polished away, so they must have been put there just today.

The Bridge was not horizontal, but arched up to the High Office so one must climb, and even with three or four people in the Bridge with me, I felt very alone. I clutched the brown paper-wrapped Imperial Book to my chest and climbed to the welcomist's desk. It was the same Yeoli who had booked my appointment moons ago.

"Ah, there you are," he said in equal to equal Arkan. "Perfectly on time. Go on in, he's expecting you."

I touched the bald head of the little statue of the Lukitzas, next to the solid gold door, for luck, dropped a gold chain into his bowl. It wasn't as if I'd need it for anything else after this two tenths. It was likely that in a single tenth bead I would either be locked up waiting to be executed, or locked up for the rest of my life.

The Highest Office... the littlest one, of a string of offices gradually increasing size along the cliff face, was a gold-lined bubble in the stone, with a vast mirror on the inside wall... behind which I knew where the watchers with their fingers on the triggers of scores of hidden spring-darts in the walls and furniture. The outside wall was clear glass, floor to ceiling, with a vast panoramic view of the whole city and part of the woods and lake as well.

In between the two, Chevenga sat, at a desk so gilded it looked as golden as the rest of the room. I caught a flash of his dark eyes over a white and gold shirt as I went down in the prostration, putting my nose on the floor as gracefully as I could. But I barely had time to get down before he had me up again with a soft '*gehit*'. I smiled at him as I got up and laid the book on the desk in front of him. "Have a seat, how are you Minakas? You've not been writing so much since you came to dinner."

I sat down. "Ay'm fine, You Whose Wit is the Wisdom of th' World, sor... ah... Imperator –" He waved impatiently at that.

"—it's Chevenga, you know me well enough."

"Thenk yeh, Ch'venga." Just as at the dinner, I found myself pronouncing it the way Gannara did. He looked well, but a lot more tired than when I had last seen Him this closely. I found I wanted to hug Him and send Him to bed. Or perhaps just fling myself on the ground again, bawling, in awe and terror since He'd been touched by the Gods but I did neither. "I brought along a gift fer 't exalted... ah... yeh..." I shifted from one up to equal to equal though I didn't want to. "Beggin' yer pardon fer 't impropriety..." I took off my gloves and opened the Imperial book and ran my hands over a number of the paper pages, back and forth to prove they hadn't been poisoned.

"Oh, you don't need to do that, Minakas!" He looked bemused but curious, his eyes bright. I had to smile. He trusted me. *Oh, Chevenga, you should never ever trust me. And I'm sorry that you probably never will again, for I've lied to you. I've lied to you and your whole family.*

"If not fer yeh, sor... Ch'evenga... then fer yer... ah... watch's peace 'o mind..." I tipped my head at the huge mirror, hiding the trap-booth, just for a moment. I slipped my gloves back on and pushed the book across the desk towards him. "'t paper cover tears off."

Looking completely intrigued he pulled it towards himself and the brown paper ripped off to show the gold cover with the Aan Sunburst over the Arkan boat upon it. His bare fingers, with the gold seals glittering on his hands, touched it and the book sang, or cried out in recognition. He leapt back as far as he could in his seat and I jumped back in mine just as far. His face was frozen with shock and I heard the hiss and snap and felt the sting of a dart standing in the big muscle of my upper arm. I could see the vaning out of the corner of my eye.

He wouldn't still have the deadly ones? Would he? Oh sh... That was my fading thought even as I saw his hand come up to signal something but I couldn't make out what it was and Chevenga grew very small very fast as if he were retreating down a long black tunnel that closed in on his face. "Mina..." and then nothing at all.

47

———

I WASN'T DEAD

Headache. That was a good thing. It meant I wasn't dead. I wasn't in any other distress so I wasn't in full restraint. Full restraint was, in and of itself, distressing. It was arms, legs and head restrained, even fingers strapped down. A chest strap and an abdominal strap to restrict one's breathing. A blindfold. A knife gag. Ears sealed with wax and felt. One would be naked and impaled upon a thin rod in one's anus and for men a wire inserted. 2nd Amitzas had illustrated it for me once, as one of his training sessions. I didn't like to remember that.

I wasn't naked. I lay, on my back, on something soft. *Why am I not in full restraint? I suppose I'm not considered that dangerous.* I heard the click of a bead clock. I wasn't on a table downstairs that was good. I opened my eyes to find I was in a room of the Marble Palace that I didn't immediately recognize and realized it must be an antechamber to the High Office itself or a room back across the Glass Bridge. I hoped not that. If Gan had seen me carried out, he'd be beside himself with worry.

Chevenga sat beside me, just turning away from the clock that showed I'd only been unconscious a tenth or so a bit more than half my audience. How was that possible? To recover from being stunned it usually took a half bead or so depending on the person. I let my breath out, thankful I would still be able to carry out my plan but I didn't say anything at first, suddenly not sure what to say.

I looked down at the glasses someone -- perhaps Chevenga himself -- had placed in my hand and didn't bother putting them on again. I really didn't have much time left, in the audience or otherwise. I'd been planning just to tell him after he looked at the Book but that plan was long gone.

"Good, you're awake. It was my fault for getting you stunned. I've had my healer make up an antagonist, and since you were stunned because I was slow I figured you deserved some. Here, take this, under the tongue. The headache will get a lot worse for a moment, then go away." He offered me the remedy from His own hand.

"Thank you." I said, equal to equal, using my own accent, that I had not used since I'd left the Mahid two years ago. It felt strange, but good at the same time, as if my tongue had craved it, even as I forced it to accept a different caste's cadence and rhythms. I took the remedy and winced my eyes closed at the bolt of pain lightning behind my eyes. But like all correct Haian remedies, it worked as well as he'd said. "I hope you didn't have me carried out somewhere across the Bridge. I have a Yeoli friend waiting for me in that waiting room and he'd worried and upset if he saw that." I found my hand tugging at my hair on one side as if I could pull it to my mouth, as I had before 2nd Amitzas broke me of the habit.

"A Yeoli friend waiting here with you?" He asked, intrigued.

"One of my best friends in the world, his name is Gannara Melachiya." He signed chalk and his hand hesitated a moment as I sat up, still looking at him straight.

"Your friend is named Melachiya?--" And that was the moment when he knew me. He blinked, as I pulled my knees up, wrapping my arms around them.

"Minis!" he said. I held my breath and waited.

Then he said the last thing I would have expected. "You've... *changed!*"

I had to laugh. It startled me enough that it hurt coming out. "Yes. A bit."

"Gannara..." He glanced at the cascade of tiny beads that marked out hundredth beads, flowing like sand into the container below. "I'll have him shown in... Don't worry. Neither of you have anything to fear from me. I got your letter. All your letters."

I had to close my eyes. He'd gotten my letter, from Haiu Menshir that enumerated what I had done to him. And he didn't have me hustled off into full restraint? He was so much saner an Imperator than the fat gu... my father. I opened my eyes again, trying to face what might be coming.

He raised his voice. "Krero? Could you..." the guard captain was in before he'd finished calling. *Here it comes. I'm ready, just breathe and submit...* He wouldn't need a full guard to haul me off to a cell. The Yeoli captain might have been in the trap-booth himself for the odd look he gave me. But Chevenga wasn't telling him anything. "Yes, Krero. There's a Yeoli boy – where did you say?"

"In the waiting room on the other side of the Bridge."

"Yes. His name is Gannara; could you fetch him here, please?" *You have nothing to fear from me,* he'd said. Another glance at the clock. "And on the way by could you have Binchera send for Skorsas, please?" *He's not called the guard captain to haul me off? What?*

"Certainly, Cheng." In that familiar Yeoli way, he signed chalk and left.

There wasn't much time left in my audience. Already the next supplicant would be making their way to the Bridge. "I... Ch'venga..." I was surprised at how choked up I was. "I'm giving myself into your hands, you realize this?"

"Yes, I realize. Minis... don't worry. You know me. Don't worry about it. Ah, here's Krero again."

Gan's eyes were wide and apprehensive and he relaxed a little when he saw me, sitting free on a chaise, next to Chevenga. His reaction... trained by Mahid... tried to put him on his face on the floor but he'd healed enough that he stiffened before that happened, took a deep breath and nodded at the Imperator. "*Semanakraseye,*" he said.

"Here I am, Jewel of the World," Skorsas said coming in on Krero and Gan's heels.

"Good, Skorsas, thank you Krero, I've got it now." And Krero, though curious as to what was really going on, left. "I have a couple of guests for you to look after, Minakas Akam and Gannara Melachiya, if you would, Skorsas. I have another audience in less than two clicks."

"Certainly, Jewel, I'll see to it." I slid my gloves and spectacles back on while all this was going on. Chevenga touched my shoulder and Gan's on the way by. He was on *faib* skates I saw as he rose and glided to the door.

"I'll see you two tonight, after my day is over," he said and pushed off, hard.

"So, would you like to see some of the Marble Palace before I show you to your rooms?" the Imperial Chamberlain asked, brightly.

48

PAST SELINAE'S DAUGHTERS

I blinked at him and Gannara said, just as brightly. "Oh, we would *love* to see the Marble Palace, wouldn't we?"

"Certainly, then. If those ones will follow...Oh," said Skorsas. "Hello, Minakas, my apologies, it took me a moment. How are you? You'll be staying at the Marble Palace, then." It wasn't a question.

"Oh, yeha. Thenk yah, sor." *I didn't want to put the fessas accent on any more. But he knows me as fessas and Chevenga introduced us that way. What in Hayel is going on? He hasn't said, exactly, what he's going to do with me now that I've turned myself in. Blast the Book for recognizing the true Imperator! It messed up everything!*

"Let's get you over the Bridge, then, and I can show you a number of things on the way down to the Guest wing..." he was addressing me only a trifle more formally than when he met me at the Hearthstone Independent.

That would still be the Fiparmukinian *level.* That was between the Imperial sections and the Administrative sections of the Palace, on the other side of the Audience -- now Assembly -- Chamber. I didn't say anything that would let on that I knew it at all. When I had lived here, father had told me to stay out of there, mostly, so as not to bother his guests, though he had few. There was always some supplicant *Aitzas* lordling from out Empire, to overawe. But I was grateful I wasn't as familiar with it as most of the rest of the Marble Ant pile.

Skorsas was friendly, asking about how my writing was progressing and I asked him about the household back in Yeola-e, all very calm. I had to keep telling myself to be appropriately overwhelmed when he showed us this or that incredible artwork, or commented on what kinds of fantastic toys the children had found down that particular corridor.

At one point I had to stop and clamp my teeth together. I'd read that 'Selinae's Daughters', by Durumas in the Past Age, had been damaged in the sack and could not be repaired, but that what remained was still so beautiful that it was left in place... I had to clench my eyes shut when we rounded the corner and were confronted with it. The ten dancing young women in mid-dance or play, the sculptor had never said, all had their heads missing and many of the graceful arms also gone.

"There is a commission trying to find a sculptor who might be able to piece the glass back together," Skorsas said, with sympathy. "The joins would show and the missing heads... well, there isn't a sculptor in Arko who wouldn't love to try and cast replacements -- even to copy Durumas's work."

"That's... awful!" I said, horrified. "Each face... they all had their own expressions they weren't just generic girls." *Oops. That sounds like I've seen it.* "M' da tol' me... he saw 't once he said and were struck by how much that 'un..." I pointed at one figure, "...minded him of ma when she were a girl."

Chevenga hadn't introduced me as Minis to Skorsas... nor to his guard captain. He obviously didn't wish to trumpet to the world that I had been caught. My covering story was thin but I couldn't make any mistakes. Skorsas looked over at the figure I'd indicated, shrugged and led us on. We should be properly overwhelmed just by being conducted by the Imperial Chamberlain himself anyway. I shut up and let Gannara ask more questions, just as if he'd not been tortured in these halls.

We were going to be put up in the Azure Suite, a set of rooms done in plain marble and simple blues and whites, with minimal gilding. It was a bureaucrat's rooms and I was tremendously relieved that it wasn't anything more elaborate. "I'll send a servant around to show you to Dinner... the High Court... you probably won't see the Imperator, I'm afraid. I'll have to put you at the other end of the hall."

"Oh, sor... that's mor'n we thought, thenk yeh sor."

"It's a less formal court than anything under the Aan," Skorsas went on blithely. "So those ones needn't fear being underdressed." He was speaking down to us, but only barely. "There will be a servant along with some light refreshment for you, shortly. The Lesser Baths will be available to you, should you wish to refresh yourselves. Just ask a servant and they will show you."

"Thenk yeh, sor. It's all so much."

He smiled at me. "Don't worry about being a little shocked by the opulence. Everyone is."

I managed to smile back. "This 'un'll keep it 'n mind, 'onoured sor." And finally a door was shut and we were by ourselves. Gannara grabbed my elbow and dragged me over to the inner room, between one of the beds and a window, the place least likely to have any kind of way of over-hearing us.

"So what in Hayel *happened*?! Does He know? Are you a prisoner? They're still calling you Minakas... what's going on!"

"He knows me. The Imperial Book knows Him... it did something weird... never mind... I got stun-darted and he got me woken up fast and then he recognized me... he knows who you are too. He wants me to stay here. He said Ili was safe and fine where he was... and we... I specifically don't have to worry about any harm from Him. So there."

He stared into my eyes for a long moment then dramatically flung himself back onto the bed with a 'pflump', hands outflung. "The boy does it again! You're all right. How do you DO shen like this and keep coming out all right?"

"I have good friends." I snorted. "Gan, he wants me to keep it quiet that I'm not just Minakas Akam, it seems."

He raised his head. "That makes sense."

"You don't have to stay if you don't want to –"

"—fik that," he snapped, interrupting. "I was thinking about that, and kind of planning what to do if they locked you up here." *Best case,* I thought. "I figured I'd help you get our stuff from the apartment... we're paid up through the end of the moon and give notice. Then when we know exactly what's going on with you... probably in rooms next to the main library, right?" I nodded. That would be a good place to live out the rest of my life. There were worse prisons. "And then I go and show up to my parents... that would be fair... and if they're grossed out—"

I had to interrupt. "—They won't be grossed out! Stop that. If I can't beat up on myself for what my father did to me, then neither can you beat up on yourself for what they did to you either!" He waved a flapping hand from the bed, not even pulling his forearm off his eyes.

"Yeah, yeah, all right. But I can always come back here with you."

"Gan... my brother..." I sat down next to him on the bed. "If I have anything to say about it... I'd love to have you stay with me... especially if you need to."

"Phf. We're talking like a couple of lugubrious old farts on a Fire-Fountain bench. I hope those 'minor refreshments' the Chamberlain was talking about have some beef rolls. I'm starving." As if by magic the servants' knock came almost on the heels of his words.

The two men wheeled in a tray with enough food on it to feed a small army, or two teenaged boys, whisked the covers off and disappeared, as silently an efficiently as they always had. War, conquest, election, the Marble Palace servants just seemed to carry on.

"I couldn't swallow any lunch myself," I said, grabbing a plate. "There are rolls. I'll arm wrestle you for your share."

Gan was serving himself from the other side, spooning noodles in cream sauce with green garnish into a bowl. "Sure, my granny could beat you arm wrestling!" I had an odd flash to my father refusing to arm wrestle Chevenga for his freedom and shook it off.

"Well, yeah, she's probably captain of the Asinanai guard!"

"Idya, mammoka diddler."

"Dog sucker, idle, flea-bitten Masker tickler."

And we stopped our mouths with the astonishing food. I had forgotten. It was as if 2nd Amitzas and his Mahid had burned the memory out of me with what I had eaten since.

49

FIRST DAY IN CUSTODY

After we ate, I called a servant to show us to the Lesser Baths. Thankfully there was no one else in there and I hid my shaking in the water and when the entire mob of Chevenga's children, and family descended, the whole group I had met at the Hearthstone, they all had to greet me and ask how I was and tell me about what pets they'd had to leave behind.

"Hey! Minakas! Hi!" It was one of the girls who recognized me first, Kila.

"H'llo serina." She giggled.

"I'm not a serina!" She said and I smiled back at her.

"Ah, t' serina wants me t' call 'er by name like 'er da?"

"Yeah! Hey everbody, Minakas is here!"

I managed to sort out who was who and introduced Gan as a friend of mine and we sat for a good part of the afternoon. I'd wanted to flee but found myself reluctant to when so warmly welcomed. They'd brought the parrots along and the one seemed to remember me enough to try and land on my head again. It was like having a huge family, even if they were just friends and very pleased to see me again. I wondered why, exactly. I had ony been at their father's house for the one evening.

After they were all called away by their teachers and care-givers and Gan and I went back to our suite. I took care to get us 'lost' once and have to ask, I also asked a servant if there were a Library I might be permitted access to, and he went off to get permissions from someone, probably Skorsas.

After sitting at a lower table in the Dining Hall we received permissions to the Main Library and were allowed to fetch two volumes with us to the suite.

Gan had a book on merchant ship design and I, of course, had a book on the period I was writing about, Notyere and Tathanas, though it was not about politics per-se but about the language shift in Arko around that time, though it could not drift too far from the Temple language.

The soft knock was all that came by way of announcement. It was Chevenga. He came in, loosening the formal ties of his overtunic, dropping it away from his neck as if to let himself breathe.

As I backed up from the door where I'd let him in, I went to get down in the prostration and he blocked me. "Gehit. I know. You want to do it. Look, Minis, let's take that first prostration you did for me in the office as a blanket one, all right?"

I nodded and signed chalk, still retreating before him. He came in and sank down in one of the overstuffed chairs. "Sit down, let's talk," he said. "I never thought I'd get done today." He had the Imperial book clutched to his chest as if he'd never put it down all day.

Gannara sat, calmly enough, and I sank as though folded. I had calmed over the course of the day, with food and bathing but now it all came roaring back. I pulled off my spectacles and gloves, that I had worn to the door, dropping them upon the table next to us.

"First of all," he said quietly. "Minis, I did…" he looked at Gannara, then at me. I guessed why he paused so I took a breath and said, "If it's about the letter to you, Gannara knows. He helped me write it."

Gan nodded, reached over to pat me on the shoulder. "This idya keeps thinking he's evil, *semanakraseye*."

"Call me Chevenga, please. Gannara I'm so glad to see you safe." He held out his hands to Gan who took them.

"I'm all right, Ch'venga. Really." I wasn't surprised at all when he got pulled into a hug. That made me feel much better right then. Chevenga would have wanted to find us, just to make sure of Gan's safety.

"I'm sure you are. And I hear you about -- Minis." There was a twinkle in his eye as if he considered repeating what Gan had called me, affectionately, and thought better of it. Gan settled back into his own chair, looking much happier about the whole arrangement. But my stomach clenched hard though I tried to sit calmly. I had told him what I had done and I was still surprised that he wasn't locking me up more than he had. After all, I was an admitted rapist.

"I don't remember it, Minis and my healer tells me I might never. Which could be a good thing." His gaze on me was perfectly steady. Steady enough to see how heart-breakingly tired he was and I cursed myself inwardly for adding to it. "But you were a child and thus not responsible."

As he paused, Gan hissed in my ear, but loud enough for Chevenga to hear. 'See, I TOLD you so!"

"And I don't blame you for it, or hate you, or want to hurt you or despise you." He held out his hands to me. "You're old to have a father-in spirit but if you want it, it's still yours."

"*Told you!*" Gan was smiling, but I couldn't take Chevenga's hands. If I touched him I'd fall apart. All that emotion. Everything I'd fought so hard to keep inside, the unseemly tears, would all come pouring out and the last thing Chevenga needed was to be looking after me.

"I am... still a boy... only second threshold..." that was true, and as a child I should still be young enough to accept some comfort... but I was the last person who deserved it from him. He opened his arms to me, offering to hug me as I sat shaking, wondering if I dared let myself touch his hand.

He leaned forward, grasped my one wrist nearest him and pulled me in. I lost all control and cried like child, like a baby for far too long. When I hiccupped and managed to gain some control back he brushed my hair out of my eyes and said. "I know... I can guess some of the things that Kurkas said and did when he made you hurt me. But you were a child and he the adult. You see me as the victim and yourself as the viola-tor, correct?

I nodded, gradually realizing that I was getting snot and tears all over his priceless white and gold shirt. "That's the truth. That's as it was."

"That's the truth Kurkas created. A violator has choice. Did you?"

The tears threatened my control again as I remembered trying to say I would rather not. But I had a choice. I could have chosen to give up my position as Heir. "I did."

He snorted. "You were a child and even if you tried to say no I think your father would have come up with a threat that would force you to do what he wanted. And if you'd still refused would he not have had you seized and held still? No choice at all."

I had to be honest here. That was the only way I could expiate my sins. "I... took pleasure in it, Che'venga."

Another laugh, not bitter exactly, but more knowing. "And you trained by Mahid! You know how they do it. Force pleasure and then convince you that because it felt good you were responsible? I was forced to feel pleasure more times than I remember, and often linked with other ugly things. Remember, the responsibility lies with the one force pleasure on you against your will. It doesn't change who you are any more than a stripe of a whip across your back makes you a different person. Even if he spoke as if it was by your will... that was the lie."

His hands on my shoulders were as warm as they ever were. He certainly believed this and Gannara was nodding, wanting to chime in with his opinion. Two sets of brown eyes that could be as alike as brothers, united in thinking I was not a bad person; and the one God-touched. I was required to believe Him. But I couldn't, quite yet. I'd have to think about it.

"So tell me what you know about the true Imperial Book." He laid it upon the table. "This is keeping me up for good reason and is without a doubt important Imperial work."

50

THE IMPERIAL BOOK

HE RAN HIS FINGERS REVERENTLY OVER THE GOLD COVER. TRULY IT was less a book and more of a gold box, with pages added into it somehow. "How old is this book, do you know?"

I shrugged. "One story my father told me was that it was the Imperial Book from the beginning when we were a small village here. From when a star fell and gouged out the Lake. Another time he told me it was from before we were even fallen from the stars. There's half a dozen different versions of how old it is."

My fingers tingled and I rubbed the tips of them together. It was so strange that this book I had kept so close to me, so silent was so uncanny... I had just treated it like any other ancient and carefully kept book... what else was it capable of? It made my neck prickle and I was thrilled and frightened of something I thought would just sit on my bookshelf my whole life.

"So that was at the beginning of all the ages?"

I could only shrug. I didn't know. I had not been taught. It was a secret that my father never passed on, though I was beginning to suspect he should have. "We were supposedly cast out of Selestialis that way. A fiery star. Two thousand one hundred eighteen years ago."

He pursed his lips in a soundless whistle and opened the Book to the first page. It didn't make that warble again, content to be as silent as any other book. "Father showed me the first twelve pages once or twice. In his hands they were alive, some of them. For me, they were always blank and silent."

"Silent? He looked up at me. "So you've heard this book make noises before?"

"Sometimes you could hear unearthly things from the Highest Office. People mostly stayed away because they were afraid."

"There is something here but it moves too fast to see," he said. The first page, that for me had been blank, and that father had never shown me, was *flickering*. It seemed as though it was the fleeting shapes of letters, machine printed letters, but no words that I could make out, and some of the shapes were just wrong. And they flowed by so fast I wasn't even sure they were letters at all. Chevenga touched the page all over but the flow never even slowed down.

The second and third and fourth pages were blank, looking like plain white paper. The sheet holding pages three and four had a bottom corner torn away. The fifth page, when he touched it made a sound. All three of us jumped, and as he whipped his hand away it went silent again. The three of us stared at each other, then at the book again.

He reached out his hand and as he touched it -- sound poured out from under his finger. A woman's voice, singing in a language I had never heard. His finger trembled a bit but didn't move and the song continued till it ended naturally the strange instruments clearly signaling an end. Then it began again.

He moved his finger and a man's voice, again in a strange tongue said something urgent. A woman's voice, in a different sounding language, almost spoken through the nose. Another man, speaking in a harsh bark.

Every finger touch started a different sound. "Can you make anything out? I can't."

"No. It's people but I don't know the tongue or tongues. None have spoken in a language I know." Gan just signed charcoal.

We jumped again as a sound like a thunderclap rumbled through the room. He put his finger back on the spot where the woman sang and listened to the whole song once more. "She's singing to us from two thousand years ago. She sounds like an angel, a messenger from Selestialis."

He tried various fingers to see if that changed the sounds, but it seemed to be the spot on the page, not which finger was used to press it. He found a type of music -- at least I thought it was music -- wild and rhythmic yet I wasn't sure there was a melody in it. It was just very strange. He held that one to the end as well, eyes intent as if there were images to go with the sounds, but the page was stubbornly blank.

His finger slid over and suddenly there were animal noises the like of which I'd never heard before mixed in with wolf howls, a low wailing noise and some odd creaking noises that Gan suddenly recognized. "Those are *daiyanal* sounds!" He said.

"Minis you try it with your finger," he said. I put out one trembling finger to this uncanny book and laid it upon the page and nothing happened, even with Chevenga's fingers upon it. It did not respond to me.

"It has to be me. I wonder how it knows? I don't think there's a person alive who knows."

I had this thing. this almost alive thing next to me, under my pillow, for years. The skin on my back and the back of my neck crawled.

His finger came down in a different place and another snatch of music began, this time measured and grand. "It knows you. That's why it sang. It recognized you as Imperator." I wrapped my arms around my middle.

"How can a book know *me?*"

"I don't know."

He got an 'I have an odd thought' look on his face. "Unless... Minis, Gannara", you didn't see me do this." He took off the Imperial seals, to my gasp.

He laid his hand upon the page and it responded, as if he were wearing the seals. "I thought it might be the seals themselves." He flipped the book to the first page and just dropped the seals upon it and again the book did nothing... even the flicker on the first sheet was gone.

He touched the book again, to pick up the seals and the page flickered on. "It's not even who wears the seals... it's *me.*" He slid the seals safely back upon his hands, took a deep breath and sat back to take a drink of water that Gannara offered him. "Thank you," he said absently.

"Your father had it... you said it did these things then?"

I nodded and signed chalk. "He showed me some of the pages. Not the noise page. You'll want to be careful of the image on the twelfth page -- the last of the magical pages. It's a picture of him, on Ascension." He signed chalk absently, still thinking hard. "In his hands, it was alive like this," I said. "In mine, it was blank and silent." *Somehow it knew I was not to be Imperator. It knew the rightful man.* How much more proof did I need from the Gods?

"It's whoever is Imperator... and it somehow knows, even if he's not wearing the seals." He shook his head, absently as if trying to shake an odd idea loose and turned back to the book.

The sixth page was blank except for a black line down the center. He looked very closely at it and gently drew his finger from the middle outward. A flickering black line followed it for the width of a finger and then faded. That sheet had been folded it looked like. So the seventh side was almost blank, with shadows of things as if they were just under the surface of the paper.

When he ran his fingers over they grew larger or smaller and it seemed as though they were trying to come clear but were covered in a pale fog. Colours became more clear in a sort of puddle around his finger but faded when he raised it. Some pictures came clearer at an angle... a tree... a bird... a tower of some kind, burning... a dragonfly big enough for an armoured man to stand next to it? A sunburst?

"It was full once," he said. "Every page. They're broken. I think." He said thoughtfully to us. "No one should ever fold these pages, or tear them."

We both nodded and signed chalk but neither of us said anything. The eight page was blank again. While the ninth was a solid blue from edge to edge and top to bottom. It had what looked like the picture of a Haian sand timer turning over and over again, slowly. A deep male voice asked something, and then there was a silence. The sandtimer turned over again and the voice asked the same. Then again. Then again.

"A sandtimer turning... means time? Passing time?"

"I have no idea," I said. "Should we wait and see if anything else happens?" Chevenga touched the page all over and it didn't change. The sandtimer flipped again and the voice asked its incomprehsible question.

"We can come back to it. I want to go on to other pages." The tenth page was an image of the Marble Palace, but only the Steel Gate and Presentation Balcony and the building immediately behind it up to the cliff. There was no wing with the Black door nor wing with the White door. No Administrative office section. No Heir's wing. There were no gold-topped turrets and the bare, unadorned skeleton of an iron tower on top was the tallest thing about it. There was no Eagle carved upon the cliff above, no hint of the Glass Bridge or Highest office.

"It looks like the Marble Palace, a long time ago!"

"The oldest section," I said. "Why did someone scribble on the picture and with arrows pointing at things?"

"You know archaic Arkan," Chevenga said, turning to me. "Can you read that?"

I squinted at the scrawled notes. "Hmmm. I think... I think this is something like an old version of 'to gehit', 'to raise or raise up' but I'm not sure."

Chevenga pointed to what looked like a drawing of the dome over the palace, apparently made entirely of smooth glass with an arrow and a single word... "Maybe it means 'to go'?" He looked to me and I had to shrug.

"It looks high, but I can't tell because there's no Eagle on the cliff to judge how big this is."

"We might never know what any of this means, as long as we live... and have to accept that." he touched all over the page but, again, nothing changed.

The eleventh page was a strange picture. It wasn't a picture of anything I recognized, but boxes connected to each other with lines. Some jagged, some straight, some with lines crossing the lines. Some boxes were connected to circles with things written inside... machine shaped letters in a language unfamiliar. Dots. All very regular. The lines were all perfectly horizontal or vertical. And nothing moved on the page no matter what Chevenga did.

"I cannot make head or tail of any of the words. It's older than any version of Arkan that I know. Perhaps someone at the University could figure it out, perhaps even Ailadas might have an idea what some of them may mean. No one had ever known, as far as I knew, what the circles, dots, lines and zig-zags meant. "The last page will be a portrait of my father as I told you. Just to warn you, again."

I could see him set his teeth as he turned the page, went pale and slammed the book shut. I flinched.

51

THE TWELFTH PAGE

"Ai!!!! *Kyash!* Shen!" He stared at me, the white showing all around his irises. "Shen, shen, *kyashin,* shen!" He was pale, and shaking all over, his arms crossed, hugging hard.

"I didn't think it would be so bad... it was him when he ascended." I wanted to reassure him, to touch him but I didn't think it would be a good idea.

Gannara had been looking at the book rather than at Chevenga and he was signing charcoal, shaking his head, no. "Um... No... I don't think it was Kurkas on that page."

Chevenga got up, paced and then sat down again. "This is too odd." The look on his face was the strangest I had ever seen. He opened the book to that page and held it up so Gan and I could see. I gasped in shock. Under the ancient sunburst was a portrait, indeed, but not of my father. It was of Chevenga, looking quizzically off the page as though he were about to burst into questions. He was dressed as he was today, as if the image had been painted the instant I handed him the book, earlier today. It wasn't painted though. Not a 'rendition' but a perfect copy. Every wrinkle in the fabric, no brush strokes, an unearthly perfect copy.

"Oh Muu... oh. Ten." It was like the portrait my father had shown me. He'd been very proud of how calm he'd looked in it. As Chevenga held the book open, his hand pressed onto the bottom of the page and the image began to fade but not to blank. Another face was swimming up out

of the blank white sheet. It was my father; the portrait I had thought was
there. Him, looking thinner, more fit, with none of the signs of poisoning
or dissipation. Aside from the paler, very bright eyes and the birthmark,
he looked enough like what I saw in the mirror to make me swallow my
gorge. "That was the one he showed me." But even as I spoke it was
fading as well. The next face that came up I knew as well. "That's my
grandfather."

Chevenga turned the book so he could see it change, not shifting his
fingers. "They're changing?"

I nodded. I know grandfather from his portrait on the Grand Allee
wall, and from the statue on his tomb." His picture fades and shows
another portrait, another Aan, in the Imperial Robe. "That's great grandfather."

"It's all the Imperators," Chevenga said.   "Working backwards."
Gannara and I hung over his shoulders like Mezem spectators, watching
the ghostly progression. Chevenga was controlling himself with main
will, the two points of red up stark on his face, breathing regularly but I
could tell it was by counting.

The next portrait was an older man and a boy together, "Regent
Idiesas and Imperator Itasas," I said.

"How far back will it go?" he wondered. I wasn't sure if he was just
speaking aloud or to us. His eyes were very bright, fiery almost. "I'd stay
up all night if I had to, for this."

The ninth image had bloody hands and blood smeared on the seals, a
spray of it across his chest. He had blood on his shirt under the Robe,
and Chevenga asked me "Succeeded by assassination?"

I thought hard for a moment. "That would have been the Imperator
Boras Lukas Aan when the Crystal Throne went to a cousin line."

Sometimes the background of these images was the Temple, in others
the Highest office, or the Golden Office, once it was the Imperial
Bedchamber in the progression backwards through time. The Imperial
Robe disappeared somewhere around the sixtieth.

"How long was their average reign?" Chevenga asked quietly as the
picture shifted one to the next.

I blinked and puzzled it through. "Anywhere from an eight-day to
almost seventy years... but the average would be around twenty."

The ninety-eighth Imperator wore a strange suit with a metal ring-
collar... he was bloody and scorched, with hair short as an *okas* yet with a
strangly military air about him. His eyes were haunted.

There were four Imperators in dark blue, with a metal wall behind them, and one wearing some kind of dark and striped tunic, a narrow red strap knotted around his neck, with a gold pin through it that showed the Arko boat. He had a window and green plants behind him. Then Chevenga's picture came back and stayed.

I took a deep breath. "I had very careful instruction in how to care for this book. Now I know why. And why it had to come home to you." Another deep breath. "There is a special place for it in the Highest Office, that only my father could open. Perhaps it will for you, now." I was suddenly aware of Gannara's shoulder next to mine and wanted to cling to him. I didn't move.

There was an odd line of writing below Chevenga's picture. Machine printed but as strange as the words. Chevenga carefully touch his own picture, here and there and the strip along the bottom reacted. The middle when he touched, said something.

"I… wait… were those numbers?" It made sense. The language might change but the numbers might not, at least not so fast. "Can you make it do that again?" He did and the sonorous voice announced again. "A five? No, not five… eight something. I still might be wrong and that might have been an archaic version of a 'four'. Four something eight something, I think."

"A date? A calendar, perhaps?" Chevenga looked even more intrigued if that were possible. He yawned, trying to suppress it.

"It could be I suppose."

Gannara said, "It could be a year… the Haian calender is four thousand nine hundred and eighty this year."

Chevenga moved his hands around the bottom of the page and it began fading back again. To my father, and the voice intoned a similar string of sounds. "There!" I said. I was almost certain of it. "I think that first sound is a 'four' something… perhaps six or sixty. And then… Four again if I'm right. Lets call it nine. Eight. zero… this year. If I'm guessing right. My father ascended in the Haian calendar… Four Nine Thirty-Seven." And the picture of my father held steady as long as Chevenga held the corner of that page. "So… perhaps, an ascension date and a death date?"

"That might be when the Book thinks the Imperators reigned?" I was quivering with… hmm… my urge to find out for lack of a better term, but then I was still under third threshold and had in effect been resting the whole day. The bead clock clicked and Chevenga sat, looking at the book as though he were too tired to even touch one more page. "It can be figured out, later, Ch'venga."

"Hmm?" He truly was so tired he could hardly keep his eyes open. "But how can a book think?"

"I think you should think about that some other time." I felt so guilty that I had had the book… prisoner in a sense, if it could only come 'alive' in the right hands.

"You're right." He reached out and closed the book, leaning his head back against the back of the chair. "So, Minis, where were you? What happened to you after you were hustled out of the city?"

"I can tell you that some other time as well, or write the story for you so you can read it at your own leisure. I'm going to have time. Right now you need to quit working and head for bed."

Gannara laughed. "You two… the poker calling the shovel black! *Semanakras'* Ch'venga… go to bed!"

Chevenga blinked and smiled. "You're right."

"I heard you do nothing but work… maybe you should call it a day? Gannara continued in his usual relentless way.

He cradled the book in his hands, nodding. "I should have a satchel made to carry this with me, in case of fire. I'd give my life to save it from destruction."

I had to nod at that. "I have the silver to wrap it in, like the books in the Temple."

I handed him the packet I had in my pocket and it made a shivering sound as I pulled it out and handed it to him. "This won't tear and is proof against water… father said it was proof against fire but I never had the nerve to test it."

"This is the most valuable thing in the world," he said quietly, sliding it into the envelope and climbing to his feet wearily. "If it were lost we wouldn't even know what we were losing." I had to nod at that. I hadn't even known what I carried, other than an Imperial record.

52

CASE CLOSED

PERISALAS SHEFENKAS PAUSED BY THE IMPERIAL SECRETARY'S DESK. "Good afternoon, I was called to see the Imperator?"

"Oh, yes, Perisalas, just wait one moment and I'll send you both in."

Both? He turned and saw Matthas, in his guise as a minor *fessas* bureaucrat, his gloves clasped primly in his lap, sitting off to one side of the Glass Bridge door. "Oh, hello, Matthas. Nice to see you again."

"Hello, ser." Matthas said. "The rain we had the other day, was certainly unusual."

"Quite."

"Gentlemen, the Imperator will see you now."

The head of Irefas and I together? This could be something big. Perisals thought. There had been no sign of the Spark in Exile or any of his possible alias's at the Gate or the *lefaeti*. Perhaps Joras Mahid had remembered something important?

"Same place, same time... must be for the same reason... any idea what?" Matthas asked softly as they stepped out onto the gold carpet leading to the High Office.

"I theorize that it has something to do with my perview... either the Spark in Exile or renegade Mahid..."

"Makes sense and is more than I know. Thank you."

In the office He Whose Timesense Is the Master Clock of The World waited... "Gehit, gentlemen," he said even as their knees started to bend. "Take seats; I have all of a tenth, and it need only be brief at any rate."

They both sat, murmuring 'Of course, Shefenkas."

"You can close the investigation on the whereabouts of Minis Aan. He's here."

Perisalas paused. His mouth actually fell open for a fraction of a second. *That pissing shennen little fikker*, was almost the first thought that managed to surface in his head. He closed his mouth and blinked several times, as Matthas spoke up. "Oh. Yes. In custody, Shevengas?"

"In effect. Skorsas is hosting him in the Imperial guest section. He turned himself in, and relinquished any claim to the Crystal Throne."

Turned himself in? Turned himself IN? "The only question that remains open," the Imperator continued. "Is where his Mahid are, and he's agreed to help us catch them. He and they had an agreed-upon method of finding each other if they got separated, and he's said he'll use it to aid us."

"I... we.... ummm... Of... course..." It wasn't like Matthas to be quite so inarticulate but the circumstance was certainly unusual enough. Perisalas could feel his lovely logic chains just evaporating in the sun. *Just the Mahid. Oh thank my Steel Armed God, no more seven foot tall Minis's on fire-horses on the moon. Just... Mahid. Mahid alone rather than Minis and Mahid.* It was one reason that Matthas had the highest job. Perisalas could sit and be quiet and think and let Matthas talk.

"So we may interview Aan, Shevenkas?" Perisalas said. "I should like to tie up loose ends in my own files if I may." *Fikken turned himself fikken IN.*

"You have all the information you need to do that... or is it a matter of wanting to know where he was and how he managed to elude you? I can tell you how he turned himself in: got himself on the audience list under the alias Minakas Akam, and waited for nearly six months. Came in here with the Imperial Book--do you know what that is?--and handed it to me, saying it should be in the right hands."

He has the gall, the nerve, the sheer effrontery to get his alias on the fikken AUDIENCE LIST and just walk into the Marble Palace, right up to Chevenga. RIGHT UNDER MY FIKKEN NOSE!

"Oh. Aras bless. The Imperial Book? Aras Bless. The sword as well? How would he have brought the sword in?"

"No, he left that at home and I sent someone with him for it later."

"Well. It is good to know that a clear threat to the Empire is neutralized," Perisalas murmured. *Yes, I want to know every move the smart-assed brat did to elude me. Calm. Every move the boy made. Better. I shall have a clear mind if I do not allow unseemly emotion to cloud my judgment.*

"That was exactly what he said; that if he stayed free he'd be a danger to the Empire even after he was dead. I think he'll be willing to talk to you about where he went if I ask him to. But no truth-drug."

"Understood," Matthas said. He took no notes but he would have the whole conversation verbatim should Perisalas need reminding. "Might we inquire about the younger brother?"

"I know where he is, too. Same house as Ailadas Koren, the tutor; you may verify that, but leave both of them be."

"Ah. As you say, Shevenkas... He is... ahem... Ilesias Koren, then?"

"For now. If Kallijas wins, then he'll likely be Imperator when Ilesias reaches majority and can publicly relinquish the throne himself, which I think is the only way to head off the danger without bloodshed. If Kallijas does not win... well, I should not tell you more. You'll still be here, subject to truth-drugging at the orders of a new Imperator."

Perisalas had to cough. *He is hardly treating the boys like public enemy the first and second. Why?* "Certainly. Thank you, Shevenkas." *It is as the Imperator wants.*

"Perisalas... Matthas... you know it's my policy that you may always speak freely... but I have a feeling it needs reiterating. Speak freely, please."

Perisalas spoke up, firmly. "I am not much given to cursing, Shevengas but my inclination is to be rather more vocal than polite at the moment. I have the idea that I have been chasing this boy all over the Empire, at great expense and he turns himself and his little brother in to us. It is a great irony, ser." *There. Calmly enough said.*

"If I'd known that I could have saved the taxpayers of Arko so many chains, I would have. But it's worse than you think, Perisalas. I actually had Minis to *dinner* at my place in Vae Arahi. He was in disguise as Minakas Akam and I ran into him in the library. I know him from his writing. I kept thinking he looked familiar--it was sending me up the wall--but I couldn't place him. He said"—Chevenga imitated a broad *fessas* accent--"P'raps in the Mezem when m' dad took me, sor?" Which was *absolutely true.*"

"Akam the journalist? He took the man's name to hide as I recall."

"There never was a Minakas Akam other than Minis. He invented the name and wrote all the articles. Now we know why it was he seemed to have so much knowledge of the Marble Palace and things Imperial."

"Oh..." his control slipped, just slightly and he muttered under his breath "*fikken kaina maruch... fikker...*" Then louder. "I see."

"It gets even worse, Perisalas... Gannara Melachiya came with him to wait for him to complete the audience. You know where they were the sixty days before my second Ten Tens? Camped out in front of the Temple. When they were carrying me out of the Temple, Gannara *touched the back of my head.*"

"In the city I knew once we captured the Mahid... oh... *fik me...* excuse my language, Shevengas."

"It's all right, I first learned that sort of Arkan in the Mezem. Can you believe it? I have you chasing him all over and he ends up right here." *Fikken, Shennen, piss-ant stinking Selestialis dump its commodes upon my HEAD!*

"By all reports he is intelligent for an Aan. He did also mis-direct his own Mahid to the north countries when he was much younger." Perisalas said, remembering the Mahid grave along the river.

"Oh, he's very intelligent. Read Minakas Akam and you'll see it. You mean when he split off from them, he sent them on a wild goose chase?" Chevenga had a quirky grin, as if he were *proud* of the miserable brat, for some reason.

"Yes, Shevengas. According to Joras Mahid, he insulted the first of the Mahid enough to enrage him too much to think straight and left the note with a dead Mahid, in his bed."

"Really! They killed one on the way out? I thought their numbers were being thinned by attrition. We're going to need to know how many they are now are they still in two groups?"

"The last that Joras Mahid knew is that there was a single group and another, independent Mahid who may or may not be out searching who is trained to feign an *okas.*"

"Joras, that's the one you just caught after the Ten Tens, right? And who turned?

"Oh, yes. He was reported by an anonymous Dyer and Serina Kyriala Liren, who recognized him."

"I think I know who that anonymous Dyer might have been."

"Hmmm." *OH, MY STEEL PENISED GOD.* "You think -- Aan?"

"Well, tell me this--did he or did he not have to be a person who recognized Joras Mahid?" Chevenga grinned slightly. "And you know Minis was in the city. Unless the Dyer was someone he sent."

"Of course. And hair dye is cheap." Matthas had one hand over his face... chagrin... he tended to use more hand motions having been in Brahvniki so long, before he held this job.

"The herb-head kid who reported was paid by this Dyer with bright blue hair and a single nose-ring on *faib* skates."

"Not a bad disguise, if you want to be in disguise but not look like you are, these days. I'd put money on that Dyer being Minis. Especially if he skated well. He taught me how."

"Truly? Hmmm. No reports of how well he skated, Shevengas but yes. Thank you for all this information. My final report will certainly be more complete." *COMPLETE IN EVERY FIKKEN USELESS DETAIL.*

Chevenga made the Yeoli brush-off sign. "I'm just guessing. You want the truth in detail, ask him. It's as I said, I don't think he minds you knowing *now*. It's all over; he's done with fleeing."

Perisals felt the unnatural urge to beat upon his own head with the palms of his hands. And just as naturally suppressed that urge along with the urgh to scream *"Aigh aigh... forzak that fikker!"* Those unseemly reactions could just sit there for a time.

"Shevengas. I was apparently much closer to apprehending this boy than I perceived. Had I had somewhat more budget or manpower I would have likely caught him much earlier than now!"

"Perisalas, it is as I said in answer to your requests, directly or indirectly; there were other things that were higher priority, such as rebuilding Arko. I understand your frustration; you're a conscientious one, who always wants to do his best, and you weren't given the resources to do quite that. But I have conscientious people in every other department as well."

He bowed his head and said nothing for a time but at last, feeling the press of time, the words did burst out. "Will you tell me the truth? You didn't want him caught all that badly, did you? Did you expect him to turn himself in? To do the right thing for Arko? He's an Aan!"

"One question at a time. Yes, I will tell you the absolute honest truth. No, I didn't want him caught all that badly; duty required it, but, by Arkan standards, duty would require me to do him harm if he was caught. I didn't expect him to turn himself in, else your budget would have been even tighter. I didn't know what he would do; he was just a kid, probably frightened, growing up now with Mahid influences... I didn't think I could predict it. You haven't asked me whether he and I were friends, but I think you want to know: yes, we were, and we still are. He has a good heart. He always did. I saw it when no one else, apparently, did. So it doesn't surprise me that he turned himself in. But I would have considered it just as likely that he'd try to disappear into a new life. I am not telling you everything... there are some things that are personal, between him and me, that informed these thoughts. But him doing the right thing for Arko doesn't surprise me at all."

KAINA MARUGH MINIREN. A friend... he's public enemy number the first and your friend.

"Perisalas, speak freely, that's an order." There was a snort of laughter from Matthas and Shefenkas scrawled a fast note while Perisalas wrestled with his sense of propriety. He handed the scrap of paper to Matthas who read it, palmed and nodded at the Imperator with a bit of a grin. It was the sense of time passage that finally overwhelmed Perisalas's decency and decorum.

"*Kaina, fikken Marugh, Miniren... public enemy the first and your friend so I shouldn't fikken worry? I needn't get my clout in a kaina mothering knot about it?*" The words finally overwhelmed his propriety. He was breathing hard, through his nose. "Well. I can just...write it all out in my final report about this and then I shall do my best to forget about my failures! The next person I am to find... I shall."

"We'll make sure it's no one that anyone above you doesn't want caught." The Imperator and Matthas, his superior, exchanged a meaning full glance, a "that's-an-order" look at Matthas who rolled his eyes and nodded, sharply. "As far as whether he's an enemy of Arko, I've told you; you can speak to him. See what impression you get."

"As you wish, Shevenkas. I shall be pleased to speak to him. He sounds like a respectible mind."

"Very. You did not succeed but you did very good work and I won't forget that." The Imperator stood up. "Thank you, and thank you Matthas also." They went down in the prostration as he rose, before he could stop them. "Gehit. Go on."

Pacing decorously down the Bridge, Matthas said thoughtfully. "You know, I do the prostration in part just to bug him. You've got to love how he squirms every time."

"Truly?" Perisalas paused for a long moment, they gave an encouraging nod to the supplicant going up to the Imperator on the other carpet. "So do I, actually."

Matthas let out a long laugh. "I wonder how many of us do? Hahahaha... You must be wondering what's in this note."

"I was, but wondered if it was eyes only."

Matthas handed it to him...and, scrawled in Chevenga's super-fast Arkan, he read. "Mat – 1000 g. C. to P as appreciation, not treas. but Skorsas, show him this - 4Che."

He stopped like he'd been punched in the gut, wheezing a little... "Wait, am I reading this correctly? A thousand? And G.C.?"

"Gold chains, Matthas said helpfully.

"A... a... oh. My... Aras bless. A... th..." He had to cough. "I... didn't expect that... I was just doing my job!"

"I think he feels bad for hindering you in it."

"Well... well. That... ahem... sweetens any kind of bitterness I might have had! Oh. That... um..." He paused again. "It's too much for the minor frustration I suffered."

"Well, notice he feels it's overgenerous to come out of the treasury."

"He is giving it to me out of his personal fortune, yes. He is a generous man and this is not something the Empire would thank me for." For all that he suddenly wished to begin capering he clasped his hands behind his back, tilting his head thoughtfully toward Matthas as they emerged from the Glass Bridge.

"Has the honourable *solas* eaten? The Sun-Chime Dining hall has an amazing late luncheon for the administration." Matthas took up his *fessas* persona immediately.

"Ah, I shall sit and have kaf with you, ser."

"I shall have to write an appropriate thank you letter." To whom he did not say, in case of anyone overhearing. "A *very* appropriate letter. I, ah, assume you would wish to come with me? I should like to speak to -- Minakas Akam -- immediately."

"Oh, certainly, ser. I shall be able to take notes for the ser." The implications of the Imperator's gracious thank you were starting to become immediately real. Perisalas, pacing gravely along, with his hands at the small of his back, allowed himself an internal jig. *From slave to wealthy solas in less than five years! I shall be able to press my suit immediately with Mapela's father. I shall be able to purchase an appropriate home for her. I shall... think on this, very carefully.*

53

A LIBRARIAN AND THE CONCERVANCY

"Atzana Jesara Mil Kallen, *Aitza!*" the old librarian had to pause and cough. Atzana schooled her features as she stood in the doorway of her superior's office immediately behind the Main Imperial Library desk, folded her hands decorously before her. Buranas Murnas, *Aitzas*, didn't quite have the 'full name' down the way her mother did, but he was obviously annoyed.

"Yes, ser?"

"Bad enough that girls may read, now-a-days, bad enough that we must *employ* them! But at least we can request that the women in question refrain from answering a query and making cow eyes at the young man requesting research materials! Stick to filing and let the men handle the requests!"

"Yes, ser," she said quietly. And just as quietly resolved to answer every request she could. "I did smile at the young man, ser. I was taught to be polite, ser, even to *fessas* scholars, ser." *Silly old man.* "Did you know, ser, that that young man was Minakas Akam? The fellow who revealed the Wall of the Lost here in the Marble Palace?"

"No! And it's not my purview!" *Of course,* she thought. *Anything outside of First Age Patronymic Nomenclature is outside your purview!*

"He was requesting some of the oldest files we have past the third portal, once restricted, ser. If I could call upon your expertise, ser..."

"Well, hrmph." She could see him consider. He could assign her to the young scholar and continue his own work, currently stacked upon the desk, or set everything aside and attend the young man himself. "Young woman, you have proven yourself capable of filing and finding most anything. Set aside the makework and attend the boy, will you?"

Thank my serene and multi-dactyl Goddess. "We shall cease bothering you, ser."

"Good. Go away."

Atzana bobbed a bit of a curtsy at him, even though he was buried nose first in his own books once more, and hurried out to where the young scholar waited.

"Ser, my superior has assigned me to attend on you in your research, he is very busy."

The young man blinked at her from behind brass rimmed spectacles. He was very young to have to wear them. He smiled at her. "Ah, yes. Then 'f yah could show me where tah begin lookin', serina."

"You said Imperial Expenditures Archives from two hundred years ago?"

"Thet's about th' right time frame, serina."

"Well, then if you would follow me, please." She led the way from the desk, down the stacks to the third spiral staircase. "Have you ever been in the Library before, Ser Akam?"

"Ah, no, serina."

"Please, call me Atzana. It will not be improper, ser, since I am an independently supporting woman and have no father nor brother to offend." His almost silver pale eyebrows went up but he didn't lose the smile.

"Merely a first name, serina? Very much like t' Imperator, Atzana, Please tah be callin' me Minakas then."

She nodded and turned to the now open portal at the top of the stair. "'th' portals 'r open, serina... um... Atzana?"

"Yes. One of the first things the Imperator repealed was the restriction of books and literature. To anyone, though as you found, I'm sure, the city libraries are much more open than the Marble Palace ones."

"Ah, yeha."

She directed him to the correct set of stacks. He looked at them, then at her. "Are there cabinets of loose papers as well?"

Even as she said, "Oh, yes, Minakas, those have been moved to the conservancy room. I've been working on restoring some of the older papers." she wondered *how did he know?* That meant a trek up to the top floor where there was a whole bank of windows and skylights, the lamp-sconces newly copied from the Press to provide maximum light with minimum smoke. "This room is new."

"Oh, tis lovely!"

"So what papers were you looking for, ser?"

He coughed, like a much older man. "Ahem. I found a series 'f letters in t'main lib'ry in Vae Arahi. Ah were hopin' ta find t' match who he were writin' tah." He thought for a moment and then named a range of dates. 'Round 't time, Atzana. Imper't'r Tatthanas's letters."

"Oh. I haven't come across anything like that," she said thoughtfully. "The loose papers were and are still in a fearful mess. A hundred people could work years to straighten it all out."

"'r yeh t' only conservat'r?" He looked at her. "It's obvious yeh love teh work."

"Oh, no, there are a number of women in my circle who volunteer here, as well as four apprentices and my superior, Ser Murnas."

"Wah then, let m' do some diggin' then an' see iffn we can't do thet w'thout destroyin' anythin'."

"Thank you, Minakas. If I might ask you, please, could you change your gloves for these?" She handed him thin gloves specifically for working with the old papers.

He was a careful searcher and she found herself looking up at him occasionally. It was the strangest thing. He was so comfortable, even in the Marble Palace, though he said he'd never been there before. Perhaps it was because it was a library.

At one point almost a bead later he pulled off his spectacles and tossed them upon the desk, leaning back in his chair, pinching the bridge of his nose, leaving a smudge of dirt on either side, muttering in Yeoli of all languages.

He found another box with some of the papers he was looking for and carried it to her desk and then, apparently, trusted her to deal with it. Unlike some other scholars who tended to hover and gasp every time she picked up the next paper, he retreated to his own box. *Why is he familiar to me?*

Like other scholars, he did tend to mutter to himself while research-ing. *He sounds like my papa, talking to himself,* she thought absently to herself as she squinted at the faded ink of a new folder.

"Ahah! There! Ah." he cleared his throat and looked up to see if she was looking. "Atzana? Hev yeh got anythin' there fr'm the Year 244 Present Age?"

"I have a folder that is supposed to be included in the bound Chronicles for that year and four pages of things that looks like personal correspondence but I should check it against that book."

He leapt up. "I'll fetch it. Is it still in the Silver stacks?"

"Why, yes. Your pass will let you into the Heir's library ..." Her voice faded. He was gone almost before she finished speaking, down to the other end of the room, to another hallway that would take him out of the Great Library and if he knew the way, to the Silver stacks more quickly than going by the main corridors.

She stared after him. *You know this place. You know these libraries. Why would you lie to me about never having been here before? Your permission letter was from the Imperator Himself, not a minor bureaucrat.* She looked over and saw his spectacles where he'd flung them. It was very strange.

When he came back, he laid the correct book on her desk and went to fetch his spectacles and settled them firmly upon his nose. "So, Minakas, might I ask what you are researching?"

His smile lit up his face. "Oh, Atzana, this 'un's workin' on an unknown connection 'tween Yeola-e and Arko. 'T looks like their disgraced *semanakraseye* knew t' Imperator Tatthanas."

"Truly?"

"Oh, yes there were a letter or two in Vae Arahi, but if I'm correct, then copies o' t' letters and t' letters fr'm Notyaras should be here."

"How fascinating!" *Or did you see them once? I... shall consider this.* "Let me compare my folder to the bound book and see if they were excised by decree or just by negligence!"

"Thank you!" He smiled at her again and headed back to his desk.

She pulled out a large magnifying glass and clamped it to its stand and adjusted it to bring the page into perfect focus. "This is a letter in Enchian, but I cannot make out the signature."

"Set 't aside for me, please, Atzana."

It was the faintest hint of accent. *Aitzas,* not *fessas.* She raised her head and gazed across at his profile. His glasses were off again as he peered at the paper in front of him. "Of course, Min—akas. Excuse me, please I will be right back."

"Of cours' o' course," he said absently. Atzana rose and exited as if she were going to the garderobe. Once out of the conservancy she gathered up her skirts in her gloved hands and ran down the hall, hoping that none of the palace fluffies spotted her or decided to chase her. Down the hall, and the wide blue marble stairs around the corner and caught herself before she ran into a guard at the corner. She slowed down and decorously walked past the guard, smiling at him.

And opened the crystal doorknob into the Chrysophase reading room. There was a painting of a young man in that room, it was of the young Spark of the Sun's Ray, in profile, over his school work. It was a portrait of 12th Amitzas Boras Tatthanas Aan and it could have been sat for by the young man upstairs bent over his mucky, crumbling papers.

Is that young man related to the Aans? If so there is only one person he could be. It would explain how comfortable he is in the Great Library and in fact where he might have know about the Wall of the Lost. The various little clues fell together in her head as she reversed her course back up to the conservancy.

But I've liked his articles... his ideas... and he has been perfectly polite to me... oh my most elegant serene Goddess. What do I do?

She worried over it even as she carefully set another letter, half eaten by spots of mold, over onto a glass topped table. Finally she turned in her chair. "Minis?" she said softly.

"Hmm?" he said in reply before he twitched as if prodded by a sword-tip. "Did you call me?" He said, trying to make as though he hadn't heard me correctly, but he was so rattled he could not keep the *fessas* accent.

"Does the Highest Office... does the Imperator... know?"

It was so quiet she could hear a distant fountain and the muffled-hoofed click and creak of a house-donkey cart and the trilling, whistling songs from the Most Splendid and Regal Wings Aviary. He rubbed his gloves together and gazed at the kernels of dirt falling into his lap. "Yes." He said, glancing up as he said it. Then he sat, looking, waiting for her reaction, for all the world looking as though he were holding his breath.

She turned back to her latest folder as if he had just answered a question about a page or a type of ink. "Oh. Good," she said. "I'll just get back to this, then, shall I? That research piece will not write itself."

54

TRUTH AND KAF

MINIS STAGGERED DOWNSTAIRS FROM THE ABSOLUTELY BEAUTIFUL conservancy room with a stack of barely legible papers, a half ten of folders and two thick books of Chronicles. And a chest... his chest...the one bounded by his own ribs, full of confusion.

Atzana knew. She'd figured it out and she finally had mercy upon him and told me where he'd slipped. It had been the Marble Palace itself that had lulled him into being sloppy. And she apparently attended Kyriala's salons. How many Arkan women were so smart? And as effective? The Yeolis kept saying so.

He asked the servant for the suite if it would be possible... if it would not be too much trouble... for a cup of kaf? He sniffed at the parochial waffling. "A pot of kaf is eminently fetchable, ser," he said. "It will be but a moment."

"Th... thenk yeh, ser."

"Oh, not at all, Ser Akam. The High Chamberlain charged us... the servants assigned to this suite of rooms, ser, with your care. We understand that you might not be used to being served. Not to worry. Just ask."

Minis nodded and blinked at him as if he were completely overwhelmed. "I'll get that kaf for you then, shall I?" And he winked before he left.

The papers he laid out carefully on the big table in the suite and sank down with the the cup of excellent kaf and put his feet up to think. Gannara was down making sure that everything they hadn't packed up was out of the house. He was probably taking advantage of the privacy with Alya or Tahatina, or Maru. Minis tried not to feel jealous. He probably would never be comfortable with boys or men that way.

There was a knock at the door and he set his cup down and went to the door, calling through it. "Yes? Who is it?"

"Perisalas Shefenkas, *solas*. May I speak with you?" The voice was precise and very calm. "I have the permission of He Whose Knowledge is the World's Safety." Minis opened the door to him and found he had a *fessas* clerk with him. *Ah, Chevenga said the investigator would likely wish to speak to me. Here he is.*

"Please, sor... ah sors..." he backed up, indicating the chairs by the fountain. "How may t's lowly 'un help 't honourable ser?" The man scanned the room automatically, even here in the Marble Palace, the most secure place in the Empire. Minis wouldn't have noticed him looking if he hadn't been watching for it.

The moment the door was closed and the clerk ensconced in a chair with his notebook folded open, the *solas* cut straight to the heart of his visit.

"As I said, my name is Perisalas Shefenkas, *solas*, Spark in Exile, I am an investigator for He Whose Will is the Support of the World, and I would like to speak with you, if I might." He looked as though he were setting his teeth into raw onions and refusing to acknowledge the bite of acid into his gums. *This man is the agent who was searching for me. I look at his calm, calculating face. Did he make the hunt for me, personal?*

Minis dropped the *fessas* accent. The clerk was obviously an Irefas man or he would not have been there. "Ah. Certainly." He said. *Why do I want this man to like me?* "You have been seeking me for quite a while." He spoke in his own accent but equal to equal. "Please, gentlemen. I just asked for the pot of kaf, may I offer you cups? I am hardly in a position to offer hospitality but He Whose Generosity is the Worlds will surely give me that graciousness."

Perisalas bowed, just slightly. "Thank you, Exalted. I have indeed been seeking you for quite some time, it seems even longer than your Mahid were seeking you."

"I am no longer "Exalted or Chip of the Light' or anything else. Please call me Minis... yes... My Mahid and I had a falling out." *If he has Chevenga's permission then this is part of my turning myself in. Honesty here.*

I am broken open in the Imperator's hands and given to those who ask. It was a relief, to be honest. No more cramped shut hiding of parts of myself from any other parts. I am free to be whole. There was no one to protect, no one to hide, no one to shield. He sipped his own kaf and savoured the rich, hot aroma, and the cream and sweetness of the chip of sugar.

"My Imperator has made it clear to me that your status, while ambiguous, was inarguably elevated, and I wished to put you at ease. I am sorry. Minis, then?"

"Thank you. Yes."

"I am eager to hear more of how you and your, ahem, the Mahid parted company, but first I would like to know more of the events right after you left the City. It would satisfy my curiosity as well as helping me complete my files and reports for the Imperator." *He needs to know. The perfect Irefas man.*

"Of course. Gentlemen." He found there were three extra cups on the tray that the superior servant had fetched and poured two cups of kaf. "Perisalas, do you take your kaf black?"

He looked startled but only for a moment. "Yes. You need not serve." Minis shook his head at him.

"Please. I have been infected with Yeoli ideas of hospitality." He set the cup down in front of him, and picked up the sugar tongs to place a single chip of sweetness upon the plate. "Should you choose to indulge yourself, ser."

He stared at him and nodded, sharply, once before reaching to touch the edge of the delicate, gold-trimmed saucer, accepting it.

"Ah, sor," The *fessas* said quietly. "Thenk yah. Cream please." *You are comfortable with this in a strange way. Who are you? I shall have to find out, just for my own curiosity.* Minis set the cup before him and turned back to Perisalas. The special investigator had not drawn any attention to the man, so ignoring him would be polite as well. "It is a long and rather tedious story."

He sipped the kaf lightly and set it down again, listening. *I am so glad I did not know this man was on my heels. What sleep I did have would not have been nearly so peaceful, had I known.*

"As you undoubtedly know, my brother and I and my betrothed were rushed out of the city in litters with an escort of fifty Mahid. 2nd Amitzas pushed us until the litter slaves collapsed and he killed the lot. You will find their bodies and the destroyed litters at the bottom of a cliff under a rockslide North East of the City."

Perisalas glanced at the clerk and then set his eyes back on Minis where he sat. *Is he surprised I no longer have anything to hide? I shall explain.* "Ser Shefenkas I have no more need to hide, no more need to run from anyone but the renegade Mahid. It is the right of Empire to know all that I know."

"I thank you for your patriotic concern, Ser Aan, for I feel a great personal need to support and work for our Empire."

Minis smiled at the man. It was a pleasure to deal with a competent Irefas man, especially since he was no longer running from him and it made him feel good to know that the Empire was being protected by good, intelligent men. "It is pleasant to find officers in the bureaucracy of Arko who are diligent and competent.

"The first morning after the flight, I -- fat, snotty little bastard that I was -- attempted to command the Mahid and found that my father had commanded I be given to their command rather than the other way around." He grimaced, remembering. "That first day of training was not pleasant and it took me all day to do fifty push-ups." He sipped, trying to be polite and still clear the pain out of his memory. "My father left letters to me and to 1st Amitzas laying out our relative status."

He sipped as Minis did, apparently unmoved by the rich kaf, finally free of bitterness. *My whole life I had been taking in the taste of corruption and madness. I was finally free of that.* "Really?" He inquired, quietly. "Serina Liren said as much to me when I asked her about those times. She described them as 'hard' and that the Mahid were not prepared for life outside the City. Would you agree? Do you feel that Second Amitzas was unprepared?

Minis had to laugh. "Oh, they had no idea. Ser Shefenkas. First Amitzas lost a dozen of his Mahid the first year! Snowblindness, lung-clot, exposure... attempting to impose Mahid correctness on wilderness. Hmmm... how do I put this? My little brother needed better food so they struggled with goats, attempting to milk them and burnt food."

Perisalas's lips twitched involuntarily at this picture. "Was this up in the mountains near Two Kills pass? The site with the small cabin?"

"Yes. Just so. He lost people in the mountain passes. Yes. After we left there -- that was just the first winter. It was a learning experience for him if he chose to take it as such."

"It seems to me that you were the one learning." *If he truly smiles will his facade shatter? No, he really is amused.*

"I should hope so." Minis smiled back at him. "I'd be a 'right knob ser'," he said, in a bit of the *fessas* accent. "If I could not learn from such severe mistakes."

"Did the Mahid train you in how to change your caste traits?"

"Oh, no. I had to adopt those after we fled the Mahid so *they* could not find us. And it was hard. I had enough incentive however."

"Ah. I had received a number of reports about *okas* Mahid, in amongst the MANY strange sightings of you, that I wondered if there was a new sub-set of Mahid who trained to impersonate lower caste Arkans, though Joras Mahid was the only one we apprehended."

"There was only one 'okas' trained Mahid that I knew of. First Matthas. Though Joras was more dangerous because he knew how to be 'ebullient'. He could smile easily."

"He has sworn to the Imperator, and is re-training under the Imperial pharmacist. I tell you so that you will not be frightened into fleeing again, should you see him in the Palace."

"Oh. Thank you, Ser. I... He swore?" *Oh Ten. Oh Ten. Joras is here and sworn? I would have sworn that the sun would fall out of the sky first. But then... Chevenga, I think, can turn anyone. He saw Chevenga do the Ten Tens,* he reminded himself. *That would hit a fanatic hard.* He swallowed.

"He swore. After a full bead of drunken fessas bawdy verse, the truth-drug took hold and he swore without reservation." The look on his face was almost painful. Of course he would have sat through any amount of ribald doggerel.

"A full bead? and without reservation?" Minis managed to choke out. "Oh. I. I saw him in the city. I paid a herb-head to report him."

Perisalas smiled again and nodded encouragingly.

"Well... I suppose I should not hate any of my relatives no matter if they are Mahid or not."

I had confused him. I wouldn't have seen that had I not been watching so closely.

"You know... Ser..." I continued. *I would let him know I did not deny any of my heritage, my mother... who... who was my mother? I had never asked.* "My father had not wanted me to ask which Mahid concubine was my mother." *Whose name on the woman's cenotaph should I honour? I didn't know. I was to have sprung fully formed from his loins but that was rank insanity. I would have to find out. I should find out.*

"At the time, that might have been one of the LEAST remarkable things one was to believe in Court." He said. *Yes, he was being that dryly humourous.*

Minis snorted and set his kaf down and wiped a drop away with his napkin. "Ha! Yes. I will not say anything directly against my father, Ser, whatever I think. I might be made to acknowledge certain things that should or should not have been but I will not speak against him. The Gods do not bless a father-hater."

The expression on Perisalas's face was interesting. Minis wasn't sure how to interpret it. He settled back intohis chair and anticipated a long afternoon. The investigator would want to know every detail.

"If I had known, ser, that you were following me, I should not have rested easy." *Tell him the truth.*

Perisalas snorted. "You, ser, misdirected me well enough. The ploy of being escorted to the city by our own road Sereniteers was nothing but brilliant. I was inclined to rip my hair out by the roots."

Minis picked up his cup again, smiling slightly. This was going to be considerably more fun than he thought it would be.

55

WHOSE NAME ON THE CENOTAPH?

I HANDED THE PRECIOUS PERMISSION TO THE IMPERIAL ARCHIVES to the librarian, rather than to Atzana. She was too diligent and perceptive. I knew the fellow -- Atzana's superior, from years ago. He was more stooped and had thinner hair. His mouth was tighter pursed but since he survived war and sack and retained his job, there was more to him than I ever gave credence to. Like everyone. People had so much more strength than I ever knew and I found myself impressed and awed by it over and over again. I had been forced away from them by my father. Then I had run, and run and run, trying to run away from people and here I was, back again. Meanwhile he, and others like him, had endured.

After gazing at me over his half-moon spectacles in a look that I think all librarians must have learned in the cradle, he passed me into the Golden Archive without a second look.

The door opened into the dim room where I, years ago, had blown through on my *faib* skates. I took a full step in and stopped, taking a deep breath. The parchment, vellum and paper and ink smell sunk into the stone seemed to fill me up in spaces I hadn't realized were empty. I had needed this place and hadn't recognized how much.

The Imperial records were in the gilded bookshelf across the whole room, set up so that one could see them, slightly higher, between the lighted corridor of stacks, the leather volumes and folios all gold.

The book I needed opened with a crackle and I was suddenly finding

it hard to catch my breath, my heart leaping up to gallop away on me. I
stared at the words appearing underneath my finger... there...

The birth of Minis Kurkas Joras Amitzas Aan, son of 16th Kurkas Joras
Amitzas Boras Aan, birthed from *an Imperial concubine.*

"Shen!" Two other scholars looked up at me, startled at my outburst.
That kind of language wasn't usually heard out loud in here.   They
couldn't be bothered to list her *name*? Of course. It was what my father
wanted. I was his alone, sprung from nothing but him. If he could have
had me without the necessity of my having been grown inside a female he
would have.

Suddenly, in my mind, I was back in the town square of Asinanai,
watching Gannara find out that his blood parents – both of them – had
died in the war. He knew. It was important that people knew their
parents. Parents, grandparents, brothers, even sisters, uncles and aunts,
cousins. Without knowledge of them, I had come to understand, you
were isolate in the world.

My father had tried to isolate me to himself alone and that way lay
madness. I *had* to find my mother's name. It was important. I tapped
my gloved fingers against the unhelpful page, as isolated from the
knowledge as my skin was from the book. This wasn't going to be so
easy.

The Mahid records were as dark as the Imperial were golden, set in a
bookshelf of blackened silver, tucked into an alcove off to one side, in the
shadow of the Imperator, one might say. The black leather books of the
years of my father's reign were too heavy to carry to the desk in one trip
but took three.

I started looking backwards from my birthday to be certain I wouldn't
miss it, though I did understand normal human breeding was nine
months – I didn't know for sure how many I was carried... if I were full
term or not.

Most of father's concubines were boys... but he went through phases.
There were times there were more girls... and there were -- two births
recorded. I had two half sisters almost my age. "Lia Mahid... Divinely
conceived on Ilanai Mahid. Born 10 Anae Year 70 PA. Amali Mahid...
Divinely conceived on Tira Mahid. Born 4 Muunas Year 69 P.A. *And one
boy.* Chosen Heir, First Minis Kurkas Joras Amitzas Aan. Divinely
conceived on Inensa Mahid. Born 1 Muunas Year 69 P.A.

Inensa. Inensa Mahid. *Inensa?* She... she... I knew where she was.
She was still alive. She *was married to 2nd Amitzas.* She had been head of

the women in my eclipse court and had laid hands on Kyriala when the men had killed Binshala. That woman was my mother?

I covered my face with my hands. I was wrong. I didn't want to know and now I couldn't un-know it. I blindly began putting the books back and spun away... then, almost reluctantly went back, my footsteps dragging. If I knew my father's lineage back more than a thousand years wasn't that enough? Why was I drawn to this?

I had to guess, because I didn't know how old she was. It was hard because I kept having to blink. I wasn't crying. That was impossible. I was half Mahid. I'd had training as one. I stopped and closed the book. I couldn't bear this. *Why couldn't she just have been some Mahid I'd never seen? Some woman who died in the sack?* It would have been so much easier if that had been the case.

My finger tracked down the lines of the Mahid clan. No... no... I checked a dozen family lines before my finger fell on her name. Her brothers... my uncles...were all on the men's black cenotaph, in the Mahid chapel. Her father... My finger froze again and I swallowed.

Her father. My grandfather, was also still alive. He was the Imperial Pharmacist, 1st Amitzas Mahid.

I could come back... I had to... later...

I managed to compose myself and walk in the halls, full of the sense of having done this kind of thing before.

Gannara was there on the bed, reading a book that I... for the life of me, could not remember. He put it down and said "Minis. What's the matter?"

I sat down as if my bones would shatter if I moved too quickly. "I found out who my mother is," I whispered.

"Oh. Um." He put a hand on my shoulder. "Condolences—"

"—No!" I leapt up to pace back and forth. "IS! She's not dead."

"Not dead? But you look like --" He waved his hands, confused.

"She's alive," I snapped. "She's with 2nd Amitzas."

"With SECOND AMITZAS?" I hunched my shoulders at his shout, turned and paced back again.

"You don't need to shout, Gannara."

"Yeah, sorry, but... You mean she was with us?"

"Yeha. Why couldn't she just be... just be safely dead, some anonymous woman, so I don't need... um..."

"*Which one???!*

I took a deep breath. "His wife."

56

SHE'D HAVE TO LISTEN

GANNARA TOOK A DEEP BREATH AND I PUT MY HANDS OVER MY ears. "HIS WIFE???!!!"

I took my hands down and paced faster. "Inensa." Why did it have to be her? The only time… the snow-fight… the look on her face when she hit 2nd Amitzas with snowballs. She was Mahid and a near perfect one. I would never have guessed. Why her?

"Kahara! INENSA is your MOTHER? That layer-forged tight-faced… um… Sorry."

"SHE's as much a MONSTER as HE is! AIGH!"

"No, she isn't. Nobody is."

My hands were clenching and unclenching and I ripped the *forzak* gloves off and flung them across the room and they fluttered down in the middle of the room. "She's…*his*… *AIGH!*" Unwilling, the memory of the sounds, the meaning of those sounds, heard while my nose was a fingerwidth above water, muffled sounds of tent canvas splitting under a knife and thunder and rain… floated up in my memory like a bloating corpse in a lake.

"That…" he said thoughtfully… "can't be any fun."

I dragged a breath in as though someone had just punched me in the gut and I was struggling to recover. "No. I knew I was part Mahid. I knew it. I knew I should know, but I don't want to know."

"You figured chances were she was dead right?"

"Yeha. I did. I... thought... I'll just find out."

"Why don't you sit down, Min? You thought you'd know whose grave to put a flower on..."

"Yeha." I did sit down but I clenched my hands in my hair, my forehead almost on my knees.

Gannara was quiet for a while but when I didn't stir, spoke up. "So... I guess maybe this might change the plans for capturing them, hmmm?"

"I... didn't think..." I actually hadn't thought that far ahead. I... she... I didn't want her dead. But... Inensa Mahid. "She's my mother." As if that answered anything or gave him any kind of useful information.

"Yes. She is. You owe her life."

"I know the fat guy's lineage for a thousand years... and now I know her's as well. I feel like I crawled out of such a cess pool."

He put his hand on my shoulder. "You're a good person, whatever you crawled out of."

I clawed at the tears staining my face. "Only the Gods know how."

"Aw, Minis…" He held his arms open for me. I turned on the end of the bed and crawled into his hug.

"*Shen*, you hear this kind of thing from me all the time. You shouldn't have to. It's just *shen*. Sorry." But since this was said, against his neck, it didn't have the force it should. I was just so tired.

"What, hear you found out your mother's Inensa? It's only happened once."

"Thanks brother." I took a damp, shuddering breath. "Yeha. And I can only have one. I need to try and plan so that the women don't get killed or kill themselves when the Mahid raid happens."

"Hey, bro, I think I'd be crying too, if I found out something like that… I bet she's nice underneath what she's required to be. You had to get it from somewhere. And your smarts, too."

I blinked, thinking that odd thought. "I suppose. You know the fat guy didn't bother putting her name in the Imperial records?"

"Doesn't surprise me," he said. "He always saw you as a little more length on his dick or something like that."

I sat up, shuddering, and he let me go, even though he kept his hand on my shoulder, a warm spot. "Maybe it was a *reward* to be married to Ice Eyes. For birthing me."

"Oooh, some reward! If that's a reward, I want a punishment."

"I…" I swallowed hard. "I…heard... some of the stuff he did, the night we escaped."

"What do you mean?" He looked sick and like he didn't want to know but couldn't help asking.

"He was beating her to get himself up, I think."

Gan stared at me in silence. "Really?"

"Yeha. I didn't care, then."

"That means she must have got beaten every time he wanted to get himself up, at least with her."

"Yeha, he never marked up her face." I turned and flung myself stomach down on the bed. "Aigh!" His hand that had been on my shoulder settled on the small of my back. It was as though it helped steady me, let me breathe.

"You didn't know she was your mama."

"I hated her for handling Kyriala like that. But she had to."

"But what's going to happen with capturing them is that Second Amitzas will either kill himself with his poison tooth...or get captured, in which case Ch'venga will kill him. So she'll be free of him."

"She... and the women have to be told not to cut their own throats... it's Mahid... she might think it a requirement to die." I clenched my teeth.

"She might chicken out of that," Gan said helpfully.

"I don't *know* her!" I said through my teeth.

"Are you going on the raid?" he asked. "You hadn't said."

"Yes. I have to. And now I have to figure out how to get to her."

"Maybe you can talk her out of it...like, 'I know you're my mama! Maybe you could *order* her as her son, and Kurkas's.

"Oh, Gods. She'd have to listen."

"And then maybe not getting beaten up and made to slit throats and so on for a while will make her turn more normal."

"I need... to figure this out." I turned my face down into mattress. "I need to know her better and her father might know her some... more than I do anyway. I need to talk to him. Um... I guess that makes him my grandfather..."

"Him? Her father? Talk to him? The only old Mahid who is alive and available for you to... talk to... is..." His voice faded away. "You... found his name in the records too? 1st Amitzas?" I nodded without looking up. "The Imperial Pharmacist? The highest, most dangerous torturer in the whole Empire? The man who nearly broke Ch'venga's mind into tiny little pieces?"

"That would be him." I said, and folded my hands over my head. "I once tore up his books and tossed one into the lightning snake's --- that's a terribly venomous snake by the way – tank. He doesn't like me very much. He must know that I'm from his daughter… he must know. Oh, my ever spinning ancestors… Sinimas what am I to do?"

Gan coughed. "Um… talk to him, I suppose?"

I lay there without looking up, breathing the hot air I had just breathed out into the cloth under my face. "Yeha. I do need to talk to him." Oh, *shen*. I had to talk to him if I wanted to have any change of convincing my newly discovered mother from not slitting her own throat rather than be captured. I had to talk to him and he didn't like me much. Surely he would help me, for her sake?

57

____

SO MUCH UNSAID

I STRAIGHTENED MY SCHOLAR'S ROBE, UNNECESSARILY. I WAS SO nervous I couldn't swallow. _I had the man on one of his own tables. He let me in to the Haians with Misahis's kit in my hands, without a word. I truth drugged him and broke his left hand. He's my Grandfather._

I felt completely unreal, walking down the stairs to the Mahid section. I stopped for a moment, looking up at the painting of my ancestor and had to smile. He looked less severe and dyspeptic, and more sympathetic to me now.

The Mahid part of the Marble Palace was changed enough to stop me again. The lights were all changed and it looked warm and there were actual rugs upon the floor. The doors were painted a dark green, far less disturbing than the blood red. Flowers. Mahid roses and Fire-sprigs actually stood in crystal vases upon tables here and it was faintly perfumed instead of smelling like sour cleaners. It was disorienting enough that I had to actually count doors to make sure that I had the correct door. Another deep breath and I raised my hand to knock.

His precise old voice called from inside. "Who is it?"

"Minakis Akam, _fessas_, sor... might this one hev a moment of yer exaulted one's time, sor?"

"Who? Who authorized you to be here?"

I pull out the note from Chevenga. He was Mahid, of course he would need authorization, even in the Marble Palace. "T' Imperator, sor. This 'un has information for the exaulted sor..."

There was silence from the other side of the door. "I'fn yeh need a note, sor... I hev one."

"Who did you say you were? Minakis Akam?"

"Ay sor." The last thing I expected to have to do is talk my way through his door.

"*Fessas.* The writer?"

"Ay, sor."

From his voice he was right on the other side of the door. I so wanted to give up, to run. I didn't want to face the man, knowing I was his grandson. What did a grandson act like?

"You're not... *getting* information? I don't have any for you…"

"Thet is indeed m' byline, exaulted sor..." *Will you just stop being stubborn, old man, and just let me in to talk to you!*

"What's this information you have for me?" I wanted to beat my head against his door.

"Aboutn' fambly exalted sor. T'exalted sor's fambly, sor."

"Mahid? You're a *fessas*, what would you know about Mahid?"

Gods and the little sugar devils! Forzak me! "M'byline sor…one could say alias, sor." Another long silence from inside. "I hev t'authorization sor. Ay'd rether not explain in a corridor sor, even in t' Marble Palace, sor." I slid the note into the slot and felt him take it.

"Hmmm… All right." He opened the door and stepped back. "Come in. Have a seat."

He slid the book he held in his hand onto a shelf, I caught a flash of pink on the cover and wondered which knuckle sucker it was he was hiding, and sat down across from me. A small table, two chairs, and bookshelves. It was just the same as it always was. Except for one small change. There was a Haian remedy box tucked away on one of his shelves.

"Information?" He said drily.

"Excuse me," I said, dropping the *fessas* accent, but only giving him the two words. I pulled off my glasses and my gloves and he twitched as if I'd disrobed in front of him.

"Excuse me!" He snapped. "I beg your pardon, Ser Akam!"

"As I said," I said. "My byline indeed is Minakas Akam. Perisalas Shefenkas was fooled long enough by the alias to keep me safe. As was 2nd Amitzas." He stared at me, silenced. "My name is Minis."

If I didn't know Mahid I wouldn't have been able to see how nonplussed he was. A quiver of eyelash, or a tightening of jaw. That was all the indication I had. But it was there.

"Spark of the Sun's Ray!" He breathed.

"Not anymore," I said crisply.

"Your illustrious self.. ...here... ...how... The Imperator..."

"You understand I couldn't just blurt out my name in a corridor."

He could not say anything to that.

"As you see, from the note, Shefenkas knows I'm here."

"Well... indeed. The Imperator... knows...?"

"Yes…it's true I came to talk about family... I turned myself in, after his second Ten Tens..."

What was I thinking? That he would throw himself into my arms? *He's Mahid. For that matter, so am I.*

"Ah." Was his only response.

"It seemed that my duty came that way."

"What are his requirements of you? If I may be privy."

"There are plans to bring in the unsworn. I shall be assisting the rightful Imperator capture Second Amitzas and the others…" I had to pause. "I hope to leave some the choice to swear."

"Some?" Amitzas asked quietly.

"Like my mother." I said. Then it was for both of us to sit, looking at one another, uncertain what was correct to say.

"That is an admirable hope," Amitzas said finally. "Does the exalted have the Imperator's permission to attempt this?"

I nodded, finally. "I do. He wishes me all the leeway he can give me, to save Inensa… and her women... if…"

"If?"

"If they are willing to swear to the true Imperator," I said firmly.

"Ah. Of course."

"I hope... to save my mother from her current husband."

"You obviously know who she is."

"I do…" I said, and swallowed hard. "And... thus... the rest of the family as well – grandfather."

"Yes." He nodded courteously, acknowledging. "Though your Mahid ancestry is irrelevent. Only your Imperial ancestry truly counts."

"I understand. I do not agree with you, however, Grandsire. So I was taught. And I reject that idea, but I find that curiously shallow. If I do not know... or acknowledge the other half of myself, then how can I have integrity of any kind?"

He blinked. Once. He was completely baffled, I could see.

I pressed on. "It is unlikely that Ch'venga will be forced to carry through with the law... he does not wish my death."

"He Whose Wit is the Wisdom of the World... you know his plans for you?"

"At the moment... only to clear up a threat to the Empire... after that, no."

"Ah. But he was a friend to you once."

"He still is." I was sitting and looking and he was sitting, gazing at me quietly. I felt like I had ants applied to my skin and had to draw on all my strength to sit as quietly as he. I wanted to run, screaming. I wanted to hide my head under my pillows and howl into the mattress, but I could do none of that. I had to sit. I had to be calm and look back into his level gaze.

"You are blessed," he said quietly.

"Yes. I am." And then we sat in an awkard silence for a while.

"If I may, ser." I held my hands out to my grandfather, so like Chevenga.

He drew back, his hands folded against his chest. "What do you wish?"

I had to pull back, he looked so much like a maiden auntie pulling his delicate parts away from a ravisher. I didn't want to laugh at him. It was the last thing I wanted to do. I drew the Yeoli gesture back to myself, folding my hands in my lap.

"I wanted your hands for a moment."

He stared at me as if I were very odd. "For what purpose?'

"To thank the hand that succored Ch'venga." I said simply. "I'd like to thank you, grandfather."

"Thank me? For what? I have done you no favours."

"I wished to thank you for your flexibility... for your compassion. You saved Misahis and the other Haians... and Ch'venga himself... the amount of pain you suffered, being Mahid, and managing to have that strength, I want to acknowledge."

He sat, staring at me as if I had grown another head upon my shoulders without noticing and then, finally, said, "Thank you."

"You're welcome." He wasn't going to bear too much more honesty. It was time to speak of things less painful. "Do you still have the lightning snake?" I looked around as if to see the tank, even though I well knew it would still be in his office if it still were in his possession.

"Yes, I do. He's just a pet now... You want to see him, don't you?" He got up abruptly. "Come."

I smiled at him as I rose, pulling on my gloves once more. The spectacles I gathered up but did not don. "I do... I remember your lecture about it being innocent."

We went to his office which was perfectly untouched since the last time I'd seen it. He made a wordless noise to my comment. I wasn't sure what he meant by it. "I can't give him away. I can't just let him go."

"You know... this room was the warmest in the whole section... because of him... Of course," I said. "He's your responsibility."

"So... I keep him, along with the rest of the menagerie and herbarium."

"I wonder if the Haians make medication from his venom?"

"Of course they do. Karaserium, they call it." *How does he know?* I made an acknowledging noise.

"Then I suppose your snake would still be useful that way if you chose." He looked sharply at me.

"Minis -- Grandson." I had to stop and just breathe. He was acknowledging me as his family. It was... like a distant, faint hug, a hand reaching out of darkness.

"Yes?"

"Would you like him?" I stilled where I sat.

"Me? Grandfather... I... would love him... but... my own place is uncertain enough that I could not. I am not even capable of maintaining a home for my little brother."

"Your little brother? Is he safe? Does the Imperator know? Your place is uncertain?" For him that was a flood of emotion.

I made the Yeoli brush-off gesture. "Ilesias is safe, but not with me, and yes Ch'venga knows where he is. Until things settle for me, would you keep the snake?"

"You are safe if He Whose Whim is the Will of the World is your friend."

"Well. This raid is not necessarily going to be the safest thing I've ever done. And the Assembly might attempt to enforce 14.8 upon me. And Ch'venga will only be Imperator another few moons."

"True. I will keep him for you."

"Thank you. I... um..." I could feel myself blushing. "I never got a chance to finish reading 'Ragged Gloves'... was it good?"

He blinked at me and took off his own spectacles and polished them meticulously, clearly giving himself thinking time. "Well..." he said at last. "I won't give away the ending." He rose and paced to a shelf and pulled a volume out of the mass. "Here."

I took the slender little volume in my gloved hands. "Thank you. I'll bring it back when I'm done."

"I'm sure you will."

I went to one knee before him, bending my head the way a grandson did to a grandfather. He hesitated long enough that I wondered if I should not have done it, before I felt his hand on my bent head. It was warmer than I thought he had in him.

"I have years of grandfather gifts to make you, ser. Please let me know what would be appropriate?"

I was close enough to hear his breath catch. "You... wish to save your mother. If you succeed, then I will be well gifted, Minis. Muunas watch over you."

With my forehead against his knee, hidden, I smiled "And you too, Grandsire. I'll do my best to bring Mother home alive."

He lifted his hand and I, my head. "May I call upon you again, Grandfather?" I looked up into his wrinkled old face, wanting something more than just the formal acknowledgement. He looked as startled as he ever did through his stone face.

"If... the Imperator permits it... and you... wish... it... certainly." He said, hesitantly.

"Thank you, ser. I and my companion are currently being housed in the Azure suite..." I said. "When I am not in the library, ser. If my honoured elder would wish to call upon me."

He sat still as if he were a statue. "I... shall consider that."

I got up and made sure I had my spectacles and the book. I couldn't help but smile at him. "I'm glad I know you, ser, for more than what you were presented to me."

He didn't answer but his face softened a fraction. No one but Mahid would have seen it. I nodded and let myself out of the room.

I made it down the corridor and up the steps before collapsing against a wall, wrung out as if I'd been doing a full workout, my robe soaked with nervous sweat.

58

——————

KALLIJAS KNOWS

Chevenga asked me to come up to speak to Kallijas... to introduce me in my real guise, late the next day and I had enough time to work myself into lather so that I spent a bead in the middle of the night in the Lesser Baths... then couldn't sleep at all. I was in my cottons, walking the halls, and found myself completely alone, standing in the Great Hall.

I stopped, looked up the Hall, up toward Muunas's face, but could not see it in the dimness. Even without looking I knew my toes were on the mark for the Spark of the Sun's Ray's ritual practice.

I stood there, just breathing, looking around. There were no guards closer that three corridors away, this deep, this far away from the Imperial chambers and it was so late that very few servants were about. I could hear wall washers distantly, so far away that their humming was like a beehive.

Surely the Gods wouldn't mind me doing rote motions, with no intent behind them? The ritual always calmed me. I might be able to sleep after... if I dared. I went down in the prostration, stretching my length on my stomach and waited to see if the Gods would object. The coolness of the stone struck upward through my cottons, cooling my overheated body. There was only silence, so I rose and began, quietly, whispering the prayers, doing the motions that I had done since first threshold, eleven years ago.

Afterward, I slipped into our rooms and to the sound of Gan's quiet breathing in the one bed, slipped into the other and managed to chase sleep down the black tunnel.

Next day, I went up the Scarlet Rosary room at the appointed time and was admitted by the guard there. It was one of the most secure rooms in the entire ant pile. Chevenga and Kallijas were both there and I took my spectacles off as the servant closed the door behind me.

Kallijas looked just as he did when I'd met him, at the Hearthstone Independent, but in the silks more suitable to an Imperial candidate. He also looked more tired. "Hello." I said... The one word wasn't enough to let Kallijas know my own accent.

"Hello, Min," Chevenga said. "Kallijas, you met this young man before, but let me make him known to you by his real name, Minis Aan."

He'd been getting up to greet me in return, and didn't check, even for a moment as he rose. He looked very formidable in dark blue silks. "It is an honour to meet you honestly. Should this one give the prostration to the Spark of the Sun's Ray?" He asked quietly, glancing at Chevenga. He already knew who I was, of course.

I shook my head. "Please, no, Ser Itrean... Kallijas if your earlier permission to make free with your personal name still holds. And it is just Minis, if you please."

He nodded. "As you wish," he said and sat down again, as I did.

"I've had my titles crammed down my throat by my own Mahid for the past few years and I find I dislike what they represent." He tilted his head, curiously.

"Truly... how so?"

"Ser. My father gave me into 2nd Amitzas's hands for training completely. In effect I began a modified Mahid training at age fourteen. He enjoyed addressing me with a grandiose title while making me do my first five hundred push-ups or doing something either demeaning or exhausting... not that that kind of training was bad... it was the association with him and his will to hurt. It pleased him to do so. It was how he could care for my status and enjoy rubbing my face in my helplessness before him."

"Shefenga said you were war-trained... for how many years?"

"Two years under the Mahid. Then on my own till now. Gannara and I trained together and I studied the books I could carry with me. Mostly only the slimmest... Five Circles was the first on one I bought after I escaped the Mahid. I couldn't carry the thick ones."

"That is a very fine book... a good choice, Minis."

"Thank you, ser."

Chevenga was just sitting, watching us, quietly, thinking. He had ideas going on behind his brown eyes but he wasn't sharing them yet. Then he spoke up. "But there were the political books too, yes?"

"Oh, every time we stopped in another town I'd go after the libraries or the book sellers in the markets, if there were any. Ilesias's Treaties, The Principles of Ieyasi was interesting because I found it quite close to some..." I cut myself off. Neither of them wanted to hear me burble about good Arkan political texts. "Sorry, it's a subject I find fascinating..."

"It doesn't bore me, and Kallijas is aiming to make it his trade."

"Yes, I am." He smiled slightly.

"Most of those books were my reference for some of the Minakas Akam articles."

"I like them," Kallijas said. "Some show very well how you think... your character. In fact they've helped my understanding." His head motion took in the whole room and all that included.

"Oh. Thank you. But the Imperial Book is a marvelous place to start," I said.

"Help yourself to a cup, Minis," Chevenga said, nodding to the service cart. I smiled my thanks and went to pour myself something warm. My hand hovered over the kaf and then I settled on the *ezethra* for myself.

"What do you think of what this mob-rule-adhering curly-hair is doing to our empire?" Kallijas asked me, completely without cracking a smile, but the twinkle in his eye gave him away. I was used to reading Mahid faces. I had to laugh.

"Marvellous! Promotion by merit was desperately needed." He smiled then. "I'm particluarly interested in how my sire and his father changed the laws in the Imperator's favor and where the checks and balances on office went," I continued.

"It goes back further than your grandfather, Minis," Chevenga said quietly. I nodded.

Kallijas continued his own thought and I wondered that the two of them were working well together to keep me off balance. "But he's making people vote, ...and making the Imperator a jumped up bureaucrat..."

"As the *semanakraseye* is in Yeola-e," Chevenga cut in.

"Ah," I said. "But the Imperator in Illesias the Great's time was exactly that, as well as a sword-buck."

"He was?" Kallijas asked, leaning forward, interested. I was suddenly reminded of General Mud, on the trail of something fascinating.

"He's an Imperator to study --- I thought. Because he understood where power truly comes from." I took a sip of my *ezethra*.

"There is a very old quote about power, do you know it?" Chevenga asked.

"The first one that springs to mind for me is 'Absolute power corrupts absolutely.'" I said.

"I was thinking of a different one... where power truly comes from," Chevenga said.

"Well," I said. "Ilesias himself wrote "All the Imperator's Power is given him by his people, without their support he can do nothing – that's from the Idylls."

"Still another," Chevenga said. "He probably knew it. True power comes from the love of the people. It's a philosopher of politics who wrote long before the first fire."

"He also wrote: The *solas* are the strength of the Empire. Keep their honor as your own." I remembered the worn little book that I had returned and left upon Atzana's Concervancy desk, without mentioning it.

"That's odd that that even needed to be written," Chevenga said.

"It was in his instructions to his son... Sinimas, before the boy died."

"Fair enough," Chevenga said. "Kall would you pass me that chocolate thing?" He pointed at a pastry and Kallijas passed it to him with a smile. I hadn't taken any pastries. I was still having nightmares about getting fat so I watched the sweet, rich things I ate.

"There's a whole list of how to treat each caste," I said, and settled back a little bit. I was talking politics with two of the most important men in the Empire. This was as close to Selestialis for me as it would get for me in this life.

"What did he write about how to treat *okas*?" Kallijas asked me, taking up a cut piece of star-fruit.

"Those who treat *okas* like animals," I quoted. "Obviously do not care to eat. Their labor feeds every caste above them. Treat them with respect or learn to grow your own grain."

"And *daifikas*?" he asked.

"Slaves are given into the hands of Arko by the Gods will, in order to preserve the best of alien races. Beware that the Gods do not decide you need to learn humility at another's hands like this. A slave is still a man.

A man who may one day be free." I nodded at Chevenga thinking that life would have been very different if my father had kept that in his mind.

Chevenga dusted his hands clean of chocolate crumbs, the Imperial seals ringing sweetly. "Because we alien races, you know, we can't preserve ourselves." His laugh invited us to join him and we both smiled with him.

Kallijas shrugged. "Well, we did learn humility at *your* hands."

My smile stretched into a laugh too. "We forgot that. Arko wouldn't have had to learn that if my sire hadn't forgotten all Illesias wrote."

"Having said that, I think Arko would do well with an Imperator who patterned himself after Ilesias," Chevenga continued.

"It would be good. There are a dozen of his books in the Archive that don't exist anywhere else, Ser Itrean. If I recall I had gathered them into the Silver stacks -- the Heir's library." I tilted my head to indicate Chevenga and said to Kallijas, "He reminds me of Ilesias the Great. He always has, even when he was a gladiator."

"But what I've done, really, is brought Arko closer to what I know best -- the Yeoli system," Chevenga said, two points of red coming up on his cheeks. "Were it up to me, I'd outlaw castes at all. Or laws that differentiate between men and women in any ways other than what's relevant to childbirth and nursing."

I caught Kallijas's eye at that and saw we were in accord there. "No, I don't think Arko would be very happy with that at all. They would believe the world was descending into chaos."

"Well, that's why I wanted to go slowly... and the schedule is all set now. I got the start on it by giving women the vote."

"That lets them vote on everything." I shrugged. "If they can vote, then they are people, albeit people who have not been trained to be independent, Chevenga. As always their men will push them how to vote."

"Well, you actually have to think of it as something that, in truth, will take more than one generation. I think maybe you underestimate their strength, Minis... I've seen cases where the woman pushed the man." He was grinning.

"That's in the God's hands." I had to smile at an odd thought. "Perhaps the Goddesses were tired of not being heard?"

"I heard them," Chevenga said, very quietly. "The first Arkan diety I ever heard was a Goddess."

That flung a certain silence in the room. Perhaps because Kallijas was imagining that he might shortly have to listen for the Gods and Goddesses. And me, sorrowing that I would never have the chance.

"Really?" I set my cup down.

"It was Selinae. I had no idea who She was at first," he said, looking into the middle distance. I couldn't take my eyes off him, thinking of the reflected glory I'd seen in the Temple. "I was thinking, it was just a dream... with no particular meaning... Who ever heard of a person with prehensile hair?"

If the Ten did not forgive, Selestialis would be empty.

"But it was too vivid... and it came back too often." Kallijas was nodding. He had obviously heard this but I never had. "She seized me with her hair. It was a very odd feeling. But that was how vivid it was... I can remember it like yesterday." His eyes were taking on more of that reflected glory, as he remembered.

"I'd never heard of the Goddesses speaking to the Imperator, just the Gods." I could feel myself blushing all the way into my hair I was so hot.

"Well, They probably thought, 'he's a Yeoli, he pays attention to females.'" He said, laughing but not losing any of that sacred glow. *How?* "You know how it is... people have their doubts... the Fenjitzas would say, it was the Selinae of my imagination, or even my intentions, if he had the nerve to say it to my face. But it had the same feeling as when I have heard the voice of All-Spirit, which I've heard since I was a child."

"I've heard the flute/voice of Aras when I've fought, but I've never heard words in it," Kallijas said. *Yes. The Gods have touched both these men, deeply. Am I disappointed or relieved that I have no such gifts?*

"You don't have to hear words," the Imperator said. "If you know what the music means. You become Imperator, you do the Ten Tens, right? You have to be listening then." I realized my hands were shaking and I tucked them under my legs to keep them still, but my whole body was shivering. I took a deep breath. "One of those things that is scary, but worth it."

I whispered, "The Ten... still terrify me."

The two men smiled at me and Chevenga said "Then stay and face him, terrified." And Kallijas said "Terrified or not, face Them." They exchanged a look and burst out laughing. I managed a thin smile.

"But most of the time it's not communing with divinities, it's nuts and bolts." Chevenga yawned, already into a long work day, though it was not yet Last Meal. "I know I could have done it all in a more Arkan way if I'd had more Arkan imperial education. But it's as Minis says, the best sources are in the archives, and I couldn't get into them when I was a gladiator."

I looked at the two of them, so different in their look, so much the same in their spirits, their souls. "The way I see it," I said. "You both live in both worlds... somehow managing the day to day, while listening to the Gods at the same time."

"You make me sound like some sort of sage," Chevenga said, grinning.

I shrugged. "You were both raised morally. That's all I'm saying. You have a basis for creating your ethics."

"The person who finds morality without having been raised with it has actually done the harder thing," Chevenga said, even as Kallijas nodded, thoughtfully.

"I had excellent examples of what not to be."

"Examples, plural? More than one? You must be counting 2nd Amitzas, as well as your blood father."

I nodded and signed chalk. "Yes, him too. He certainly whipped me into shape physically."

"But morality, you weren't going to get from him. Not his strong point." He was teasing me. *He's taking a great deal of time to converse with me and Kallijas, to introduce us properly. Why is that?*

"He is a sadist and a fanatic as well. I find it very hard not to hate him. I struggle not to hate. For a number of reasons. Even outrage is something for me to be very, very careful of."

"You know, I see it in Arkans all the time... and part of me never knows what to make of it... so many of you are afraid of yourselves. As if you cannot choose what you will do... with anger, outrage, fear, what-have-you."

"My sire did what he wanted with his and look where that got him and Arko."

"I am sorry if I am sounding like the oh-so-pure Yeoli here... I don't mean to." Chevenga shuddered. "Your sire... was not normal." I just shook my head, not in negation. "The world was not real to him. I actu-ally think people like that are relatively rare." Kallijas was just listening quietly. "It's not as if I haven't seen others... but they are few."

"Very few people have no controls and no conscience."

One of Chevenga's eyebrows rose toward his hairline. "So do you see controls and conscience as the same thing? ... as if every desire is evil?"

"Aren't they?"

"No, of course they aren't. Conscience is doing what is right."

"Perhaps it is just for me. After all, look at my blood."

"But, Minis, every moment you are choosing."

"The will to hurt or be careless or just selfish is there. It needs to be recognised and controlled."

"Maybe I need to ask it like this: why is it, 'I must enchain my desire to hurt,'" Chevenga said. "Rather than, 'I just won't hurt that person'?"

"No one right now, but if I were presented with 2nd Amitzas..." I looked away and shrugged.

"But everyone feels that, with someone who's hurt them so badly. That will happen every time."

"Do Yeolis not feel that the child is born bad and must be trained to good?" I really wanted to hear this one from his lips. I had read this but I couldn't feel it down to my bones.

"No. Why would a child be born bad? That never made any sense to me. You feel the Gods are all-wise, yes? And good?"

"Yes." This time both Kallijas and I spoke together.

"Why would they create children bad, so that the children must suffer to be made good?"

I shook my head. "No, people create children out of their sinful bodies and out of a sinful act. Their souls yearn to the good but their bodies are rooted in the dirt."

"Everything we eat is rooted in the dirt! Minis...... what we eat..... is GOOD. I shouldn't... I've had this debate with so many Arkans... 'How can you think pleasure is a *good* thing?' they'll ask me." I was just shaking my head, listening to him. "I'm thinking, 'How can you think pleasure is a *bad* thing?' And pain is good? Did your nerves grow in backwards or something?"

"Ch'venga... is there no difference between body and soul?"

"There is difference between blue and red, but does that make one bad and the other good?"

"Sex and the body are a reflection of the mortal earth, the idea of death and dying, control and chaos. The soul is above all that."

It was his turn to sign chalk. "I hear the words, but I don't get the idea."

"The Sainted Distinas wrote that paradise lies between shit and piss and I believe he meant more than just symbolically!"

"To my mind, getting pain and pleasure mixed up is madness."

I nodded. "Granted, I got a lot of this training from 2nd Amitzas and 3rd Eforas and both of them have those two firmly tangled together."

"I suggest that what they taught you, you ignore. Unless you would live your life as they live theirs, that is." I just shuddered. Not something I wanted to contemplate. I did *not* want to live my life like a Mahid.

I turned to Kallijas. "Ser Itrean, with your permission, may I observe when you train?" Mercifully, he picked up on my hint.

"Oh, certainly. I can give you some teaching, if you like." I smiled wide enough to feel my cheeks stretch.

"Thank you!"

"So can I, for that matter," Chevenga said and the two of them looked at each other in that way that had them together like sword and fighting chain.

"Well, then, Muunas has heard my prayers." I said, thrilled. *The two best warriors on the earth sphere offer to teach me?* I was breathless with my good fortune, laughing. "When, where and how often can I presume?"

59

EVERYONE IS THE WRONG HEIGHT

GANNARA STOPPED AND SAT DOWN ON THE BENCH UNDER AN OAK,
tugging at his shirt. I sat next to him, leaned forward, picked a long hair
off Gan's shoulder and brushed an invisible dust-speck off his sleeve.

"You look very Yeoli, my brother," I said. He looked so odd, with all
the colours in his hair over-dyed with black. "You look fine. Don't worry
about it. I'll wait here for you but you don't need to come running out
again. You'll know where I am and I won't worry if they don't want to let
you out of their sight for the first little while. They'll want you to stay."

"I want them to meet you."

"So bring them to the Azure suite with you, later. Then they can meet
the real me." We were speaking Yeoli, since my accompanying guard was
Arkan. Gan sat for a while longer, in silence, looking at the sign over the
door on the other side of the street.

GreenHills Shipping and Merchant House

"Gan?"

"Yeah?"

"What's it like to have family?" I wasn't even sure why I was asking.
1st Amitzas was hardly something one would call 'a family'.

He snorted. "I. I can't remember so well. You're better to ask
someone else."

"Ah, *shen*." I seized him in a hug. "I'm sorry I asked."

He hugged me back and then fought me off. "Hey! You'll wrinkle the shirt!"

"Considering that it's crinkled cotton, it's not hard!" He took a deep breath. "It's all right."

"I wish you had never met me... I wish you had never met my family."

"I don't wish that. I mean the meeting you part. I could have done without your dad."

"Yeha. The fat guy."

"About family. You could ask Kallijas Itrean, since we were introduced."

"I just met him, really-- but yes. He has a sort of normal family."

"Or you could ask Ch'venga, if he has time. He always makes you feel better."

I sighed. "Yeha. But...um... Yeolis..."

"You don't see Yeolis as normal?" He started grinning at me, looking a little less nervous. I started blushing.

"Four parents as the most usual family? Not normal at all." I smiled back at him.

He laughed more than my little joke warranted. "I had four parents. I knew a guy who had eight."

"Oh, my beloved ancestors spare me."

"You can't get away with *anything*. There's always at least one of them around!"

"I'd hate to bring a girl home to that... like your friend Fari... something?"

"Farasha. I wouldn't mind. I think they'd like her. What do you know about bringing girls... or boys... home to the parents, anyway?"

"I used to read about how hard it was... to... umm... be... 'checked out?"

"Riiiight..."

"We're stalling." I pointed across the street to the office. "You need to get this over with." I put my hand on his shoulder. "They're in pain and so are you. Go on."

"Yeah, brother." He covered my glove with his hand and got up. "I'll see you... probably in a few days."

"Sure. You can do it, Gan."

I watched him let an express chair pass in a blast of whistle, throw his shoulders back, step into the door and disappear.

~

I could feel Minis watching me as I stepped through the open gate. It led to a courtyard with a garden office in it. A greeter… a boy a little younger than I was… stood up… and he looked familiar to me but I couldn't remember.

"Can I help you, kere?" The greeter asked politely. Was that… my little brother? I… I could't… I thought…I had to cross my arms across my chest. "S…ss…ssach…er…ao?" He stopped, his smile replaced by round eyes.

"PAPAAAAAA!" He yelled. A man at a table desk leapt to his feet, ready for trouble. He took two steps and stopped, staring.

"GANNARA?" I had time to draw breath, maybe, before I was enfolded in the biggest hug and I remembered it. I remembered and started crying.

"Shadow-papa! Shadow papa!" I managed to gasp.

Then my little brother piled in and was hugging me and shadow papa nearly deafened me yelling, right in front of a client or two, not caring in the slightest… 'TISHA! IT'S GANNARA! HE'S HERE! HE'S HOME!"

The shriek from inside was nearly as deafening and it wasn't like shadow-mama at all but she came tearing out, her hands covered in ink and flung herself on the pile of us and there were other people but I couldn't see them all I started crying harder. I was bawling hard enough I couldn't see.

"GANNARA! Oh, kahara, where have you been—what happened to you—you were on Haiu Menshir—we were there the same day!—Duma, run and let Auntie Rao and Great Uncle Cham—we're closing!—you look just like your father! Look at you! You're so big! That awful boy let you go! Are you all right?…" and on and on a flood of words and questions I couldn't answer or even then it wasn't until I was cried out that I could even think about answering any of them.

"Sh--- sh---shadow mama, Sh-shadow papa," I tried to say, and my tongue locked up tight. I couldn't say anything but cling to people until I was cried out and even then. I had snot running down my face and no more tears and I couldn't even sob… I was so happy and scared all at the same time.

"Everybody… everybody back up a bit," shadow-papa said. "He's here, he's not going to disappear from under our hands, he's safe… let's let him catch his breath."

"I've got the wine case you set aside dad," a voice… Erano-e, my older shadow brother's voice. He was… a year older than I was, I remembered.

"Good lad, kerel,--" Without letting go of me he managed to turn to the clients in the office garden. "Our son is home after being lost for years… I'm sorry but our business day is done."

I didn't have to talk. But I did manage to say, "Shadow-mama, Shadow-papa, I'm… I'm… I… I… I…m all right." *Forzak that Mahid stutter.* "Min isn't an awful boy, he saved me… I…I'm." I smacked a fist on my own thigh. "*Kahara* I hate this… I'm sorry, I was scared… you… I… I don't know why I was scared."

Shadow-mama patted my cheeks with a handkerchief, wiping the muck away. It felt so good. "Gannara. It's all right. Sit down and have something to drink and let your shadow papa hold onto you. Linasika, he's shaking… I'll get everyone organized, when Duma gets back…"

They got me sitting down and more family was coming in… more than just shadow-mama and shadow-papa had come to the city. The business was doing well I guess. I kept blinking because I was wrong about having cried myself out. Shadow-papa's hug was just wonderful and I hung on hard. I held onto shadow-mama's kerchief and sniffled and smiled and tried to unlock my throat. My voice was coming back.

I was crying but I had a huge smile on my face at the same time. My chest was loosening and I could take a deep breath. "I'm back, shadow-papa. I'm all right. I'll tell you all about it." He let go of me with one hand to sign chalk and then charcoal.

"Wait until everybody's here, Gan. You don't want to keep telling everybody over and over."

I turned my big, teary grin on him. "Yeah, shadow-papa. I love you."

"We love you too, my lad." He was a lot shorter and balder than I remembered. Everybody was the wrong height, either too tall or a lot shorter.

60

THE WORM OF ERROR

I left Gan in the arms of his family, I could see and hear
they were immediately celebrating so I nodded at my guard and came...
well, home.

I had something on my desk that I had to send up to Chevenga, rising
out of his question about what I wanted to do with my life. I had sat
down and taken up my pen a ten of times and couldn't come up anything.

What came out of my mind wasn't a 'plan' it was -- poetry, and I
didn't understand it. It annoyed me. It was not a logical answer to
anything I had been asked. So finally I thought I needed to send it to
him and perhaps he would have some kind of explanation.

The poem...

The world is full of the worm of error
And I am seized with the wild wind of possibility.
Pulled between the heavy worth of earth and

Oh thou wild
Oh thou unlimited inhibited and swept by
Wind and world and...

I tried to explain my trouble with it, in the note, but finally, in frustration, just sealed it and sent it.

~

The woods around the city are thicker than I remembered. I am running under the trees and see the Fire-flowers everywhere. There are eagles soaring above me, so high above the Rim that they are flecks of solid gold in the sun.

I am running and the golden flecks are suddenly falling toward me. Not falling, diving. I hear the eagles scream and I run faster. They are after me. They are eagles bigger than a man, bigger than a horse... big enough to carry off a man on a horse and carry them into the sky. To them I am a mouse in the grass.

I dodge and dodge and am surrounded by the thunder of wings. The screams beat in my ears. I fall flat as if I am prostrating myself. Then I am up and running again. They are above me again and I hear them screaming. They stoop on me again and this time something big comes up crashing behind. I'm afraid, but not, all at the same time. I run faster as if I can escape and I see sharp, bony points come out around me and I realize there is an enormous deer about to scoop me up in her horns.

I know she is a she. The horns are white. White as snow. White as teeth. White as bone. I am lifted up in the cage of them, swinging up and up as the horned doe runs into the sky, I cling to her horns with my hands, jolting and laughing and terrified all at the same time.

I am safe in her horns. I want to hide from the eagles and it is as if I am invisible, but she cranes her neck and bells at the eagles to no effect. They swoop and screech and search. What are they looking for? She carries me through the arc of her enormous leap and we are back on the ground, in the greenwood.

The horns are warm in my hands and I grasp them in bare hands, and lean out and down and stare into her wide, brown eye. "Can I get down now?"

The doe flings her head and I hang by my hands, flapping like a flag, over the rim and I lose my grip. I fall down toward the roof of the Marble Palace and fall past the image of the Eagle cut into the cliff. But it has been re-gilded. The golden image peels up off the rock, the paper-thin and perfect, searching, seeking. I catch the edge of a hair-thin neck feather with one hand as I fall and, like the time I was drunk as a child, I hang from it above the slate roof.

It folds itself down and sets me safe on the roof. "Miiiiiiiiiiiiinnnn" It shrieks and folds up to put itself against the rock once more but I notice the gilding running from its eyes like tears.

I wake up in the middle of the Great Hall, apparently in the middle of doing the Ten Tens. I can feel the echoes of whispers in the ceiling of the last of Risae's prayer. I should not stop. I should no longer be doing this. But it is not right that even the practice be stopped once begun, so I go on to the Cunning Mikas's part of the rite. Then Dimae, Sera of the Wild Wood and… in the appropriate place, in the dim light of the moon shining on Muunas's head I put my hand on a sword. The Imperial Sword. Chevenga had sent me to get it from our lodging and not demanded custody of it, saying I had kept it well so far, and asked me to keep it until he asked me to give it back.

Steel Armed Aras. I had brought a sword with me, in my sleep, to the Great Hall, to do the Ten Ten's practice. I picked it up. The Ten obviously wanted me to do it, so I would give it every scrap of my will. As They willed. But I could not stop the tears running, in the dark, where no one could see, or hear me.

The Temple must, for me, be forever empty. I had submitted myself to the true Imperator's hands, surrendered all claim on the Crystal Throne. This practice, these motions, in my hands, in my body, were illegal enough that the penalties for doing it were horrific. Chevenga would not care, trusting the Ten to mete Their own justice. The dark made it easier. *The Temple must be silent for me. My punishment for being Aan will be to be exiled from that light, from that glory.*

I would finish and go back to lay my head down in the bed once more, hopefully to no more dreams. Gannara was still home with his family so I hadn't disturbed him with my night walking.

I managed to keep my calm enough to do the rite well, all the way to the end, and I could kneel in the middle of the floor with my hands over my face in the dark. There was no one there to hear me weep.

Next day Gannara came back and said he'd wanted to bring his shadow parents up to meet with me but thought he should let me know, so I could be prepared. "Thanks, Gan."

"You look tired. You having bad dreams again?"

"Dreams, sure. But not really bad."

"Right." He didn't sound convinced. I liked the way he looked. He looked lighter, more whole. More comfortable in himself and I loved seeing it.

"I trained on the roof this morning… with Kallijas. He's being very gentle for someone with his tremendous reputation as a warrior… I was scared shenless. He acted as if he could see all the training scars Ice Eyes left on me. He's… um… cracking me loose, he says."

"Oh yeah?" That diverted him and I was able to regale him with tales of all the odd things Arko's greatest champion was having me do, and stopped Gan from asking about the dreams.

～

'… there, where the two men first met, when they were boys. The Spark of the Ineffable Light and the Yeoli *anaraseye--*" The knock at the door made me jump but I was lucky and didn't blotch my page.

The servant handed me a note from Chevenga, in his awful short-hand scrawl, asking me to bring Gan, if he was with me, to the Scarlet Rosary Chamber that evening.

61

SUCH A MORON!

Gan was back again before the evening meeting. "I'm going to be going back and forth for a while. Farasha wants to meet the family. That means you too, once we figure out what's going to happen with you," he said. Oh. Of course. I pasted a smile on my face. Things just kept getting more and more complicated.

~

This set of Scarlet rooms was becoming familiar. We were let in, with no more ceremony than the corridor guard opening the door for us. Chevenga was already there, still dictating something to his secretary.

"… that should be sufficient, Ch'venga," he was saying, packing up his lapdesk. It was big enough that instead of being a true lapdesk, it had to be put on wheels to carry all the seals and inks and pens and other things an Imperial Secretary needed.

"Thanks, Binchera. Hello, Min… and Gannara."

I began bending my knee to go down and he said 'Gehit!' before I could even start to do the prostration. I heard the door closed behind the secretary and Chevenga waved us over to chairs.

"I don't have a lot of time, Minis. I need to ask you. Did you know about Compartment Fourteen, section Eight?"

My guts clenched. I had hoped that it was one of the laws he had done away with. Obviously not. There was a settling, a kind of finality to everything. It was right. The Gods wanted me here and here was where my life was going to end. "14.8" I quoted. 'If a man or boy by reason of his ancestry or birth is likely to, or likely to be seen to, make a claim to Imperium, the Imperator shall arrest him and his immediate male kin, and execute them publicly, in such a way as to produce firm proof of the death of all.' It was Eleventh Filias Aan who enacted it," I said, trying to state it calmly, trying not to shake. "232, Present Age, to legitimise executing his grandson Twelfth Filias by his first son Ninth Amitzas, whom he had disinherited."

His brows drew together almost in a single black line. "You didn't come here and reveal yourself to me thinking it was still on the books, did you?" He asked me. I shrugged. I hadn't checked. It hadn't seemed important after the Ten Tens.

"I thought you'd gotten rid of the oppressive laws." There, that was neutral enough and didn't make me sound like a complete idiot.

Gannara's eyes widened. "It's... it's... still..."

"You mean... it's still a current law? The Assembly would want that law still there, specifically for me. You didn't take it off?"

"I didn't *mean* not to." Chevenga looked chagrined.

"You were probably too busy to notice if it was there or not and Arko would have been afraid of me and my eclipse court... all my Mahid. We were a danger." I kept my eyes on Chevenga, but I could feel Gan glaring at me. I knew he wanted to yell at me.

"Of all the crack-brained, idjit things to do!" Gan said finally. "You *didn't check* to see if this law you knew about... that would MAKE the *semanakraseye*...your friend... KILL YOU?"

I just shook my head feeling so tired. "I would have come anyway. For the sake of Arko, now and into the future. It's as I said: I put my life into your hands." Perhaps I'd be able to rest once he killed me. I remembered the snatch of dream I'd had about walking to the headsman's block. Perhaps it was presentience.

Chevenga looked away from me and took a deep breath... then smacked his hands on the arms of his chair and sprang up to pace as if the room weren't big enough. "Either you disappear again, and do your best to do it in such a way that no one can kidnap and make a puppet of you, or claim to be your descendant—or we try to talk for your life to Assembly. I don't like either of them, but at the moment at least I see no other... do you?"

"Chevenga, would you have me leave and become a threat to my country, my home, again? I can't do that. Against Arko, I am nothing at all. As are you." I didn't understand why it was so hard for him to understand that. He was the one who had taught me that kind of responsibility.

He signed chalk, hand out to one side so I could see it, even as he had his back to us, the other hand clenched at the small of it. "Yes. *Kahara*—your father should have had a *hundredth* of the sense of responsibility you have."

Gannara turned away, and pressed his face into the plush back of his chair, hands clenched in his long hair, silent.

"I can speak for you," Chevenga said. "You know I will do that. If anyone will be believed about you, it's me, who suffered so much at the hands of your father."

"I know you would." I said it as quietly and as calmly as I could. Somewhere in me some part of me was screaming that I didn't want to die. I told that part to shut up. "Thank you."

"And no one knows you're here except the three closest to me, and I told them to keep it quiet, so that gives us time to try to think of something else." He turned around and his face had relaxed somewhat, as had his shoulders. "Minis—you gave an answer to my question, what do you want to do, but it was a small one: finish some works of Minakas. I want you to answer it more completely. What do you want your life to be?"

"I only thought as far as here, Chevenga," I said "And that note I sent you. Nothing more."

"Think further. If you had fifty, sixty years of life ahead of you: what would you want to fill them with?"

Gannara turned around and his eyes were red-rimmed and he had his sparring stare on. I felt as if they were two brothers staring at me hard, as if I would run away from such a question. I flung up my hands as if to push their gaze back. "I… I said finish the Minakas works…" I gulped, hard, my mouth dry. "If I could live, I would probably make a middling-good political scholar, tucked away here in the archive. That would be a good life." What a dream. I'd have to live to see it and 14.8 ensured that it was only a dream.

"Never mind 'if you could live'" he snapped. "—I'm asking, if every option were open, if nothing were stopping you from doing whatever you wanted. Tell me that."

"Every option…" I looked over at Gannara and then back to

Chevenga. There was no escape from this question, however much I wanted to run from it.

"Even if it seems like only a dream. Tell me."

I licked my lips. "A… a family… would be nice. I always thought I would have one."

"And your work?"

"Something…" I pushed back into the wing-chair wishing desperately that he had not asked me that question, wishing I could just quietly vanish and cease being such a problem and a trouble. "…political." I managed a whisper.

"To what end?" *WILL YOU JUST LEAVE IT ALONE!* I wanted to scream. *WHAT DOES IT MATTER? I'M DEAD ANYWAY!* I shook my head.

"Answer him, crack-brain!" Gannara reached out to nudge me and I realized I'd gone still as well as quiet, holding my breath as if hiding from a predator. Like the eagles I'd dreamed of. I was a mouse under their combined looks. I managed to pull in another small breath. "For the good of Arko… administration… maybe Kallijas, or whoever wins, will need someone like me."

He signed chalk, decisively. "Good enough." He looked almost satisfied. "Let me think on it, and you think on it too. We're not doing anything public until we deal with your Mahid anyway."

"Oh, yes." That made my middle relax. That would take a little time to plan and execute. I flinched away from that word in my mind. "There's time."

～

"SOMETIMES, FOR A SMART PERSON, YOU'RE JUST SUCH A MORON!" Gan had a lot of stamina. I had to give him that. He'd been yelling at me for almost a full tenth and hadn't lost any volume at all and he'd never repeated himself once, nor said anything that would give my identity away if someone heard him, either outside or in a spy-tunnel. "YOU COULDN'T CHECK THE LAW?"

"It didn't matter, Gan. I told him. I'll tell you again. It wouldn't matter. I'd still have done it."

"It's not right. I'm willing to bet it's one of these laws that could be argued was never valid. I'd be willing to stand up and argue it, because it targets innocent people, babies, kids… I'll bet there's an advocate who would be able to make a case that it's an invalid law!" He finally got a little quieter.

"I… suppose." He grabbed me by the shoulders and shook me before putting his nose almost up to mine. His next words were whispered.

"You listen to me, First Minis Kurkas Joras Amitzas Aan! You did your *fikken* duty by turning yourself in. It doesn't mean you have to die, got that? You are going to stop this *fikken, shennen, kyashin, kaina marugh meniren,* wool-knot picking, goat diddling, Gods and *kahara forzak* crapping on yourself once and for all! Do you hear me?"

His eyes were flecked with tiny bright gold spots. This close, I couldn't help but notice. I'd nod except I'd bump our foreheads if I did. "Yeha. I hear you." I couldn't close my eyes.

"You told Chevenga the hideous thing your father did that you've been blaming yourself for, and he doesn't hold you responsible, you're not tainted or evil or vile or *forzak* or any other nasty thing you think of yourself, got that? Zinchaer liked you and told you the same thing. I love you and I've been telling you that for years. Your tutor and Binshala and Kaita and Kyriala and Ilesias… we're not stupid people. Give us some credit for seeing the truth, okay? We *all* wouldn't love an evil person, so quit telling us that we're deluded! Do you understand how much you're insulting our judgment when you argue with us?"

I could only blink at him. "Oh. Um. I'm sorry. Gan I didn't mean to insult any of you. I guess… I suppose… It seems too easy for me to let go of that. Too easy on me."

"Well, stinkin' listen for once. Ch'venga has or is coming up with some kind of plan, that was obvious. So I'll trust that it all works out for the best for you and for your precious country too… though if I had to choose between your country and you, Minis, I'd want you."

"Thanks Gan. Thank you. You've -- given me a lot to think about." I felt as though he'd taken a hammer to this enormously thick glass wall inside me. It wasn't broken through yet but there were huge cracks in it, finally.

"And my family and Farasha are going to want to meet you, over dinner, so go scrub your brain out in the bath and get a good night's sleep for once?!"

"But…" He smacked fingers across my lips, shutting me up.

"Shh!" He said, firmly. "We are going to keep on as if 14.8 has already been solved. No negative words, no arguing, no worrying. It's in

Ch'venga's hands and he's shown that he can solve the impossible situation over and over and over again."

All I could do was nod, and I smiled against his fingers, warm across my mouth. He smiled back. "Do I have your word on that?"

When he took his fingers away so I could answer I had to find the air somewhere. "Yes. I will not worry."

62

KAF AND MUSIC AND CREME CAKES

"Kyriala? Are you paying attention to your guests at all?" Her mother hissed discretely in her ear. "I thought you wanted to have these gatherings to improve mind and attention?"

She snapped her fan open and fanned herself more vigourously than absolutely necessary. "I was just thinking, mama."

"Think later, my daughter. I do believe that young Benthasas Monnen has just arrived and you and I need to greet the man!"

Oh dear. Oh dear. Benthasas, again. He's very good looking. He was wounded in the final defense of the city. Oh dear. He's charming. He's nice. I do like discussing the implications of women voting with him. But... he's predictable. After all this, the madness in the Marble Palace, the insanity in the wilderness... when did 'he's predictable' become 'I'm bored talking to him?' When did my standards of 'interesting' change?

"Of course, mama. Oh look, the butler just let Ormanas Tafan and Hikinian Fidaren in as well, let's go greet them all." The men would be obliged to be polite and speak to each other and wouldn't be able to hang on her sleeves all during the salon. The looks they were covertly giving each other made her hide her mouth behind her fan. *Am I a female cat to be fought over by all the rude toms?*

She looked around the garden room. Her guests -- technically guests for her little brother who was twelve now and most interested in the cream cakes -- were chatting together over cups of *kaf* all the way out the

open doors to the wide stone terrace with its shade sails, the garden and
the smooth green lawn beyond. A superficial glance over the elegant little
scene might make one think the city hadn't been sacked so few years ago.
She caught Laisa's eye across the room and her friend tipped her own fan
back at her, the barest quiver of the end, and they smiled at each other.
She was in a similar position as Kyriala with her mama pushing that she
be betrothed again, but Laisa had her grandmamma on her side, coun-
cilling 'wait'.

If one looked closer, the signs of war recovery were there. The cups
and saucers were mis-matched and anything new was quite plain, for her
mother's taste. The damaged and replaced wood trims were not quite
matched to the old, the coloured window glass scenes had been replaced
with plain, clear glass. Mama bemoaned having lost so many things but
Kyriala found she didn't miss it much. "Once you're wed, the family will
make up so much that we lost, Ky!" *It is not hardship to have to drink out
of ungilded cups.* That kind of money worry made Ky very tight lipped
about some things.

For instance, the scarf that she had worn around her waist full of
money chains and gemstones. Minis hadn't mentioned it as he'd said
goodbye and she'd been wearing it so long she'd forgotten that she still
had it. She hadn't realized until she'd disrobed late that night that she
hadn't been able to give it back to Minis. She'd risked a note to Ailadas
and he'd written back saying Minis had left instruction that she keep it,
just as Kaita was supposed to. *I haven't mentioned the little hoard to mama.*

The scarf, knotted tight, like a narrow, lumpy snake lying along the
top of her bed canopy, was going to be her independence once she
reached her majority. *Mama's frantic to have me safely wed before my third
threshold which is coming up much too soon for her.*

She snapped her fan -- one that Laisa had actually made for her, with
slender steel spines hidden in the hollow spars – closed and followed her
mother to the entry hall where the new arrivals all waited.

"Gentle Sers," Daurama Liren said and surreptitiously nudged her
distracted daughter with her toe.

"Ser Benthasas, Ser Ormanas, Ser Hikinias," Kyriala restrained the
urge to whap her mother on the back of her elaborate hairstyle with her
fan. "Do come in. May I pour *kaf*?"

Their polite murmurs of greeting to mother and her followed as she
turned, not letting Benthasas offer the back of his hand to escort her. Let
mama sigh.

She paused on her way across the room to speak to another friend. "Oh, yes, shall I freshen your cup, Skala?" Her friend was very properly gowned but the hair at the crown of her head was bright pink and fanned out from her head like a short upstanding peacock's tail, the rest flowing down her back to brush her hem. She was talking to a girl with her hair cut *okas* short and dyed in indigo and bright blue stripes. The Dyer was just explaining, "… I'm not really *okas* I cut my hair to spite my father and betrothed…"

"Thank you, Kyriala… In a click…" Skala bent her head to listen, smiling, as Ky lead the new guests to the faux *kerulan*-style table where the *kaf* service sat. She sat down and poured. *As long as I'm fussing with kaf and cups they can't really talk to me.* But that ploy could only last so long.

"I'm looking forward to hearing your reader, Serina," Benthasas said. "Thank you, cream only. Ormanas here mentioned your reader was going to be presenting a selection from "The Elegant Solution.""

"Why, yes, Ser. That will be later on, allowing people to meet each other." She raised her eyes from the cup she was just pouring and to her friend Skala who was just approaching. "Skala, will you introduce me to your friend?"

"Oh, certainly. Kyriala Liren might I introduce Riala Kien. Riala, this is my good friend Ky, Ser Benthasas, Ser Ormanas and…"

"I already know Ser Hikinian," Riala cut in. "If you're pouring, Kyriala? I take my *kaf* black." She smiled at Kyriala, half turning her back on Hikinian, who glared at her. "Nice to meet you. And Sers…"

Ormanas just blinked through his spectacles and his hand shook, making his cup rattle in its saucer.

"It's nice to meet you Serina," Benthasas said calmly. "Serina Skala, what interesting friends you have."

"Oh!" Ormanas gulped and coughed as if he'd just swallowed too big a mouthful of hot *kaf*. "Serina Kien? Are you related to Professor Kien? The Under Chancellor at the University?"

Riala sipped her *kaf* . "That is nicely brewed. You may as well dispense with the 'Serina'. Just Riala or Kien if you want."

"Thank you, Riala," Kyriala said. "You may call me Ky. Might I ask why you are asking us to dispense with polite forms of address?"

"Oh, that's an archaic form of address that I don't want to have to hear. I'm considering dropping my father's name since I don't wish to carry it, ever since he disowned me."

"Ah." There didn't seem to be anything to say to that. But Kyriala liked the twinkle in Riala's eyes. "You might want to talk to my friend Laisa Si Rusa… I'd like to introduce you…" Ky looked around the room at the various conversing groups. Mama was speaking with an older lady… one of the Puriren, new to the city, that Ky didn't know but she couldn't see Laisa immediately. "Later."

"Thank you, Kyriala."

"I think the stripes are amazing… I like it," Ky continued. "My mother would be scandalized if I should dye so much as a single strand of mine." *I shall have to look into that tomorrow.*

Hikinian, looking as though he'd swallowed a wasp when Riala snubbed him so rudely, cleared his throat. "I think your hair is lovely as it is, Serina."

"Thank you for the compliment, Ser Hikinian."

"Dye washes out," Skala said, taking a sweet crème bun from a servant. "Cutting is …permanent."

"My dear friend… hair grows back, especially if one wishes… it is hardly a scandal any longer, but more a statement." Ky said quietly, thinking of how hard it had been to cut Minis's hair.

Riala smiled. "True, though there are some things that, once cut, will never grow back. Yeoli women have never been cut that way, yet they seem to be more blessed than we."

Kyriala was astonished to find herself actually speaking a thought she'd thought before, out loud. "If any parts of our bodies are incorrect, why did the Gods put them there in the first place?"

The three men looked tremendously uncomfortable, standing with their delicate gilded cups in their hands, for once exchanging glances that showed them in accord rather than rivals, at least for the duration of this conversation.

"So, says the Voice of the Gods on the Earthsphere," Riala said quietly. "The Pages have been running those stories of women coming forward with the harm it has done them… Including the Fenjitza."

Ormanas leaned forward, looking a little like a crane, eyes wide and round behind his spectacles, swallowing nervously and enthralled to hear such shocking viewpoints expressed so openly. Hikinian pressed his lips together on more than one swallowed wasp if one went by his expression. Benthasas sipped his *kaf* and listened attentively.

Kyriala surrendered the pouring to her Auntie Rue and took up her own cup. The little group went with her to the shaded and curtained terrace outside. Benthasas held her chair for her and as she sat down Socks came panting up to sit upon her feet. "One must realize that those Pages stories are not the moon-sprite and glass goose stories that used to be published... don't you agree Ser Benthasas?" She said to him.

"Sometimes it is hard to know whether to trust the pages." He responded mildly, neutrally. "But the voices of the Gods... the Imperator Himself... and the Fenjitzas and the Fenjitza all speak out against the long-held tradition."

"It is a little different," Ormanas gulped.

"Actual people," Skala said drily, the pink spikes standing up behind her head like a divine sunburst shining upon her hair. "Not 'reports say' or 'it is said'."

"This is excellent *kaf*," Hikinian said, glowering at Bentharas. "... and such fine porcelain."

"Thank you, Ser. The pattern is my mama's favourite." *What's left of it. I will take your clumsy change of topic.* "So I just read that a scholar once wrote that philosophy is the highest music. What do you gentlemen think?"

"Well, I think that 'highest' is perhaps not the most interesting catagory to rank sciences, Serina, but if philosophy is music then logic must sing?" Ormanas smiled and ceased gulping, having been presented with a philosophy question rather than the shocking or the uncomfortable ideas. Since everyone was now looking at him he gulped and shrank into himself once more, sipping his *kaf.*

Kyriala fanned herself abruptly with her snapped-open fan. *Did he realize the double entendre? Did he mean to suggest...?* "Sing?" She coughed. "Skala do you play the table harp? Since Ser Tafan mentioned singing... I shall..." She practically leaped to her feet, Socks jumping up, beginning to bark. Ormanas stared, confused, picking at a spot of ink dried into the ends of his hair. Benthasas and Hikinian were both hiding smiles, Benthasas into his cup, Hikinian more openly behind a raised glove. Riala snorted. "Ser Ormanas did you mean to make a sexual joke?"

Skala burst out giggling as she and Kyriala actually fled inside to the table harp, so as to not laugh right in the young scholar's face. "He... he didn't even realize what he was saying? Did he?"

"No. He just never learns. Perhaps Raila will enlighten him. Laisa, I am so sorry to interrupt your conversation, but I have a request for some music. May I request you help us?"

After 'The Chestnuts of Arko' 'Rim Dawn Hymn' and a little humorous piece called 'New in the City', Ky begged off singing and sank down in a chair beside the garden windows, fanning herself, listening to her guests discussing who should play or sing next. Laisa ended up choosing an old lament, 'The Fallen General', and persuaded Ser Iliar to play the harp for her.

"Serina Kyriala." Benthasas stood to one side, his *kaf* cup exchanged for a wine glass.

"Ser Mennon," Kyriala jumped. She hadn't heard him come so close. Laisa and Iliar prepared to do the song, while everyone else stayed clustered around the harp, with the ladies sitting on the settees and light chairs, and the gentlemen standing behind. Ky caught mama's eye as she checked to see where she was, but rather than moving closer, her mother merely settled next to Auntie Tekka, folding her gloves under a lap scarf, preparing to listen. *Was that... approval in her eyes? Oh...*

"I'm sorry to have startled you, Serina Kyriala... may I call you Kyriala?"

"Ser... Benthasas... it is rather forward..." She flipped open her fan again and used it as a shield, put it between him and her.

He set the glass down on a tall spindly little table next to mama's new, ugly little fluff-fern. "Let me come immediately to the point. You are an intelligent woman, as well as beautiful. I shall be tremendously blunt and tell you I believe any children will be phenomenally attractive –"

She couldn't let him go on... "Ser!" Let him think she was offended, even if he were following the new, open fashion for people to speak to each other.

He smiled and didn't answer immediately and her heart sank. He was attractive. He had a nice smile and he had been a warrior who fought even the hopeless last battle to keep the city from being sacked. His hair was fine and long and strong and bright and he had a slight cleft in his chin, but she found herself searching for dimples, which he did not have.

Benthasas made the formal two-hand spread wide bow to her, as her breath caught. There was only one time that an Arkan man ever, ever bowed to a woman. When he came up from his bow he held out his glove – the open palm to her. On it was the split, empty glass wedding ring. "Kyriala... will you do me the honour of accepting my suit? Will you fill my ring with your marriage lock?"

63

A MERCY, A MERCY

I'm climbing the steps of the Presentation platform. Ilesias is there. I kneel on the platform and wrap my arms around him. He will not see me executed, he will die first, I know it. Oh, a mercy, a mercy... 1ˢᵗ Amitzas is there and he has his kit spread out. My brother will be unconscious before Ilesias Mahid cuts his head off.

The crowd is making an ugly noise full of their fear of me and my innocent little brother. They think we are corrupt as our father. They... the Assembly of Arko... insisted on enacting the law despite anything Chevenga could do.

The Imperator... isn't Chevenga... this is after the vodai... I don't recognize the Aitzas who is now the Son of the Sun...He has the look of a Kallen... I see Ilesias's eyes close, in my arms, as the drug takes him away... Rest in Selestialis little brother... I make my fingers let go as they lift his limp little body away from me. Now I will pray. Now I will beg the Gods to take him straight to Selestialis. I cannot watch from where I am kneeling, my hands at my temples. My eyes are squeezed shut but I cannot close my ears and I hear...

I was sitting bolt upright in the bed in the Marble Palace suit, blinking, with the sound of the head'sman's axe cutting through my little brother's neck still thudding in my ears, in my bones. *When is it? What day is it? Is it early morning or... my head is full of confusion. It's in the middle of the night and I can't breathe.*

My bare feet on the rug looked unreal as I climbed out of bed. I splashed water from the basin on my face. *When am I?* I threw my robe over my cotton nightclothes, caught up the Imperial sword and went out, heading for the Great Hall. The sentry at the end of the hall nodded at me as I headed toward the Lesser Baths. "Good morning, ker. You know you don't need to be armed in the Marble Palace?"

"Thenk yah, ker. I've a sword-exercise... ker, ah can't sleep." She nodded. At least the Yeoli sentries understood that explanation and didn't wonder why a *fessas* would want to train with a sword at all.

"Good meditating, ker." She stepped back and let me go. The stone under my bare feet felt wonderful. There was a bead clock in a niche over the stairs. It was so late it was early. I shouldn't be doing this but it was one of the only ways I could settle my head enough to try and sleep a bit more.

I would be training with Kallijas on the roof later this morning and I was starting to wonder if I should bother. I was trying to act as if 14.8 no longer existed, the way Gannara said. Gan... he was with his family so I hadn't disturbed him with my waking. I would be meeting with his family for dinner tomorrow... yes, tomorrow.

I would be able to go out again to meet them, with a guard in tow, of course. For dinner. The way my guts felt right now the thought of food was nauseating. I tried to breath through it, stopped at the entrance to the Great Hall. I didn't think Chevenga would mind that I was still doing the Ten Tens in the middle of the night. It wasn't as if I was a pretender to the Crystal Throne anyway, so my intentions were not treason.

The Hall was full of dark, and echoing cool. There was enough light from the moon and stars coming through the roof window for me to go to lay the Imperial sword in the correct place and pad back to my starting mark. My toes knew it. All the way up to and past my heart.

I was able to begin calming my mind by the time I got to Imbas's part. I filled my mind with how it must have looked when Chevenga did it... In the darkened hall my mind filled with light. If I could cling to that I could calm myself enough to swim and then sleep after.

～

The thump of a knock had me sitting bolt upright again, just as I had earlier. "Enter, please." The servant came in and set a breakfast tray down. Since I would be training it was earlier than the formal First

Meal. I gulped a cup of *kaf* down and sniffed my cottons... they would do.

The chef had made foamed eggs and porridge and I couldn't gulp it down. I knew enough that I had to eat something or I would not be able to train but if I gulped or gorged I'd end up vomiting. 2nd Amitzas had trained that into me.

Every lesson was terrifying because I was afraid I'd fail and failing such a teacher made my heart sink. I was both exhilarated to have Kallijas willing to teach me, but I was also afraid. I knew that I would not be good enough. The old whip strokes across my back felt tight and hot.

It was before rim-dawn when I and the sword emerged onto the Marble Palace roof, with the evening damp cold underfoot, the mist fading fast. My heart was in my throat and I realized I was a trifle late anyway, since the *solas* on the roof were just lining up. *Oh ancestors.*

Kallijas came trotting over from the group. "Minakas. Good you're just in time." *I was?* "First things today... I need to find out more about your conditioning and what you know. Just keep up with me, hmm? I'll call it."

Just keep up with him? He's going to do the exercises with me rather than standing over me? We did all the exercises that I knew, and a good half dozen that I had never seen before. He ran me up and over the Eagles's tower and I had to smile to myself remembering the last time I'd climbed it. At least this time I wasn't drunk.

Spots were swimming in front of my eyes when he called me to kneel. "You're about to pass out, lad."

Honesty. "Yes, ser."

To be so honest, kneeling in front of Kallijas whose likeness was reflected in so many icons of Aras himself, his eyes chips of gemstone they were so bright... was hard for me to do. His spirit shone in every inch of him and I so did not want to disappoint him with my performance, since he'd agree to teach me.

He just nodded. "I will take that into account." *Really?* I was surprised that he hadn't just run me to passing out. Then he really surprised me. "Hold out your hands." He reached over to a basket he had beside him, flipped it open, reached inside and drew out a fluffy ball of white and dropped it in my hands.

I caught the kitten and it flipped over and clung to my sweaty gloves with all four paws, biting and pawing as if it could kill my fingers, play-growling. I gaped at it and then at Kallijas. "Play with that kitten for a half-tenth." I sat frozen and he smiled. "Truly. Play with that kitten for a half-tenth," he repeated.

The kitten was too young to actually be able to bite or claw me through my gloves so I used my covered fingers to tickle the belly and twiddle all four of its feet. It was the oddest exercise I'd ever had to do. *My teacher is smiling and telling me to play with kittens. Am I dreaming? This makes no sense.*

He held out his hand for the kitten after what felt far too short a time. "Now. Tell me three things you've learned about fighting, from playing with this young cat."

I blinked. "Ser? This cat... um..."

"Quick! Three things... don't think too much!" He petted the kitten and set it in the now open basket where it immediately leapt out ran behind me and began attacking my toes.

"Ow! Tenacity! Um... fluid... ow... fluidity... and um... no boxes!"

"Good, up! Don't step on the kitten. Put your sword down there and we'll start empty handed."

Sparring? Oh Sin. Kallijas smiled when he sparred. 2nd Amitzas had smiled too but this was different. It was pure joy. It was light and even as he was teaching me some of the oddest moves I'd ever seen it was as though... it was the strangest thing. It was as if he loved what he did and... loved me – even... even as I took the place of an enemy.

We went faster and stronger, and even as I thought I had nothing left in me and was cursing myself for being too sloppy, too slow... I... was having fun. Terrified fun but still fun. And... he... didn't seem disappointed in what I could do.

He took me to the point where I thought I was going to fall over but never past that first point where I almost fell over... and kept me there for far, far longer than I thought possible. "Don't step on the kitten," was his most frequent teaching and the silly ball of fluff insisted on playing with our feet while we sparred.

"Cease! Good," Kallijas said and I straightened out of stance as he did. He wasn't sweating at all and I was soaked. At that point the fluff-ball decided she wanted to get more height and climbed up my back and under my braid. I did my best not to flinch. *Good?* I'd sparred and worked out as nimbly as a spavined destrier. "I'd like you to keep your training partner there, for a while, hmmm?"

He nodded at the kitten on my shoulder. *Was the man mad? I'd spent most of my time trying not to step on the forzak thing while one of the greatest warriors in the world pounded on me...* His eyes twinkled as I nodded. "Yes, Teacher."

"I have a little more to do, if you care to watch." As if I would go away when he'd let me watch.

I sank down on the slate tile and listened to the chorus of training calls coming from across the roof where the elite were still working out and Kallijas did this wild, flowing dance, with his sword in his hand, singing to himself in Yeoli... but a Yeoli I didn't recognize. It was eerily beautiful and I could see... it was the wildest thing but it was as though he was being the Mountain and Stars.

He was winded when he stopped and looked up. "Noon," was all he said and sank to his knees. I was recovered enough to roll up from sitting to kneeling and put my hands to my temples and sing the Noon prayer with him and the others kneeling all across the roof and all across the city. The silence afterwards was no longer polluted by the screams of children.

"You should see the old Yeoli lady who taught me," he said when we all rose. He was grinning and seemed cleansed even more if that were possible. "I am not fit to hold her stick while she does that, but I just need forty or fifty more years to be as good, perhaps."

"An old Yeoli lady?"

"I was with a woman by the name of Sukala Iri for a while in Yeoli. Shall we get cleaned up and eat something?"

"Yes, ser... ah... Kallijas." His lips quirked but he didn't say anything.

64

A FRAUGHT DINNER PARTY

I sat in the same park across from Gan's parent's business. *Greenhills Shipping and Merchant House* The letters swam in front of my eyes. Gan and I talked it over and figured out it would be easier for the family if I came down and there was no reason to hide so they could meet me as Minis straight off. *Oh joy.*

My guard was waiting for me to enter the building before leaving and would be waiting for me in two beads, should I be ready to leave by then. *More likely I'll flee screaming inside a tenth. They hate me. They must. And this girl Gan's sleeping with? Why am I doing this? I'm going to get four-teenated and won't have to worry about it any more!*

This was worse than what was described in most knuckle-suckers... the 'meeting the family' scenes. Most back alley trash heroes or villains didn't have the family already to hate his shadow. Gan peeked out the gate and grinned. I could see that all the way across the street. He waved 'come on' at me.

I gulped, and the guard said, "I'll see you in, *ker.*" *Here we go.* I made my shaking legs raise me up and walk me over. I had to wait for a courier to whip past me, whistle shrilling, and then I couldn't delay any longer.

At the gate I said, "Hi, Gan," faintly. He flung his arms around me.

"Minakas, you *idya* it'll be fine!" The guard faded, and I inexplicably wanted her back. *Don't be silly, you don't need a guard to protect you from Gan's family!*

With his arm still around my shoulders, he turned me around to face the people in the courtyard, standing next to me. His girlfriend wasn't there yet. The older man's hair was light brown, almost blond, and thinning, his wife dark haired, dark eye'd, almost as dark as Gannara. The three boys with them... I could see the youngest looked most like Gan with black hair. I felt like I was going to just melt away under their combined gazes and longed for that to happen, so I could flow away through the cracks in the stones of the courtyard and not have to keep standing there.

In Yeoli he said. "Shadowmama, Shadowpapa, sibs, I'd like you to meet my best friend in the world," I didn't have the nerve to poke him.

"Minis." It was so hard to not flinch at hearing my own name just spoken out like that. Thank goodness I could manage speaking Yeoli.

"*Kerel*," I managed. His shadow father stepped forward with both hands out. His shadow mama stood slightly behind, looking stiff under her calm surface - but she beamed when she glanced at Gan.

"Welcome to our house, Minis." I took them, feeling his fingers warm through my gloves.

"Thank you, Ser... um... sorry... Ker..."

"I'm Linasika. Tisha come say hello." She gave me her hands as well.

"Welcome, Minis. It is....a pleasure to meet you at last. Please, come into the shade," as she gestured to a bench in the courtyard. She didn't seem to be forcing the words out, but she *did* seem uncomfortable, and her hands trembled slightly.

"Min, this is my shadow sib, Erano-e, my shadow sib Dumaryae, and my younger blood sib, Sacherao." It was the usual overwhelming bunch of handclasps and I tried hard to smile at everyone.

"I'm... so happy Gan got home..." I managed. "He was worried about me and I couldn't convince him he should..." *Oh shen, how stupid. Did I have to say that?*

"Gan?" That was Sacherao. "Oh, you mean Nara!"

"Nara," Gan said. "That's what the family calls me... I'd forgotten and then forgot to mention it to you."

"Nara," I repeated, dutifully. *I'll never remember. But I guess I'll have to try.* I took a deep breath. *Best get it over with.* I looked straight at his shadow parents. I wanted to talk to Linasika but Yeolis had different ideas and I should speak to her, not him. I made myself address his shadow mother. "Ker Shae-Ara. For the stress and pain my family caused yours, I owe you and your family more than just an apology but I do not know what would even begin to pay. I am in your debt, more than I can say. Gannara saved my sanity more than once and my life also."

"Oh, that went both ways!" Gan said. "There was a time when the Mahid were going to flog me..." I saw him shiver and flung my arm around him. "Let's just say, it went both ways. I don't think we could have got out of it alive if it had been just one of us."

"Yeha. That time... we stood there for two days..." It looked as though she wished to hug her shadow son but was holding back. I let go and moved away.

Tisha's hand covered her mouth and her eyes widened when Gan spoke, and she looked even more surprised to see me hug her shadow-son. "I, I don't know what to say. This is not how I....well. This is not how I ever pictured meeting you, Ker Minis. I am so glad that 'Nara has returned to us, and it seems like I need to thank you for that." She moved a step towards me, stopped, and turned to Gannara and stroked his hair back off his face.

"Awww... mama..." But he leaned into it. "It's all right."

"Ker, just Minis, please. I'm just glad he's home with his family. I shall consider myself in your debt, nonetheless."

Linasika said quietly "Gannara tells me that you are his brother-in-adversity, and thus family. There is no debt in family." As he spoke, tears filled his eyes and ran down his face. He wiped his cheeks, and reached out to touch Gannara's shoulder, as if to test his solidity.

Tisha winced slightly, but then nodded her agreement. "Gannara has told us about you and your escape from the Mahid. Are they in custody yet?"

I wasn't going to argue any longer about it... but they hadn't convinced me. "Not yet. Soon, though. Everyone is in danger as long as they are loose."

Tisha turned to Lin, "See, I told you that we need to keep our watch rotation. It is not safe here."

"I shouldn't say... but I will let you know immediately when they are captured or killed... or Gannara can, but he won't be coming with me to see them captured."

"What?" That was Gan. "Nobody told me anything! Are you crazed?"

"Gan, the Imperator assigned an elite unit to the problem... and they need me to draw the snakes out of their hole, that's all. You don't need to go into any kind of danger... and I think you should stay here... at home... I mean, with them!

"Of course you shouldn't go on a raid against the Mahid! You are not *Darya*, you need to stay here!" A flush began to creep up Tisha's neck, and points of color flared in her cheeks. "The war is over at last, and we need you here!"

"Mama... didn't you say you needed to keep an eye on the fish?" Erano-e broke in, glancing at us before looking innocently back at his mother.

"Oh! My fillets!" Tisha jumped up, ran to the door and darted into the house.

Dumaryae leapt up to follow, "Let me help you, mama," he said and followed her.

Linasika groped for a new topic of conversation. "So, Minis, Gannara tells me that you bought a house in the *fessas* quarter. How do you like that part of town?"

"I actually gave that house to my tutor."

"Oh. You bought a house and gave it away? *Kahara*. And I was going to ask if you were growing a garden there."

"Oh, Ker Linasika. I'm a terrible gardener, as likely to rip up the vegetables thinking they're weeds... I'm so impractical a person I once bought an extra frying pan instead of a kaf pot. Gan-nara was fit to be tied."

"Just Linasika, please." He smiled. "Gannara used to drive his mother to fits when he played in her herb-pots...marching his toys through her rosemary."

I looked at him sideways, trying not to laugh, even as Gan groaned. "Papa..."

"Shall I pour us all a glass of wine?" Linasika said, getting up. At that point there was a knock at the door.

"Oh, that will be Fara!" Gan jumped up and hurried to greet her. *Oh good.*

"You gave away a house?" Erano-e said quietly. "Do you have any more?"

I brushed it off with a very Yeoli wave. "No. This girl, Farasha, have you met her yet? Do you like her? She's one of the Gibyr... those wandering teachers..." I shut up as Gan brought her into the little circle of chairs and couches.

"Erano-e... this is my friend Farasha. Fara, this is my big brother...

shadow brother really... and this is my little brother Sacherao... Sach for short. Minis you've met... though it was as Minakas. His name really is Minis."

She smiled at all of us and we all said hello with the hands... even me. Her eyes were twinkling and I was happy to see she was wearing a shirt this time. Linasika came back with glasses and welcomed her and went off again to fetch her a glass as well. I was so glad to be able to sit and listen to them all begin chatting with her. Maybe this was why Gan invited her... to draw their attention between the two of us.

I grabbed Gan's elbow and hissed in his ear. "I shouldn't *be* here!"

He grinned at me. "Shut up. Next I want to get Fara to meet Kyri-ala. I think they'd like each other a lot."

The thought had all the blood draining out of my head. I sat down hard, gulping. *Farasha and Kyriala? Together? With Gan, chatting over kaf? Oh... well... that ... that would be good. Especially if they got to be friends, if I weren't there. Gan's acting like I'm trying to find out if a four would work.*

Linasika returned with a glass for Fara and an extra bottle of wine. "This was a wonderful idea Gannara, all you youngsters make the house so much more full of life, and energy." He was smiling big and warm. He looked truly happy, looking around at all of us. "Look at you! All alive and hale after so much trouble! *Kahara* bless us!"

Tisha and Dumaryae came back right then and called us all in to the table. I was so glad it was fish. I might be able to swallow something. *Compliment the cooking, even if you can't eat.*

Tisha called to Sach and Erano-e to help carry dishes. "Since this is a rather large party I decided to serve dinner in the Arkan-style, so this is just the first course. I hope everyone is hungry!"

The fish was astonishing and I didn't have to fight to swallow at all, creamy and perfectly cooked... a sea-faring family, of course... "Ker Shae-Ara, this is amazing!"

Linasika beamed. "My family recipe but Tisha cooks it even better than my father did."

"Never! He was the master of just the right seasoning." She looked pleased at the compliment.

"Oh you should have seen some of the things the Mahid tried to cook," Gan said, smoothly. Suddenly we had everyone's attention. "Or when they tried to milk goats."

I had to laugh. "Those goats left a bunch of them on the ground, clutching their privates! Excuse me, for being so crude."

"Really?" Sach said. "They butted them there?"

"Oh, yes," I said. "Then the nanny trotted right over one Mahid's prone body, trampling him and hitting him in the head with the log she was supposedly tethered to." I thought I saw Tisha's mouth twitch. "And then she turned around and 'baaaaaaaaahhhhed' right in his face."

Farasha giggled right out. "Oh, I've had to herd goats before. I can just see it!" I threw a grateful glance at her.

"Ker Shae-Ara --"

She interupted me. "Just Tisha, Minis, please."

I cleared my throat like Ailadas, and Gannara smirked. "Tisha... thank you. I'm not used to such phenomenal cooking anymore. Thank you for this."

"Well, compared to the Marble Palace it's not fancy, but there is nothing better than good food with family and friends." I blinked and looked down, my throat suddenly knotted tight. *True. I just wish I knew better how to do it.* Linasika caught my eye and winked at me, just a little.

65

THE QUALITIES NECESSARY

Kyriala looked at Benthasas's face, then down at the split ring lying so innocent in his gloved palm, as if it were a tiny, poisonous, jewel spider. She could feel mama's eyes on her, and the aunties, and Hikinias and Ormanas, even as they pretended to be paying attention to Laisa, preparing to sing the Lament. She could feel the pressure of their desires, the aunties and mama to see her safely wed to a good man, the other suitors to see her refuse.

"Why, Ser Benthasas… this… I…" She could see his smile start as she fumbled, thinking he knew what she was going to say. Her spine stiffened. "I'm sorry. I was just taken aback by your munificent offer, Ser Benthasas. But I am not worthy of you. I'm sorry. No."

The smile – *why do I think it is a self-satisfied smirk?*—fell off his face as he realized what she'd said.

"Serina." He gulped, his hand shook as he thrust it toward her as if he could push it past her 'no'. "What do you mean?"

She reached out gently with her closed fan and tapped under his outstretched fingers and as they twitched up, followed them and folded them over the ring in his palm. Then over to his thumb and directed it to complete his fist around the ring. "I said no. Ser Benthasas." The fan tapped his now closed hand. "No. I will not be your bride." *Does he not hear what I say? How many times do I have to say it?*

"Surely, Serina, I mis-heard… May I repeat my request?"

Obviously he is hard of hearing when it comes in a woman's voice. "Ser Benthasas. Did you wish me to say this louder? So that everyone in my salon may hear?" He straightened. *As though I'd thrust a rod up his... spine.*

"No, Serina. But..."

She kept her voice down. "But? Ser. I have said I am unworthy of you. Let that assuage your...spirit. Should anyone dare to inquire, you may use the information as you see fit. Ser, let this never have happened and neither of us need say anything." *Either for, or against, the other.* "Let this be as if no such words ever passed between us and both our reputations will be perfectly intact."

He blinked at her and then down at the hand fisted around the empty wedding ring. "Of... of course, Serina. Will you sit?" The arm bent to offer Kyriala his elbow and she laid her fan upon it to let him escort her to a seat near the table harp. She could feel her mama's eyes upon the side of her face, questioning, and she turned her head slightly to catch her eye.

She is quivering like a sight hound with prey on the ground. Kyriala shook her head, fractionally and all the energy went out of her mother's posture. *Poor mama.*

⁓

Gannara was with me and we were called to the Scarlet Room, yet again. Apparently Chevenga had something he needed to speak to me about that was important enough to see me immediately upon us getting back from the family dinner. Something was looming. Why else had Kallijas gotten so much more intense while training? It had to be about 14.8.

The tension over dinner had eased considerably as the courses continued and both Linasika and Tisha showing their amazing skill as cooks, especially of seafood. Gan... no Nara... I had to remember... was unbuttoning his waistband. "*Ashapapa's* fish stew is just as I remember! Oh, I ate too much."

"Nara—"

"—Gan." He broke in. "You've always called me 'Gan' and I like it."

"Oh. Oh... all right. I thought I was going to die. You were joking about introducing Farasha to Kyriala, weren't you?" I yawned. It had been a long day.

"No, I think they'd really like each other."

My mouth dropped open again but before I could start an argument,

Chevenga let himself in, still talking over his shoulder to Binchala…. "—you know how to present that best, with the rest of that paragraph. They won't find anything to argue with it… thank you. I'm starting early tomorrow, Binchera, why don't you roust one of your apprentices and sleep in a little, you're looking too tired. Thank you again… Get some sleep…" The door closed on Binshala's goodnights and remonstrance's that Chevenga should get some rest as well.

"Hello, Minis, Gannara… how are the two of you?"

"Good, *sman'kras'ye*," he said, smiling. It was like looking at siblings… even more now that Gannara was older. I nodded.

"Aside from Gan trying to kill me with embarassment by introducing me to his family, fine." *As if fourteen eight did not exist. As if everything were not done, over finished and I'd end up on a head'sman's block like my dream.*

He sat down and I and Gan reached to pour him a cup of *ezethra* at the same time… looked at each other and snickered. Gan let me pour it. I set it by his hand and he smiled as he thanked me. He did look tired and almost gray. This vote could not come fast enough. Surely he would be able to rest afterwards.

Gan was pouring cups for the two of us as Chevenga came to the point. "So Minis, I'd like your advice since you have such a unique perspective. What do you think of these qualities for an Imperial candidate? Someone who is intelligent, war-trained, broadened by hardship, intellectually curious, knowledgeable in Arkan law and politics, open-minded, committed to the good of Arko, with a lineage that would make even the most rigid of traditionalists consider him legitimate on the throne, yet a willingness to embrace the new way, so that he combines the best of old and new in one?"

My smile grew as he listed quality after quality and hid the grin in my cup, sipping. "I'd say you must have commanded open the gates of Selestialis so that this person could walk through on golden-winged feet and descend to the Earthsphere on a stairway of sunlight," I said. "Which is beyond even your fantastic abilities, I suspect." Gannara sputtered and giggled.

But Chevenga was solemn as if he were officiating in the Temple. He'd sipped his cup and set it down with a click. "Not at all." That was when I caught the trace of a smile in his eyes, as I stared at him. Gan was staring as well. "…well, except for the Selestialis part. But he does exist and he's in Arko, so I could ask him any time."

I had to cough. *He was talking about a real man? Other than Kallijas Itrean? Kallijas... his lineage was what had some people choking on the idea of voting for him... the other things... well he could learn the political but who on the earthsphere was he talking about?*

"Perhaps I know him."

He was very serious. "You do, actually… perhaps better than most would at your age."

I looked down and put my face in my hand, thinking. There wasn't *anyone* I could think of who fit all those criteria. "I just cannot bring to mind any single one of the Fortunate Fifty that fits those standards, Chevenga. I mean -- the best candidate I can think of is Kallijas Itrean and he hasn't had the political training that most of the born *Aitzas* have. Mind you, that might be a good thing, seeing that they slid along with my father's corruption far too easily."

"*You*," he said quietly.

-31-

PREVIEW: MINIS NEVERBORN

Like "Burning Crystal"? Here's the first chapter of book six: Minis Neverborn.

CHAPTER 1: ONE SOLUTION TO COMPARTMENT 14 SECTION 8

Chevenga… the Imperator of all Arko, my friend, my father's enemy, Conqueror. Voted in Imperator, blessed by the Temple had just suggested that I was a fit candidate for the Empire's throne.

Oh my Ancestors. Sinimas did he just… Oh no… My heart leapt up with an evil little 'yes!' I squashed it even as I tried to draw in a breath through a chest gone to stone. No. No. No. It was a hideous idea. A horrible one. Arko would never want me, the little monster, on the Crystal Throne. I had a vision of one of my nightmares… my eyes in the fat guy's face, clawing the flesh off in gobbets, trying to get out.

"You." I couldn't get enough air to talk. "Aren't." Another breath. "*Serious???*" Only my hands clutched to the arms of the chair were keeping me upright, though I still felt rigid against the too-soft cushions. I couldn't see him clearly, even staring straight at him, as if through a fall of water over a pane of clear glass.

His hands turned up. "I am absolutely serious. Do you dispute any of the qualities I named?"

Serious. I couldn't look at him any more, his eyes that could only see the good in me, the hard-earned, rote learned goodness plastered over the rot put in me by my father. My hands were up over my eyes and I could finally move, bending over as if to fold over a gut wound. *He's serious.* At least bent over my suddenly aching gut I could answer him. "I… No.

Not as you stated them… but the character behind them cannot be trusted."

"What, you've turned dishonest since the last time I spoke with you?"

"Raik—Shevenka!" I was reverting to the first names I'd ever called him. The world was spinning end over end.   I gasped in another breath. *Don't faint.* "Please… don't joke, I'm serious. *You* of all people should know I would never survive the Ten Tens, even if all Arko should want me as Imperator!"

Even if I went along with his mad scheme… even if I could win this *vodai* in the few days left of the campaign… even if all of that… the Ten would smash me like a slug on marble. I was *forzak*. How could I even consider approaching Them?

"What are you talking about? You actually *know* how to do it," he said, leaning forward with his elbows on his knees so when I looked up I was almost nose to nose with him, startling when I took my hands down. I stared into his intense eyes a little frozen now by how much he felt about this. He was inspired. "I didn't. I already told you I'm serious. The only problem is that you're two years or so too young; so what I propose is that Kallijas act as regent until you get to third threshold. If you agree, he'll be the next person I speak to." He might already be considering that given the way he'd been training me in the mornings. Kallijas wasn't stupid.

It was about three more breaths, nose to nose before I couldn't bear it any more and cringed back into my chair, burying my head in my hands again. *"Aigh aigh aigh no!* It would be blasphemous for me to even try!"

"Why? Because you are Kurkas's son? You are *you*, not him. Just because he called you his addendum all the time doesn't mean it's actually *true*. Don't you remember, he lied about a thousand things?"

"You think the Gods, having set you in the Crystal Throne, would accept the Aan bloodline back? Are you out of your mind?" The dark behind my eyelids wasn't enough to drive that image away and the spots of false light made by my hands pushing on them somehow made it worse. I reverted to a much younger child and curled my legs up under me, knotting me tighter into my own chair. I remember vaguely the creak it made as I shook.

I heard his chair legs scrape slightly on the floor as he shifted it… closer I imagined. "Minis. Look me right in the eyes."

He waited for me and wasn't going to stop till he got his answers. I set my feet upon the floor once more, pulled my hands down though it felt as though I should not, prying my eyes open, feeling the pressing tears. They were like pressure in my head like a reservoir pipe over-stressed. *I have to say no, don't you see this? I have to. If I say yes I'm starting on the same route to corruption that my father tread. I have to say no. Sinimas, Ancestors... please intercede for me with the Ten and make him stop.*

I was close enough to feel him breathing. Like Gan his dark black eyes had threads and speckles of gold in them. I could smell the sweet green scent of the *ezethra* on his breath. "Forget everything else. The Gods' opinions, as if you can know them, the people's opinions, as if you can know them any better, the Ten Tens, all of it—"

No, no. I whipped my head side to side as if to throw off his words, turned to Gannara who was sitting quietly, watching, his hands over his mouth. I couldn't decipher the look on his face..."Gannara!" I called him as if asking him to throw me a line as I drowned in this insane idea. "Can't you tell *your semanakraseye* to stop this insanity of me running for Imperator...?"

His hands came down and he was smiling. *He agrees with this shen?* Chevenga spoke again as if I hadn't tried to wiggle out of his verbal grip and my eyes snapped back to his. "Forget all that, put it out of your mind," he said, quietly intense. "Look at me, Minis, and tell me, everything else aside and if there were no obstacles at all, on your hope of *Selestialis*: do you *want* this?"

I did. I wanted it. But that was wrong. Tears flooded up to make his image wavery and as I clenched my eyes shut once more, I felt them overflow onto my cheeks, hot as blood. I... he'd asked me and I wouldn't lie to him. "Yes."

"Why do you want it? Tell the truth."

"That I want it, alone, is enough to make me a bad candidate." *Why didn't he understand that? I'm Mahid trained, I'm a Mahid as far as my blood is concerned, a Mahid or an Aan and neither one is good.*

He took me by the shoulders, gently considering how intensely he was speaking to me. "*Look* at me, Minis. Why?"

I looked through the drops hanging on my eyelashes. "I... this will sound insane."

"Something I've learned recently: if a person tells the truth that is deepest in him and therefore scares him the most, it sounds insane to his own ears. So say it anyway."

I managed to swallow against the glue in my mouth. I found one of my hands pulling my hair toward my mouth but it wouldn't reach. I had no jewelled buttons to worry on my clothing. "I… I love Arko," I managed to whisper. "I love… every one of them. I turned myself in to die if that was best for them… but if I could *live* for them…" I clenched my eyes shut again, against how much saying that hurt. It was as if my heart were clutched hard.

"You used to hate everyone." His voice was very soft. I nodded and flipped my hand over in the Yeoli chalk sign at the same time. My chest jerked and quivered as it fought me trying to draw breath.

"When I hated them… they hated me." That had been when I was much younger. "When I found out that I could choose to hate or love, when I learned to look at a person and see him as someone who wished as much and fought as hard as I did, for life and happiness…" *I'm just a fessas boy and people just treat me nicely because I'm just another fessas boy.* "When I could *see* them… I could feel for them, I could like them, I could love them. All of a sudden everything made sense… out in the country, once we'd got away from the Mahid, and I was just a *fessas* boy… I could just *talk* to people, like every day was *Jitzmitthra*." The yearly festival of madness and fools. That sense of freedom was good to remember. I would never have managed to be so happy as a Dyer if I'd not had the little first freedoms taught me as a *fessas.* "And so many people were so kind, they'd do me kindnesses even though I was nothing but *fessas*, just because… just because I was *there*. It was as though I was freed from a prison. If I could do something for all of them… that they can't do themselves, singly, as you said… I know, it's insanity, it's all *insanity*." How dare I love people so much? How dare I? Where was this flood of words coming from? Had I been holding all this inside?

"Let me ask you this," Chevenga said. "Why did your father like being Imperator?"

I shrugged against his hands. That was easy. "He loved having the power. There was no one to restrain him, least of all himself."

He stared at me and then said something I thought he never, ever would. "Being Imperator *is* power. You should love having it if you want to do it. You think I don't love it?"

I ripped back out of his hands though he let me go the instant I pulled, staring at him. "No! No no—that's backwards! It's the *responsibility* that should be loved."

"Ah," he said. "You're separating the two in your mind. I say power, I mean responsibility too, because they are one and the same. It's a misnomer, in truth, that they're even two different words; in Yeoli, they aren't." It was a relief -- there was the Chevenga I knew. I could finally draw a deep enough breath. Talking about politics without this awful idea he was pushing was a respite.

"You taught me that all those years ago. Loving power with no responsibility makes my father," I said. I wasn't sure why I needed to tell *Chevenga* that.

"What did he get out of it?" He was baiting me... I was suddenly certain of it. He knew all this.

"Anything he wanted!" If he wanted me to say it out loud I would. Even if I had to be ashamed for my own blood. Perhaps he'd realize I knew why I was fighting him. "He had and loved power and threw away all responsibility and in that sense made himself a God, or rather a demon, for he did it for no one but himself."

He smiled, just a little. "Right. Now, just to reiterate, for whom would you be Imperator, again?"

Both he and Gannara were smiling at me. I'd just made their own argument for them, out of my own mouth. I would be Imperator for my people if they would have me. I covered my treacherous mouth with one whole hand, the other went over my eyes again as if to take back the words and not see the consequences. But I couldn't make them go away.

"Sheep-brain, will you *listen* to him?" said Gannara, with exasperation. "Quit trying to tell him you're evil!"

Chevenga actually flashed a grin at him. "Don't worry, I won't let him," he said to Gannara. "Or listen. I asked for the truth."

I had to make myself into stone to say what he wanted... the truth. It was as if I were answering Ice Eyes. "I would be Imperator for my people and the Gods." My face and throat were stiff as stone, forcing out the truth. He ignored the way I said it, waving his hand and sitting back as if he'd won his argument... he had. I'd won it for him. It was my duty if I cared about Arkans so much. How dare I deny them if I could?

"So you see the difference, between you and him? It's definitive."

Mucus clicked in my throat. "If Arko would ever want me in a thousand years!"

"That's up to Arko. I can't hand you the seals; only *they* have the power to do that, now, through the vote. The *vodai*."

"If the Gods, or Arko, want me... then it's my duty no matter what I want or fear."

"You don't know what the Gods want. Or the people, until the election. The important thing is whether *you* want it, for the right reason. Which you do."

"It's my duty to try?" I felt a little like a child asking if there wasn't a way out of this.

"All too often, Arkans hide what they want behind duty," He told me. "You want it even more than you're letting on; I hope it's only me, whom you can't fool, who you're trying to, and not yourself, whom you can. Your life is your own, ultimately, and the law recognizes that. Even in Yeola-e; if I wanted to resign, I could. As always, you choose."

Just listening to him brought out my emotion. I curled back into the chair again, my hands fisted over my eyes. "I want it too much!" Arko wasn't *safe* from me, how could he not see that? After what I did to him? A sob shoved its way out of me. "I don't trust that in myself!"

"How much is too much? Minis, I wanted it enough to fight all the way here for it, and talk an army and a nation into doing so with me— some at the cost of their lives." This was all wrong. I couldn't get away from him and this insanity. This idea... I wanted desperately to run and all I could do was leap up and start pacing back and forth from wall to wall back and forth, hands clasped behind my back, head down. Gannara leaned over to Chevenga... as if I couldn't hear the loud whisper.

"Wanting it *at all* is too much, he thinks."

I whipped around and glared at him. "For Arko's sake!" I yelled at him, "Not MY sake. Never MY sake. For Arko's!"

Chevenga, of course wasn't intimidated by my yelling at him. "As it turned out, yes," he said almost as quietly as Gan. "Once I knew what it was in my heart I wanted, I set out to make it real. It's not bad in and of itself to want power; it's good or bad depending strictly on what you want to do with it. Now—your and my purpose in being Imperator would be different, how?"

I grabbed my hair on either side of my head. "*Aigh!* Shevenka—I... I can't be Imperator because --" Suddenly it came to me. There was no way I was eligible to be Imperator. Arko would want an Imperator who could found a good line, an Imperator who could engender heirs.

I couldn't. I was safe. I took a deep breath, able to straighten. I closed my eyes. "Arko requires an Imperator to have Heirs. I'm incapable."

ABOUT SHIRLEY

Shirley Meier has been writing professionally since the 1980s and lives in Toronto. As well as being an award-winning author, she is an artist with several book covers to her credit. Her archery, horse riding and other hobbies have to take distant third place!